Mike:

?

The Raid

A Novel

Ken Merkley

Thank you for the great web-site. I hope you like the book as much as I like the site!

Ken

Note for Librarians: A cataloguing record for this book is available from Library and Archives Canada at www.collectionscanada.ca/amicus/index-e.html
ISBN 1-4120-9309-0

Printed in Victoria, BC, Canada. Printed on paper with minimum 30% recycled fibre.
Trafford's print shop runs on "green energy" from solar, wind and other environmentally-friendly power sources.

PUBLISHING™

Offices in Canada, USA, Ireland and UK

Book sales for North America and international:
Trafford Publishing, 6E–2333 Government St.,
Victoria, BC V8T 4P4 CANADA
phone 250 383 6864 (toll-free 1 888 232 4444)
fax 250 383 6804; email to orders@trafford.com
Book sales in Europe:
Trafford Publishing (UK) Limited, 9 Park End Street, 2nd Floor
Oxford, UK OX1 1HH UNITED KINGDOM
phone 44 (0)1865 722 113 (local rate 0845 230 9601)
facsimile 44 (0)1865 722 868; info.uk@trafford.com
Order online at:
trafford.com/06-1063

10 9 8 7 6 5 4 3 2

The police raid described in the Prologue is based on a real event. Nevertheless the characters are entirely fictional. All the characters and events in the remainder of the novel are entirely fictional. Any resemblance they may bear to real persons, experiences and events is illusory.

Care has been taken to trace the ownership of copyright material used in this book. The author welcomes any information enabling him to rectify any references or credit in subsequent editions.

Grateful acknowledgement is made to the following for permission to reprint previously published material: Cover Photo CBC Vancouver

Acknowledgments

I would like to thank Valerie Harlton for generously providing her time to edit this book. Her valuable suggestions and careful attention to detail has made my job as author so much easier. I would also like to thank RCMP Staff Sergeant (ret'd) Bruce Brown for his advice on RCMP organization and operations and Doug King, ex B.C. Legislative Security Staff, for explaining the intricacies of B.C. legislative security. Taninder Hundal was kind enough to provide assistance by reviewing my list of Indo-Canadian characters and suggesting some appropriate changes. Suzanne Bowen's proofreading services are also greatly appreciated. Finally, I especially wish to thank my wife Bernadette, as her patience, encouragement and advice has been "above and beyond the call of duty."

Prologue

IT IS DOUBTFUL THAT ANY other provincial capital in the western world can be as quiet as Victoria at 6:00 a.m. on a Sunday morning between Christmas and New Year's Eve. Normally, the respectable citizenry and misinformed tourists would all be snug in their beds, safe from the cold winds and drizzly black skies that generally prevail at this darkest time of the year. This particular Sunday was different, however, in a lot of ways. For one thing, it had been clear overnight and unusually mild, with the temperature hovering well above the freezing point. The warm night had uncharacteristically resulted in a few hardy souls wandering aimlessly down Douglas Street in the vicinity of closed bars and open, but barren, coffee shops, wanting one last holiday season drink and not quite finding the courage to sober up with a stiff jolt of caffeine. Finally, this Sunday was different because an event was to take place that would change the city and the province forever.

Douglas Street runs through the commercial centre of the city. Not that there is much commerce, but a few banks and credit unions have optimistically built five- or six-story office buildings, appealing for tenants on their middle floors and striving for an impression of size and stability. Many of the offices on these floors are leased by financial specialists, such as investment councillors, stock brokers, insurance agents and the like, all eager to assist the large and often naïve senior community to part with its pensions and savings. The rest of the street embraces a confused collection of travel offices, newspaper stands, hotels and family restaurants. A few small struggling department stores still exist, but most of the larger ones have long since moved to the malls in the city's suburbs.

Generally the tourists don't spend much time on this street, preferring the imported baubles to be found closer to the harbour in the shops on Government and Wharf Streets to the east of Douglas. Even at the best of times the main users of Douglas Street are suburbanites attempting to sort out screwed up financial statements, commuters waiting for late-running buses, or the night crowd, crossing the street on their way to the restaurants, prostitutes and nightclubs to the east, or the movie houses to the west. The whole downtown area has the desperate air of an aging lady of the night doing her best to maintain an attractive appearance, but starting to show a few too many warts and blemishes.

In an attempt to gain as little attention as possible, the combined RCMP/City of Victoria Special Police Unit had chosen to drive down Douglas on a date and at a time when virtually no one would notice. With no apartments or houses along the street, there usually wouldn't be any early morning dog walkers to become curious as to why a convoy of vans and police cruisers would be making their way through the heart of the city at this ungodly hour.

The raid on the legislature had been planned for weeks. As early as two years before, the RCMP had become alarmed about the increased drug activity in Victoria, its connection to organized crime and motorcycle gangs and its brutal effects on the vice trade in the province's capital. Only recently, however, had potential links to officials in government been established and evidence surfaced that perhaps party membership buying, influence peddling and contract rigging were tied to local drug dealing. The Mounties had quickly determined that the scope of suspected illegal conduct was much too complex for them to handle alone and they had enlisted the assistance of other law enforcement agencies, including the Victoria and Saanich Police Forces, to map out and conduct a counter-offensive. The resulting combined investigating team included members of the RCMP's Commercial Crime, Drug and Organized Crime Units, as well as their counterparts from the City of Victoria.

Tireless hours of planning and intelligence gathering had led to the formation of the Special Unit. Maximum security was required at all stages, as connections to not only the Provincial, but also the Federal Government, were strongly suspected. Other than the B.C. Attorney General, the senior justice officer in the province, no cabinet ministers, or even the premier, could be informed of the raid. Likewise, no information could be provided by the RCMP to federal government officials. Discretion was required to obtain search warrants for the many private and government offices where links to possible illegal activity had been established, and aside from The Speaker, who was consulted to ensure that parliamentary privilege was not being violated by the raid, no legislative personnel were informed.

As the convoy crept through the early morning darkness of late December, street lights shone accusingly down on their ominous black vehicles, resisting their attempts to remain discreet and inconspicuous. The convoy ploughed persistently on, leaving behind the few hapless street wanderers, who stared balefully, but with little curiosity, at the passing parade.

At the bottom of Douglas they turned right and made their way between the Provincial Museum and the Empress Hotel. Except for the lead vehicle, the procession turned left on Government and then right into the driveway between the legislature and the annex, stopping behind the East Block entrance. Meanwhile, Special Unit Commander Sergeant Tom

O'Brien, and his driver proceeded across Government Street and up to the entrance of the main building.

On a clear, sunny day, the legislature, often ostentatiously referred to as the Parliament Buildings and colloquially as "the ledge", is a beautiful building. If one looks down from the upper commercial offices along Government Street, the legislature sits in front of the shimmering waters of the Juan de Fuca Straight, with the Olympic Mountains soaring picture perfect behind them, providing a majestic and striking backdrop. At night, with all its lights ablaze, profiling its stately and symmetrical domes, the legislature is also a spectacular sight, standing upright against the darkened sky. The reflection of the lights and building are transposed onto the sailboats and docks of the inner harbour, creating a post card view that has been captured by photographers from all parts of the world. Even here from the entrance, with its wide spacious front lawn glistening under the glow of its silhouette lighting, the building looked down benevolently, as if welcoming this invading force.

As he arrived at the wide arched doorways of the main entrance and into the foyer, Sergeant O'Brien was met by a sleepy and very surprised Legislative Police Constable, Jack Lawson.

"Good morning, constable. I'm Sergeant O'Brien and I and a few fellow officers are here to take a gander at a couple of the offices in this fine building. Here is a warrant authorizing our right to search the premises. We shouldn't take up more than about six or seven hours of your time."

"But I don't have any knowledge of this," Lawson sputtered. "I'll have to check with my superiors to see if this is okay."

"That won't be necessary, constable. This warrant makes it okay and we'll just keep it as quiet as we can for as long as we can, shall we? No point in getting the reporters and tourists all excited any sooner than we need to."

From the foyer, O'Brien and the constable walked left to the East Block where Tom directed Lawson to unlock the breezeway doors, permitting the task force direct access to the block.

"Alright men, you know the drill," O'Brien shouted. "Harrigan, I want you and your group to go straight up to the second floor, secure it and proceed directly to the Cabinet Minister's office. Because he's the minister responsible for Crown corporations, the files in his office are bound to contain lots of information relating to the privatization scandal. Remember, the warrant lets us search the entire office, including the inner office, and while his aide is our main target, we need to go through the whole suite with a fine tooth-comb. Meanwhile, the rest of us will head down to the other Minister's office and go through the same routine there. Remember, we need to haul everything away with us, so make sure you are properly armed."

Dressed in their black, nondescript coveralls and armed with flattened file folder boxes, the Special Unit headed up the stairs and down the corridors, looking more like an army of bureaucratized ninja warriors than a group of her Majesty's finest. As he moved into the minister's suite, O'Brien directed his group to the filing cabinets, desks and computers of both the inner and outer offices. A cursory search of the files was made first, then a careful placement of all selected materials into the file boxes, followed by a thorough sealing and labelling to indicate the contents and sequencing of each box.

"I always knew I would end up with a desk job if I stayed with the City of Victoria long enough," jaded Traffic Section Sergeant George Wright quipped to his work partner, Mountie Bill Evans.

"Think of it as a favour to the taxpayers, George," Evans countered. "We could have had the government mail us all this stuff, but instead we provide free pickup and delivery, thus saving tons of packing and courier costs. Not only that, if you get tired of police work you will be qualified for both provincial government employment and moving company jobs."

"By the time I pack all these boxes out of here I will likely be more qualified for disability allowance."

"Don't be too disappointed, lads," said O'Brien. "If you weren't lazing around this cold empty office, you would probably be at home, forced to fix your kids' broken Christmas presents or watching some boring American college football game."

By eleven o'clock the local media had gotten wind of the raid and were soon clamouring around the site, taking pictures and attempting to interview anyone wearing black coveralls or looking even slightly officious.

"Come on, Sergeant O'Brien," pleaded the CBC's Legislative Reporter Phil Brown. "There must be something you can tell us."

"I can say this much, Phil. What are you guys doing here, standing around in the cold? I thought you all had nice cozy offices in the basement where you could be keeping warm and writing stories about the premier's holidays. As for the boys and I, we heard there was a late Boxing Day sale here and we thought we would arrive real early to take advantage of the specials. Judging by the boxes of stuff we're leaving with, we've done exceptionally well, don't you think?"

While O'Brien was speaking to the media, some of the officers from the unit were moving boxes out of the East Block and loading them into the waiting vans.

"Okay, so what's in the boxes and where are you taking them, Sergeant O'Brien?" asked Canadian Universal Media Reporter, Helen McIver. "You can't just storm the legislature, fill up a couple of vans with boxes of files, or whatever you've taken, and leave us wondering what the hell is going on."

"In due time, Helen, in due time. Right now that is exactly what I am going to do. Just the same, I am sure one of our fine spin doctors from the Divisional Office will have a word or two for you later in the week."

With that, the members of the Special Unit climbed back into their vehicles, and under glaring sunshine and along streets now busy with church goers and sightseers, made their way quickly back up Douglas Street and away from downtown Victoria. Their vans were loaded with 37 boxes of electronic and paper files. Under a separate warrant, members of the Unit had also quietly removed from the government computer server the electronic equivalent of 97 compact discs. Over the course of the day, other search warrants were executed by the Special Unit and visits were made to a minister's aide's home and to the homes or offices of a number of executive members of the federal governing party.

Ken Merkley

Part One

Traffic Services

Some dreams live on
And some, they don't
All that's left to know
All that's left to show
Are flowers by the side of the road

Katrina Elam: "Flowers by the Side of the Road"

Chapter 1

IAN POOLE AND DOUG HAWLEY were doing what they usually did at this time of the afternoon – nothing. Since graduating from Belmont High the year before, the two of them were in a period of what they referred to as "transition". Because they had been popular at school and gifted athletes, they were finding it difficult to come to grips with the idea that nobody really gave a damn about their earlier reputations. They had spent the past year working at odd jobs, looking for trouble or hanging out at Ian's parents' place, drinking beer and playing pool.

Ian's father, Jack, was a realtor and developer who became rich as the son of wealthy parents that owned a huge portion of the finest properties in the West Shore. He never had to work too hard for the benefits he received, the consequence of which Ian clearly understood and enthusiastically took to heart.

Doug, on the other hand, came from a family that was dirt poor. During his high school years he learned he could cash in on his athletic prowess to become accepted as a member of the in-crowd in the student pecking order. When he was younger, he did a few after school jobs to give him spending money, but later he discovered fencing marijuana and speed was a lot easier and made him even more popular than simply being a good basketball player. He was well on his way to a life of serious crime and drug dealing, but he found Ian's generosity and easy life-style much to his liking and endeavoured to stay in his good graces.

Both boys were tall and lanky. Ian was blond and wore his hair long in front. He had the habit of continually pushing it off his face, a habit Doug found irritating. In fact, Doug found a lot of what Ian did irritating, including his ever present sense of naïve optimism, but he kept it to himself. With Ian's access to easy money, he wasn't about to ruffle the feathers of the golden goose.

Doug, on the other hand, was dark and cynical. He knew that Ian was attracted to his penchant for seeking out danger and his reputation for being connected to Victoria's criminal element. He played on Ian's desire for adventure and continually found things for them to do that were either against the law, or were sure to cause someone else grief. He would instigate fights in bars, plough down traffic signs, or run other drivers off the road, not so much because he received a big thrill from doing these things, but simply because it amused Ian to be involved in them. Having little or no initiative of his own, Ian was always eager to keep Doug's company and to follow his lead on these menacing exploits.

Now the two of them were discussing the evening's activities. It was their habit to start off at any of a dozen favourite watering holes and then make their way to one of the nightclubs on Wharf Street in downtown Victoria, where they would continue drinking, maybe take some drugs, pick up a couple of young women, and hopefully get laid. Along the way, they would engage in one of Doug's "impromptu" initiatives and perhaps late, late in the evening, they would seek out something really sinister – something that actually hadn't happened up to this point. They could afford to indulge in this late night lifestyle as they shared a preference for sleeping in until at least noon.

"Care for another beer, Doug?" asked Ian, knowing full well he wouldn't refuse. In fact, he couldn't think of any occasion when Doug had ever refused anything he had offered him, except for the job his father had proposed, showing condominiums to the public at open house sales.

"Twist my arm, Ian. Got pale ale in the fridge? Maybe you have a nibbly to go with it?"

"Okay. The old lady keeps some chips in the cupboard here somewhere. Here we go. Would you also like a kick in the ass to get your jaws moving?"

"So, Ian, what would you like to do tonight?" Doug asked, ignoring the jibe. This was the lead-in he used every afternoon before a night out.

"Well, Doug, what do you say we head down to The Post later, suck back a couple of brews and watch the football game? In the meantime, do you want to go for a swim? It's getting hotter than hell and I need to cool off."

After almost an hour of lolling in the heated pool, they got dressed and leisurely headed out to the garage, slid into Ian's Pontiac Grand Prix and cruised down Veteran's Memorial Parkway into Langford, stopping in front of The Post. The Post was one of those trendy places where the jock crowd hung out. Starkly furnished and cold, it had televisions hanging on every wall, with others suspended from the ceiling or sitting on high counters. They were all turned to the same sports event which, depending on the season and time of day, was usually golf, skiing, hockey or football. As they walked in, the same Canadian football game was blaring out of about a dozen TV sets.

They chose a booth rather than one of the tiny tables wrapped around metal posts and surrounded by overgrown highchairs that the more extroverted patrons preferred. This allowed Ian and Doug to easily watch the game and still keep an eye on the comings and goings of the other customers. They ordered their beer, noting that Calgary had a twelve point lead on Toronto early in the third quarter, and got back to discussing their favourite subject – what to do next.

"What say we head into town, maybe cruise down Wharf and watch the show at Winnie's for awhile?" queried Ian, watching Doug's reaction, knowing that most times Doug had his own ideas of what they should do.

"Sounds okay to me, Ian, but let's watch the end of the game and then I have a small errand to do. We should be able to get to Winnie's by about nine, which is plenty early. The good peelers don't come on till later anyway."

Through the fourth quarter, Toronto made a comeback with a touchdown and two field goals and for a while led Calgary by only one point. The game finally ended in a squeaker, with Calgary pulling off a field goal on the last play of the game for a two-point win. As die-hard Western fans, Doug and Ian had watched nervously through the quarter and were elated by the near win. Doug in particular was pleased, as he had placed $100 on Calgary with his on-line booking service, money he would have hated to lose. Over that last 15 minutes of playing time they had also managed to down another three pints each, as well as consume a well-balanced meal – a burger and fries for Doug and a Philly steak with onion rings for Ian.

Leaving The Post in a jovial mood, Doug asked Ian to drop by an address in Colwood where he had some business to look after. After ringing the doorbell, a small spectacled man with greying unkempt hair and a dirty white undershirt answered.

"About time, Doug," he challenged. "If you're gonna be in this business, you hav'ta learn to get here on time. You can't expect a customer to wait forever when he's in the mood for a small snort."

"Sorry, Al," Doug lied, handing him a zip-lock freezer bag filled with white powder, knowing full well that as a dedicated coke addict, Al Whitelaw was always in the mood for a snort and rarely, if ever, was it a little one. Nevertheless, feeding Al's habit was good business for Doug and kept him in ample spending money, so he conjured up contriteness, rather than allowing his true impressions of Al to surface. "We were held up because we had a little trouble with Ian's car," he lied. "It's working fine now, though, and we came here as soon as we could."

"Okay, but just don't let it happen again or I'll find another supplier. While you're here, I heard about a little deal you might be interested in. A friend of mine knows a guy who has started distributing crystal meth in Victoria on a steady basis and is looking for someone like you to supply his West Shore customers. You interested?"

"Maybe. Where do I find this guy?"

"Drop by Sam's and ask for Dick Walker. Tell him I gave you his name."

"Thanks, Al. We might just drop by tonight. Ian and I haven't been around Sam's in a while and the grapevine tells me he has all kinds of new stuff."

After leaving Al's, the boys elected to drive through Colwood by way of the strip. Colwood is politely referred to as a bedroom community for Victoria. At one time, all the West Shore towns, including Colwood, Langford and Metchosin were so designated, but lately, under a business-friendly council, Langford had become a destination for big box stores, main drag boutiques and new and revamped retail malls. A concerted effort to doll up the downtown with the demolition of eyesore buildings, widened boulevards, tree planting, fancy street lights and a new city hall had given the place a new look. As such, it had shed its reputation as a "town full of yahoos with pick-up trucks, all with a rifle rack across the back of the cab, a bimbo in the passenger seat and a big dog in the back." Now it was referred to by Victoria's business community as "the place where the action is."

Colwood, meantime, still appeared content to let the world go by, presenting quiet streets of ranch style houses and bungalows built in the 60s, small aging malls filled with pizza joints, barber shops, privatized liquor stores and dry cleaners. Nothing moved very quickly in Colwood, particularly the commuters heading to or from their white collar jobs in downtown Victoria. At these times, the old highway through the Colwood strip is referred to as the Colwood Crawl, providing the slow-moving motorists the opportunity, once again, to study the latest acquisitions in the never-ending line of used car lots.

At this time of the evening, the highway was quiet. Ian quickly passed by the auto lots and was soon on the four-lane Trans-Canada, heading south into Victoria. The Grand Prix was five years old, but it was Ian's pride and joy. His father had bought it for him when he graduated from Belmont the summer before, with the understanding it would come in handy for Ian when he helped out with his father's real estate deals. Instead, it had served Ian well for a month or two as a way to impress his school chums. After most of them moved out of his life, leaving for university or new lives in Vancouver or Calgary, it allowed him and Doug a highly suitable vehicle for their evening exploits.

Ceaselessly trying to find ways to make an impression with Doug, Ian pressed on the accelerator and soon had the Pontiac up to 140 kph. The stretch from Colwood to Victoria was very open with one or two easy curves and wide traffic lanes. It was rarely patrolled by the RCMP and was subsequently a favourite for would-be race car drivers. There had been some horrific accidents along the highway, but this never seemed to deter others from "burning the carbon out."

"I thought this old bucket of bolts was capable of a little speed, Doug," yawned Ian. "What say we take her out to the Pat Bay Highway later and see if it's qualified for more than taking your granny to church?"

"That sounds good to me," Ian answered uneasily, slowing down as they rapidly closed onto the approaches of the city.

The north side of Victoria becomes the terminal for a confluence of roads which funnel into the Trans-Canada and become Douglas Street. Once in the city, the traffic becomes much heavier. The city sits on the southern point of the Island

and is heavily congested, with a dense population in a very small geographical area. The only saving grace has been the insistence by a long line of city councils that the downtown buildings be built no higher than thirteen stories, a decision that has mainly been honoured and has saved the streets from becoming one big parking lot.

Leaving Douglas, Ian made an easy right onto Government, went a couple of blocks before turning right again and then left onto Wharf Street. Wharf is where the action is. A parade of nightclubs, restaurants, pubs and hotels line both sides of the street from Pandora south to Fort Street. Ian located a place to leave the Pontiac in a city-owned parking lot just off Wharf and then he and Doug returned and walked back to Winnie's. Winnie's advertised itself as an exotic nightclub, but it's actually a pub with two separate bars, one with an endless stream of female strippers, and another periodically enticing Victoria's women with a select stable of male studs, appearing mainly during weekend early evening hours during the summer months.

Doug and Ian arrived in time to see a reasonably alluring, but obviously bored, white twenty-something stripper named Jewel begin her routine. Showing an affinity for oldies, she had selected Donovan's Mellow Yellow as her theme music, a number popular before most of the young male crowd were conceived. Displaying a healthy interest in a vertical metal post running from the ceiling to the stage, she gyrated to the music while running her body up and down its length, all the while discarding various colourful necklaces, brooches and earrings, obviously as some kind of sacrificial offering, either to the audience or the post. Having exhausted her outer ornaments, she turned next to her few items of clothing, each festooned with various baubles, ribbons and pins, all likely intended to convey a relationship to her adopted stage name. Her coup de grace, after adorning the metal post with her glimmering bra and panties, was to display her admirable body to the crowd, with nothing remaining except two strategically placed rubies and a large shiny sapphire. Then she scampered offstage to a less than thundering ovation from her limited attention span audience.

As the next act got under way, and while Ian ordered a replacement round, Doug carefully scanned the crowd. He knew that a fair amount of reasonably discreet drug trade took place at Winnie's and he had heard rumours that here, as well as at Sam's, a variety of designer drugs were becoming available, including the increasingly popular gamma-hydroxyl-butyrate (GHB). GHB is a depressant drug with anaesthetic properties, which in small doses allows the taker to feel pleasantly relaxed. Doug wanted to find a supplier as he believed it might go over well in the pubs in the West Shore. He recognized two or three past contacts and made a note to have a chat with one of them in particular the next time he went to the men's room.

It was about then that Ian's attention was distracted by a couple of exuberant youths standing between him and the stage, thus blocking his view.

"Sit the fuck down," he yelled, while raising an index finger skyward.

"Screw you, dickhead," the smaller of the two responded. "My buddy and I want our money's worth and no shit bag like you is gonna stop us."

"Why, you little prick. I don't think you know who you're dealing with. Now sit down before I sit you down."

"Try and make me," the youth taunted, sneering confidently, judging that his larger companion would make short work of Ian, should anything come of their disagreement.

With that, Ian shoved him into a chair and the youth lunged back up, fists raised and arms ready to swing. Ian then suggested they go outside and settle it in the parking lot. Doug followed the three of them nonchalantly, somewhat bemused by Ian's unexpected show of initiative.

The parking lot behind Winnie's was surprisingly empty and quiet. The other patrons had paid little attention to the altercation and no one had bothered to follow them outside. Ian and the youth squared off in an empty area behind a dumpster. Ian soon got the better of the battle – that is until the larger one decided to interfere with an unexpected and brutal clout into Ian's right kidney. As Ian started to crumble, he followed up with a knee to Ian's chin.

Having determined that the dispute was proceeding a little unfairly and could soon lead to serious harm to Ian, Doug discreetly slid a hand into his right front pocket, popped a blade open on the knife that found its way into his palm and smoothly inserted it into the stomach of the interloper. With a smashing blow to the chin, he then disposed of the smaller youth, got Ian to his feet and walked him away from the parking lot and quickly back down Wharf Street in search of further engaging adventures.

Chapter 2

CORPORAL TIM MURPHY wasn't sure why his career in the Royal Canadian Mounted Police wasn't going anywhere. Perhaps it was because of his impetuous nature, which tended to get him in trouble more often than not. But then he had always been impetuous. He was involved in more than his fair share of fights in high school, usually as a result of defending himself from some perceived slight that on closer examination, or after he had cooled down, he would see as not having been all that important.

Or maybe it was the result of his willingness to accept almost any dare, simply because it gave him a sense of power to defy death. There was the time, for instance, he had been on detachment in a remote native community in Northern Ontario, when he had walked blindfolded across the outer railing of a narrow railway trestle, simply because a couple of fellow officers had suggested he was too chicken to do it. He had been able to feel his way along the railing with his feet easily enough, but his Detachment Commander had gotten wind of it. He had not been amused and had written him up for it.

But then, as far back as he could remember, he had wanted to be in the RCMP. Growing up in Northern Alberta he had observed how a small detachment of police officers could quietly maintain peace and order in a large chunk of the province, retaining the support of the law-abiding citizens and the respect of those who weren't.

He had also seen the police force as a way of escaping his rural upbringing and ensuring he was not coerced by his father to join him in his commercial fisheries vocation. Tim had joined his dad on the boat for the summer between his last two years of high school and had managed to get seasick over half the time, including one long stretch of 21 days. He blamed it on the need to look down all the time to pick fish out of the nets, even though he recognized that neither his father nor younger brother shared his tendency for upchucking.

By the time he was in high school, he had made up his mind to enrol in the RCMP. He did so within a month of his graduation and it even required the permission of his parents, as he was still shy of his nineteenth birthday.

Tim breezed through his basic training, thriving on the tough disciplinary approach of his instructors and soaking up their no-nonsense attitude concerning their duties. He also found the camaraderie to his liking and formed many life-long friendships with his fellow cadets. By the time he graduated and was posted to his first operational assignment, he was proud and contented with his choice of careers and enthusiastically looked forward to a life of variety and service.

For the first few years it appeared he would be a star. Willing to accept the most unglamorous assignments in the most remote detachments in Western and Northern Canada, he was a favourite of his superiors, receiving glowing evaluations and recommendations for promotion. It wasn't until his characteristic of trying too much to be popular and "one of the boys" surfaced that problems started to arise.

There was, for instance, the time in Slave Lake, Alberta, when he and two other of the local detachment's younger off-duty Constables joined in a beach party with a group of under age locals. That, in itself, would have been enough to get him in hot water, but then he made the situation even worse. Having noted that the amount of beer on hand was getting alarmingly low, Tim and one of the other officers drove back to town, put on their uniforms and went out on highway patrol. They stopped a few cars and quickly and efficiently confiscated a good-sized quantity of open cases of beer and brought them back to the party. Unfortunately, while it was illegal to have open cases of beer in your vehicle, one of the men whose beer was taken heard later that the beer had been provided to the youths and he raised a complaint with Murphy's Commanding Officer. That and a couple of similar blemishes had slowed down his career advancement.

Still, he took his duties seriously, and after one notable event in which he convinced an irate husband not to use his .22 calibre rifle on his wife, himself, or Murphy, he received a commendation and was promoted to Corporal shortly thereafter. Twelve years and a large number of tough and varied assignments later, Tim, now 38 years old and still a Corporal, was a little worried that he wasn't about to receive any further promotions. Many of his Regina classmates were now senior to him in rank and had received more glamorous or important assignments.

Generally, however, Tim was satisfied with his career and his life. Eight years previously he had met Gloria Dawson while posted to Fort Nelson in northern B.C. Gloria was a nurse and had worked at the town hospital for six years before Tim arrived. She was of medium height and had the most alluringly dark eyes Tim had ever seen. He decided he was in love with her the first time those eyes met his at a dance at the local community hall.

Gloria had enjoyed her time in Fort Nelson, but when Tim proposed and he had completed his posting assignment, she was ready to move on and let life take her to wherever the RCMP decided they should call home. In the years since, employment was always available to her, and as children were not making their appearance, she and Tim lived a comfortable life and had even saved some money toward their eventual retirement.

When Gloria developed kidney disease three years after they married, it had seemed at first as though they had suffered a terrible setback. The disease progressed slowly, but inevitably Gloria was required to begin dialysis treatments. The RCMP was understanding and had posted Tim to the Sidney Detachment, near Victoria, where in-hospital treatments were readily available for Gloria. She was able to continue working for a time, but the treatments gradually wore her down and she was forced to quit work and lead a more sedentary life, relaxing at home when she was not undergoing her hemodialysis "runs." These consisted of sitting in an easy chair with her arm connected to two tubes hooked to a machine that pumped blood out of her body, through a filtering device and back into her body again. The process was slow and Gloria was required to endure the treatments for four hours at a time, three times a week. Tim would drive her to the hospital and pick her up as often as he could as Gloria often felt very weak and dizzy after finishing a run and would frequently get severe leg cramps when the treatments dehydrated her too quickly.

They soon adapted to the routine, and although Gloria missed her nursing career, she enjoyed being at home and was able to prepare meals for the two of them. This was something

Tim appreciated, as they had often eaten separately and hurriedly before she became ill. They were now able to spend much more time together, and while they often talked about how things would be back to normal when Gloria received a transplant, both of them were able to make the best of their current situation.

Unfortunately, though, their routine was affected again three years after their arrival. After a run-in with a speeding cabinet minister, Tim was reassigned from traffic services duties at the Sidney Detachment to his present position in the Vancouver Island District Headquarters as officer in charge of the RCMP's South Vancouver Island Commercial Vehicle Safety and Enforcement Team. The position, while rather mundane, meant that Tim was often required to travel to detachments all across southern Vancouver Island, as well as to weigh scales and other vehicle inspection sites on Vancouver Island and the Gulf Islands.

Today, Tim's schedule meant he would be spending a busy Friday. He had an early appointment with Jim Urquhart from the Commercial Vehicle Safety and Enforcement Division in the Ministry of Transportation. Later he would be visiting two of his team, traffic patrol members with small detachments, one in Ganges on Saltspring Island and the other on Pender Island. These visits were to be followed by a stop at the weigh scale on the Pat Bay Highway on his trip back into Victoria from the ferry terminal. Leaving the house at 7:30 a.m. in order to make his early appointment with Urquhart meant Tim wouldn't be able to drive Gloria to or from her Friday dialysis treatment.

"You know if you don't think you're up to driving, take a cab. It's not going to break us and the good citizens of Victoria will appreciate your not fainting and running them down."

"Don't be ridiculous, Tim," Gloria answered with rising exasperation. She often found Tim's over concern a little irritating, and while driving after a treatment was tiring, it was only about a thirty-minute drive and she had found that Tim's current work schedule meant she was taking herself to the hospital more and more often. "I'm capable of driving myself. Now get out of here and go to work."

Tim wasn't out of the house five minutes before his mind was straying to the day ahead and it wasn't work he was thinking about. During his time on regular traffic services duties, he had tumbled into an affair with a fellow traffic services officer. Sheila York was tall, blond and gorgeous. Tim wasn't sure why she should be interested in him, but she had made it clear at a staff party one night that she was. Tim had never considered himself as particularly desirable, and while he managed to get laid from time to time during his single days, only Gloria had ever admitted that she had a hard time keeping her hands off him. Many of Tim's fellow officers had a go at getting Sheila into the sack over the years, but as far as Tim knew, none of them had ever succeeded. She had, of course, occasionally been accused of being gay by the more malicious of her would-be suitors. It wasn't until later that Sheila confessed to Tim that she had been maintaining a discreet relationship with another married officer, but he had been transferred shortly before she started up with Tim.

Flattered and bothered by Sheila's interest, Tim had at first kept his distance. It was difficult to do, as she was often part of his daily routine – present at work briefings and frequently assigned to ride with him during traffic safety patrols. The sight of her walking down an office hallway or languishing beside him in the patrol car would get his blood stirring and he more and more frequently began imagining being alone with her in more delightful surroundings.

Adding to his emotional upheaval was his relationship with Gloria. While he loved her dearly and was comfortable with their home life, the burden of her kidney disease was slowly taking its toll. In addition to feeling lethargic and tired most days, and particularly before and after dialysis treatments, Gloria's interest in sex had slowly waned. Tim took it in stride and did his best, but more and more, lovemaking lost its pleasure and became a duty to her. As a result, Tim's advances were frequently rebuffed or accepted resignedly, so that over time he attempted to initiate something less and less frequently.

Tim's traffic services unit had often made it a habit on Friday evening to drop by their favourite watering hole, the Brass Rail. It was probably inevitable that Tim would find himself alone with Sheila one evening, after a few too many drinks and after everyone else had gone home or in pursuit of other interests. Drink by drink, his concern for Gloria's welfare was inversely linked to his increasing awareness of Sheila's charms. Determining that he was probably in better shape to drive than she was, he finally offered Sheila a ride home. Arriving at her condominium, she said, "Perhaps you should come up and get some coffee. Some bad police officer is liable to stop you and arrest you for driving under the influence."

"I suppose you're right," agreed Tim. "But it will probably take about eight cups and even then I might be accused of being a wide-awake drunk."

Sheila's place wasn't the typical starkly furnished bachelor flat that is often associated with single police officers who are rarely home to enjoy it anyway. She had always taken pride in maintaining a suite where she could leave work behind and relax in cosy and pleasant surroundings. Pastel walls, plush carpeting and large, lightly patterned sofas were complemented by a diverse collection of paintings, ornaments and assorted well-made pieces of art that, taken together, seemed to invite visitors to unwind and feel at home. Tim did so while Sheila left to prepare the coffee and extricate the various pieces of officialdom, including her gun, badge, handcuffs and uniform that let the world know she made her living as a law enforcement officer. In their place, she slipped on a halter-top and loose fitting pair of slacks and was back before Tim could figure out how to work the stereo.

"Do you have anything in jazz or blues?" he asked, pretending not to notice how good she looked out of uniform.

"How about something light and instrumental, say, Miles Davis or Herbie Hancock, or maybe the soothing vocals of Diana Krall?"

"Diana Krall sounds great. And speaking of great, this is a first-rate place you've got here. I hope you're finding the time to enjoy it."

"I'm enjoying it right now, thanks. Come and dance with me while the coffee perks."

Tim hesitated for as long as it took her to walk across the floor, but still managed to get to his feet before she reached him. He felt a rush of excitement immediately as he put his arms around her and felt her body against his. He leaned into her and began kissing her. Sheila responded instantly and they collapsed onto the sofa with his hands quickly finding their way under her braless halter top. She eagerly tugged at his belt as he deftly removed her top and pants. His mouth and hands were all over her body as she made short work of his uniform and began caressing his highly receptive skin. He drove his tongue into her and she responded, gasping with delight, moaning and thrusting into him. When he felt she was ready for him, he moved up and into her. Their mutual delight was at such a peak that, unable to slow themselves, they pounded at each other and quickly came in a synchronized wave of pleasure that washed over them. Later, they took more time and found that their craving for each other was only heightened by delaying their climax.

Now, as Tim reminisced about their first night together and all the evenings since, he thought pleasantly about his upcoming visit with her today. Their affair had gone on for almost a year before their senior officers got wind of it, and in typical fashion, posted Sheila to Saltspring Island where traffic duties were, to say the least, less than hectic. She had been forced to sell her condo and now lived in a much more humble, although roomy, apartment in Ganges. Tim had been permitted to remain in Victoria, but was reassigned to his current Commercial Vehicle Inspection duties, ostensibly as a result of the aforementioned run-in with an irate provincial cabinet minister. Gloria, meanwhile, either did not get wind of Tim's affair, or chose not to know.

Tim and Gloria had elected to buy a house in Metchosin, a rural suburb of Victoria that kept him far away from the office on his time away from work. Now it meant he had about a forty-minute drive to Jim Urquhart's office in Selkirk. He decided to take the Old Island Highway route, meaning he would have to face the "Colwood Crawl," but would still get to his destination about the same time as if he had taken the more hectic alternative of the Veteran's Memorial Parkway and Trans-Canada Highway. He found the Old Highway route to be a much more pleasant drive, once he was through the Crawl and could enjoy the scenery of the aptly-named View Royal and the winding meander along the Gorge Waterway.

By the time he got to the entrance of Selkirk he was in a fairly relaxed mood, until he remembered he was coming here to see Jim Urquhart. Tim found Urquhart to be pompous and arrogant, typical, he had determined, of many lower ranking officials in the Provincial Government, holding positions of questionable public value. Urquhart was an analyst in the Commercial Vehicle Safety and Enforcement Division. His job was to maintain coordination with the RCMP and other police forces in the province, ensuring that officers who had received Inspection Enforcement training were current on Vehicle Inspection regulations and practices. Tim had determined early in his new assignment that he could easily stay up-to-date by occasionally scanning the applicable website.

After finding a place to park in the lot assigned to the Division, Tim resignedly obtained a parking permit from the front desk commissionaire, placed it on the windshield of his four-by-four Ford Explorer and made his way into the labyrinth that held the staff of the Division hostage from eight-thirty to four-thirty for five days a week. The building was tall, cold and sterile on the outside, and bleak, characterless and unappealing on the inside. Like many of the government buildings in Selkirk, it was built at a time when the politicians had decided to move government employees from downtown to help ease overcrowded conditions in the heart of the city. Selkirk had been a confused mess of old gravel piles, rotting wharfs and decaying welding and machinery shops, and the city was grateful that the Provincial Government had been willing to clean it up. It should have been an attractive area to work in, located along the entrance to the Gorge, with a background of treed parks and walkways, but somehow the architects had missed the mark and created a series of stark, puerile towers, perched above narrow, winding and generally foliage-free, pedestrian-hostile streets.

Inside the building, the interior reflected the typically stupid decision of the current government to reduce the size of the government public service about the time the office towers were being completed. Pockets of small offices and panel-divided cubby-holes were separated by huge, empty, unfinished spaces, holding nothing but stale overheated air. Tim hadn't been to Urquhart's office before, and after receiving directions from the commissionaire and a visitor's pass from the receptionist, made his way down a long zigzagging corridor to the elevators located at the far end of the building. Disembarking on the third floor, Tim was forced to obtain further directions before locating Jim Urquhart in a small, featureless office hidden behind a vacant meeting room.

"Good morning, Tim. Before we get started, help yourself to a coffee from the machine in the meeting room behind you, if you like."

"No thanks, Mr. Urquhart, I got my fill before I left home this morning. I think I will just coast for awhile."

"Please call me Jim, and let's get to business then. As you know, our vehicle inspectors rely very much on the services of the police forces in the province, especially the RCMP, to keep an eye on the commercial vehicles on the highways, in particular those operating in smaller municipalities and the more rural areas. Since downsizing, our inspectors are pressed just to maintain the scales and ensure that the carriers are properly licensed. I know some of your officers in traffic services are trained to carry out inspection enforcement, but I sometimes wonder if they place as much emphasis on that job as they do in catching speeders, or whatever."

"Well, Mr. Urquhart," Tim replied, noticing he was already losing his temper, "you are not the only organization with stretched resources, but you can be assured that our officers are aware of all their responsibilities and give them the attention they deserve. Do you have a particular example you wish to discuss?"

"As a matter of fact, I do. Some of our inspectors along the Pat Bay Highway think maybe a few trucks are making their way around the inspection station and across the ferries to and from the Gulf Islands with some goods they shouldn't be carrying, if you know what I mean. Now I know you have detachments on some of the Islands, so maybe they could do more to check up on them."

"Well, perhaps if you have a specific request, you should channel it through proper channels and my Sergeant can provide me with the authority to devote some time and attention to looking into the matter. In the meantime, I was under the impression your duties were to do with training and communications, and I came here this morning with the understanding we were to discuss any new rule changes that may have occurred since we last spoke."

"No need to get put out, Corporal. I'm just passing on a friendly tip. I know this information will make its way through the pipeline in due course, but in the meantime there is some reason to believe a few bales of the wrong crop are making their way to Vancouver Island and onward. And yes, there are a few changes to the Motor Vehicle Act Regulations we need to talk about. I'm sure you appreciate how important it is that all our inspectors and our police partners are up to speed on these changes."

After their meeting, it took a little time for Tim to put Urquhart out of his mind, and he had to concede that as he was going to a couple of the Gulf Island detachments anyway, he could pass on the request. The brass had become concerned lately about the increase in drug traffic across the province and if they could bust a carrier or two hauling illegal shipments, it could help Tim get back in the good graces of his Inspector.

Traffic was light as Tim made his way out of Victoria along the Pat Bay Highway. He made it to the ferry terminal with about thirty minutes to spare until the next sailing to Fulford Harbour, the closest landing to the Ganges Detachment. He took the time to go into the cafeteria and fetch the coffee he had turned down from Jim Urquhart. Back in his vehicle, his thoughts returned to the rest of his day's schedule, especially his upcoming meeting with Sheila. It was about four months since he had seen her last and he was eager to make up lost time.

As he boarded the ferry at Swartz Bay, Tim noted with some relief that the winds were light and the seas calm. The ferry crossing was as smooth as silk. The warm day and gorgeous scenery allowed Tim to relax and enjoy the journey. Clusters of bright modern houses stood out amongst the rolling hills bordering the shores. Further north, the ever-changing shades of the many species of coniferous trees created an endless mosaic of green, overlain with a clear blue sky penetrated by a sun that made every detail stand out in stark relief. Ahead of him, the peaks on Saltspring Island rose boldly out of the water, like sentries guarding the inner valleys and rolling plains of the terrain between them. He could see eagles circling the peaks and at one point a pod of killer whales making their way up the Georgia Straight back to their summer home at Robson Bight after a short hunting excursion.

Tim arrived at Fulford Harbour about an hour after leaving Vancouver Island. The road to Ganges, about 30 kilometres to the north, was winding and narrow. While his RCMP four-by-four was hardly of racing car stature, he enjoyed peeling around the corners of the lightly-travelled route. He pulled into the detachment on the approach to Ganges just before noon and had the receptionist, Judy Collins, page Sheila for him. She arrived quickly and they headed off to the Driftwood where they had earlier agreed they would go for lunch. Settling into a booth across from her, Tim could see that Sheila was nervous and uncomfortable. He asked her what was wrong.

"Things have changed, Tim. I have met someone here that I have been seeing a lot. He lives here now, but works in Victoria and wants me to move there with him as soon as we can both arrange it. It means I wouldn't be able to see you again, especially if I can get posted back."

Dazed and with his expectations shattered, Tim asked, "A bit sudden, isn't it? You didn't give me a clue about this when we agreed to meet here today."

"Just what did you expect? Perhaps you wanted an official e-mail or a personal letter to your home for Gloria to intercept? Just how was I to say anything when we both work with nosy police officers all day? I couldn't exactly call you at home. It was hard enough talking to you to arrange this lunch with half the detachment listening in."

"So why lunch at all? We might just as well have met at the detachment and discussed business, if you meant to cut me out that abruptly."

"Come on, Tim. I will miss what we had as much as you, but it wasn't ever going to be anything permanent, you know that. Gordon is offering something long-term and, frankly, I am ready for it. You know how much I like you and I hope we can still be friends, especially if I can arrange to transfer back to District Headquarters."

Tim lapsed into a moody silence, eating as quickly as possible and never tasting a bite. Angry and disappointed, he drove Sheila back to the detachment. For the rest of the day he worked in a daze, meeting with the other officers to discuss Commercial Vehicle Inspection responsibilities and forgetting to pass on the information that marijuana was possibly being smuggled by truck back to Victoria.

By the time he had made the trip to Bedwell Harbour and headed back to Swartz Bay on the last ferry from Pender Island, Tim felt exhausted and totally depressed, and he still had the stop at the Pat Bay weigh station to look forward to. He gulped down a late supper at a fast food joint in Sidney and arrived at the weigh station close to midnight. The inspector on duty would normally close the scales at that time, but tonight the station was staying open until the wee hours of the morning. This was done periodically to catch any drivers who might be trying to sneak through to the ferry terminal with unsafe or overloaded trucks. By doing this, a driver could catch the first ferry to the mainland in the morning without ever being weighed or inspected. And while Tim's visit was to discuss coordinating arrangements between the Ministry inspectors and the RCMP traffic services officers, he had agreed to do it tonight so that he and his vehicle's presence might "persuade" passing commercial drivers to stop at the scales.

"Good of you to come in personally, Corporal Murphy," said Jack Hanson, himself a senior inspector who would normally work a more civilized shift. "I know this is not the most ideal time to be meeting, but it's a good way to kill two birds with one stone. As you know, the incidence of illegally loaded trucks is causing concern with both our organizations and with inspection and police forces across the country. It seems that organized criminal gangs have noticed that resources devoted to inspection services have been reduced in recent years and are trying to take advantage by moving illicit and stolen goods, virtually under our noses."

Tim nodded absently. He knew all this and realized that Hanson was just making conversation, but his mind was not really focused on their meeting. He replied cursorily to Jack's attempts to communicate and soon settled into a pattern of reviewing their joint coordinating details, interspersed with long periods of silence while he wrestled with his private thoughts. It wasn't his intention to stay through the night, but he felt he should maintain a presence at least until three or four o'clock, knowing it would still seem like forever.

EARLIER THAT DAY, the Captain had also given fleeting attention to commercial vehicle inspections. Pacing across the vast expanse of his huge headquarters, high atop an office building in downtown Vancouver, he prided himself on his ability to focus on the many details of his various enterprises. He stared down from his wall of windows across Burrard Inlet to North Vancouver, observing the many merchant vessels arriving and departing from berths on both sides of the harbour. In the near distance he could see more traffic cruising under the Lions Gate Bridge and further out to the far edges of English Bay. Along the eastern wall of his office, another bank of windows gave him a view of the docks, warehouses and offices of the industrial section of the harbour. He often thought of his office as the bridge of a large carrier, controlling and protecting the movements and operations of all the ships making their way to Vancouver from other cities all over the globe.

While these grand thoughts exaggerated his importance, The Captain was, nevertheless, a very wealthy and powerful man. He was the surviving member of the third generation of a family that had created the largest and, by far, most important import-export business on the west coast. In addition, he owned his own shipping line and a fleet of trucks carrying imported goods to the interior of the province. In recent years, he had added shipping containers and expanded his warehouse holdings along or near the harbour. He had also gotten into the automobile insurance business and had set up offices in a number of B.C. communities. Finally, he was a name to be reckoned with in the inner circles of the federal Progressive Party.

To The Captain's mind, commercial vehicle inspections and enforcement were too rigid and had made it difficult for him to maximize profits from his trucking operations. A few years earlier, a disastrous accident at the Horseshoe Bay ferry terminal had occurred, when a heavily loaded runaway truck with faulty brakes crashed into a line of vehicles waiting for a ferry. A public outcry had lead to stricter regulations and in many cases a smaller load limit. It was time, The Captain decided, to see about having the regulations eased. He was confident the province's business-friendly government would be sympathetic.

Chapter 3

AFTER MAKING THEIR GETAWAY, Ian and Doug wandered aimlessly along Wharf and Government Streets for awhile, which gave them a chance to cool down. Shortly after ten o'clock, Doug finally decided it was probably late enough to visit one of the nightclubs back on Wharf Street. He chose the Bang-Bang House, knowing that by now the band would be in full swing and the girls would have had a chance to settle in and knock back a few drinks. After they entered, they lingered along the wall for a few minutes to case out the room and finally agreed on two comely young women at a table by themselves near the dance floor.

"I like the blond one," Doug asserted, knowing that Ian would be agreeable, as the brunette across the table was also easy to look at.

"I hope you don't mind if we join you," Doug stated, as they dropped casually into two empty chairs at their table. "It's a bit crowded in here tonight and if it's okay with you, we thought we might share your space."

"I know what you mean," answered the brunette, as she scanned the half-vacant room. "There's hardly an empty chair in sight."

"Now that you're here, perhaps we should have a drink to celebrate the occasion," the blond added, pointing to the concoction in her more than half-full glass. "I'm drinking whiskey sours."

"I guess we could spring for that," Ian chimed in, waved down a passing server and passed on their orders. "By the way, I'm Ian and my mouthy friend here is Doug."

"Hello, Ian," answered the brunette. "My name is Diane and this is Diane."

"Ah, we are in the company of the goddesses of love, no less. We shall refer to you as Diane 1 and your blond friend as Diane 2, without any suggestion of order ranking."

"That's fine with me, as long as you don't call me late for breakfast."

"I can see we are going to get along very well. Let's drink a toast to the evening ahead."

The time passed quickly as they danced to the raunchy music provided by the three-piece rock band, and in time they had consumed another three rounds of drinks. Sometime during the evening, Doug came up with an ecstasy pill for each of them and this had helped put everyone into an even better mood. By one o'clock, however, the band stopped playing and the bar closed. Doug suggested that they move on to Sam's where the after hours action was always interesting and where he was sure a good party would be going on. After receiving agreement from the apparently game for anything Dianes, they clambered into the Grand Prix and headed out to the suburbs of Cadboro Bay where Sam's was located.

Sam's Supply Shop, as it was unofficially called, was a large house in a residential area of Cadboro Bay, not too close to the water, secluded and a fair distance from the closest neighbours. A long driveway through a stand of large firs provided cover for the many cars that frequented the house, especially after midnight on weekends. So far, the police hadn't learned about the various activities that went on at Sam's and its strategic location was probably the main reason why they hadn't.

Doug's reasons for coming here had less to do with entertaining his fellow revellers than with seeking out sources for expanding his drug trade. He was particularly interested in a secure supply for his growing crystal meth business and he wanted to hunt down Dick Walker. The drug was becoming ever more popular and to date his current suppliers had only been able to provide him with the drug on a hit and miss basis. In addition to crystal meth, though, Doug wanted to provide a wider variety of substances for his West Shore clientele and he was hoping to find someone who specialized in the so-called "designer" drugs, especially GHB.

Ian and the Dianes were pleased enough with the action at Sam's. There was a crowd of about thirty people seemingly enjoying themselves, a small dance floor and a good quality sound system. There was also plenty of booze available and access to almost any recreational drug that might strike their fancy. Still high from the alcohol and ecstasy pill, Ian took turns dancing with the Dianes while Doug networked the crowd, seeking out the allusive Mr. Walker. Finally, their cautious host, the bartender, acknowledged he knew Doug's contact, Al Whitelaw, and slipped him a telephone number. He also steered him to a part-time supplier who sold Doug a small quantity of crystal meth, enough to meet his customer's needs for a week or two. Doug then went off to the bathroom long enough to sample the wares, a questionable way of ensuring that the supplier had provided him with the proper product.

Around 2:30 a.m., Doug started to become restless and suggested to Ian that they should take the girls for a ride. Ian agreed and even went along with Doug's suggestion that he should take the wheel as Ian thought this would give him an opportunity to become better acquainted with Diane 1 in the back seat of the Grand Prix. They wound their way around Mt. Douglas Park for awhile until Ian began to notice that Doug was driving the steeply curved roadway somewhat erratically and politely suggested a change of drivers.

"Relax, Ian, I told you earlier we need to see what this bucket of bolts is made of. I'm going to take her up to the Pat Bay Highway now and give it a little test."

"Okay, but keep it down until we get there, so we can live long enough to find out."

Doug soon left the Mt. Douglas area via Mackenzie Street, turned onto the highway and pressed down on the accelerator. While Ian continued to worry about the behaviour of his usually unflappable friend, the two Dianes appeared not to notice and seemed to enjoy the sensation of the rapidly accelerating Pontiac. By the time they reached Elk Lake Road, the Grand Prix was clocking 150 kph and increasing.

Almost the entire distance along this section of the Pat Bay Highway is a divided four-lane road with barriers on both sides, separating the northbound and southbound lanes. There are a few cross streets, with turning lanes and lights at each intersection, but generally the road is restricted to straight ahead driving. Also, in the wee hours of the morning the highway is almost deserted and there is almost nothing to discourage committed drivers from moving at the speed their vehicles will allow them to go. "Yahoo! Yahoo!" Doug shrieked, pounding on the steering wheel and bouncing up and down on the seat, obviously intent in determining just what that speed was for the Pontiac.

Ian didn't know that the combination of alcohol, ecstasy and crystal meth was profoundly affecting Doug physically and mentally. What he could understand was that he was now acting totally differently than normal. "Pull over, Doug," he pleaded ineffectively.

"Go you motherfucker. Go, go!"

"Jesus, Doug. There's a cop behind us. For Christ's sake, stop this thing."

As they passed McTavish Avenue, the turn-off to the airport, Ian realized that Doug wasn't going to stop and they were in serious trouble. He continued to plead to no avail, noting they were now moving at 190 kph. The girls had gone deathly quiet, no longer enjoying the ride. Soon Ian could see flashing lights ahead on the approach to Sidney and prayed this would get Doug's attention.

It did. Doug jammed on the brakes and the car fishtailed as they slowed dramatically to a fraction of their earlier speed. Ian slumped in relief just as Doug cranked the wheel and spun the Grand Prix around and headed back toward Victoria.

As they began to gather speed once more, Diane 2 came to life and pounded on Doug's shoulder and head and grabbed ineffectively at the steering wheel, which Doug held with a grip no one could have broken. Meanwhile, Diane 1 huddled up against the back door and whimpered in horror at the awful turn of events.

"Get this bitch off me, Ian," Doug yelled, staring straight ahead, but continuing his dreadful bouncing.

Reacting almost hypnotically, Ian obeyed as he reached forward and clipped her across the jaw with a smashing left hook that sent her sprawling against the side window, where she now lay quietly with her head down on her chest.

"For God's sake, Doug, we're on the wrong side of the road. Stop the car! Stop the car!"

Not a single vehicle came towards them as they continued to rocket forward. Time almost seemed to stand still for Ian as the scenery flashed past in a hazy and surreal blur. Almost in a trance now, he had the eerie feeling he had been on this nightmare ride forever and that it would go on endlessly. Thoughts of his youth, his parents and his wasted summer, all this and more flashed through his mind in a jumble of vignettes and confused recollections. He was incapable of concentrating on their predicament and what he might do to resolve it.

Then a flood of relief washed over him as he made out a police vehicle across the road well in front of them, all its lights flashing and blinking, creating an obvious barrier that would be impossible for Doug to ignore.

Ignore it he did. The Pontiac sped relentlessly toward the RCMP four-by-four as if nothing but a shadow across the highway was impeding its progress. Only in the last second did Doug react, pulling the Grand Prix to the right, aiming for a small opening between the parked vehicle and the barrier to the median.

He almost made it. The Pontiac clipped the four-by-four's back bumper by only the smallest of margins, just enough for the car to ram the barrier at a forty-five degree angle. At a speed of 185 kph, this caused the Pontiac to bounce upward and back left, flipping over on its roof and crashing back onto the road, sliding about 50 metres before stopping very suddenly against the other barrier on the outside edge of the road and disintegrating from this final test of its structural integrity.

Chapter 4

BY THREE O'CLOCK, TIM had enough. Bone tired and frazzled, he called an end to his meeting with Jack Hanson, rationalizing that it was unlikely any commercial trucks would be out on the highway for the rest of this extremely quiet night. As he climbed into his Ford Explorer four-by-four, his only thought was to make the long trip back to Metchosin and then to sleep through most of Saturday if he could get away with it.

Just as he left the weigh scale parking lot, a red Pontiac Grand Prix whizzed past him, heading north like a migrating goose worried about missing mating season. Acting on his spontaneous instincts, he went after the car, lights flashing and siren howling. He stayed behind the Pontiac, but unable to close the gap, he called the Sidney Detachment on his radio and requested they set up a road block. He eased back then and waited for Sidney to acknowledge they had apprehended the fast moving travellers. Instead, the call he received explained that the Pontiac had made a 180-degree turn just before the road-block and was now heading back on Tim's side of the road.

Without giving it a lot of thought, Tim pulled his four-by-four across the highway along a reasonably straight stretch in such a way as to block a goodly portion of the two usually northbound lanes. With no turn-offs along that section of the road, he judged that the Grand Prix would finally be forced to stop. He then realized that legitimately northbound drivers could be in jeopardy if they failed to notice in time that his vehicle was blocking their passage. He reached for his flashlight and a couple of flares he had handy in the van and sprinted up the road, hoping to set up a signal far enough in front of the four-by-four to give oncoming traffic an opportunity to stop safely.

He had only run about 50 metres when he heard the Grand Prix coming. The roar of the engine was relentless and the headlights quickly became larger as the Pontiac streamed up the highway towards him. He could see then that the car was not going to stop and he decided to beat a tactical retreat to the side of the road. He clamoured over the highway-edge barrier and across the ditch, just as the car crashed into the four-by-four, and quickly exposing its underbelly, skidded forward to join him. After coming to a sudden stop at the barrier in front of him, a crumpled pile of steel lay on the side of the road, with only a slight ticking sound emanating from its contracting metal to hint that a fully functioning automobile had just been effectively transformed.

Tim ran to the car, dreading what he would find. In spite of all his training and exposure over the years to mutilated bodies, he still found the sight of bloodied and battered individuals difficult to take. While it was unlikely anyone could survive such destruction, it was his job to make sure. As he knelt down by the driver's side, he could see the roof had been squashed down to the bottom of the side windows. Shining his flashlight into the interior, the carnage was terrific. Doug's upside-down and now headless body was wrapped around the broken steering column in a macabre lover's embrace. Beyond him, spattered blood and body parts were everywhere. Front-seat Diane was now part of the side door and Ian's remains were scattered about the back like a shopping bag that had its contents tipped over. Diane 1 now looked more like Diane 0.5, but miraculously, Tim was sure she was still breathing.

But how could he help her? He ran to his vehicle, radioed the Sidney detachment and quickly reported the situation. Next he hastened back to the other side of the wreckage and peered into the compressed space. Somehow, in spite of being the only one of the four with her seatbelt done up, Diane 1 had managed to huddle into the back right-hand corner and curl her feet under herself before the crash. Her seatbelt had prevented her from having her head scoured into the roof, and while her arms and shoulders drooped awkwardly and her body bled profusely from numerous cuts and abrasions, her chest moved up and down rhythmically.

Tim pulled out his pocket knife and reached through the shattered rear window and quickly cut into the seat belt. He was able to get one arm under her, and as the belt gave way he gently began to lift her through the narrow space. He had difficulty straightening her legs enough to get her past the window posts, which caused him to wonder if one or both legs had been broken in the impact. Eventually, by twisting her sideways, he got her out, carried her to a spot in the ditch adjacent to his vehicle and covered her with a blanket that he retrieved from the Explorer. He did what he could to stem the bleeding as he listened with relief to the sound of ambulance sirens heralding advancing reinforcements.

STAFF SERGEANT RALPH TOMS was steaming mad. "Corporal Murphy, I have a mind to suspend you right now until my investigation is complete. Just what in hell did you think you were doing? You endangered the lives of everyone northbound on the Pat Bay Highway and ended up killing three young people for no good reason. We have more than enough of them doing it to themselves without you aiding and abetting."

Staff Sergeant Toms was in charge of RCMP Traffic Services for South Vancouver Island and would become responsible for putting a Criminal Crash Investigative Team in place. The crash had occurred in Central Saanich, a municipality with its own police department, so one of their members would ostensibly be in charge, but most of the resources would come from the RCMP and from the Saanich Police Department, both with much larger complements of traffic service officers.

This morning, Toms was trying to determine how an accident this horrific could have occurred. Lately, a number of similar crashes had taken place around Victoria and the public was screaming for an increase in traffic surveillance measures to reduce the carnage. As always, an inadequate budget devoted to traffic safety made this next to impossible and his anger at Tim was a result of this pressure, in addition to his lack of understanding about Tim's actions.

"I regret what happened as much as you do, Staff Sergeant, but my actions were totally necessary at the time to prevent a bad situation from becoming even worse. The actions of the driver, including his excessive speeding and the manoeuvring of his vehicle into the counter-flow lane occurred without any provocation from me. And far from aiding and abetting, my decision to place my vehicle in his way was done to protect the northbound traffic, not endanger it."

Predictably, Tim's temper was getting the better of him and challenging Toms's interpretation of events was only serving to raise the temperature in the room.

"Just how were straddling two lanes of traffic with one four-by-four going to stop anyone intent on avoiding arrest? It seems to me the only thing you accomplished was to create a danger for legitimate traffic driving in the proper lane. And to top it all off, you didn't stop this fool from attempting to get past you anyway."

"All of this is well and good, Staff Sergeant, but it could have been a hell of a lot worse if he had driven unimpeded into an oncoming vehicle. In addition to the three that were killed, God knows how many others could have been as well."

Toms decided he needed to cool down and talk to Murphy after he had more information from the crash investigation team. "You may go now, Corporal, but I want you to remain on office duties until I can decide what, if any, role you can serve in this investigation and what effect your actions may have for your future."

He considered what he would have done in the same situation. It was clear the Pontiac was a grave danger to other traffic and needed to be stopped. If Murphy had contacted the other police departments, Saanich and Central Saanich, was it possible a team could have reached the scene in time to block off the northbound traffic and place a spike belt across the highway? Considering the speeds involved, probably not. And was he simply angry because Murphy's actions had not been successful? And what about the effect of the crash on Murphy? He would have to live with his decision, no matter what the investigation concluded. It might be best to recommend a transfer for Tim to another department with new and different responsibilities. The more he considered the situation, the more perplexed he became. One thing was obvious – the investigation team would need to find out what caused the driver to act so insanely. Another was not so clear – why the relentless pattern of young people killing themselves on the highway continued unabated across the city.

THE OFFICER IN CHARGE of traffic safety for Central Saanich was a Corporal. Eventually the various jurisdictions accepted Staff Sergeant Toms's decision that a Sergeant from the Saanich Police Department would head the team. They settled on Sergeant Amar Singh Ranga, head of Traffic Services and an experienced member of the force who had served on many investigative teams in the past.

Ranga was a quiet man and very thorough. He was well aware of the carnage caused by young drivers in B.C. This was the third such accident he was required to investigate in the past year where three or more vehicle occupants were either killed or seriously injured. He was also aware that crashes are the leading cause of injury and death for young people in the province and that impaired driving contributes to 30 percent of all traffic fatalities each year.

After assigning members of his team to the accident scene to analyze the circumstances of the crash, and to the Sidney detachment to debrief the officers involved in the road block, he decided to talk to the sole survivor himself. Diane was still in the Victoria General Hospital Critical Care Unit, but while still in much pain, her condition was said to be improving and she was soon to be moved to a regular recovery room. She had suffered a broken right shoulder, a broken hip and a fractured pelvis, in addition to a number of severe cuts and facial lacerations. Nevertheless, faced with the need to understand what had caused the crash as soon as possible, he decided he wouldn't wait for her to get any better.

By the time Sergeant Ranga reached the hospital, Diane had been moved to a recovery room. She was conscious as he walked in, but did not immediately acknowledge his presence.

"Hello, Diane," he said gently. "I know you are not feeling too well right now. My name is Sergeant Ranga. I am hoping you can help me understand what happened last night so that we can try to find a way to make sure it won't happen to anyone else."

Diane had earlier been told some of the details of the accident and that the others in the car had been killed. She agreed to tell Amar Singh as much as she could. While she had difficulty in focusing on many of the details, Ranga was able to grasp the significant points. She outlined how what at first seemed like a thrilling joyride had turned into a nightmare as Doug's personality change took place. He listened carefully as she described Doug's frantic screaming and bobbing up and down in the driver's seat of the Pontiac and the horror she had felt as he turned the car around at the road-block. She also recalled the nightmare of speeding along the wrong side of the highway and how Doug seemed totally oblivious to the pleading of the others for him to stop.

Singh was particularly interested in her observation about Doug's yelling and bobbing movements. "I know that Doug had been drinking," he said. "But did he or the rest of you take any drugs during the evening?"

Diane admitted to the ecstasy, but as she had not known that Doug had sampled crystal meth before the drive, she denied that any of them had indulged in anything else, other than the alcohol.

After a few other questions and a sincere expression of condolences, Sergeant Ranga said goodbye to her and left the hospital, mulling over her recollections of Doug's strange behaviour. The crash investigative team was also to learn that indeed Doug did have a package of crystal meth in what was left of his pocket and a blood test confirmed that it was in his system at the time of the accident.

Later, after receiving a full report from Sergeant Ranga and his team, Staff Sergeant Toms recommended to his superiors that a larger investigation be initiated to focus on the increased linkages between highway crashes by young drivers and their use of illegal substances.

Chapter 5

DUNCAN HENDERSON LIKED TO THINK of himself as a very pragmatic man. Others may say that he lacked principles, but he preferred to believe that remaining flexible and keeping his options open would help to ensure that the interests of the province, not to mention his own, could be best served. He was also an ambitious man and his interests were very well served indeed.

Duncan had moved with his family from Alberta to Victoria when he was sixteen. Highly aggressive and with a powerful bulldog shaped body, he excelled in contact sports, particularly rugby and soccer, and quickly became popular in his new high school. His father was a corporate lawyer who made a good living by serving the interests of those who sought business contracts with the Provincial Government and Duncan decided early that he would like to follow in his father's footsteps. By the age of 24, he had graduated in commerce and law from the University of Victoria and began his career by accepting a position as an administrative officer in a small municipality. On the surface, the position seemed hardly one to get him started on his chosen path, but in his versatile way, he used it to make many helpful contacts with business owners, politicians and public officials who dealt with the municipality on a day to day basis.

He was also prone to allowing his sense of arrogance to come to the fore from time to time, which did not always endear him to the general public. A good example was his decision as town clerk (a promotion he achieved within two years of first employment), to restrict access to a local beach. He did this because it was difficult for him to find a place to park when he wanted to take his dog for a swim. As a result, he arbitrarily banned all parking along the access road, with the exception of three spaces that were to be kept open for town officials in "the course of fulfilling their municipal responsibilities." While he received a good deal of static from the public on this and many similar issues, he intimidated the elected council into supporting him in his decisions.

It was during his employment in the municipality that he became interested in party politics and joined the federal Progressive Party then in power. Because he wasn't always sure which way the political winds would blow, he also joined the provincial Progressive Party. He was one of the few people who seemed comfortable working within both party organizations, not really caring, as the two party wings did, in whether the province's assets were owned and controlled by British Columbians, other Canadians or outsiders. As a result, he often served as a liaison between officials from the two party organizations, each believing Duncan represented their interests. The contacts he made served him very well and he was selected at the ripe old age of 30 to become Western Regional Vice-President for the Development Bank of Canada. The position required him to move to Vancouver and it was here that Duncan first met The Captain.

Duncan had quickly become a working member of the team of volunteers who looked after the Federal Party's interests in British Columbia and he was soon seen as willing to work hard to maintain and expand those interests in whatever capacity the party wished to make use of his services. He possessed a latent talent for fundraising, and with his outgoing and aggressive personality, he was able to penetrate many organizational hierarchies made up of young and dynamic business leaders that the old guard had difficulty relating to. As a result, he tapped into a significant source of new party funds. Within three years this allowed the party to noticeably increase expanded membership activities that would contribute to the party's electoral fortunes in subsequent elections.

When The Captain first interviewed Duncan, it was with the intention of determining whether he should be made a member of the inner circle that controlled these activities. As was his fashion, he extended an appointment to Duncan to join him in his inner sanctum high over Burrard Inlet.

Sitting across the desk in the accustomed position The Captain liked to place his visitors, Duncan did not experience the sense of nervousness that most did when The Captain began his careful scrutiny and formal interrogation. The Captain's desk was big, black and formidable, and he always ensured his guests were directly across from him at eye-to-eye level. He knew he had the ability to make many of his associates uncomfortable by doing this and it gave him a feeling of power to observe their unease as he carefully scrutinized their faces and their reactions to the most innocuous of questions. However, Duncan's own well-developed self-confidence and natural arrogance made him immune to The Captain's techniques, and while he remained polite in the face of his inquisitor, he was more bemused, if not amused, than he was intimidated. Nevertheless, The Captain appeared to be oblivious to his guest's lack of nervousness and plodded through the interview routinely.

"I have asked you to join me today," he began in his standard opening address, "because I have heard from others of the good work you are doing on behalf of the party and wished to extend my personal appreciation for your efforts. You seem very young to have made such an impact, but I am assured you know what you are doing and are able to use your young age to your advantage to improve the party's fortunes in the province."

"Uh, thank you, but I'm not sure my age has too much to do with it. I believe I can help the party in any capacity that may be useful. Being in my thirties has helped because of the emergence of a new group of entrepreneurs who are taking the stage in the development of the province. My connections through the Development Bank have probably been more useful than my generational connections."

"Nevertheless, the results are impressive and we believe you may be ready to take on more senior responsibilities."

"I'm certainly prepared to do that if it will help the party, but I'm not sure I can take the time away from the Business Development Bank to take on more responsibilities. Also, while I enjoy the job, I would like to find a more senior position in the business world to give me the kind of influence that a senior position in the party may require."

"Hmm, well I might have a solution that could help both you and the party. We are interested in getting some party loyalists in senior positions within various Crown agencies and corporations, both provincially and federally, that may be ripe for privatization. This might seem unrelated, but the Great Forks Zinc Corporation is looking for a new CEO. Now, I know that the Provincial Government is preparing to sell off BC Hydro and many of its operations will be purchased by local power companies prepared to expand. One is the Cascadian Power Corporation, which is also a Crown corporation, but the province also wants it to become a private company and look after power distribution in their region. Great Forks Zinc uses a large amount of electricity and has a sweetheart deal with BC Hydro to obtain power at a very low price. We could get you in there and you would be in a position to be part of the consortium to take over Cascadian. This would help to ensure Cascadian stays in Canadian hands and that Great Forks will continue to prosper by having its own power source."

"That could work very nicely. Great Forks Zinc has its headquarters here in Vancouver, meaning I could continue to look after party interests, while increasing my profile with potential party contributors."

"You might also start thinking of cashing in on that profile by running for election. Get some time in with the company and look around for a potential seat. Some of the Greater Vancouver seats are pretty safe for the party. As long as you are prepared to support the party's position on corporate ownership, you would make a great candidate."

"Alright. I am, of course, always prepared to support the interests of the province."

For the next three years, Duncan Henderson, in addition to running his new company with ruthless efficiency, was able to line his own pockets nicely, thanks to the very generous salary, bonuses and stock options he received. The low cost of electricity provided through the Cascadian Power Corporation ensured that Great Forks Zinc had a distinct advantage over its competitors.

True to his word, Duncan also continued his party work and raised significant amounts of money from like-minded business interests in Greater Vancouver. About the time the Provincial Government decided it was ready to privatize BC Hydro, he resigned from his company, placed his holdings in trust and became a member of the Board of Directors for Cascadian Power Corporation. However, before the arrangements were made to implement the privatization process, the new Prime Minister called a federal election and Duncan decided to throw his hat in the ring. He chose a safe seat in West Vancouver and was handily elected with the full support of the party apparatus.

Part Two

Drug Squad

My neighborhood's a shooting gallery
Because of crack dealing scum
Another kid blown away
Thirteen years young

What's your pleasure, what drugs did you do today?
Because of your habit, who died along the way?

Drug dealers, death dealers, life stealers,
junkie breeders.

Destroy: "Lethal Habits"

Chapter 6

AFTER HIS DRESSING DOWN from Staff-Sergeant Toms, Tim spent the rest of the weekend at home with Gloria. He wasn't good company. He hadn't felt more despondent, tired or depressed during any previous period of his career. Gloria's attempts to cheer him up or to get him to talk about the events of Friday went nowhere. When he went back to his office on Monday morning he did so with great dread, which was compounded when a message left on his desk indicated he was to report to Staff-Sergeant Toms as soon as he came in.

Toms's mood had changed from their last meeting. "Come in, Corporal Murphy. Take a seat. Since we talked on Friday I have received some preliminary information from the crash investigative team, indicating that drugs may have played a big part in the Pat Bay accident. It's likely that the investigation will be broadened and I've decided that, if you are up to it, you should be part of it. In the meantime, I have already spoken to Inspector Fields and he agrees that you should be relieved from your current duties, at least temporarily, and reassigned to the Drug Squad to provide some, uh, independent probing to help us understand where this Doug Hawley character was getting these drugs he was carrying and supplying to his friends. Now I know that this a bit sudden, but assuming we can get the transfer okayed by Human Resources, we think you might be in the best position to work independently on this and at the same time give yourself a chance to think about something else, other than the accident, for the next while. Of course, you will still be interviewed at some point by the investigative team, but at least you won't have to constantly deal with it as you would by remaining in your current position."

Tim was stunned. Saturday morning he was not sure whether he would have a job much longer and now he was being offered an assignment in a new department and one which would remove him from the routine office work associated with coordinating Commercial Vehicle Inspections. If he could move into the Drug Squad permanently, it meant street work, undercover assignments, detailed investigations and anything but routine. "I will be pleased to assist in any way I can be useful," he answered dryly, a response that seemed to satisfy them both.

Tim decided a good place to start would be to pay his own visit to Diane. After reading Sergeant Singh's preliminary report, he wanted to know more about Doug Hawley and just how involved he was with drugs. It seemed to Tim that having encouraged the others to try the ecstasy and Doug's own use of the crystal meth meant that he might have had more than a cursory knowledge of Victoria's drug trade.

Diane was a little less than pleased to find that another police officer wanted to interview her. But once realizing her latest visitor was the officer who had pulled her out of the crushed Pontiac, she became more forthcoming and did her best to recall the experiences of Friday night.

"Diane, I know it's hard to go over this again, but I understand you told Sergeant Singh that after leaving the Bang-Bang House, Doug took you to a place near Cordova Bay that he called Sam's. You also described Sam's as an after hours party house that sold liquor and may have had drugs available for purchase. What made you think that there might be drugs available?"

"I didn't have to think. Doug told us that we could get just about any recreational drug there that we could want to try. I wasn't particularly interested, but I overheard Doug asking some people at Sam's whether they knew a certain dealer who apparently could get Doug a supply of crystal meth."

"Do you remember the name of the person that Doug was trying to find?"

"No, but I do remember hearing him ask the guy working the bar where he could find this person and mentioning to the bartender that he knew someone called Al something or other. I think maybe it was Al White, or White something, maybe Al Whitehouse or Whitehead, something like that?"

"Sounds like you have pretty good ears. Do you recall the name of the bartender, or what he looked like."

"Yeah. Well, I was curious about this place we were in that I had never heard of before and I kept wondering why Doug was so busy asking all these people questions all night. But I never did hear who the bartender was. It seemed kind of funny, though. All those people asking for drinks and no one using his name. Usually the bartender is the best known person in the room. But he's pretty easy to describe, very short and stocky, curly black hair, about 35 and even though they didn't use his name, everyone seemed to know him."

"What about the location of the house. Can you remember how you got there?"

"Sort of. Most of Cordova Bay is pretty hilly, but this place seemed to be in a fairly flat area to the left of Cordova Bay Road, heading away from downtown. There was a long driveway and the house seemed to be hidden from the road. I'm not sure how far along Cordova Bay Road we drove, but it didn't seem all that far from the University and I think it was before the golf course."

"Did Doug get you or the others to try the crystal meth like he did with the ecstasy?"

"No. In fact, I didn't even know he had it with him, or that he had taken it himself. Later, though, when he started acting crazy, I figured he must be on something pretty wild. That's when I freaked out. Then he turned the car around and …."

At that point Diane began crying uncontrollably and Tim decided to end the interview. He knew he could always visit her again if he thought there was more she could offer, but he was sure he had learned most of what she remembered and it was obviously the right time to leave her alone.

"Thank you, Diane," he said gently. "You have been very helpful. I am extremely sorry for what happened. You can be assured I will do what I can to find the people who supplied Doug the drugs and to make sure this doesn't happen to anyone else."

Tim was certain he could find Sam's very quickly. But he doubted there would be much point. After the accident, the newspaper was quick to come out with the details. The reporter even speculated that drugs were the cause of the crash and Tim knew that Sam's would be quick to shut things down until the whole matter blew over. Later, they would likely set up in another location, but for now he was sure he would discover nothing but a quiet residential house on a quiet residential street.

Finding Al Whitesomething was probably a good place to begin, but the white pages were full of Whites, Whitelaws and Whiteheads. By narrowing it down to the West Shore, the list was considerably shortened, but he had little reason to believe that Al came from there, other than the fact that he was Doug's contact and Doug made Langford his home. Next, he checked the RCMP files and hit pay dirt when he discovered an Al Whitelaw from Colwood who was "known" to the police. The files on him indicated that Al had appeared in court on two occasions, one after an accident involving alcohol and the other after refusing to take a breath analyser test. While there was no reason to think this Al Whitelaw had graduated from booze to drugs, the information seemed very promising. Tim jumped into his four-by-four and made for Colwood.

As soon as he answered the door, Tim knew that he had found his man. With pupils the size of saucers and as twitchy as a Mexican jumping bean, Al Whitelaw was the personification of a man high on cocaine. As he backed rapidly into his living room, eyes wildly scanning the surfaces of his own furniture, Tim could easily read guilt from a man with something to hide. That something wasn't hard to determine. A small zip-lock bag lay open on an end table near the television, its white powder contents as obvious as sand in the Sahara Desert. Al dove for the bag as Tim's eyes converged on it, but Tim was faster.

"My name is Corporal Murphy. Perhaps we might have a little talk, Al?" he asked conversationally. "I might not even wonder what's in this bag, if I get the right answers to a few questions."

"You can't just barge in here and grab my personal property. I know my rights. You need a search warrant to do that."

"Oh, so this is your personal property! The prosecutor will be pleased to know that. By the way, I don't need a search warrant when the evidence of criminal activity is right before my eyes. A search is hardly necessary."

"Alright, what do you want to know?"

"That's better. Do you happen to know a young man by the name of Doug Hawley?"

"Do you mean the young guy who was killed in that accident last week? Why should I know him?"

"You tell me. Maybe it's got something to do with the contents of this little bag?"

"Okay, I knew him. He sold me some coke from time to time, but that's all I know about him."

"That's not what I heard. The word has it that you gave him the name of a supplier in town who could fix Doug up with some crystal meth and maybe some other delightful concoctions as well. What's his name?"

"I don't know what you're talking about."

"All right, have it your way. Let's take you and this little bag and go have a longer chat down at the station."

"Not so fast. I'll tell you as long as you don't let him know that I gave you his name. He might not like it too much if he finds out it was me that ratted on him."

"You can count on it, Al," Tim replied, glibly. "We wouldn't want anything to happen to a fine upstanding citizen like you."

"His name is Dick Walker and all I know is he often hangs out at a place called Sam's. I also heard that he knows how to get his hands on a steady supply of meth and maybe some other drugs as well."

"Who are you hearing all this fine information from, Al?"

"Just the fellows down at The Post, shooting the breeze. I can't remember who in particular might have said it."

"Okay, Al, but I might be back. In the meantime, try and recall who gave you the name, or I might forget you asked me not to let this Dick Walker know you gave his name to me."

"If I can remember, Corporal, I'll let you know," Al answered hurriedly as he led Tim to the door.

Chapter 7

SERGEANT SINGH RANGA'S REPORT was only one indicator of a rapidly growing problem, not only in Victoria, but across the country. The capability of criminals to transport illegal drugs across the Canadian border had increased at the same time that they had learned how to produce them at home and abroad more cheaply and much quicker than in the past. As well, the willingness of Canada's youth and young adults to experiment with drugs had also increased. The popularity of softer drugs such as marijuana and ecstasy had grown as never before, but now the use of such stalwarts as meth-amphetamine and cocaine were on the rise. In addition, experimentation with the newer chemical drugs had lead to an alphabet soup of mind-altering substances such as ephedrine, pseudoephedrine, phencyclidine, ketamine, dextromethorphan, codeine and gamma-hydroxybutyrate (GHB).

The lucrative monetary rewards that are gained from the drug trade had led to innumerable traffickers. Some were individuals, others were loose associations of like-minded delinquent groups, and many were part of highly organized criminal networks. In British Columbia, the trade was often organized around ethnic groupings, such as those of Vietnamese heritage controlling large sections of the marijuana trade, or those of East Indian and other Asian descent involved in the manufacture and export of ecstasy and methamphetamine. Biker gangs were heavily involved in the manufacture and distribution of the synthetic drugs, especially crystal meth, and more recently, GHB. Disagreements between these groups led to increased violence and attempts by powerful organizers to coordinate the actions of the lesser players.

The investigation in Victoria into the drug trade may have been initiated by the increased carnage on the highways from the misuse of various drugs, but it was only one of many similar investigations in mainly larger centres across the country. Law enforcement agencies in some cities formed cooperative organizations to combat the problem. Victoria was one of these. The RCMP and Victoria City Police initiated an investigative drug squad to look into not only the linkages between increased drug use and traffic accidents, but all other effects of drug trafficking on the public. Sergeant John Anderson from the Vancouver

Island District Office was appointed to lead the squad and Corporal Tim Murphy was made a member.

Soon after his appointment was approved, Tim was called to Sergeant Anderson's office for their first meeting. Anderson's office was in the District Office Headquarters on Nanaimo Street, located on the northern approaches to downtown. At one time E Division Headquarters, the centre for RCMP operations across British Columbia, had been in downtown Victoria housed in an old college building on Johnson Street. But E Division Headquarters had since been moved to Vancouver and the city had taken advantage to buy up the building and sell it to a major bank. District Headquarters Offices had been created across the province after the move of E Division and Vancouver Island District Headquarters was one of these. The newly-built Nanaimo Street building provided ample space for the RCMP staff assigned to the Headquarters. Sergeant Anderson's roomy office was located on the third floor with a view of Blanshard Street, which at some indeterminate point heading out of town became the Pat Bay Highway.

Sergeant Anderson was a grizzled, long-in-the-tooth, dedicated police officer who had spent most of his career in narcotics operations, including lengthy stints in undercover work in Regina, Winnipeg and Vancouver. He had been pleased with his transfer to Victoria late in his career, as until recently Victoria could hardly be described as a hotbed of illicit drug activity. But he looked upon this latest assignment with some reluctance, not possessing a lot of faith in the ability of city police forces to respond effectively to drug use within their restricted jurisdictions. He recognized that the increasingly sophisticated ability of organized criminals to operate internationally made a mockery of any attempts by a single city to deal with the problem. Nevertheless, through the RCMP network, he would be in a good position to share experiences with other cooperative teams set up in other cities across the country, so perhaps something could be accomplished through this new initiative.

He welcomed Corporal Murphy into his office somewhat warily. After reviewing Tim's record, he was not sure what to make of him. He appeared to be an effective, intelligent and hardworking officer, who nevertheless had a tendency for getting into hot water without a whole lot of effort. He knew Murphy's transfer into anti-drug work was not exactly looked upon by his superiors as a promotion, but he had also learned that these same superiors were confident that he would be an asset to the squad.

"Please have a chair, Corporal Murphy. I see from this report from Staff-Sergeant Toms that you have already been investigating the drug connection in the recent Pat Bay Highway crash. Are you making any headway?"

"Good morning to you, too, Sergeant," Tim replied, somewhat bemused by Anderson's blunt manner. "Well, I have uncovered a couple of leads. I guess the main thing I have learned already is that there may be a fairly large network of dealers working loosely with each other across the city. Until recently they operated through a house in Cadboro Bay called Sam's, but I believe they may have moved to another location, which as yet I haven't found. I am also attempting to find a man by the name of Dick Walker, who may be supplying dealers across the city. That name is probably a pseudonym as he doesn't appear to be listed anywhere."

"It doesn't sound like you have learned that much, Corporal. Anything else?"

"I have a description of a bartender who appears to have a good deal of knowledge about various suppliers operating out of Sam's. According to the surviving woman from the crash, she overheard a conversation with the driver, Doug Hawley, and the bartender. She learned that the bartender knew this Walker character, whatever his correct name, and was able to steer

Hawley to another supplier in Sam's at the time, who supplied him with a bag of crystal meth."

"And you're going to tell me you have tracked this bartender down?"

"Not yet, but Victoria's not that big. He'll show up. One more thing. The man who gave me Dick Walker's name, Al Whitelaw, said that he was in the habit of discussing drug suppliers with some of his cronies at The Post, a pub out in Langford. It might be an idea to grill Al a bit more and perhaps go undercover there and see what we can find out."

"Okay, I'll assign someone to do that. As for yourself, Tim, you're part of the special drug squad now and I want you to work with Constable Craig Ballard, a member of the Victoria Police Force. I want to see if the two of you can track down these elusive characters that, as you say, are bound to show up. Craig has spent time undercover, knows the city well and might have some ideas on where to look for these guys. Also, if Sam's has moved to another location he may be able to help us find it. Oh, and just so you know, Corporal, the rest of the squad will be focussing on finding out where the drugs are coming from. Lots of crystal meth is manufactured in Canada now. It's pretty easy to do and for all we know, they could be making it here in Victoria, right under our noses. In addition, I'll be talking to E Division staff in Vancouver to see if they can tell us anything new about drugs coming across the Georgia Straight, or even directly into Victoria from the States. As you can see, we've got lots to do, so get to it."

AFTER LEAVING ANDERSON'S office, Tim called Constable Ballard. They agreed to meet in an hour in Tim's office. Craig Ballard turned out to be a lanky, long-haired man about thirty-five who was the personification of casualness. Slouching into Tim's office, Craig barely acknowledged an obligatory introduction before leaning unceremoniously against a filing cabinet, ignoring Tim's invitation to take a seat. His eyes roamed over the sparse contents of Tim's office, alighting fleetingly on a picture of Gloria, before focusing through the lone window, onto the side street below.

"Nice office you've got here, Tim. I always wondered what it was like in the hallowed halls of the RCMP's District Headquarters," he drawled sardonically. "Sort of reminds me of my office downtown, especially the great view of the alley outside your window."

Momentarily taken aback, but reacting quickly, Tim replied, "I thought you guys all worked underground in your line of work. Your only view would be the far end of the mole hole."

"Hey, that's undercover, man, not underground," Craig laughed. "Sometimes, I even get to see the sun, at least when I'm not hanging out with Victoria's late night crowd of riff-raff."

"And that reminds me why my illustrious Sergeant has asked us to get together. He thinks you can lead me through the sin bins of the city and ferret out a couple of shady characters involved in the drug trade."

"Looks to me like we have some work to do before we can take you downtown. You're a little spiffy for this kind of work. We will need to grub you up a bit before we start cruising bars. Luckily, that short hair of yours is in fashion. Maybe we can cut it even shorter and get you an earring."

"Hey, there's a limit, but I'll try and do enough to pass myself off as a new customer from the suburbs looking for a steady supply."

"Sounds good. When do we start?"

"Does tonight seem soon enough?"

They spent the rest of the meeting discussing the details. Tim went over the information he had gathered from Diane. Craig seemed particularly interested in the closing of Sam's and thought that if there was a replacement place it shouldn't be too hard to find. Many dealers would also be out looking for the location and if he and Tim started asking around, that may not seem at all suspicious. Craig thought that a good place to start would be the Devonshire Hotel, a large downtown place where much of Victoria's fast crowd hung out and where Craig was just another familiar figure. They agreed to meet there at 9:30 pm.

Gloria was amused at Tim's new assignment. She had difficulty picturing him as an undercover agent, but agreed to help him prepare for the role. She was able to cut his hair to about a half inch, reasonably evenly across his head, but instead of an earring, they settled on a casual suburban look, with jeans, running shoes and a plain tee shirt. He looked like Joe Everybody, maybe even an off-duty police officer, but with no particular reason for anyone to suspect that he was.

The Devonshire is a big hodgepodge of a hotel, mainly catering to Victoria's drinkers. Tourists, regulars, suburban shoppers, hustlers or new-age trendies, they each have a bar in the hotel where they can feel at home. Tim made his way to Mad Mike's where he and Craig were scheduled to start their search for dealers. Mike's is the hangout of the regulars, locals who have been drinking in Victoria's bars since it first became common. While the odd tourist wandering into the Devonshire may find his way into Mike's by mistake, generally the people know each other and know the city. Craig was accepted here, but the patrons would have been amazed to learn that he was a police officer. They just thought he was one of the boys, here to pass the time and swap stories with the rest of the regulars. He was able to introduce Tim without anyone getting too curious. They could understand that he was looking for a little extra to compliment his alcohol intake, and while no one was willing to admit they knew anyone who could sell Tim anything, except for a little grass perhaps, one of them finally recommended they try the Racket Room, where the new-age crowd were more likely to know a few traders.

It wasn't called the Racket Room for nothing. It catered to a much younger and more energetic set than at Mike's and everyone seemed to enjoy talking at the same time. Except for a large and boisterous crowd along the bar, the drinkers were divided into groups of about six or eight, all crowded around individual tables and generally oblivious to the revellers around them. It was easy to talk to the mainly male imbibers at the bar, an easy-going group who didn't seem to be bothered that the two new interlopers were older than themselves. Craig was soon swapping stories and steering the conversation around to his and Tim's apparent interest in recreational drugs. Craig was adept at the game of one-upmanship and soon had the others trying to out-macho each other by relating their various drug experiences.

"Reminds me of the time a few months ago when I scored with old Dick at Sam's," related Craig, inventively. "He got me a bag of GHB. Talk about dream city, I felt like I was on a cloud for a week. Man, I sure miss that place."

"Yeah, it's just not the same since they moved the house to James Bay," a muscular, thick-headed youth named Bobby piped in helpfully. "There are too many houses around, no place to park and you always have to keep the noise down so the neighbours won't complain."

"Well, it's still better than nothing," agreed Craig. "But I've been working in Vancouver the past couple of months and haven't had a chance to get out there. I'm not even sure if I know how to find the damn place."

"Hey, it's easy man," obliging Bob replied. "It's the third last house on the right before the water on Clark Street. If you go, say hello to Dick for me."

"Sure, Bobby. What's your last name again?"

Tim could hardly believe their luck. Once they determined they weren't going to get anything else out of Bobby or the others at the bar without raising suspicions, he and Craig downed their drinks and left the hotel. They decided there was nothing like the present and made for James Bay.

Chapter 8

FOR AS LONG AS HE could remember, Barinder Chohan felt that he was under pressure. His parents had been born in India, but had come to Canada to work in Barinder's uncle's lumber mill in Surrey shortly after they were married. Barinder's father, Amrit, had done well in his brother's company and was presently responsible for all trucking operations. Amrit, and especially Barinder's mother, Manjit, were very devoted to their Sikh faith and customs and expected that Barinder should be as well. They also required that he do well in school and would endlessly enquire about his class standing.

Barinder's schoolmates also had expectations. Many of the other Sikh students westernized their appearance in an attempt to fit in with their classmates and subtly hinted that Barinder do the same. The white students, on the other hand, were much more brutal and especially ridiculed his turban and long hair. While Barinder desired to fit in, he was still respectful of his parent's wishes and maintained his traditional garb.

In time, Barinder became resentful of his parents' and teachers' expectations and began to hang out with a tough crowd of Sikh youth, more interested in fast cars and petty crime than in grades and parental wishes. By the time he had completed high school, Barinder was working full-time driving a truck for his father by day and helping to break into cars by night. Somehow he was never caught, and while he bowed to his parent's demands that he attend university, his criminal friends never allowed him to break free from their own set of expectations for him.

In university, though majoring in engineering, Barinder discovered politics. He quickly learned that he could garner favours by aiding aspiring politicians to gain office. After graduating from the University of British Columbia, he was rewarded by receiving a minor position in a federal Progressive Party constituent office in Surrey.

Here he encountered a new set of pressures. In order to further his own career, he was expected to sell party memberships and help party bagmen raise donations from the Sikh community. At first the work was straightforward and Barinder was able to persuade a sizeable number of his friends and acquaintances to become party members. Soon, however, in order to satisfy party organizers, he was directed to raise monies to pay the membership fees for community members who would agree to join the party, but who were unwilling to pay the nominal fee of $25 to do so. While $25 didn't seem like much in order to increase the party membership in a significant way, Barinder had to resort to creative ways to find the money.

With the assistance of a party organizer, Barinder arranged for one of his former classmates to get a job with his father, hauling lumber across the border to Washington and Oregon. From time to time, the driver was given an additional package to take with him, well hidden in the middle of a large load of two by fours. On his return trip, he was given a much smaller package to bring home, this time hidden in a small compartment under the driver's seat, especially constructed by an associate of the party organizer. Barinder's father was never made aware of these special deliveries, nor was he informed of the existence of the special compartment. Barinder was provided a portion of the proceeds from the sale of these packages in order to fund his membership fee assignment. The arrangement worked well and Barinder was able to considerably increase Progressive Party membership in his Surrey riding. The party thought highly of Barinder's results and eventually a job was found for him in the Provincial Government in Victoria, where he was given the position of aide to the Minister of Economic Diversification.

Barinder soon found that the pressure in his new job was as intense as ever, maybe more so. While his duties as aide were taxing in themselves, he was also expected to organize Federal Party membership recruitment drives for Vancouver Island and to raise funds for membership purchases across the province. In order to brief Barinder on just how he was expected to perform these duties, he was paid a visit by Roger Kent, an influential fund raiser who was responsible for Party matters across the Island.

"You have done some excellent work for the party in the Lower Mainland, Barinder. As you know, we were able to recruit enough new party members in Surrey in the recent election to take the nomination away from the sitting MP, Harb Dhillon, who was becoming a liability to the party. We want you to do the same thing here and at the same time keep an eye on the provincial Party. We're not always sure that the Premier understands how things should be run."

"Thanks, Mr. Kent. I'm happy to do what I can, but I'm not sure how I am supposed to raise the money required to increase federal party memberships across the entire province."

"We have a lot of friends here on the Island, Barinder, and we feel that with your help, they can assist us in raising the funds. The party will provide you with some seed money, which we are going to ask you to give to certain people. Maybe you also know of others you can approach? The idea is that these people will use the funds as a down payment for a mortgage on properties here in Greater Victoria and up-Island. The properties will then be rented out to other friends of ours who will be expected to make some pretty generous rent payments. These payments will then be used to pay the mortgage and to help you with your membership responsibilities."

"Not many people I know can afford large mortgage payments," Barinder observed. "Where are they going to get the money, month after month?"

"Oh, you don't need to worry about that. In fact, you don't even need to know the real names of the people who will be renting these places. But if you have any relatives or acquaintances who would like to own a nice piece of property and obtain a good, steady income on the side, you should approach them. About the only requirement is selecting people who can keep their mouths shut."

"I think I am getting the picture," an enlightened Barinder Chohan replied. "I have a cousin who just might be interested. He's with the Victoria Fire Department. Give me some time to think about it and I can probably come up with another name or two. How many do you think we need altogether?"

"That's the spirit!" beamed Kent. "We only need five or six and I have two for you already. Now, let's go to the business of your provincial job. The two levels of the party work quite closely together at times and your new boss, Jack Perrier, owed us a favour, which allowed us to get you the position as his aide. Jack's okay, but you will be in a good position to know exactly what the Cabinet is up to and we need to know that. In order to make sure that the Provincial Government is onside with Federal Party interests, we may need to find some replacements at the next election. The current Premier, in particular, will need to go. He seems to think the only requirement of his job is to reward his Howe Street friends, and that bunch doesn't always have the best interests of the country in mind."

"Well, again, I will do what I can, but I don't know if I can figure out everything the Cabinet is up to alone."

"You will be getting some help. We have also found a position for a buddy of yours, Alan Diwan, who is to become the aide to Shelley Peregrine, Minister of Public Works. The two of you will be able to work closely together."

As Barinder left from his brief meeting with Roger Kent, he felt like he had just inherited a whole new set of pressures.

THE CAPTAIN WAS PLEASED with the efforts being made to increase membership in the federal Progressive Party. He knew that the Asian communities were becoming a larger and larger percentage of the population and that they tended to vote as a block. He also knew these new members could usually be manipulated, and by doing so, he could ensure particular candidates were selected at nomination meetings in a significant number of Lower Mainland ridings. He also knew that he had the ability to work from behind the scenes to ensure the right candidates were chosen in the first place, that is, ones who would support his plans for the party. He had arranged a meeting with Paul Husband, a campaign manager for Federal candidates in the province. It was also convenient that Paul was married to Marlene McIntyre, another Cabinet Minister in the Provincial Government.

Paul Husband was a wiry, high energy man who very much enjoyed the organizational work required for party nominating meetings and especially elections. He was a born net worker, adept at the glad-handing, back-slapping aspects of his job. He generally felt at ease with the powers of the party and felt most comfortable in their presence. The Captain was the exception. He made Paul feel uneasy and he could never relax during their thankfully infrequent meetings. He wasn't sure if it was The Captain's immense wealth, his reputed power, or his ability to make others seem inferior in his presence. He supposed it was all of these, but in addition, an intuitive feeling about The Captain, a sense that the man used others strictly for his own purposes, which always caused him to be cautious whenever they were required to meet.

The Captain led Paul to a seat on the opposite side of his immense desk and sat himself directly across from him. From this position, Paul had his back to the window and the glorious scenery far below them, while The Captain could carefully watch both Paul and the passing marine traffic.

"I was very pleased with the outcome of the election result in Surrey last month, Paul, as Harb Dhillon's loyalty was becoming very suspect. He seemed to have more interest in the provincial opposition party than his own federal party responsibilities. It's clear the new guy won't be a problem."

"Thanks, but the real credit has to go to Barinder Chohan for signing up so many new members in the Indian community."

"True. We think we can also get him to increase memberships in other ridings where enough votes in the right direction will make a difference. As you know, the situation in Parliament is pretty unstable and we expect another election to be held in less than a year. It will be up to you to put the organization in place to use the money that Barinder raises to fund new memberships in those key ridings. Not all of them will have significant Asian minorities and you will need to pinpoint other groups willing to support our candidates. Roger Kent, Leif Johannsen and I will determine where new candidates will be required and who those candidates will be. It will be your job to ensure they get the party nominations."

"That's a pretty tall order. The constituent organizations usually favour the incumbent. It's not always that easy to get them to switch to supporting a new candidate, especially if they see that person as an outsider."

"That's right, Paul, and I am sure by the time the election is called you can guarantee that the constituency organizations in those ridings will each choose an executive that understands the situation."

"Okay, give me a list of the ridings we need to focus on and I'll get to work."

After Husband left, The Captain considered what he had said about the constituency organizations. He could see that in some cases the executive members would need to be replaced. He foresaw that a change of president would be enough in most problem ridings and he was confident that he could persuade the current incumbents to step down and arrange for others to take their place. He would see to it that Husband was provided the names of the individuals who were willing to take over as president. It would be up to Paul to ensure they were elected.

The Captain turned his thoughts to the membership/funding problem. The right individual would be required to organize the production and sale of marijuana crops on the rental properties arranged with Barinder Chohan. Reluctant to become directly involved with the more powerful organized gangs who could easily make the arrangements, the Captain determined that he would steer Roger Kent to an intermediate-sized operation already active on the Island as the best option.

While it was never ideal to work with criminals to raise money, he couldn't possibly use his own wealth for funding memberships, as it would be much too difficult to launder the amount required. Nor did he wish to use his existing contacts in Vancouver who currently handled the trucking operation into the U.S. as they would not have enough familiarity with the Island. After carefully exploring various options, he settled on the Desperados, originally an eastern-based motorcycle gang, which had slowly set up new chapters in the west in recent years. The new chapter in Victoria had only been operating for two years, but had already made inroads by selling marijuana and certain chemicals to American operatives in exchange for cocaine and an assortment of recreational drugs which they peddled throughout southern Vancouver Island.

Chapter 9

JAMES BAY IS IN A SEDATE, well-established section of Victoria whose residents pride themselves on their community-mindedness. Enclosed by the Harbour to the north and the legislature and Beacon Hill Park to the east and south, the land is flat and the houses are close together. Many of the original inhabitants of Victoria chose James Bay as a superior section of the city to settle and an impressive number of their descendents are still there. In recent years, however, a significant number of the houses have been divided up into small suites and boarding rooms and the occupants are generally transitory. The large clapboard house located on the right side of Clark Street, only three houses away from Dallas Road, appeared to be a typical example.

The house was recently purchased by a rather nondescript individual, Mr. John Smith no less, but in fact it was owned by a very wealthy businessman who lived in Vancouver. Still, it wasn't a typical gang headquarters and the occupants maintained a quiet orderly-looking residence, at least as it appeared from the outside. Inside, the same activities that took place at Sam's went on here, only a lot less boisterously. Patrons of the house, which had as yet not been blessed with a name, were required to park in one of many small parking lots on nearby Dallas Road. If the neighbours were aware of the frequent visitors to the house, they didn't seem curious, assuming they were fellow transients without cars who were forced to live in crowded bachelor apartments and rooming houses.

Craig Ballard parked in a residence-only spot about a block north of the house and he and Tim sauntered casually up the step and rang the doorbell. The man who answered the door seemed satisfied with their reference to Dick Walker and let them in. As they made their way into the lounge area and approached the bar, Tim knew their luck was holding, as the bartender matched the description that Diane had given him. They paid for their drinks and stood around the bar making conversation with the bartender. Finally, Craig casually asked, "Is Dick Walker around tonight?"

"Nope, I haven't seen him. It's still a little early for Dick, though. Are you looking for a little stuff?"

"My buddy here might be interested."

"Well, be patient. Dick's a reliable guy and I'm sure he can fix you up. In the meantime, enjoy the scenery."

A few couples were dancing in one of the other rooms, but generally the house was pretty quiet. Tim assumed the house wasn't well known yet, and while some of the regulars had already made it part of their routine, a lot of the casual patrons had still to locate it.

After about an hour, having gone back to the lounge, Craig and Tim were waved over by the bartender, who pointed out a man who had recently entered.

"That's Dick. Just let him know what you want. He's pretty easy to deal with."

Tim was a bit surprised by that. Obviously, the initial public reaction to the Pat Bay accident had died down and while it had led to the subsequent transfer of the club's operations, the owners and dealers were confident that business was back to normal. Just the same, he let Craig approach Dick first, as they had previously agreed to do, while Tim remained with the bartender.

Dick didn't appear to find anything suspicious about Craig and after a short conversation he nodded at Tim to join them.

"Your friend says you're interested in a little coke. Is this for yourself or are you planning to start your own business?" he asked, only half jokingly.

"I just need enough for me and a few friends to relax once in a while. I'm not planning on starting a new enterprise. I've got enough to do bossing a construction crew," he added, seemingly convincingly.

"Okay, here's the deal. I sell it by the gram. A five gram bag will cost you $400 and that should last you a little while. Come back and see me when you need more and if five is not enough we can increase it. I have a room in the back where I handle the transactions and we can go there now. I will ask that your friend stay here, as I will only deal with one customer at a time."

"Sounds good," agreed Tim.

They left Craig at the bar and strolled to the back of the house where Dick maintained a locked office. He unlocked a secure cabinet in the corner of the small room and brought out a previously prepared bag of cocaine. Tim handed over the money and the deal was done.

It had all been too easy, but this was only step one. It was Tim's plan that he would establish Dick's confidence before they made an arrest. He wanted to know more about Walker and how he operated before trying to trap him into disclosing his suppliers. He also wished to determine what other drugs Dick handled, and in what quantities. The more serious he could eventually make the charges against him, the more he was sure he could get Dick to cooperate in naming his accomplices. He wasn't sure how far up the chain he could get by using this approach, but in the meantime, by gaining his trust and visiting the house from time to time, he hoped that he and Craig would learn more than they knew now.

After the transaction, he and Craig left, and after securing the bag of cocaine at District Headquarters, Tim went home to Metchosin. By the time he got in, Gloria was fast asleep, and as he found himself doing more and more these days, he undressed in the darkened bedroom and slipped quietly into bed.

In the morning he was pleased to find that Gloria was in an upbeat mood and was studiously reviewing tenant tax receipts. The previous day was a dialysis day and often the day after was a relatively good one for her. He admired that, in spite of suffering from very low energy levels from her disease, she attempted to maintain as normal a life as she could. She even made a point of going running at least two days a week, even though a kilometre was all she could handle and likely didn't contribute much to her overall level of fitness.

Being used to rural assignments before being posted to Victoria, Tim and Gloria had decided to live in Metchosin, even though they could hardly afford to do so with Tim's Corporal's salary. Although only about twenty kilometres from the centre of Victoria, Metchosin is a surprisingly rural community and the inhabitants have worked hard to keep it that way. Time and again the residents have been forced to organize in order to thwart the ambitions of covetous developers, eager to replace the municipality's existing bylaw requirement of five to ten acre property holdings with one that would permit city-sized lots.

Nevertheless, a loophole in the bylaw allowed a property owner, after owning the property for more than five years, to carve off up to an acre to be sold to a direct relative. Of course, once the relative had taken ownership, he or she was at liberty to resell it. On paper this had been done, allowing Tim and Gloria to purchase an acre from a property holder's father, who had owned the land for one whole day. The loophole had been closed shortly after they had purchased their one acre, and Tim often joked that he had lobbied hard for the change, in order to keep other riff-raff like himself out of Metchosin.

As Gloria was not able to work, she had looked for ways to keep busy and to earn some extra income. Hoping that one day she would receive a kidney transplant and be able to have children, they had decided to build a larger house than they required. She determined that, in the meantime, renting out a portion of the house to tenants would give her something to do and provide her with a small but important cash flow. Tim had agreed and in the three subsequent years they had already had four tenants.

Working her way through a pile of receipts, Gloria began to laugh. "Do you realize, Tim, that we have never had nice boring tenants that simply went about their lives quietly and routinely? First there was Stan and Noreen. They had that cute Rottweiler pup that soon grew into a huge monster that destroyed the backyard and by the end of their time here he was determined to kill our dog, Groucho. Then there was that young guy, Jeff, who smoked marijuana after we told him that we didn't want him smoking in the house."

"I guess he figured it wasn't carcinogenic so it didn't count," recalled Tim. "You think he could have shown a little respect. He knew I was a cop and yet he smoked the stuff all the time. At the very least, he could have slipped me a joint once in a while."

"Yeah, right. Then he split and left his girlfriend here and she moved out after chucking all his clothes and tools in the trash. Then when she was gone we found out her cats were still here and we had to track her down and make her take them away."

"And what about that old guy from Saltspring, Gloria? He seemed so laid back and calm to begin with. Then you told him we were repainting the bathroom before he moved in. He didn't show up when he was supposed to take possession and two weeks later you finally got a letter from him, saying that he is allergic to paint and can't live anywhere for three months after it's painted! This in spite of the fact he already gave you a deposit and post-dated cheques for six months."

"I think we should be thankful he didn't move in. Anyone that eccentric would have probably been a bit much to live with."

"Your new one, Helen, seems nice enough. Let's just hope her ten-year-old son doesn't burn us out."

"Now, Tim, you know it wasn't him that set her last place on fire. She told us she had a candle going and fell asleep and it caught the curtains on fire."

"Okay. Just make sure the fire insurance is up-to-date."

"Speaking of fire, Tim, I think there are a few embers glowing in the old furnace. Are you doing anything this morning?"

"Not anymore, you wanton hussy," he teased, calculating that it had been at least three weeks since they had last made love.

Chapter 10

DREW PEARSON HAD LEFT TORONTO in a hurry. The Satan's Sirens had moved in only the previous summer and the Desperados had fought hard to maintain their operations, but they were no match for the much larger and better organized gang. Drew had lost two Desperados' members before he resigned himself to a strategic withdrawal. He chose Victoria, as it was relatively unorganized, but was still large enough that the potential was there to make a good living. He had avoided Vancouver, where a number of gangs were busy sorting out boundaries, figuring he could use a rest from the inevitable bloodshed. Besides, the Desperados weren't in any shape to be challenging for a piece of the action in the much bigger city.

Drew had grown up tough. His father, Robert (Bud) Pearson, had owned a downtown magazine stand, but his real source of income was a bookie operation that provided his clients an opportunity to bet on almost anything, particularly sports, of course, but even politics and election results. Everyone knew about Bud's backroom enterprise, especially the police, many of whom were his best customers. He only found himself in trouble when a long-shot Toronto mayoralty contender came up the middle to beat out two establishment candidates and a cash-strapped Bud couldn't come up with the money to pay his new "protectors." They had hired a local bouncer to beat it out of him, but in his enthusiasm, the bouncer had managed to create enough damage that Bud had died from internal bleeding.

His mother had done her best to raise Drew properly in a seedy section of East Scarborough, but by his late teens he had established himself as a steadfast member of a youth gang and was totally engulfed in the petty turf wars that characterized that section of the city. He was smart and ambitious, and soon established himself as the leader of his group which, after four successful years of criminal activity and a few organizational changes, became a chapter of the Desperados motorcycle gang. Drew enjoyed being the head of a criminal group and the money and perks that came with it. He tried to avoid the violence, typical of motorcycle gang life, but his successes inevitably attracted the attentions of the police and other criminals.

In the three years Drew had now been in Victoria, the Desperados had done well. Drew was proud of his organizing abilities and he had worked hard to establish their business. He had determined quickly that the so-called recreational drugs had the greatest potential for growth. The demand was burgeoning and the existing suppliers were all small operators, required to buy their products from the mainland. Drew established a methamphetamine lab in Saanich, a large suburb of Victoria where the hard-working residents were rarely at home and paid little attention to the comings and goings of the neighbours. By-passing the need to smuggle his product in from the Lower Mainland, he was able to provide his own dealers with a reliable and steady supply.

Drew was a stickler for quality control. He had carefully learned about the manufacturing requirements for crystal meth and he knew that some of the ingredients were exceptionally lethal and needed to be handled and stored very carefully. He also recognized that a toxic reaction to the drug could easily kill his patrons, which would not only be bad for business, but would gain the attention of the various police forces in the city. Unfortunately, his less-organized competitors were not nearly so scrupulous and this contributed to the decision to initiate an inter-department police drug squad investigation throughout the region.

Once the lab was providing a healthy income to the gang, Drew began exploring further avenues for growth. Marijuana cultivation was an easy one. Vancouver Island was one of the biggest sources of the drug in the western world and it was grown on farms and in houses everywhere. Shipping and trucking operations were in place to move the product to the mainland and into the United States. One of the most common methods of transport was by small fishing and sailboats that could come and go across the border without careful scrutiny, simply because of the huge numbers engaged in these activities legitimately and the impossibility of inspecting them all thoroughly. Because the risk of detection was low, it was not difficult to find boat owners willing to transport the product.

Drew used the proceeds from the sale of crystal meth to set up a number of grow-ops, mainly in smaller up-Island communities, where rural houses were able to cultivate the crops without much chance of detection. He had also hired an electrician who easily by-passed the meter at each house, so that the increase in electrical use would not be detected. Reliable friends of gang members were willing to maintain the grow-ops, as Drew and his gang tended to avoid the violence and intimidation typical of many groups involved in marijuana production.

Next, Drew turned his attention to increasing the supply of pseudoephedrine in the gang's lab. This chemical is used in the production of methamphetamine and there was a big market in supplying the substance to "super-labs" operated by Mexican trafficking networks in California and the other southwestern states. The absence of regulated chemical controls in Canada made it easy to smuggle pseudoephedrine across the border. Drew was able to do this by simply incorporating a business in Victoria, ostensibly manufacturing chemical products used in various medicines. Within a few weeks, the gang was making regular trucking runs across the border, without ever encountering the slightest suspicion from customs agents. There was no point in having the trucks come home empty and that led to a lucrative cocaine business. Soon the Desperados, while still small and low profile, were becoming very prosperous.

It was through a part-time fisherman, Terry Sawyer, that The Captain had discovered the Desperados. An amazing number of small boats were involved in smuggling marijuana and occasionally one would get caught. Considering the number of boats crossing the border between B.C. and Washington State each day and the limited resources of the Coast Guard and Customs officials, the odds were low enough that many individual boat owners were willing to take the chance to make a quick buck. Terry had been willing to be one of them and he had previously made four successful trips. He had learned not to ask for the identity of his contacts on each end of the trip, but to simply take his money and keep his mouth shut. After he was arrested, he refused to disclose the very little information he did know, including the name of one of the more junior members of the Desperados. Later in prison, Terry was persuaded by a fellow inmate to disclose what he knew, enough for The Captain to discover the existence of the Desperados and their operations.

DREW AGREED TO MEET Roger Kent in mid-afternoon on a weekday at the Five Mile Pub. The Five Mile was a large, rambling historic building in the West Shore with many rooms, each with its own atmosphere and unique arrangement of oddball furniture. The pub was not a place that either of them usually frequented but it offered the privacy for their discussions that each wanted. The pub's clientele were the usual mix of dedicated alcoholics, unemployed youth, sales agents between appointments, retired couples and bored housewives that one finds in suburban drinking establishments all over North America. The other patrons paid them little attention as they arrived separately and found an appropriate table in a room at the back, close to a noisy video game machine that easily masked their conversation.

Drew was not pleased about the meeting. Terry Sawyer had never warned him, either directly, or through any other gang member, that he had been forced to admit to his connection to the Desperados. Nevertheless, if this man, Roger Kent, had some knowledge of their activities, he had better find out just how much, so that he could determine what he would need to do to protect the gang's operations. He had been scrupulously careful to distance himself from any arrangements with non-gang contacts and he felt that someone within the Desperados must have talked to Kent to allow him to know as much as he appeared to when he first called for a meeting.

Kent appeared to be the slickest person that Drew had ever met. He was slim, very tall, and moved confidently with sure and athletic movements. He also had dark black hair, a friendly looking smile and icy cold blue eyes that erased any thoughts that he may have actually been friendly. Drew's initial reaction was a desire to keep his back to the wall to stop Roger from getting behind him. While oozing charm, Kent had the ability to make you think he was holding a huge threat over your head that could be used at any time.

"I wish to thank you for agreeing to meet with me," he began politely. "I realize this must be difficult for you. Nevertheless, I think when you hear me out you will agree that it will be very much to our mutual benefit to work together. Our research has determined that your operations here in Victoria are working well for you and your associates and my only desire is to help you make them even more successful."

"I am not sure what operations you are referring to," Drew answered uneasily. "Your so-called research should tell you that I am simply a small businessman who runs a very humble medical chemical production company. I think you might need to find a new researcher."

"And a very nice cover I must agree," Kent countered. "We have been watching your operations now for some time and believe that your periodic hauls to Seattle and California alone are amongst the most efficient we have ever observed. However, we are also impressed with your ability to arrange discreet grow-ops and it is that end of your, uh, medical business that I wish to talk about. I am sure you will find that my associates and I also believe in maintaining the utmost discretion in any arrangements we might come to."

"I don't know what you and your associates think you have uncovered here, but you obviously have me confused with someone else."

"Oh, I don't think so, Drew. Otherwise, why would you have even agreed to meet with me at this out-of-the-way establishment? Curiosity? I don't think so. Perhaps these photographs of your truck unloading at a warehouse on the docks of Seattle will help? Notice how nicely your logo shows up in the pictures."

While realizing this smooth stranger had a great deal of information about the Desperados' operations, Drew still stubbornly refused to concede his involvement. Instead he asked, "Who are these associates you keep referring to? Why would I even wish to discuss my company's business with you, never mind agree to any arrangements you have in mind?"

"Perhaps it's not important who my associates are at this time. Let's just say that I represent a person who could make life very uncomfortable for you with very little effort. But let's look at the positive side. All we are interested in is your agreement to expand your cultivation business a little and see that the product gets safely to market. Helping us will help you. We can arrange for your shipments to cross the border hassle-free. All we need from you is a certain percentage of the proceeds - let's say half, in order to meet a few business costs. I am sure you will find the terms of our agreement will be very satisfactory."

"Let me get this straight. You come up with a few locations where a crop can be grown and we put someone in place to grow and harvest the crop and get it to market and then we give you fifty percent of any money we make. Tell me again why this is a good deal for me?"

"Well, first we own the properties, so you don't need to come up with up-front money to establish the grow-ops. Next, you won't need to worry about any curious government officials interfering in your growing or shipping operations. And finally, we can help to ensure that other organizations don't get too interested in your business operations either. A very satisfactory arrangement, wouldn't you agree?"

"What if I don't agree?"

"Then you won't hear from me again and within a week you will be out of business and unsuccessfully attempting to raise bail money. Certain law enforcement officials will be very grateful for the self-explanatory photographs they receive anonymously in the mail. Again, Drew, try to focus on the positive."

Drew wasn't confident that Kent could prevent either the police or other gangs from trying to put him out of business, but with the incriminating information he had of the Desperados' operations, he could see he had little choice but to go along, at least until he could find out more about Roger Kent and his "associates."

"So what happens next?" he asked.

"It's a pleasure to sense your interest. Here is a list of the registered "owners" and addresses of the properties. You provide me with fake names for the "tenants" who will cultivate the crops at each location and who will see that monies received from the sale of the crops are provided to the owners to cover the, uh, rent payments."

"Will you be assisting us in transporting the goods?" Drew asked. "I gather you found out about us as a result of a fishing boat being nabbed. How are you going to ensure that we get across the border undetected?"

"You give us too much credit. Nothing is guaranteed, but by using trucks from your medical chemical business and transporting over the border crossings we provide you and at the times we indicate, the border agents will be much less curious than they are normally. You can understand that we will not be directly involved in your business and after this meeting you won't be talking to me again. The list I gave you shows the amount of rent payment required at each grow-op. It will be up to the tenants and you to ensure enough marijuana is grown and sold to double that amount in profits, in order to maintain our fifty-fifty agreement. The person I represent will not understand if the rents are not forthcoming in full when they are expected. In the meantime, you can do whatever you like with your other grow-ops and the rest of your business."

"It's clear enough, but it doesn't mean I have to like it."

"That's your prerogative," Roger replied with a broad smile as he stood and reached across the table to shake Drew's hand. "It has been a great pleasure to meet you and I wish you every success in all your endeavours."

Drew remained in the pub for a long while after and mulled over the conversation. While not at all pleased with the requirement to share the proceeds from his expanded marijuana enterprise, he could rationalize that the expansion would not likely have happened otherwise. The biggest problem he faced was finding new locations that were safe from outside scrutiny. Even if any of these new grow-ops were detected, he was sure they could not be traced back to the Desperados, as the only connection they had was with the tenants, whose refusal to provide information to the authorities could be reasonably assured. Also, who was to say for what price his produce was to be sold? The rent payments did not look that unreasonable and he was confident that a big enough crop could be harvested at each location to ensure the Desperados of a better than fifty-fifty split. Finally, if he could get his trucks across the border with a reduced chance of detection, his other enterprises could be expanded in a growing-demand market. All in all, Drew Pearson decided he could work with the devil he didn't know.

Chapter 11

AFTER HIS SUCCESSFUL ACQUISITION of cocaine from Dick Walker, Tim periodically made arrangements for further purchases. By week three, he let Dick know he would be interested in trying some crystal meth.

"Pretty old guy to be so interested in all these drugs," Dick observed with a tight smile. "It's usually the kids who want meth."

"Yeah, well, as I said before, when you're straw boss to a gang of construction yahoos, you do what you can to keep them happy and in line. They're a rowdy bunch and they expect me to do the dirty work. If I don't get them the stuff, they will just go work for someone else, and the owner says to keep them happy. Good construction workers are getting harder and harder to find and they can easily go work for someone else."

"Still, it's your ass in a sling if they get picked up."

"I get paid pretty well to take that chance," Tim shrugged.

After the sale, Tim judged that Walker probably had access to any of the more common drugs his customers might want. Two weeks later, he tested Dick once more by requesting a small bottle of GHB.

"Why would your guys want that stuff?" asked Dick. "Couple good sips and they will just want to find a place to sleep."

"That's fine with me. After a good night's sleep I might get more work out of them."

"Yeah, well, don't let them take too much, or you won't be waking them up. Anyway, I don't have it in the office. If you really want it, I will have to get some for you."

This was a break that Tim and Craig were looking for. Craig put a tail on Walker and the next evening he followed him to a condominium in Victoria West, a small section of the city sandwiched between the City of Victoria and Esquimalt. The condo was owned by a Victoria businessman, Ross Stubbs, who was known to police. Stubbs had been arrested for fraud three years before. Unfortunately, the prosecution had botched their case. Stubbs had gone free and to date had not been picked up for further contraventions of the law. While the investigative drug squad did not have enough information to get a warrant on Stubbs, they decided to maintain surveillance on him, at least long enough to find out if he was a conduit from larger suppliers to Walker.

Stubbs' condominium was located in a section of the city that had been reclaimed from an industrial wasteland. Located across the Gorge Waterway from Selkirk, the new properties were highly valued and their owners willing to pay dearly for the privilege of living here. The condominiums, called The Shipyards, were tall, thin and multi-coloured, looking like a flock of brightly-plumed flamingos standing in a stately row along the banks of the Gorge. The view from inside the condos was spectacular, looking across the Galloping Goose Trail and the Gorge to the office towers in Selkirk, which from this distance looked much more picturesque than they did close up. One fact was apparent. In order to live here, Ross Stubbs had to be very well off.

Walker did not visit Stubbs again over the next two weeks and during that time a tail on Stubbs had not discovered anything suspicious. If Stubbs was dealing, it likely meant he either provided Walker with a large quantity of GHB from home, or he was able to redirect Walker's request to another location.

Meantime, Tim started a paper trail on Stubbs. He soon learned that Stubbs was the owner of a recreational vehicle dealership and that he obtained his RVs from a company in Spokane. Tim also learned that some of the RVs were brought in on a consignment agreement, kept in a display yard in Sidney, and if not sold within a certain timeframe, usually one year, were returned to the American company. A detailed check of Stubbs' business records indicated his sales were very low and many of the consigned vehicles were returned. He was obviously not maintaining his affluent lifestyle on the proceeds of his RV business.

As usual, Tim decided there was no time like the present to find out more. He would drive to the RV lot and under the guise of an interested purchaser, size up Stubbs' venture. Because it was close to noon he quickly consumed the brown bag lunch that Gloria insisted he take to work with him whenever he was scheduled to be in the office for the day. After gulping down his coffee, he left his office, chose an unmarked cruiser from the vehicle compound and drove the Pat Bay Highway to Sidney. He was already dressed in his new uniform, similar to the one he had worn with Craig when they visited the house in James Bay, which would allow him to pass as just another suburbanite with dreams of escaping the doldrums of everyday working life.

The yard was located in the middle of recreational vehicle heaven. For whatever reason, anyone in Victoria who had ambitions to make a living in the RV business chose the same stretch of land beside the Pat Bay Highway, adjacent to the approaches to the airport, to set up shop. Perhaps the sight of departing commercial aircraft and the knowledge that the ferries to the mainland were just down the road caused would-be buyers to be subliminally attuned to the thought that escape from the Island was easily within reach. It didn't matter that Victoria may be one of the greatest cities on earth to live in, just the idea of being confined to an island, any island, gave many people a strong desire to travel.

Stubbs' business was the third one in the line. There was no specific reason why a potential buyer would choose this particular establishment to purchase an RV; they all looked the same. Nevertheless, having a choice provided the illusion that consumers could make comparisons. Should they look closely they would learn that all the vehicles were very similar and all of them were overpriced.

As he entered a small trailer on the property, which apparently served as an office, Tim was met by a beefy man in his late fifties, dressed in khaki pants, a checked yellow shirt and a garish green tie hanging loosely around his burly neck. The man seemed surprised to see Tim, perhaps because he received few customers on weekdays. He wiped crumbs away from the stubble on his ample chin, causing Tim to wonder if he too had a wife who made him brown bag it.

"Good morning," he grunted, "or I guess I should make that afternoon. My name's Bill. Do you want a look at our fine recreational vehicles? We've all the latest models with all the modern features that make road travel a real joy. It's as comfortable as living in your own house when you take a trip in one of these babies."

"Uh, sure," Tim answered, trying to drum up some enthusiasm for his assumed role. "I would like something that I can go on the road with a couple times a year for about two weeks. I work in the construction business and once in awhile I just need to get away from buildings and work and just get out of town and away from cities and big hotels."

"I have just the thing you need, a big Class 'C' motor home that provides plenty of space and comfort."

"Can I tow that behind my truck?" asked Tim, who had obviously focused his attention too much on commercial vehicles in his traffic patrol days and not enough on recreational ones.

"What kind of truck do you have?" a suddenly less enthusiastic Bill asked. "We have a great selection of fine fifth wheelers."

"It's a three-quarter-ton pickup with a good hitch on it. It should do the job," replied Tim, picturing a fifth wheeler as something tiny with very small wheels.

"Well, I think you need a good look at our light weight models." Bill took Tim outside and showed him the display stock of fifth wheelers.

While he explained the virtues of each model, Tim scanned the yard, looking for signs of RVs that may have been moved in or out recently, or that might look like they could be used for moving drugs.

"What kind of turn over do you get with these babies," Tim asked casually, nodding at a group of Class C motor homes.

Why does he want to know that, thought Bill. The guy comes in here and says he's looking for an RV for himself, but now he's asking about our business. "Depends," Bill replied carefully. "Many of them barely get to the lot before they are sold, some are ordered in advance and others may take awhile.

You never know for sure what will be in fashion, but most models move quite quickly," he added, faking enthusiasm.

"Sounds like an interesting business," Tim added, trying to make it sound like he was just making conversation. "I was just wondering. If someone who owns an RV and wants to sell it – can they come to you and ask if you can try and sell it for them?"

Bill contemplated where these unusual questions were coming from. In his experience, unless he was close to the end of a deal and was worried about his warranty or thinking about future trade-ups, a customer's enquiries would be about model characteristics and prices. "Yes, that's a sale on consignment," Bill replied slowly. "We bring it in and display it for a period of time and take a percentage. "Why, do you have one for sale?"

"Oh no," Tim responded quickly. "I was just curious. Like I said, I am new to all this."

"Well, we certainly do what we can to meet the needs of our customers, whether they are buying or selling. Look, why don't you keep looking for one that you like. You have reminded me that I promised one of our customers I would call him about now. I'll be back out right away."

Bill returned to the office and quickly dialled Ross Stubbs at his home phone, knowing he was only to do so when it was important.

"I have a guy down here, about 35 or so, who says he wants to look at our RVs when he doesn't seem to have a clue about them," Bill explained breathlessly, as soon as Ross answered his phone. "He seems to be asking me more about our business than about the stuff we sell. Also, he's dressed casually, but he has the manner of a cop to me. I know we get a few guys his age down here during the week not really knowing what they're looking for, but this guy doesn't seem right at all. He even wanted to know about consignments even though he doesn't own an RV. Right now, he's outside looking at the light-weight fifth wheelers, but he doesn't know a fifth wheeler from a motor home."

"You sure you're not just a little paranoid, Bill? Just because our business is a front doesn't mean we need to get all jumpy every time someone asks a few innocent questions."

"It's not only that. He says he works in construction, but he walks tall like a cop and he stares at me when he asks a question, as if I was being interrogated or something."

"Okay, I doubt it, but you might be right about him. That's all we need is some noisy cop snooping around. Keep him busy until I get there and don't let him leave. If he is a cop I can probably tell. I've had to deal with enough of them in the past. If he's police, I will need to think of something to keep him from getting too curious about our business. In the meantime, try to give him the impression that you're really busy, but you want to make sure he has had a good chance to look over all the stock in order to help him make up his mind what might be best for him."

"How soon can you get here?"

"In about half an hour at the most," Ross answered, reaching for his car keys.

When Bill returned to the lot, Tim was still poking through various fifth wheelers. "See anything you like?" Bill asked nonchalantly.

"Uh, not yet," Tim replied quickly.

Bill led him around the lot, attempting to keep Tim occupied by looking at various motor homes and even the campers and travel trailers. At first Tim thought he wasn't going to learn too much more after observing that there appeared to be a lot of inventory around, which obviously hadn't been moved for a very long time. Most of the units were covered with thick layers of dust on the windows and there was heavy grass growing around almost all the campers and other RVs. Then he noticed a group of three large motor homes in a back corner of the lot that looked like they had been placed there recently. As well, the ground under these homes was bare, indicating that other vehicles had likely been on the same spots in the near past.

Tim casually leaned down alongside one of the motor homes and scanned the bottom, hoping to get a better look for potential hidden compartments, but pretending to determine the reliability of the undercarriage. "I guess these axles can carry a pretty heavy load?" he observed, calling upon his commercial inspection experience.

This guy is really making me nervous, thought Bill. Why is he asking about motor homes, now, when he has already all but ruled them out? "Are you thinking you might go for a bigger rig after all?" he asked.

"No, just dreaming I guess," Tim laughed, but he thought a better look at the office might provide more evidence that the business was merely a front for moving drugs in and out of the city, so he attempted to convince Bill that he was now interested in a particular travel trailer and would like to arrange the paper work on it now and bring his truck down later to pick it up.

This made Bill even more suspicious, of course, but it fit into his requirement to keep Tim around until Stubbs showed up, so he agreed.

As he opened the filing cabinet to bring out a sales contract, Tim could see that there were very few files, at least in that drawer. As Bill began to fill out the contract, Tim idly asked which type of RV they mainly sold.

"Well, we do a good business in all our product lines, Tim, but I guess most customers start out with a camper or travel trailer, but soon they want something bigger and then they get into the fifth wheelers and motor homes."

"You know, after looking at them, I really like the travel trailers, but I am still not completely decided. Maybe I could also take home some literature on the fifth wheelers?" Tim asked, hoping to see if the other drawers in the one filing cabinet in the office were as bare as the first one.

Sure enough, as Bill opened another drawer to drag out some product advertising and trade specification literature, he could see that the drawer was mainly empty and the few narrow file folders inside were crisp and unworn. He decided that he had learned as much as he could at the lot, and told Bill he thought he might think about it some more and take the literature away with him to consider buying something bigger than a trailer.

"Wait," the panicky salesman exclaimed. "Maybe we could have another look at the larger units, seeing as you are already here."

"No. I have enough for now and you can rest assured I will get in touch again," he answered dryly and turned to leave.

A searing pain shot through his head as he turned the door knob to leave the trailer. As he fell unconscious to the floor, Bill gazed carefully at him to make sure he was really out. He had never used the fake umbrella handle in anger before, but he marvelled at how well it had done its job. He had kept it there to fend off would-be thieves and troublemakers, who might feel that an older man alone in an isolated RV lot would be an easy target. Not that the trailer held anything worth robbing, but Bill was overly nervous after years of associating with drug dealers and their sometimes desperate clients, who might think that drugs were kept on site.

But what was he going to do now? He realized he hadn't really thought it out when he struck Tim, but knew that Stubbs would have been very upset if he had let him get away before he arrived. A quick check of Tim's pockets revealed his badge and ID, confirming that the police were likely onto their operations, and while Tim was only one cop, more were sure to follow.

Bill looked around the office in search of something he could use to tie up Tim. He settled on a roll of heavy duct tape that came in handy for a thousand uses around the lot. Make that a thousand and one, he thought ironically, realizing he and Stubbs would likely be out of the RV business in the very near future. He wrapped the tape securely around Tim's arms and legs, pinning them tightly to his body, as if preparing him for a long life in the hereafter as a stylish Egyptian mummy. Still not satisfied, he balled up a sheet of paper towel, shoved it in Tim's mouth and bound it securely with another chunk of the versatile tape.

Just as he finished, Russ Stubbs walked in, startling Bill, who had been so engaged in his taping procedure he hadn't heard him arrive.

"Jesus Christ, Bill, I said to keep him occupied. What in hell are we supposed to do now?"

"I was thinking maybe we could take him somewhere and keep him hostage until we can get the motor homes shipped back to Spokane. The head office is equipped to remove the shipping compartments and once that's done, no one can prove that we were moving drugs."

"What about this cop, you idiot? We can't bump him off, and where in hell could we hide him? Somebody will know he was coming here."

"Maybe we can remove all traces that he was here. Later we take him to another spot and arrange it so he can get away after we are long gone. Sure, he will have us arrested, but it will be his word against ours. They won't be able to prove a thing and they'll have to let us walk."

"That's the stupidest plan I've ever heard. His fingerprints must be all over the place, not to mention footprints and tire tracks. What about his car? What are we supposed to do with it?"

"Alright, so we say he was here and he left. Then we ditch his car somewhere. Maybe we could even get one of the pros down on View Street to say he was with her all that time?"

"There's not a hope in the world that dumb plan can work, Bill."

"Well, about the only other choice we have is to make a break for it, but I don't know where in hell we could go that they wouldn't find us. Maybe it's not much of a plan, but you tell me a better one."

"Christ, Bill, why couldn't you have just let him leave, if he wanted to go so bad? No, I'm afraid you and I are out of the drug-smuggling business here in Victoria and we will have to arrange to disappear. We'll let the Spokane office know what has happened. They have a contingency plan and the whole operation can be shut down in a few hours. As well, they can arrange new identities for us.   Meantime, we need to think of a place to hide him and his car, in case some other cops show up. Got any clever ideas?"

"There are a lot of side roads up in the Highlands where his car wouldn't be spotted for awhile. Maybe we can get Thelma to help us. She runs drugs from the warehouse to the suppliers and she's game for just about anything as long as there's enough money in it for her. She can take him in his car and leave him there, tied up and blindfolded for the rest of the day. We can get Dick or one of the other dealers to pick her up. Then Thelma can call the cops without telling them who she is and let them know where they can find this guy. Meanwhile, we make our arrangements to disappear."

"Okay, let's give it a try," a very doubtful Ross agreed. "The first thing we need to do, then, is get him the hell out of here. We'll take Murphy in his car to the airport and store him in the parking lot and hope we can get Thelma to agree to pick him up. I will follow you and pick you up with my car and we can proceed with the plan to escape. We can call her after we have dropped him off, and if she can't do it, we can either get someone else, or just take a chance and leave him there. "

Slowly regaining consciousness, a very groggy Corporal Murphy kept his eyes shut while taking in most of this fascinating plan. He cursed himself for not letting anyone know where he had gone, but as long as he faked unconsciousness he didn't think he was in any real danger.

Chapter 12

AS HE LISTENED OUTSIDE the thin trailer walls, Constable Craig Ballard couldn't help but be amused that the two drug dealers had concocted such an elaborate plan for nothing. Earlier, Craig had been able to arrange and maintain continuous surveillance on Stubbs and had been in the "repair van" parked down the street, outside his condominium, when Stubbs had received the telephone call from Bill. While he felt that Tim was in no immediate danger, he knew he had to get to him before anything rash could happen. Craig asked the officer on duty, Constable John Farquharson, to end his listening surveillance, start the van and be ready to tail Stubbs when he left the condo.

As they followed Stubbs north on the Pat Bay Highway, Craig was not aware of their destination, as Tim hadn't taken the time to share that information with anyone. He asked Farquharson to keep a good distance and not to let Stubbs know they were following. Perhaps by surprising him at the lot, they could glean additional information to assist in their investigation. They watched Stubbs park in front of the trailer and hurry inside. They were able to quickly park the van at the next display yard and walk quietly back to the trailer.

Now, as Craig listened to them discuss the intricate arrangements, he devised his own scheme. They would wait until the two vehicles had left for the airport and follow them. After they parked Tim's cruiser, Craig would direct John to follow Stubbs and Bill to see where they would go next. He would stay and free Tim, as well as arrest Thelma and arrange for another police unit to take her into custody. As soon as they could, Craig and Tim would contact John on the cruiser's police radio and join in the surveillance of the two would-be fugitives.

Because Craig had learned that Stubbs would be making his escape plans with someone higher in the drug trade hierarchy, by tailing them and listening in to their conversations, they might be able to learn a fair amount about the Spokane-based smuggling venture. At the very least, they would have enough evidence to send Stubbs away for an extended holiday, which might convince him to cooperate by providing additional details of the drug smuggling operation. Craig and Tim could maintain radio contact with John and move in when it was appropriate to do so.

SOON AFTER PARKING the cruiser and leaving in Stubbs' car, he and Bill stopped at a gas station on the highway where Ross called her from a payphone. Thelma was on her way out the door when she received his call.

"What's in it for me, if I agree to do this," was her immediate response, after Ross had explained his request and why it was necessary.

"I'll arrange for Walker to pay you a grand, just as soon as we have left the Island."

"That's not a whole lot, considering we won't have a drug source for our operations once you have left."

"Don't worry about that, Thelma. The Spokane office will arrange something else soon enough. In the meantime, Walker can keep things going with the stuff on hand."

"What about you and Bill?"

"We're out of here for good. They will set us up somewhere else in due time and someone else will be assigned to run things in the Victoria area."

"Alright, I will do it, but first I have to run an errand for Dick. Just leave the car at the airport and leave the keys on top of the front right tire where it won't be seen. Put him in short term parking, where cars are coming and going all the time and I will be there in about an hour. What does his car look like?"

"It's an unmarked, dark-blue Chevy cruiser with a typical cop car look. You'll spot it in a minute."

"A cruiser? What are you planning on doing, sticking him in the trunk?"

"Naw. Bill's got him trussed up like a turkey ready for Thanksgiving dinner. He will be in the backseat, covered with a blanket. Nobody will get curious. He can't move a muscle."

"Well, good luck to you Ross. It's too bad the RV business is coming to an end. It was a great way to move drugs across the border."

"That's the way it goes, Thelma," Ross shrugged. "All good things have to end some time."

CRAIG HAD FOLLOWED the cruiser into the airport parking lot and watched as Bill parked and left the keys on the front tire. Then he quickly jumped into Ross's car and the two of them sped away. Thelma was nowhere in sight. As soon as Stubbs and Bill had left with John tailing them with the van, Craig found the keys and unlocked the cruiser. "Well, well," he exclaimed, as he pulled back the blanket covering Tim. "It looks like Christmas has come early. Who's this, all packaged and ready to be put under the tree? Why, I do believe it's my old self-reliant buddy, Tim Murphy, busy wrapping up another case, so to speak. Let's see what he has to say for himself," he added, as he not so gently ripped the tape away from Tim's mouth.

"It's about time you got here," Tim said hoarsely, as he rubbed at his burning mouth. "Now let's see if you can undo the rest of this tape, a little more gently, if you please."

"You know, Tim. I really don't think you're cut out for this undercover stuff. Maybe it worked okay pretending to be a customer looking for a few recreational drugs, but Christ, there's no way a guy who has been on regular cop duties all his career is going to fool veteran drug dealers pretending to maintain a front for drug smuggling. Why couldn't you have just waited and explained your idea to me?"

"I didn't really want to wait that long and I was sure I could pull it off," Tim replied weakly.

Craig just rolled his eyes and, as he removed the tape, he told Tim about his idea to tail Stubbs. Once the tape was off, they quickly drove off to catch up to the van, with Craig driving while Tim got on the radio and established contact with Farquharson. John was able to report that Stubbs was driving back to the city.

They followed his car up Blanshard Street, along Superior and left on Government into James Bay. Tim decided they were returning to the house on Clark Street. He assumed that it was their intention to get their hands on some cash before making a break for it, either by returning to the ferry terminal or the airport.

"I don't think we are going to learn much more, but Stubbs doesn't know you, Craig, so why don't you follow them inside and watch what happens? He may attempt to talk to the bartender, Dick Walker, or someone else involved in their operations. If he does talk to Walker, they may connect you to me pretty quickly, so John and I will follow within five minutes. It's more likely, though, that they will make a beeline for the backroom and we should be able to catch them drawing money out of the safe. Either way, we now have the evidence to convict them and we can use that as leverage to implicate others."

As it was early afternoon, the house was almost empty. After explaining the plan to John, they parked and Craig remained alert as he sauntered in, but only the bartender and a couple of drinking customers, including a beautiful raven-haired native woman, were in view. It was obviously much too early for partying, revelry and drug dealing, Craig thought. Craig ordered a beer and kept his eye on the door leading to the backroom, only bringing out his gun as Tim and John walked in.

"Okay, everyone, just stay where you are, except you, Mr. Bartender. You can come away from the bar and don't try and push any buttons or do anything else silly. Now, come over here with your customers and sit down. John, you stay with them while Tim and I have a look in the back."

The backroom door was closed when Tim and Craig got there, but they could hear men's voices inside. Craig slowly turned the doorknob, but the door was locked. He nodded to Tim, stepped back, kicked forward and the door splintered and popped wide open.

"Well, well, look at all this money," Tim exclaimed as Dick Walker, Ross Stubbs and his assistant, Bill, stared up at them from the safe, unable to react enough even to empty their hands of the wads of cash they were holding. "You boys weren't thinking of going somewhere, were you now? If it's a change of scene you desire, do we have a deal for you! Now come with us and we'll head down to police headquarters for a little chat."

Tim marched the culprits back to the bar while Craig went quickly through the other rooms in the house, satisfying himself that no one else was there. Before he rejoined the others, he called the Victoria Police Department, explained the situation and asked that a team of officers be dispatched to the house to secure and search it and bring the bartender and his customers in for questioning.

They escorted their prisoners to Victoria Police Headquarters on Caledonia Street. The headquarters building was a large, comfortable two-story structure, strategically located on the approaches to the downtown area, just off Blanshard and close to Douglas Street. The building was the pride of the city and its police force, containing large, comfortable offices and plenty of meeting space. Once inside, Craig booked the prisoners in, charging Stubbs and Bill for kidnapping a police officer, and

Walker and the bartender with peddling narcotics. They escorted Ross Stubbs immediately to an interrogation room and began to grill him while he was still off guard and before he could start demanding his right to call his lawyer.

"Well, Stubbs, we know why we are here," Tim began. "Let's get right to the point. Thanks to your brilliant idea to kidnap me and having outlined your plan to keep me hostage, we have learned a fair amount about your drug dealing business and the way you have it organized. We have enough information to shut down a sizable chunk of Victoria's imported drug trade. We also know about your connection to Spokane and the way this motor home container business operates. Because you haven't yet been able to warn them, we will be able to nab your suppliers red-handed and stop the inflow of drugs into other Canadian cities. A little cooperation on your part will help ensure that your supplier leads us to others further up the food chain and may get the charges against you reduced substantially. On the other hand, if you are unwilling to help us, you will be a very old man before you leave prison."

"Better a very old man than a very dead man. Forget it, Corporal. Just get me my lawyer."

Tim resigned himself to working with what they had, arranged for Stubbs to be brought to a cell and began the process to inform the American authorities about the Spokane operation. He was now bone tired and his body ached from his earlier confinement. He called Sergeant Anderson and received his approval to delay his debriefing and to complete his report the next day. Still, it was late by the time he left for home and he knew he had a long story to tell Gloria when he got there. Nevertheless, his thoughts turned to the inevitable invitation he would soon receive to chat with Inspector Fields.

Gloria was waiting for him when he made it home, but she was not well. She had completed her dialysis run late that morning, but had experienced severe leg cramps and dizziness ever since. She had taken a taxi home and left her car at the dialysis unit and her keys with the receptionist, meaning that Tim would need to arrange to get it home. Since the hospital had privatized the management of its parking lot, the new operators were ruthless in towing away expired vehicles and charged exorbitant amounts to get them back. Just another example of our government's insatiable desire to privatize all services and make the user pay, thought Tim. A few slots were available for dialysis patients, and while these were free, the parking company was authorized to tow vehicles away from them after eight hours.

It was a forty-minute drive to the hospital and Tim just couldn't face arranging someone to go with him and pick up Gloria's car. Finally, he called a fellow officer who lived near the hospital and he and his wife were able to take Gloria's car to their place. He could now wait until the next day before worrying about picking it up.

Well, I guess I won't have to tell Gloria about my routine day at the office, Tim thought ironically. He made her as comfortable as he could, ate a peanut butter sandwich, had a quick shower, dropped into bed, and in spite of everything that had happened, was asleep in two minutes.

Chapter 13

INSPECTOR ERROL FIELDS was a calculating, methodical and very analytical officer who lived by the rules and had crafted a successful career by being on top of his assignments. He had grown up in London, England, studied criminology at the University of Toronto and, after completing his basic RCMP training, was posted to E Division headquarters in British Columbia after only one field tour.

His analytical skills served him well in an era when police work had become increasingly complex and required the cooperative efforts of many police forces. He helped create the Lower Mainland District Integration Initiative, which greatly assisted in the development of a bold, new organization, capable of employing technological advances and proactive approaches. He was also a leader in organizing the Combined Forces Special Enforcement Unit in B.C., dedicated to improving efficiency in combating organized crime in the province. He followed this up by encouraging his superiors to develop better cooperative arrangements with other police forces and more sophisticated communications methods and procedures.

Field's promotion to Inspector at the age of thirty-five was accompanied by a posting to Vancouver Island District in charge of the newly-created department called Combined Operations, amalgamating two previous departments: Federal Operations, which focused primarily on drug trafficking and white collar crime, and Criminal Operations, responsible for violent crimes, including homicide cases. The new organization, reluctantly accepted by his superior, Superintendent Rita Chan, gave Inspector Fields a position of much authority. It also allowed him a practical opportunity to put his teamwork approach to the test.

Corporal Murphy was a very good test subject. He welcomed Tim into his office coldly and politely. With a slim build and a slightly protruding stomach, in spite of very concerted efforts on his part to exercise it away, the Inspector offered a pleasant looking image that was, nevertheless, highly deceptive. Convinced of the advantages of cooperative group effort, he found Murphy's inclination for working alone very unfavourable. He had read Tim's reports, noted his ability to produce excellent results when not getting in trouble, and concluded that the man could be a great asset to the force if he could be convinced to work more closely with his peers.

"Please sit down, Corporal Murphy. I have been briefed on your little adventure yesterday and, frankly, I am not impressed. At one time our mounted police force was just that, comprised of lone individuals on horseback, responsible for policing huge territories with no assistance and very few resources at their disposal. And that was fine. Society was loosely organized and those with criminal inclinations were wild cards and usually worked alone or in very small groups. Men like you could fit in very well, matching wits and abilities with those working outside the law. You must be aware that it is not like that anymore. Society has become highly complex and organized criminals work in large gangs, and with other gangs, to commit crimes that weren't even heard of as recently as ten years ago. You must learn quickly to appreciate that those who don't work closely with their fellow officers are a detriment, creating more work through their individual actions than any positive results they may temporarily gain. Yesterday, you not only put yourself needlessly in danger, you disrupted a surveillance operation when they were required to break it off and rescue you. As a result, you may have ruined an undercover operation that was beginning to show much promise. I recognize that you and your partner, Constable Ballard, are responsible for that early promise, but now an entire joint operation has suffered a large setback and we will need to seek a new approach to salvage its objectives."

"Yes, sir." Tim had never been reprimanded with such a long speech before and couldn't help but be impressed. He was convinced that he better make amends quickly or his job would be on the line. "I believe I fully understand the consequences of my actions, Inspector, and I can only apologize for my behaviour. If given the opportunity, I will work cooperatively with the other special force members to get the investigation moving forward again."

"And just why do you think that is possible, Corporal?"

Tim recognized there was no point in attempting to hoodwink the Inspector into believing he had more leads than he did. Nevertheless, he believed they had made a major advance in finding out who was behind the drug smuggling operations and he wanted a chance to continue pursuing it.

"I believe that we have uncovered some promising leads that can help us, sir. From what I overheard, the motor home operation in Spokane was delivering into other Canadian cities and whoever is responsible can still be identified if we can convince the U.S. authorities to mount a sting operation, rather than simply shut them down. Also, Dick Walker and Stubbs' agent, Bill, at the RV lot may be persuaded to inform us about the other dealers they were working with here in the city."

"Is that it?"

"No, sir. Stubbs contacted a woman named Thelma, who he has apparently worked with in the past. She was to keep me hostage until nightfall. There was an implication that she acts as a runner for the drug operation and knows a fair amount about Victoria's criminal activities. Coincidently, she was picked up yesterday at the drug-dealing house we raided and brought in for questioning. There's no record of her ever being arrested before and doesn't appear to be known to the police. I am hoping she may be willing to make a deal."

"Sounds like a very long shot to me, Corporal."

"Yes sir."

"All right, then, that's what you can do. It's obvious the presence of the woman at the house you raided was no coincidence. I will inform Sergeant Anderson to keep you on the special drug squad for now, but only on the condition that you restrict yourself to learning what you can from this woman and sharing it with the other squad members. Is that understood?"

"Yes sir."

"Then get out of my office."

Relieved and chagrined, Tim went to his office and filed a long report on the previous day's activities. He then left District headquarters and drove over to the Victoria police station, where she was now being held, to interview Thelma. He would like to have met with Sergeant Anderson to find out what, if any, developments had occurred in the case since last night, but decided he should keep a low profile, at least until the dust settled a bit. Besides, he wasn't too keen about being the object of another senior officer's wrath. That could wait until Anderson had heard from the Inspector and had a chance to calm down.

Craig Ballard was at police headquarters when he arrived and he was pleased to share the little he knew with Tim. "We interviewed both Dick Walker and the bartender and neither are talking much at this point. I don't think the bartender knows as much as we first thought, but I believe Walker, whose real name is Nicholas Pace, by the way, has been selling for a long time and may have a lengthy list of clients. We know that he maintains a front as a door-to-door insurance salesman, providing him a cover, as thin as it may be, for driving all over the city and visiting various houses and offices, day and night. He has an office downtown, but again, we haven't found anything of value there."

"Okay, and as you remember from yesterday, Craig, we now know there is another location, a warehouse, somewhere in the city, that Stubbs probably used to drop off the goods from the motor home and that maybe Walker, and others, including Thelma, has access to where they load up their supplies. It would also explain why a search of Stubbs' condo didn't turn up anything. Which begs the question, why did Walker visit Stubbs when we first put a tail on him?"

"Maybe we just got lucky?"

"Except if we had been a little more patient, we may have found the drop-off point," Craig added ruefully.

"So what has Anderson got you doing now?"

"We agreed we need to keep working on Walker. Based on his sales to you, we have him for selling a variety of illegal drugs, which automatically makes him a major dealer. We hope to convince him a deal can be made with the prosecutor to restrict the charge to one drug, probably the cocaine, which carries a shorter sentence. In the meantime, I am to maintain surveillance on the house and tail anyone who might be looking for drugs. What about you? Has Anderson taken you off the case?"

Tim described his meeting with Inspector Fields, ending with his assignment to interview Thelma.

"Wait until you talk to her," Craig laughed. "You're in for a treat."

Tim made his way to the cells. While he had seen her briefly at the bar during the raid the day before, he hadn't had time to size her up. Now he could see what Craig meant. Thelma was a knockout. Tall and slim, with long straight hair that she wore below her shoulders, she stood and leaned easily against the far cell wall, looking relaxed and as much at home in her holding cells as most people would be in their own living room. Her sign-in sheet showed that her name was Thelma Frank, she was thirty-one years old and she was a full-blooded member of the Songhees nation. She had been brought in as an accessory to a planned kidnapping, but as yet had not been charged. At this point, such a charge would likely hold as much water as a coffee colander. Tim knew that if he was to make a deal with her he would need to be very convincing.

"Hello, Thelma. I hope you're finding the accommodations to your liking. I'm Corporal Murphy, the guy you were supposed to kidnap. Too bad it didn't work out."

Her intelligent dark eyes took Tim in with one quick glance and dismissed him just as quickly.

"Kidnapping is considered a very serious charge," he continued, already unnerved by her rejection. "However, if you are willing to tell me what you know about Ross Stubbs, I believe I can get most of the serious charges against you dropped."

Thelma had a beautiful laugh and if it hadn't been directed at him, Tim would likely have found it very pleasant. "I have absolutely no idea what you're talking about. You guys get a kick out of arresting some poor Indian for nothing. Picking me up during your stupid raid and bringing me down here for no good reason. Then you come in here, nattering about a kidnapping. Give me a break. You know damn well I haven't been charged. Now get me the hell out of here before I charge you with false arrest and harassment."

Tim was impressed. He also knew she was probably right that a kidnapping charge could not be brought against her, as she wasn't present when they rescued Tim at the airport. While he thought that they might be able to charge her for being an accessory, Tim decided that for now, it would be in his best interest to have her released. He still felt he could make a deal with her, but it would need to be on her terms. As Stubbs had said, Thelma was game for anything, as long as there was money in it for her. It only took him a few minutes to arrange her release. The officers who had brought her in had been doubtful that anything was to be gained by arresting her to begin with, and no one at this point was prepared to press charges, least of all Tim.

He only waited for two hours after her release before paying her a visit. She lived downtown on the third floor of a tall condominium building on View Street. Tim buzzed the building manager and after identifying himself, made his way to Thelma's unit without informing him as to his destination. Thelma came to the door freshly showered and wearing a bathrobe, and quite apparently, nothing else. Still, she didn't appear to be surprised to see him.

"Still harassing me, Murphy? What do you want now?"

He quickly outlined what he had heard from Stubbs and explained that he thought she very likely knew a fair amount about his operation. As Stubbs had been arrested, she wouldn't be working for him again and it might be in her interest to assist the police in their investigation of the case. There would be no need to expose her, or ever call her as a witness, and she would be free to carry on, unhindered, with her other activities, whatever they might be.

"Well, that about levels the playing field. What's in it for me, other than to run the risk of being exposed and bumped off by another player?"

"There's no risk. Only you and I need know about it and I have access to, uh, contingency funds to assist in the investigation. It wouldn't be much, but all in addition to your normal sources of income."

"Just how much is not very much?" It appeared Thelma had become more attentive at the suggestion of money.

"It would depend on what you can tell me. Anything that would significantly increase what we know now would certainly be appreciated."

"Maybe you should come in and we can find out how much I can be appreciated."

Tim wasn't sure what she meant by that, but he followed her in, willing to find out.

"Find a seat, Tim. Can I call you Tim? I was about to put on the coffee pot and find something to eat. That excuse for a breakfast the city offered up this morning wasn't much of a treat. I'll be back shortly."

Tim nodded that it was okay to call him Tim. After she had left he looked around at his surroundings. It was a low maintenance place with high quality furniture which mainly appeared as if it had just come from a display room. Except for an interesting collection of family photographs on an expensive looking mahogany china cabinet, the only pictures to be seen were the kind hotels put up to keep the walls from looking bare. The sofa was a long, modern, dark mahogany, leather affair, accompanied by a matching chair. These were adjacent to a much more comfortable looking recliner that appeared to be the only piece of furniture in the room that was ever used. On the opposite wall, staring directly at the recliner was an enormous television set that looked like it had just been unpacked. Tim dropped into the recliner and tried to stare down the one-eyed monster, which appeared to be watching him accusingly from across the room.

As they shared coffee and sandwiches, Thelma explained how she had become involved in Stubbs' organization. She had been raised in Victoria by very poor parents who couldn't afford to keep her in school after her sixteenth birthday. After scrabbling for a living for two years, working as a waitress or a cleaning maid, she had realized that in order to escape her life of poverty she would need to turn to crime. Her choices were drugs or prostitution and while sex was fine with her, she was totally appalled by the idea that men could rent your body to use as they wished. That left drugs.

She had begun by selling small quantities of marijuana on street corners, but over time had become a distributor, selling to other dealers. Soon, she was permitted to carry other drugs, including cocaine, heroin and, finally, crystal meth and other so-called recreational drugs. In addition, Stubbs eventually began to entrust her to perform other services, including carrying drugs from the RV site to his main distribution point and from there to Sam's and more recently the house in James Bay.

"Tell me about the main distribution point," urged Tim. "What is it?"

"Tell me again about the contingency funds," Thelma retorted.

"I am pretty sure I can arrange up to a thousand for the details," Tim replied carefully.

Thelma slowly nodded. "It's a warehouse in the industrial area out in Royal Oak. Only three people, in addition to Stubbs, know that it exists: Dick Walker, Jack Grey and me. When the consigned motor homes came in, Bill and Jack would unload the drugs and Jack would take them to the warehouse."

"Wait a minute, who is Jack Grey?"

"I hope you remember later that you are paying for this information," Thelma smiled. "Jack Grey is another distributor, like Walker, except his territory is up-island. Jack has a printing operation in the warehouse and actually employs an accomplice to print manuals, mainly for training companies that operate here in Victoria. The warehouse is large, but divided by a partition into two main rooms. The printer and the printed manuals are in the first room and supposedly the second room is only used to store binders, paper and printing supplies. But in behind the binders is a locked office and that's where the drugs are sorted, stored and distributed. Dick Walker would come to the warehouse on a regular basis to pick up the drugs he needed and Jack would look after the rest of the Island. As a result, Jack was rarely around and, as he controlled the key, the office contents were often unavailable."

"Which may explain why Walker went to Stubbs' place when he needed the GHB and led us to the operation in the first place. But then why would you know about the locked office?"

"Well, somebody had to go to the laundry," Thelma smiled. "We couldn't let all that nice money pile up on the shelf. I would come in on a regular basis and get the money from Jack and take it to an accountant who would clean it up and see that it was properly invested."

"And are you going to give me the name of this accountant?"

"For a price." Thelma rose from her chair, stood in front of Tim and reached for his hand. "But maybe we need to, uh, cement our relationship, first. After all that time in jail, I'm a little restless."

Taken aback, Tim mumbled that he should be going, but as she stared at him with her deep dark eyes and loosely held bathrobe he remained riveted. She slowly helped him to his feet and moved in closer, kissed him gently on the lips and began to guide him out of the room.

What am I doing? Tim thought, but mesmerized by her scent and the lingering feel of her lips, he allowed himself to be led to her bedroom.

She kissed him passionately as they tumbled onto the bed. She was a tiger and she was all over him, pulling off his clothes, climbing on top of him and kissing him hotly on the mouth and down his body.

Tim tried to take control, but she rolled him over and lay stretched out on his back, moving slowly and teasingly along his whole body until he felt he couldn't take it. But then she moved him again and he felt her lips caressing down across his chest and stomach and down to his groin. She took him deep into her mouth and sucked and kissed him as her tongue swirled across the knob and shaft of his deeply swollen cock. But before he could get too much pleasure out of it, she was moving again, reversing her body and guiding his mouth into her, engaging him in a mutual pleasure that he thought he could never sustain. Again, before he could get too used to it, she pushed away and then sat upright on top of him, thrusting him deep inside of her, moving rhythmically and expertly to control the pace of their lovemaking. She slowly increased the tempo, but then more frantically until, with a series of deep gasps he felt her come and he let himself burst into her, coming as well with deep gushes of pleasure that left him spent and totally satisfied.

Later he lay beside her, guilty but also puzzled. "Why me?" he asked her.

"Because you were here, Tim, and I was attracted. I told you I could never accept the idea of prostitution, but not because I don't enjoy sex. I especially enjoy being able to control what happens and I kind of felt you might just let me have my way with you, especially on my turf."

"Now I feel like I've been used."

"You have," she laughed. "Just think of it as a first instalment on what you owe me. But rest assured I'm still expecting plenty of cash."

Chapter 14

AS HE DROVE AWAY from Thelma's, Tim attempted to make sense of what had happened. He was ashamed that he had so easily let himself be seduced by her. Yes, she was extremely attractive, but he knew that he loved Gloria and she would be very hurt if she was to discover what he had done. It was enough that she had to cope with the vagaries of her disease; she shouldn't have to put up with his cheating as well. He couldn't rationalize that Gloria's low energy levels and lack of interest in sex justified his behaviour. She did her best and he knew that she loved him dearly. He vowed that this was the end of it and he would endeavour to be faithful from now on.

Next he thought of Thelma and her explanations for wanting him. He couldn't believe that such an extremely attractive young woman would desire him simply because he was handy and she was horny after only one night in jail! In fact, she had been a very amenable informant, especially when no firm agreement of how he would get her the promised money had been arrived at in their negotiations. It may have even been dangerous for her to disclose the information she had. She had even told him the accountant was named Bill Taylor before he had left. He concluded that she had chosen to be an informant for reasons he didn't understand and these reasons would probably surface soon enough.

In the meantime, though, he knew he should move quickly on her information before the warehouse operation could be shut down and Jack Grey and the accountant could escape. It had only been the day before that Stubbs and Walker had been arrested and there was a chance that Jack Grey had not been informed. The stern lecture from Inspector Fields still fresh in his memory, he decided to phone Sergeant Anderson and brief him on what he had learned from Thelma.

"Well, well, Murphy, you have finally decided to let me know what you are up to. Are you finally arranging to come to my office to give me a full report?"

"With your permission, Sergeant, not right now." Tim quickly explained what he had learned and suggested that officers be assigned to raid the warehouse and Taylor's office immediately.

"That still doesn't explain why you can't come to my office."

"I think that I should be there when Grey is arrested. Also, I would recommend that Constable Ballard be present when Bill Taylor is picked up. We can brief the officers on the situation and ensure that nothing is said that would allow them to know how the information was obtained. At the same time, by leading the raids, we may learn something more about their operations during the arrest that may not have significance to others that haven't been as involved. Also, time may be of importance and I can drive to the warehouse directly and try and determine if Grey has been tipped off yet."

"Okay, you can go to the warehouse, but don't do anything on your own until the other officers arrive. I will dispatch two cars with four officers to each location, after I brief them on their assignments. We'll keep it discreet and you can lead the raid on Grey's operation."

"I'm on my way, Sergeant."

In fact, Tim was well on his way. As he talked to Sergeant Anderson he had driven down Blanshard and onto the Pat Bay Highway to Royal Oak. The industrial warehouse area was just off the highway. Typically, the warehouses were used by moving and freight haulers, large retailers and various-sized distributing companies. They mainly catered to businesses that required a distribution point handy to the ferries and all parts of the city, as well as the Trans-Canada, which connected to the up-island towns and cities.

The Triple-A textbook publishing company, housed in a relatively small warehouse on Vanalman Avenue, was right at home here. Tim parked about a half block from the warehouse and noted that only two cars were in the small parking lot in front of the building. With no obvious activity occurring, Tim removed his seatbelt and resigned himself to waiting for the other officers. But just as he started to get comfortable, the office door to the warehouse opened, a man peered out furtively and for no apparent reason, ducked quickly back inside, closing the door behind him. Tim wondered if he had been spotted and decided he should investigate immediately, in case the man was contemplating a getaway. Tim ran to the office door, pulling his gun as he approached. The door was locked. He moved quickly to the loading dock and tried the large sliding warehouse door, but it too wouldn't budge. Next, Tim ran around the side of the building, looking for other exits.

As he approached the back of the warehouse he was struck by a bullet, which hit him in the right shoulder, forced him to drop his gun and pitched him into a shallow ditch surrounding the warehouse. He rolled to his side and noted the small window above him where the gunman had obviously been waiting. He quickly ducked around the corner, saw there was another small window on that end of the building and also a small door right in front of him. It was unlocked, and knowing he was an easy target where he was, he leapt inside, hoping for the best. He was able to get behind a stack of shipping boxes off to his right, just as another bullet ricocheted into the door jamb next to his head.

His shoulder burned with pain and he was bleeding profusely. He knew he would need to do something quickly before he passed out from the loss of blood. He could hear the other man approach, confident that Murphy was badly wounded and in no position to defend himself. Tim scanned his surroundings quickly, looking for something he could use as a weapon. A hand-held dolly leaning against another stack of boxes gave him an idea. He quickly grabbed it with his good arm and got behind the stack. He waited until the gunman was almost on him before he pushed the dolly out the right end of the stack, moved to the left end and located his attacker.

He was lucky. The gunman had swerved toward the dolly, expecting to get another shot at Murphy, who was able to tackle him before he could swing the gun back toward him. As they crashed to the ground, his shoulder racking in agony, Tim managed to get his good arm around his assailant's throat and pinned his arms against the floor with his body, making it impossible for him to use his pistol. Tim hung on desperately until the gunman finally ran out of breath and passed out.

After using his wounded arm to remove the pistol from his would-be assassin, Tim cautiously released his throat, switched the gun to his left hand and climbed unsteadily to his feet. He observed that his detainee was still not moving, so he put the pistol down, ripped off a large chunk of the man's shirt and was able to fashion himself a reasonably adequate tourniquet before re-arming himself.

Within a few minutes, his prisoner regained consciousness and Tim ordered him outside and around to the front of the building as he watched warily, worrying that the man might have an accomplice. He dug out his handcuffs and locked his prisoner to the steering wheel of his cruiser, sat down unsteadily against the back right wheel of the car and fell unconscious to the ground.

WHEN TIM AWOKE in a recovery ward at Victoria General Hospital, he wasn't sure at first where he was. He finally focused on Gloria, sitting quietly beside him, looking pale, tired and worried. He rolled toward her, felt the pain from his injured shoulder and the whole event rushed back to him.

"How long have you been here?" he asked her, rolling onto his back. "Who brought me here? What happened to my prisoner?"

"Ssh. You're supposed to rest, Tim. Now lie quietly and I'll tell you as much as I know. Sergeant Anderson called me from the Division late yesterday afternoon and told me you were here. It's about eleven and I've been here since he called me."

"Wait. Shouldn't you be on dialysis right now?"

"I was able to rearrange it to the afternoon run. Now please shut up so I can tell you what happened. Apparently you were supposed to meet some other police officers at a warehouse in Royal Oak, but when they arrived they found you unconscious beside your car. They called an ambulance and got you here right away. They told me you would be all right, but I didn't believe them. Oh, Tim, why do you always have to try and do everything by yourself?"

Gloria sobbed uncontrollably for what seemed forever to Tim, as he struggled unsuccessfully to sit up again in order to comfort her. He finally sank back onto the bed feeling helpless, guilty and ashamed.

"I know, Gloria. I was supposed to wait, but I was worried that he might get away and it was my fault that he knew we were on to him. It seems that every time I get a lead I feel like I have to act on it right away or I will blow the investigation. And then something goes wrong," he added weakly, "and I have to do something else to try and make it right again." All his recent personal and police officer responsibilities flashed through his mind and caused him to look at himself as a total failure.

Gloria stopped crying and smiled at him. "Don't you think I know what you're like? It's that sense of obligation that attracted me to you in the first place. I also know how impetuous you can be. And your senior officers know that you are only trying to do your best. Craig Ballard was here earlier and he said the boys on the line look at you as a real hero. Sure, you might get chewed out by the brass over this, but Craig says you stopped the local leader of a major drug operation from escaping."

"Really? But I thought Jack Grey was just another distributor?"

"No, no, they mean Stubbs. It's clear now that he ran the local operation, although it was initiated from Spokane. Anyway, it seems that it wasn't Jack Grey you arrested. Craig says he will come to see you this afternoon and tell you what happened. He was here up to two hours ago, but had to go back to work. Apparently they arrested an accountant named Bill Taylor yesterday and he had to go in to question him. He also said that you were responsible for finding out about Taylor, so you see everyone thinks you may have broken the case wide open. I think he said one of the people arrested earlier may have agreed to talk to you?"

"Uh, yeah. I think that one of our suspects decided it would be in their interest to become an informant. What time do you have to leave?" he added quickly.

"Oh, my goodness, look at the time. My dialysis treatment starts at twelve and it's already twenty to and I have to get to the other hospital." She quickly kissed him goodbye and promised she would be back as soon as her dialysis run was over.

Tim lay quietly for several minutes after she left, wondering what he had ever done to deserve her. No matter what the circumstances, he vowed that he would never look at another woman again.

Craig was at his sarcastic best when he arrived a half hour later to fill Tim in on what had happened. "Well, well, our one-man police force is awake and ready for action. Or will a bullet in your shoulder slow you down for a day or two? I don't know why the rest of us don't just retire. With good old Corporal Murphy of the Mounties on the job, the whole city is in safe hands."

Tim smiled weakly. "I guess I've done it this time. I hear you picked up the accountant," he added quickly, eager to change the conversation.

"Yep, he has an office on one of the streets behind the Mayfair shopping centre. He's not talking much yet, but we believe he has been arranging loans and investments for a number of individuals willing to go along with this scheme for a cut of the proceeds. We're bringing an expert in from Vancouver to trace his entire money laundering operation and find out which financial institutions he is working with."

"What about Jack Grey?"

"Oh, we picked him up just after we sent you here. He came back to the warehouse, and, seeing us, he tried to get into his car and make a getaway right under our noses. We nabbed him within a couple of blocks."

"Well, that explains the second car in the parking lot. Where was he through all the action?"

"That's the interesting part. It seems he was the target of the guy who shot you, who, by the way, appears to have been a hired hit man. Obviously, not a very good one if you were able to bring him down. Grey had simply gone down the street for a coffee so he wasn't around when you showed up."

"So the hit man thought I was Grey?"

"Well, no. We think he figured out real quick that you were the law and he was just trying to take you out of action so he could make his own hasty retreat. You seem to make a habit of being in the right place at the wrong time."

"Why would there be a hit man there at all?"

"At this point we think that, since we picked up Stubbs, someone higher in the operation was tipped off about our investigation and sent in the hit man to clean up the loose ends before anyone could arrange a deal. Grey may have only been one target and not a particularly important one at that, but killing him would serve as a reminder to Stubbs and the accountant to keep their mouths shut."

"Is Grey talking?"

"Singing like a canary, but it seems he doesn't know a whole lot. I think we have cleaned up their local organization and shut down their drug trade here completely. What we don't know is where they were getting their direction from. Stubbs appears to be the key, but he still refuses to talk, probably worried about his own life and willing to take the rap for the whole Victoria operation."

"What happens next?"

"Well, cowboy, if I were you I would lay real low. Sergeant Anderson will probably be the first to be over to pay his respects, so to speak, but I am sure some of the other brass will not be far behind. The boys on the task force think you are a bit of a hero for knocking this thing wide open, but I don't think that's shared higher up the chain."

With that, Craig rose to leave. "Craig?" Tim said quietly as he reached the door.

Craig glanced back, quizzically.

"Thanks," Tim smiled ruefully.

"Don't mention it, old buddy. Just try and behave yourself for a change."

Part Three

Organized Crime

Mr. Greed Mr. Greed
Why you got to own everything that you see
Mr. Greed
Why you put a chain on everybody livin' free
How do you get away with robbin'
Did your mother teach you how
I hear you got away with murder
Did you do your mama proud

John Fogerty: "Mr. Greed"

Chapter 15

THE CAPTAIN DIDN'T think of himself as a greedy man. Of course, there were times when he was impatient with the steady, but relatively slow, increase in wealth that his many businesses provided. No, it was just that in order to accomplish all the things he felt compelled to do he needed more money than his legitimate companies would supply. In addition, there were frequent occasions when it would have been inappropriate to use his earned money, such as when paying for party memberships, buying or rigging votes, or covering the costs of bribes and payoffs for illicit pursuits. Thus, he saw engaging in illegal activities as a necessary evil.

The irony was that it was easier to hide the source of money from these activities than from legal ones. So, while he was somewhat reluctant to become involved with criminals, The Captain was frequently required to do so in order to raise the untraceable funds he needed. His recent arrangement with the Desperados was an example, but he had many others. And now one of those was drawing the attention of the RCMP, and, as he had often been required to do in the past, he had to take action to hide his involvement.

For as long as he could remember, The Captain had felt compelled to make arrangements that increased his control over others. He guessed it was a reaction to his lack of control in his youth when his parents, particularly his sadistic mother, had dictated his entire waking day and had disallowed him all but what he considered the most basic of creature comforts.

Oh sure, he had gone to a private school and had lived in a palace in West Vancouver, but he was denied money, friends, after-school activities (except where they were accompanied with rigid discipline, such as the martial arts program his mother enrolled him in at nine when she decided he would need to know how to defend himself in life) and even a job until he was old enough to work in his father's businesses.

She accompanied her strict control over his life with constant chastisement of his many faults, as she perceived them, until he was driven to hate her with a passion. His hatred became an obsession after she pushed him down the stairs landing after spilling his milk on the living room carpet. She would accompany these belittlements with endless reminders of his privileged position in life and how superior this made him in comparison to his acquaintances and most especially the "common citizens" of the city.

She was killed in a car accident when he was only fourteen, struck broadside at a busy intersection in full daylight by a thirty-year-old woman, high as a kite on vodka stingers. He had felt a range of emotions, especially a lethal mixture of relief and guilt. While forever retaining the sense of relief, over time he blamed his feelings of guilt on the drunken driver, so that the guilt was slowly transposed to a lifelong hatred of women. He never married and the women that were part of his life, without exception, would learn to regret ever having met him. This included a long line of caretakers his father had arranged to look after him, while he focused his attentions, days and most nights, on his thriving businesses.

His father gave him little thought and was quick to enrol him in a university business program as soon as he completed high school, even though he continued to live at home. An inability to participate in the more popular team sports was impossible, as his left leg never did heal properly after his stairs "accident." He had developed a fervent interest in sailing, initially as a way to make up for his lack of popularity, which he blamed on his inability to engage in other sports. His prowess in sailing never did make him any more popular with the elitist boys from his school, who later also attended the University of British Columbia, and who had written him off years before. Nevertheless, he found sailing fascinating and he discovered it allowed him to practice controlling the movements of his fellow crew members. Even in high school, when he first took up sailing, he was sarcastically referred to as The Captain and even his school year-book used the nickname. Still, he liked the nickname and preferred it to his given name. He continued to use it for the rest of his life, even though others avoided the moniker and usually called him boss or nothing at all. While in university, except for sailing, he engaged in few extra-curricular pursuits, but he excelled in his studies and was agreeable to his father's suggestion to continue at university in an MBA program.

After graduation, he began work in the company and absorbed an understanding of its complexities the way a sponge sucks up water. He moved up the company hierarchy the way a young firefighter clambers up a three-stage ladder. At the age of thirty-four, when his father was hit by a stroke, he was more than ready to assume command. In the next seven years, he had significantly expanded the company's legitimate businesses and quickly added a number of less than legal ones. Along the way, he had joined the federal pro-business Progressive Party, where he had since become very influential. He was now the party's most important behind-the-scenes authority in British Columbia. He had used his power effectively to create an intricate network of important contacts and he controlled the lives of many, many people across the province in many different occupations. He also had a myriad of contacts providing him information for various salient purposes.

The Captain's source of information in the RCMP's Vancouver Island District Office was not very senior, but he was aware of most of the district's headquarter's activities. He was Chit Batra, a young civilian employee strategically located as a dispatcher in the operations centre. Batra had been recruited by Roger Kent. Kent had learned through gang informants that Chit had grown up in the Lower Mainland and in his youth had been connected through friends to a drug smuggling gang operating in the Surrey-Cloverdale area.

Somehow, despite the usual background checks, the RCMP had never discovered this aspect of his past. Chit had been active enough that, had the Mounties known, he would not have been recruited to the Force. He had gone to work for the RCMP in an attempt to escape the violence of gang life and had hoped that, as a police civilian employee, he would have the security to remain out of their grasp. Instead, he found himself subject to the demands of Kent and The Captain in order to keep his past a secret.

Batra had learned early about the RCMP decision to work with American police authorities to investigate the Spokane-centered drug smuggling operation, and through the chain of command was able to warn The Captain long before the American authorities could close in. As a result, the Spokane operation was closed down and the head of the operation was able to go into hiding before he could be arrested. Nevertheless, the flow of drugs to Victoria and other Canadian cities was cut off, and for awhile this made a significant difference in the volume of recreational drugs imported into western Canada.

KENT KNEW THAT Stubbs' operation in Victoria was now history. Any evidence of its activities that could be tracked back to him would need to be removed. A hired killer would be used to eliminate Grey and Taylor, but they would need to wait until Stubbs entered the prison system before he could easily be dispatched. In the meantime, he was fairly certain that killing the others would help to keep Stubbs' mouth sealed. Unfortunately, the individual normally hired to look after their killings was out of the province on an assignment for someone else and Kent had been required to bring in a substitute on short notice. He had turned out to be somewhat ineffectual and had been captured by Corporal Murphy. Roger Kent was not looking forward to informing The Captain. He decided to fly to Vancouver and confront him immediately.

As he stepped into his office, Roger knew The Captain was unhappy. Not rising to greet him, he waved him to his usual seat with his back to the view.

"You certainly have made a mess of things in Victoria, Roger. Hiring a substitute killer was only supposed to happen with my authority. Can you tell me why that didn't happen?"

"I had to act immediately and obviously we couldn't discuss it on the phone. Word would have been out in no time and our regular contractor wasn't available. Grey would have been the first to know and could have gotten away quickly, so I determined that he should go first, followed by the accountant, Bill Taylor."

"Nevertheless, only Stubbs and Taylor are aware of your involvement, not Grey?"

"Yes. If the man had done the job properly, he would have had plenty of time to get to Taylor. There was no way that he could have known in advance what was happening."

"So now we have a hell of a mess. Losing the motor home operation is not a big deal. We can easily organize a replacement operation, but your involvement in this one puts you very much at risk. Both Stubbs and Taylor can identify you and they are now both in police custody. Just what are we supposed to do with you?"

Roger felt fear, probably for the first time in his life. Theirs was a lucrative business where he had power and where he was able to do the work he enjoyed, organizing others to carry out his wishes. Now he had made a mistake and if he didn't correct it quickly, his own life was on the line.

"I don't believe we need to worry about my being identified," he replied hurriedly. "Stubbs won't talk and Taylor will be in prison soon, where he can be dealt with. In the meantime, he won't be saying much, as he has a lot to lose by exposing his laundering operations. It will take the police months to figure it all out, and at any rate, none of his manoeuvrings can be traced back to us. Yes, I have talked to him face-to-face, but he doesn't know my real name and he has no way of identifying who I really am."

"Where is Taylor being held now and can you get to him there?"

"He's being held in the Victoria City Police jails and we can't get to him until he is charged and moved to remand in the Vancouver Island Regional Correction Centre on Wilkinson Road."

"You have one month to figure out a way of getting to him and it better be untraceable."

"It will be done."

AFTER ROGER LEFT, The Captain turned his thoughts to his need for additional financial resources. He had earlier established an offshore bank in the Caymans and this provided him a base for his money-laundering operations. At this point, the bank was not so much used for laundering as it was for parking his ill-gotten gains and using these, as needed, to finance his illegal operations in B.C., such as purchasing properties for the marijuana grow operations on Vancouver Island.

Soon, however, he would need substantial funds to buy marketing and advertising services to fund the Progressive Party in the upcoming Federal election. It was his intention to reverse the pattern in B.C., where the federal seats tended to split between two or three of the major parties. Instead, he would substantially increase the share of seats for his party, seats that would be filled with Members of Parliament selected by him and supportive of his objectives. Along with population growth, British Columbia had steadily increased its proportion of seats in Parliament over the years. B.C. results could now determine the outcome of most federal elections, providing a majority of the province's seats were from one political party. Determining the outcome of an election would provide The Captain with significant influence at the Federal cabinet table.

This was not to say that the amount of illicit funds collected by The Captain was insignificant. Owning a shipping line, trucking company, container business and chain of insurance firms provided him with many opportunities to engage in illegal activities. To date, he had largely focused on trucking and shipping. He had been able to carry marijuana crops into the United States using a pool of "independent" truckers, mostly Indo-Canadian, who had been recruited from youth gangs in the Lower Mainland. These truckers were financed by The Captain and the proceeds from the drug trade flowed into his coffers. The truckers arranged their border crossings for times and locations supplied by The Captain when customs agents on his payroll were on duty.

From time to time, a trucker may decide to keep a portion of the proceeds from crop sales for himself, but for his next run he would be provided with a crossing time when a law-abiding customs agent was on duty. As all transactions were arranged through a pool of intermediaries, the truck's ownership could not be traced back to The Captain and even to release the name or description of the intermediary that worked with the trucker would lead to certain death. This served to keep most of the truckers in line and very few were sacrificed to the gods of cross-border trade. In a similar fashion, The Captain's shipping company was used to carry crops to other markets, such as Japan, Korea and Indochina.

In order to raise the ante, The Captain decided it best to enlist the support of an organized criminal operation that he could rely on. He continued to be impressed with Drew Pearson and the Desperados gang in Victoria and decided that Drew was his man. Thus he called Roger back, briefed him and had him arrange another meeting with Pearson.

DREW PEARSON ALSO CONTINUED to be pleased with the Desperados' operations on Vancouver Island. Within only a few months, the gang had established a prosperous cross-border operation, particularly through the growth of pseudoephedrine sales. The California market, in particular, was insatiable and as yet no one in the state had set up a significant competitive business. This was mainly because the manufacture and sale of over-the-counter drugs required to produce pseudoephedrine were much more tightly controlled than in Canada and partially because of the rigid discipline required to produce the substance safely and consistently.

The only concern the gang presently experienced related to the increasing number of trucks returning back to the Island empty. The cocaine business had stabilized and the Desperados were receiving competition from unknown sources. In addition, they had encountered difficulty in finding American dealers willing to supply the gang with other recreational drugs that could have made up for the poor cocaine sales.

When Roger Kent called, asking for another meeting, Drew was a little concerned that he had discovered that the Desperados were keeping more than their share of profits from marijuana crop sales than had been agreed to. Thus he went to the rendezvous at the Five Mile House somewhat worried, but also more than a little annoyed as Kent had earlier explained that future meetings between them would likely not be necessary.

Kent was waiting when he arrived and Drew was quick to take the offensive. "I am more than a little surprised to see you again, Roger. It seems to me our joint operation is running smoothly, so why the meeting?"

"Relax, Drew," Roger smiled beguilingly, his icy blue eyes negating any possibility that Drew could calm down. "Yes, everything seems to be working very well. In fact, I would say exceptionally well. So well, that I wanted to determine your interest in expanding our agreement."

"There's only so many safe houses one can find to set up a grow-op, Roger," Drew retorted, not wanting to be burdened with supervising the expansion of this part of the gang's enterprises, as crop sales of marijuana were proportionately less lucrative than their other operations.

"You're probably not aware that a new market has become available, Drew," Roger answered, ignoring Drew's comment. "A significant supplier of cocaine and other drugs here in Victoria has just, uh, gone out of business and the market in this area will now be wide open. I think you will soon see a much larger demand for your coke, but you might also be interested in obtaining a greater variety of recreational drugs. GHB in particular is becoming very much in demand and I can ensure that you receive a reliable out-of-country source of supply."

"And just why are you so interested in the prosperity of our businesses here in the Victoria region, Roger?"

"Hey, Drew, you're our partner! If you do well in your business, we do well in ours. I'm only interested in your welfare."

"What else would you like from us, Roger?"

"There is just one small thing. And again, I am just thinking about the prosperity of the Desperados here in B.C., of course."

"Of course," Drew interrupted dryly.

"You guys have done such a great job increasing your pseudoephedrine sales into the States that I thought you might like a chance to expand overseas."

"You've been monitoring our operations, I see. We have never had any discussions about our other product sales into the U.S."

"Oh, we were just curious. You've gained a reputation as a reliable supplier of a product that is often handled very poorly. Anytime methamphetamine can be made to a consistent and safe standard, the manufacturer becomes very much in demand. You know more than I do that pseudoephedrine is the key. Make it properly and the rest falls into place."

"Our lab is going full tilt, now. Even if I was interested, we don't have the capacity."

"That's easily fixed. We can set you up in a warehouse in Vancouver that is totally secure and more than ample for the expansion we have in mind. And this time we will look after transport and arranging the sales. All you have to do is expand your medical drug supply business to Vancouver, which will account for your need for the increase in ingredients and then to actually manufacture the stuff. I will ensure the rest is looked after."

"What about the proceeds?"

"We are prepared to work within our current arrangement, fifty-fifty."

"Why so generous?"

"Let's just say we want a steady supply of increased cash and we need to work with a reliable partner to get it."

"Who is we?"

"That you don't need to know."

"Let me think about it. I have no desire to move to Vancouver and I would have to ensure I can find someone capable of managing an operation there to the same standards as we do here. Also, you will need to protect us from other gangs. I don't need the hassle of turf wars, and from what I can see, the Lower Mainland is one big turf war."

"I can assure you that other gangs will not be a problem."

"Well, that is an amazing assurance. If I was sure you could do that, I would be more than pleased to work with you on this deal."

"I can promise you that the gangs in Vancouver will never know this is even happening."

Drew smiled coyly as he got up to leave. "You must work for a fascinating organization, Roger. I will be very interested to see how well you can keep that promise. I can assure you I will be very disappointed if you don't."

As he left, Roger noted to himself that he had now been threatened twice in only two days.

Chapter 16

CORPORAL TIM MURPHY was not looking forward to his latest "chat" with Inspector Fields. As Craig Ballard had observed, Sergeant Anderson had been around for a visit and while he had remained calm and even congratulated Tim on breaking up the drug ring, he made it clear he was not in the good books of the District. He suggested to Tim that he call the Inspector for an appointment just as soon as his recovery permitted it.

Tim had recuperated at home with Gloria for a week before reluctantly calling. Gloria had remained sympathetic in spite of her earlier unhappiness with his hasty decision to go after the gunman. He had enjoyed being home with her and would have appreciated having more time off, but with his shoulder healing nicely, he decided he better face the music.

As usual, Inspector Fields was all business. Tim had been able to write his report at home and it was clear the Inspector had read it carefully.

"Your report suggests that while a local drug organization may have been eradicated, you believe that those responsible for arranging their activities are still at large. Why is that?"

"Well sir, the organization in Spokane has been broken up, but apparently the leader there got away. I would suggest that, because the authorities in Spokane have determined the motor home operation only extends into Canada, the leader is a Canadian who was only operating from an American city to have easier access to American-produced drugs. Hence, it is likely we have the Canadian leader still at large, as well as a larger organization responsible for providing the drugs in the first place."

"That's right, Murphy, and now we have little hope of ever finding out who they are. We have to recognize that by locating the warehouse and Jack Grey, you helped to clean up their local drug organization, but you have also made it impossible to catch the bigger fish from outside. The fact that a killer was sent here to eliminate Grey means they were tipped off and it is now unlikely we will get Stubbs or anyone else to talk."

"What about the would-be killer, sir? It should be easy to make a deal with him in exchange for providing us the name of the person who hired him?"

"That's already been tried and he's not talking. Now let's get to you. I warned you earlier that under my command the combined drug squad operates as a team. You have made it clear you have no ability to be a team player and you have been removed from the drug squad and placed on probation until your future can be determined. In the meantime, I am arranging for you to return to your traffic services duties, including your responsibilities for commercial vehicle inspections. Do I make myself clear?"

"Yes sir." Tim was crushed. He was sure that busting up the local drug operation would allow him to remain on the drug squad, in spite of his actions at the warehouse. The Inspector's earlier speech on teamwork just hadn't gotten through to him. He realized now that he and the Inspector were so different in outlook that he would never be accepted by him, in spite of Tim's individual accomplishments. In fact, he would be in disfavour with the man because of his individual accomplishments. Tim was also sure that he would not be able to change his nature, and while he would try to work in a collaborative teamwork environment, he knew that given a situation where there was a need for immediate action, he would take it, rather than wait for reinforcements. He sadly faced the fact he was destined to remain a Corporal in the force, assuming, of course, that he would even be allowed to remain at all.

AFTER TIM HAD LEFT his office, Inspector Fields turned his thoughts to Victoria's drug scene and to organized crime in general. It was clear to him that while the motor home drug bust was an important success, it was only a small part of the action now taking place in the city. Repeatedly, his officers were making arrests involving one or more of a large variety of illegal substances. Heroin use hadn't gone away, cocaine was being consumed in ever-increasing volumes, and now the so-called recreational drugs were more easily available. In addition, ecstasy and marijuana use were everyday occurrences that the police hardly bothered to try to enforce.

The use of all these drugs across the province was leading to other criminal activities that were also of great concern. Individuals were prone to steal cars while high on meth or coke, break into homes and attempt bank robberies in order to pay for their expensive habits and to engage in acts of senseless violence while under the influence of all kinds of mind-altering substances. Youth gangs had also increasingly turned to violent behaviour, fighting turf wars in attempts to control the supply of drugs in their neighbourhoods, and ethnic and motorcycle gangs were becoming increasingly vicious in ensuring suppliers and distributors met their ever-increasing demands for more product or profit.

Worst of all was the expansion of criminal activities by the major drug suppliers, who turned to other crimes to finance their drug operations and to maximize their significant profits from drug sales. Examples included the smuggling of people and cigarettes, telemarketing scams, juvenile prostitution and money laundering. Particularly susceptible to laundering operations were businesses that routinely dealt with large sums of money, including financial institutions, life insurance companies and casinos, as well as legal, accounting and real estate firms. Instances of homicide were also on the increase, with organized criminals arranging the murders of prison and border guards and gang members of rival gangs. Increased violence also led to more intimidation of public officials, law enforcement officers, witnesses, jurors, journalists and other citizens.

The Inspector realized that Victoria's crime levels were low in comparison to larger cities, such as Vancouver from where he had recently been posted. Nevertheless, the rate of increase meant the city, and Vancouver Island generally, now had a serious problem and it was his responsibility to do something about it. He decided his next step would be to increase the size and composition of his drug squad operation, and in cooperation with other Island police forces, initiate a combined organized crime force capable of working together in a concerted, highly efficient fashion.

Inspector Fields was eventually able to receive the support of his Superintendent and the Chiefs of Police in the various

Greater Victoria and other Island city police forces. Within short order, his Combined Organized Crime Unit was in operation with representation across the Island, with a total strength of 68 officers working part-time, and in some cases full-time, on organized crime activities.

TIM WAS EVENTUALLY informed by Human Resources that he was to return to his traffic services duties. He did so reluctantly. It wasn't that the job didn't have its advantages. Being one of the officers responsible for providing traffic service liaison for South Vancouver Island meant he had a good understanding of how the various RCMP detachments and city police forces worked together to most effectively investigate traffic accidents across Greater Victoria, the Malahat and the Gulf Islands. In addition, having specific responsibility for RCMP Commercial Vehicle Inspection (CVI) meant he could set his own hours and spend much of his day on the road, visiting detachments and inspection sites. On the other hand, his short time on the drug squad had allowed him the unpredictability and lack of routine that his nature craved. He hoped he could find a way to go back.

As Tim's CVI position had not been filled during his short period of duty with the special drug squad, he found that there was a fair amount of catch-up work for him to do. Office correspondence, for instance, clearly showed that Jim Urquhart from the Ministry of Transport's Commercial Vehicle Safety and Enforcement Division was perturbed that the RCMP had left Tim's position vacant during his absence. Grudgingly, he decided he best meet with Urquhart and attempt to mend fences.

Tim left his home in Metchosin in plenty of time to make his ten-thirty appointment with Urquhart. It was one of those magnificent fall days that Victoria habitually experienced, where it seemed that having finally figured out how to bring summer to the city, Mother Nature was now unwilling to let it go. He decided to take best advantage of the crystal-clear conditions and take the drive into the city along the Gorge Waterway. The road wound along the Gorge, hugging the shoreline like a lover melding into his partner's body contours. A narrow strip of landscaped lawn provided some separation between road and water, beautifully framed with a variety of colourful bushes, trees and flowers. Walkers, many with dogs and baby carriages, and runners of all shapes and sizes, strolled and jogged along a narrow path on the very edge of the water.

The waterway alternately narrowed and widened, and as Tim drove slowly down the road he was able to watch canoe and kayak paddlers leisurely gliding along the shore. He could also observe Gorge Park and its natural setting amongst the oak, maple, fir and cedar trees on the far shore. Some of the leaves on the deciduous trees had already changed, showing streaks of yellow, brown and even a little red, amongst the predominant dark green background. The scene was always peaceful and Tim loved to take this route. On this occasion, it helped immensely to ease his disappointment about his return to traffic duties and his trepidation about visiting Jim Urquhart.

The drive along the Gorge ended suddenly at Tillicum Road and from there it was only a short distance to Urquhart's office in Selkirk. After experiencing the usual frustrating routine with the commissionaire and receptionist, he made his way through the maze to Jim's office. As usual, Urquhart was impersonal and officious, wasting little time before complaining about the lack of support by the RCMP for commercial vehicle enforcement.

"We receive less and less funding from the government to carry out our responsibilities, Tim, and there almost seems to be an attitude that it has become low priority to enforce the Commercial Vehicles Act. Weigh scales are open for fewer hours and more and more commercial vehicles wait for closures or simply by-pass the scales by detouring on secondary roads. Fewer and fewer trucks are being inspected, yet an increasing percentage of those that are can't pass safety tests. Through it all, assistance from the various police forces is becoming less and less. During the time you have been away from your liaison duties, I don't know if any commercial vehicles in Greater Victoria have been pulled over for suspected violations of the Act. The situation has become shocking and we suspect that crime operatives are taking advantage by moving marijuana and other illegal substances in and out of the city. In particular, it has been known for years that grow-ops are operating all over the Gulf Islands and now there are reports that they are being discovered north of the city, over the Malahat and along the lakes. "

During Urquhart's tirade, Tim guiltily recalled their last meeting and how he had forgotten to pass on to the Gulf Island detachments the need to more thoroughly inspect trucks destined for Vancouver Island and the mainland. He had to admit that Urquhart made a convincing case and he decided he would initiate a program aimed at increasing commercial vehicle inspections. Besides, with the increased evidence of organized criminal activity in Victoria, this may become an additional method of gathering information about their operations. He left Urquhart's office with a renewed sense of purpose.

AS USUAL, BARINDER CHOHAN was feeling pressured. He had persuaded two family members to take out mortgages on properties that were now operating successfully as marijuana grow-ops. He had recruited his cousin, Jaswinder Chohan, a firefighter with the City of Victoria and another cousin, Harnam Gill, who had earlier assisted Barinder in recruiting new party members on the Island and was now a member of the local Federal Constituency. The problem was Jaswinder, who felt he should receive additional monies to compensate for the risk he was taking. Barinder couldn't comprehend Jaswinder's thinking and had decided to meet with him at his place in order to come to a better understanding.

Jaswinder lived with his wife and two small children in View Royal, a small suburb of the city, located about halfway between downtown and the West Shore. He had worked as a firefighter for the city for twelve years and was proud of his job. Nevertheless, his family ties were strong and when Barinder had first approached him with his offer he had agreed without hesitation. It didn't hurt that the deal would help provide financial security for his growing family.

Barinder felt little guilt for having gotten Jaswinder involved. "You do understand, Jas, it is your property and when it is no longer required as a grow-op, you will be able to do what you want with it, sell it or live on it, whatever you decide."

"And meanwhile, I don't know what is happening. I don't even know my tenant, who he is or what his real name is. By the time he is done with it, whenever that is, maybe nobody will be able to live there. How do I know I will even be able to sell it if I want to?"

"Come on, Jas. We talked about this before. These guys know what they are doing. Nothing will happen to your place and it will be left like new."

"But what if someone finds out about the marijuana? The police can come after the owner, even when the owner doesn't know what the tenant is doing. I don't even know the tenant and I could go to jail, not him!"

"Please, Jas, that's not going to happen. You don't want to know too much about these guys, but no one will find out what is happening."

"But what about the money they are making? I take the risk and they get the money. I think I should get some of the profit."

"But you are, Jaswinder. Property values where your house is in Sooke keep going up and up. That's profit. You have a big house in the country and lots of secluded land, and when you sell, you will make a fortune. In the meantime, your mortgage payments are all looked after. It's a great deal and you know it."

"Nothing better happen, Barinder, or you will be to blame."

"You know I wouldn't have got you involved if I thought you would be at risk. But you are involved now and so am I and we will just have to wait until the crops are no longer needed."

As he drove away, Barinder realized the Jaswinder had asked one question he couldn't answer honestly. When would the properties no longer be required as a grow-op? Roger Kent had never promised an exit date and he decided he best find out how long they could expect the operation to continue. Surely they would be able to make enough to cover the cost of membership purchases quite quickly? What Barinder didn't know was that even Roger could not predict the end date. What the two of them had failed to appreciate was that The Captain had no intention of ending the operation as long as it was making money.

OVER THE NEXT few weeks, Corporal Murphy returned to his traffic services duties with a renewed vigour. His zealous focus on commercial vehicle inspections was a cause of wonderment throughout the District, but in individual meetings with the various detachments across the city he was able to convince the officers with vehicle inspection training to increase their surveillance. Within two weeks, the results were noticeable as seven trucks were written up for safety infractions and their drivers ordered to have the vehicles undergo a full garage inspection. Many others were obviously overloaded and were ordered to the scales for weighing where they were booked for load limit violations.

At the end of the second week, an officer in the Colwood-Langford detachment made the first criminal arrest when a large stake truck loaded with live poultry was found with a sizeable consignment of marijuana located beneath a false floor partition on the bottom of the truck. The truck was ostensibly destined for

Surrey and the smell of the chickens was enough to cover the
odour of the marijuana, so that the illegal cargo was being
transported, literally right under the noses of the inspectors. Only
a thorough visual inspection had given it away. Regrettably,
however, the driver wouldn't disclose to the drug squad where
the load had originated and even denied he had known it was
there.

Nor would they know that rather than going to Surrey, the
driver was scheduled to rendezvous at an out-of-the-way
warehouse that the Desperados used to receive their marijuana
shipments. From this warehouse, the marijuana crops from the
various renter operations were then loaded onto one of the large
medical chemical supply trucks for transport into the United
States. Because they had arrested the driver before he was able to
deliver his cargo to the warehouse, they wouldn't discover the
gang's existence, but at least now Corporal Murphy had the
evidence he needed to show that commercial inspections could
serve as a useful tool to get to the criminals who ran illegal grow-
ops.

His plan was to continue vehicle inspections, but to maintain
a low profile while doing so. He didn't want the grow-op
organizers to realize that stepped-up enforcement was occurring,
as this may cause them to curtail shipments. In addition, there
was the suspicion that someone within the District office was
acting as an informant, so as few officers as possible were to
know of the plan. He expected that increased inspections would
eventually lead to another marijuana discovery, but this time the
driver was not to be made aware the load had been discovered
and the truck was to be allowed to continue on its journey. By
tracking the truck, they would discover where the shipment was
being unloaded. In addition, the truck would be followed until it
returned to pick up another load. Only then would arrests be
made. For a change, Tim brought his ideas to his superior
officers and he was even able to receive approval from Inspector

Fields to go forward with his plan. Operation "Grass Watch" was launched with absolutely no fanfare.

While waiting for results, Tim was relatively content to work on a nine-to-five routine, allowing him to be home on a regular and predictable basis. He found he had more time to spend with Gloria and to fit into her dialysis schedule. She was now doing her dialysis runs in the afternoon and she could take the bus to the hospital. Often, Tim was able to drive her home, which was certainly preferable to the bus ride, as after a treatment she would be exhausted and often nauseous.

Also, during this period, Sheila York was posted back to the District from Ganges. She had been able to arrange a transfer into Traffic Services, which had become sorely understaffed as a number of officers had been seconded to the Combined Organized Crime Unit. Tim found that he was able to work comfortably with her in spite of their earlier affair. They became close friends and Sheila was a strong supporter of his initiative for stepped-up commercial vehicle inspections. Eventually, after discussing it with Gloria, he asked her and her new love, Gordon Seppola, over for dinner.

Sheila had not disclosed her relationship with Tim to Gordon, but she had let him know that they had worked closely together in the past. And while she had known about Gloria, she had never met her, so she looked forward to the dinner with some anxiety. The long ride to their place in Metchosin seemed to take forever and her nervousness continued to grow.

While the distance to the Murphy's place was not that far from the city, to get there it was necessary to follow a succession of ever-narrower country roads. Metchosin citizens jealously guarded their rural lifestyles and had refused any attempts by council members or developers to initiate zoning changes that would allow significant population expansion. As a result, most properties were large, and their owners, most of whom had lived there for many years, were land rich but often money poor.

Properties were set back in the trees and to Sheila it seemed that they were on a country road to nowhere.

Suddenly, however, they discovered the proper driveway. As they wound their way up to the Murphy's large two-story house, she could see why Tim and Gloria had chosen to live here. It was completely secluded and very quiet. Located in a small valley with tree-covered hills on all sides, it was as if they were the only people in the world. Nevertheless, within this small valley, there were at least twelve other properties, all with the same sense of seclusion and isolation.

Tim and Gloria, like many Metchosinites, had taken in tenants as a way to cover property costs and provide some extra income. It wasn't totally necessary in their case, but with Gloria unable to work it ensured they could better meet all their living costs, including the significant transportation expenses associated with Tim's drives to work daily and for getting Gloria to her dialysis appointments. At any rate, their current tenants seemed to be good people and rarely home, and except for Tim's lingering concern that the son might be an arsonist, they experienced a reasonably peaceful lifestyle and their sense of remoteness was largely unaffected.

Tim met Sheila and Gordon at the large entrance to their house and led them up the staircase to their living space on the second floor. Nervously, he made the introductions, but was surprised to note that Gloria seemed to take to Sheila almost immediately and they were soon chatting amiably. Gordon, while initially reticent, was also soon at home and made it clear he would prefer to be called Gord. Even though it was now well into September, Tim had elected to barbeque steaks for dinner, in order to make it easier for Gloria, and after getting drinks for everyone he invited Gord to join him on the deck while he cooked.

"How long have you known Tim, again?" asked Gloria, almost as soon as they had disappeared outside.

"I guess about four years," Sheila replied guardedly. "Why?"

"Oh, it's just that I remember he used to mention you sometimes before you transferred to Ganges and he seems pleased that you are back. He doesn't talk too much about the people at work and I was just wondering. I know he doesn't have a lot of friends and I was a bit surprised when he suggested having you and Gordon over."

"Well, we have been working together quite a bit since my return on this stepped-up commercial vehicle inspection campaign and I was pleased to accept his invitation. Plus, I was interested in meeting you. He talks about you quite a bit, too, you know. He's always bragging about how well you cope with your kidney disease and dialysis treatments. Do you find it hard?"

"Sometimes. On my good days, which are usually the day after a dialysis run, I want to do things, so I have joined a patient support group to help out some of the other patients who are not coping as well as I do."

"What does your group do?"

"Things like buying small TVs to watch during dialysis treatments, plus better chairs, extra blankets and anything else to make them more comfortable. We all suffer from anaemia and are always cold, and our cheap hospitals won't provide anything to make life easier while on dialysis. Also, many patients are not well off and we try to arrange transportation for them. It's just awful having to take the bus after you've finished a run and you just want to get home and get into bed."

"Can others join your group? I have spare time on weekends and often in the evenings. Maybe I could help?"

"That's awfully sweet of you. Sure, we have lots of healthy people that help out. If you want, you could come to one of our meetings and see what we do."

"I would like that. Now what can I do to help get dinner ready?"

After they had finished eating, Tim was able to get Sheila alone in the kitchen for a few minutes. "How are you two getting along?" he asked. "It seems to me you are like two long lost buddies."

"I like Gloria very much, Tim. I'm glad you had us over. She's got me interested in helping out with her patient group."

"You're not feeling guilty or anything, are you?"

"You flatter yourself too much sometimes, Tim," she replied angrily. "What happened between us shouldn't have happened, but at the time that's what I wanted. That's well over and how I choose to live my life now has nothing to do with the past. I like Gloria for herself and it has nothing to do with you or what we did. Is that clear?"

"Absolutely," Tim smiled.

Chapter 17

THE ACCOUNTANT, BILL TAYLOR, made his first trial appearance in early September, after the police had gathered enough evidence to charge him with investing in the proceeds of crime. The Victoria City Police had conducted an investigation into his activities and had generally discovered how his money investment scheme worked. Basically, working on behalf of his clients, he made deposits into their bank accounts, as well as purchasing stocks and mutual funds in small amounts from a variety of brokers and investment dealers. As none of the transactions were over $10,000 and many different banks were used, the suspicions of the police had not been raised.

Withdrawals by the local players involved were also done discreetly and in amounts that would not cause anyone to become curious. Taxes on interest and capital gains were paid as required and no one had connected the amount of investments by each player with their respective incomes. It was their intention as business grew to start laundering funds offshore, but to the point where they had been discovered this had not been necessary. The majority of the profits, however, were forwarded in cash by an anonymous carrier to The Captain and these were laundered by him separately.

The Captain's regular hit man, Roy Carpenter, was a nondescript slightly-built man who had the canny ability to receive absolutely no attention from others, either while walking down the street or standing in a group of people. He could blend into his surroundings as effectively as a praying mantis and was just as dangerous to other members of his species, although rarely bothering to have sex with them first.

Roy had been raised by a brutal father who had taught him through many painful lessons to never invite attention, as it would bring nothing but trouble. He ran away at fourteen, and, growing up poor in East Vancouver, had learned to look after himself and to never trust anyone. He had also learned how to be extremely careful and conscientious and was able to apply this effectively in his chosen vocation as a hired killer, a profession he was well suited for, as he had no conscience and no feelings of any kind for his victims.

The Victoria Courthouse is located in a relatively quiet section of downtown with little to no parking. A grey, monolithic three-story affair, the courthouse has been efficiently processing the area's lawbreakers for many decades. Cold and impersonal, large outer doors open onto a small desk, behind which an officious-looking commissionaire demands the nature of your business before granting passage. Inside, the high ceiling corridors are filled during the day with small knots of desperate looking families huddled on benches and whispering with their ne'er-do-well offspring, while bored defence lawyers make fake noises of assurance as they wait for their court appearances. Along the corridors, endless doors lead to small, stuffy courtrooms where overworked judges hear endless cases dealing with driving and drug possession infractions. The whole atmosphere serves to intimidate all but the most hardened criminal.

As the accountant's trial got underway, Roy was able to hang around the courthouse without notice. He learned that during the afternoon recess, Taylor would be brought to the men's washroom and allowed inside alone while his guards remained outside the door. He also learned that a storage room with internal locked doors connected the women's washroom with the men's.

He made his move on the third day of the trial. Dressed as a janitor, he placed his earlier confiscated "washroom closed for cleaning" sign outside the women's washroom only five minutes before the afternoon recess. He then deftly and quickly picked the locks into and through the storage room to the men's washroom and waited behind the door until he was sure Taylor was alone. After entering, he quietly slit his throat and dropped him gently into the urinal and made his way silently back through the women's washroom, stopping only long enough to remove the cleaning sign. He then strolled calmly back down the corridor, smiled politely at the commissionaire and walked unnoticed into the street.

A RELIEVED ROGER KENT reported Bill Taylor's murder to The Captain as soon as he heard. While pleased, The Captain was aware that it was never a good thing to gain the attention of the police. Still, he was confident that connections to his Island operations had been severed or silenced, and he decided he was now in a good position to move ahead with his plans to increase his financial reserves. He had already made the arrangements for the Desperados to begin production of pseudoephedrine in Vancouver, and by early October he had made his first shipment into Japan where the market for crystal meth was well established.

As a result of his shipping and import-export businesses, The Captain had many Asian connections. Time and experience had allowed him to determine which of these was willing to engage in illegal activities, and yet could be trusted to honour any contractual agreements that he might make with them. He screened his contacts carefully and was soon able to make arrangements to export high-grade marijuana and pseudoephedrine to China and Taiwan in exchange for falsely-packaged cigarettes and fake-brand merchandise. Many unethical wholesalers in Seattle and Vancouver were more than eager to absorb as much of these products as he was willing to provide them. By carrying them along with his legal shipments and through the application of large bribes to selected officials, The Captain was able to move them easily past border inspectors and through port customs' offices.

As time went on, it seemed The Captain's ambitions and creativity had no limits. He persuaded Drew Pearson to expand his product line by becoming a major B.C. player in the ecstasy business and then arranged to supply the Desperados with sodium borohydride, a precursor drug for ecstasy that was manufactured in Shanghai. He engaged in the people-smuggling business, carrying up to a dozen Chinese and North Korean would-be immigrants into Vancouver each month, where they were trucked to Ontario and Quebec for further smuggling across the U.S. border. He even dabbled in the prostitute supply trade, arranging deals with Vancouver's Asian gangs to bring in new recruits from China.

And, oh, how the money rolled in! But now, The Captain's money-laundering experts would need to find a way to make all this money appear to be legitimately earned. This was the trickiest part of the operation, but as The Captain would need millions of legal dollars to buy voters and to fund a major advertising and marketing blitz during the next election, it couldn't be avoided. He arranged a meeting on his motor yacht with his chief financial officer, Michael Chan, to review their current investment strategy and to determine how it should be expanded.

Michael Chan had been with The Captain since he first took over the corporation from his father twenty years before. Michael's father had been an accountant with the firm and he had easily persuaded Mike to follow him into a financial career. Now forty-five, Mike had gone to the same school as The Captain and had majored at the University of British Columbia in Commerce, followed by an MBA at the Los Angeles campus of UCLA after receiving a substantial scholarship. An ambitious and hardworking student, he had focused on financial management topics and had developed a specialty in foreign investments currency trading.

In his early years with The Captain, Mike Chan had shown an amazing ability to expand the company's fortunes by arranging buyouts of smaller firms and through investing in innovative areas of technology related to the corporation's expanding businesses. He had particularly shown his worth by convincing The Captain to become heavily involved in ship containers and container carriers. Over time, as The Captain had become increasingly interested in illegal trading activities, Mike had shown his loyalty by supporting him unflinchingly in more and more daring initiatives. He had been rewarded by being promoted to Chief Financial Officer two years earlier.

Michael Chan was now the only person alive who knew as much about The Captain's business as he did. Nevertheless, his motivation was in making money and he was not particularly interested in the reasons The Captain wanted to accumulate so much wealth. Thus, he remained almost totally ignorant of The Captain's political ambitions.

The Captain kept his motor yacht in the West Vancouver marina, where it was convenient for quick jaunts around Howe Sound or into the Second Narrows, scenic routes that he never tired of cruising. He came to the top of the catwalk to welcome Michael aboard his beautifully crafted 82-foot Hatteras twin-engine yacht on which he spent much time, both for business purposes and for his own pleasure, often combined. The Captain was an ardent boats' man, and in addition to the motor yacht, he owned a magnificent 60-foot Vanguard sailboat, which he often entered into major sailing competitions, including the Swiftsure, a race he had won three times in his class and once overall. He took pleasure in escorting Michael to the large enclosed aft deck that was warm and comfortable on this mild fall afternoon. Knowing his tastes, The Captain poured each of them a large single malt scotch and settled into the comfortable deck chairs next to the bar.

"Well, Michael," he began formally, "I've asked for this meeting so we can review where we are in respect to our current financial trading arrangements. I also want your views on the strategies we are following to legitimize a significant percentage of both our on-and offshore money holdings. They will soon need to be even more liquid and accessible for both large and small payments for, uh, political reasons."

"Okay. I have prepared an up-to-date summary for you," Michael quickly responded.

"Good, good. To start with, most of our onshore holdings have already been legitimized through smurfing. Our employees and other trusted accomplices regularly receive amounts under $10,000, which they deposit into their own accounts with the understanding they can use the money as they wish, but are required to return it, except for interest, any time we need it. It is returned to us in small amounts to keep the bank authorities from becoming curious. Are you prepared to start doing that?"

"Yes. I have put in place loan-backs where the money is now being loaned back to the company where it can be used in any amounts. Also, in cases where we are paid by clients in small amounts, the funds are being conveniently "refined" by trading small bills for larger ones. I have also followed your instructions to conduct real estate flips for those properties we have held at least half a year. They are especially attractive in the rising market that we are now experiencing."

"Okay, what about offshore?"

"Our best weapon is still the overseas bank we own in the Caymans, particularly as it acts as the hub for all other cross-border transactions. I especially like it because it allows electronic banking access to international services for wire-transfer message traffic, especially SWIFT. I prefer SWIFT because it lets our agents transfer money abroad using funds disguised as proceeds from your legitimate businesses and then repatriating the money, when needed, through false loan repayments or forged invoices. These have proven to be a good cover for the laundered money. Also, as you have directed, I am depositing cash in the overseas banking system through our bank and others. I have organized a complex web of transfers that have made the tracing of the original source of funds virtually impossible."

"Are you completely convinced you won't draw the attention of the authorities?"

"It's highly unlikely we would be exposed or even come under suspicion, in spite of the volume of money we launder. The Canadian anti-laundering agency, the Financial Transactions and Reports Analysis Centre, has great ambitions but it is highly ineffective. FINTRAC only identifies about 180 illegal transactions a year, for a total of $2 billion, out of tens of thousands of criminal transactions and an estimated total of $500 billion to $1 trillion worldwide."

"Okay. Finally, what about the agents we hire to invest this money for us? Are you still confident you can trust them to do it right?"

"Hey, this is what I'm here for! We have a trusted group of people, all thoroughly tested over time. Our investment agents are careful and conscientious and each is familiar with many techniques and knows how to be flexible. The vast majority of other agents that get caught attempt to rely on only one or two techniques and attempt to launder too great an amount in one transaction."

"As usual, Michael, you have convinced me that you are on top of things. You can get on with it. Now, how about another scotch?"

Chapter 18

PROBABLY NONE OF IT would have happened if Parbeen Dhariwal had not been so efficient. Certainly it wouldn't have if he had not been persuaded by Barinder Chohan's cousin, Jaswinder, to get involved in the marijuana business in the first place. Jaswinder had still been upset that he had allowed Barinder to convince him to become a paper landlord under the arrangement he felt now he had only agreed to reluctantly. Of course, he liked the extra money that the grow-op business provided, so he had decided he could do better himself, arranging partnerships to grow and sell crops independent of his deal with his cousin. He and Parbeen had been close friends since high school days and he was able to get him to agree to the arrangement very easily.

Parbeen owned his own large property east of Sooke, and as a fast learner, he was convinced he could soon grow his own crops and thus he would not require a renter. His commercial fishing business provided an excellent cover and this would allow little chance of his being detected. Also, because he had his own truck, he could transport the marijuana crop directly to the buyers. So when his latest harvest was detected along the Sooke Highway beneath a covering layer of loaded fish boxes, a series of events was triggered that would eventually lead to the discovery of a major criminal operation in the province.

The usual procedure for those who fished commercially along the Juan de Fuca coast was to have a fish transport company load their catch at the docks near Sooke where they maintained their boats. Parbeen had instead purchased his own truck to transport the fish to the transport company's Royal Oak fish packing plant, thus saving the significant costs associated with a pick-up at the docks. Because this was not done by others that fished commercially, the patrol officer who had stopped Dhariwal had done so because he was curious why he was transporting the load on his own, much smaller, three-ton cargo truck. Even though Par's explanation appeared to make sense to him, the officer noticed his nervousness, thus leading to his decision to check the load.

The patrol officer was able to radio in his find without letting Parbeen know his valuable cargo had been detected. An unmarked car was sent to intercept the truck after Parbeen had been sent on his way, but the driver was quick to observe that, rather than stop in Royal Oak where the fish plant was maintained, the truck continued north along the Pat Bay Highway. He followed it to a small marina in North Saanich where the contents of the truck box were loaded onto a large-sized fishing trawler, which quickly departed in the direction of Vancouver. A small aircraft was despatched to keep track of its movements and to learn the destination of its more valuable cargo. The unmarked patrol car then followed Parbeen back to his East Sooke residence where a stakeout was quickly orchestrated.

Parbeen had arranged to have the marijuana delivered to an Indo-Canadian gang he had known since his childhood days in Surrey. Ironically, while all these arrangements were made without his knowledge, this was the same gang that Barinder had been a member of in his own youth. A thorough investigation by the Vancouver-based organized crime unit would eventually shut down the gang's marijuana smuggling operations, but this would have no bearing on the discovery of the Desperados' businesses in Victoria.

The stakeout of Parbeen Dhariwal's place in East Sooke never led to anything either. While he would ultimately be arrested, his insistence he was working on his own did not allow the combined drug force to determine the existence of any other growers, or even of Jaswinder's involvement. It was only Corporal Murphy working on his own with dogged determination and a strong desire to return to his drug squad duties that would lead to a break in the case. Irish luck, or perhaps fate, also played a hand.

DESPITE THE TWO arrests, Tim's initiative in stepping up commercial vehicle surveillance and inspections did not enable him to get back in Inspector Field's good books to the point where he could expect a secondment back to the drug squad, never mind the Combined Organized Crime Unit. Nevertheless, he persevered in his current duties and, in addition to focusing on his regular routines, he found time to think about how he might be helpful in learning more about the, by now quite apparent, significant number of marijuana grow-ops on the Island. He was confident that the two truckers arrested so far were not operating alone and he turned his attentions to learning more about them.

It was a frustrating business. The poultry driver contracted his services widely and observations of each and every chicken farm that he hauled for led to the conclusion they were totally legitimate. Either the driver was making a pick-up somewhere else on his route, or one of the farms was better at hiding its grow-op than Murphy could imagine. The drug squad had analysed power consumption records for each farm to no avail and even used infrared to try and detect unusual heat sources in each and every building on every poultry farm, still without success.

The driver was certainly not growing the stuff himself, as he lived quietly with his wife in a two-bedroom apartment in downtown Langford. He kept his truck at one of the poultry farms, so that also provided no clues. Except for his poultry hauling business, he appeared to have no other recorded sources of income. Finally, neither threats of a long sentence, nor promises of a shorter one for cooperating with the police, led anywhere. No doubt, an easily interpreted message passed discreetly from Drew Pearson had encouraged him to remain silent.

Still working separately from the drug squad, Murphy then turned his attentions to Parbeen Dhariwal. He followed him for days. He had even been at the scene when Parbeen had been followed by a separate unmarked police car as he made his next visit to the fishing boat in North Saanich with his illegal cargo. He researched his movements with a vengeance. He spent countless evenings parked outside his East Sooke home, prepared to follow him to each of his appointments. He listened to tapes of his monitored phone calls and e-mail messages. Again, to no avail.

At work, Tim would pore over the information the drug squad had dug up on Dhariwal, including any information they had discovered about his past and his connections to other people in the Victoria area. They had learned about his activities and friendships and his ties to various Indo-Canadian community organizations in the city. Tim would research each of these in an effort to find a lead. He even began to follow Parbeen's wife and children in order to learn more. Eventually he discovered that Parbeen's wife, Taninder, made regular visits to a home in View Royal, which Tim soon learned belonged to a long-time friend of Parbeen's, Jaswinder Chohan, and his wife, Reena. This was just one more piece of a huge file he had accumulated and it would be some time before he was to discover its significance.

SINCE MAKING HIS LATEST deal with Roger Kent, Drew Pearson was busier than a one-armed paperhanger. He had reluctantly agreed to arrange for his best manufacturer of pseudoephedrine to set up an operation in Vancouver. This meant he was required to work closely with his second-in-charge in Victoria to ensure that quality and safety standards were maintained. Meanwhile, the marijuana grow operations were producing unbelievably large crops, thanks to the disciplined cultivation practices his "renters" had been trained to follow. Also, there appeared to be little or no competition in the cocaine trade, and while there were a few nuisance operators in the recreational drug business, they were not big enough players to get too steamed up about. Finally, the drug squad appeared to have absolutely no knowledge of his gang's existence and he was reasonably sure he could maintain their anonymity.

On the down side, getting the marijuana crops to market was becoming a concern since the increase in inspections of commercial vehicles on the Island. While Drew was confident that the poultry driver would never disclose the locations of the grow-ops or of his warehouse, he still had to find a way to bypass the inspections. He was able to arrange what the gang referred to as "pick ups by pick-ups" because trucks of this size were unlikely to be inspected. However, this was highly inefficient and meant that he ran the risk of arousing suspicion when he had these small trucks continually unloading at various marinas where small boats would haul the crops to the mainland for loading onto the medical supply trucks before transporting them into the United States. Ironically, this process was necessary, as the chance of detection was now higher on the Island than it was at the American border, thanks to the arrangements made by Roger Kent with certain border guards and customs agents.

An even larger concern was the inevitable decision by other gangs to make a move on his operations. Already, he was hearing reports that the largest motorcycle gang in British Columbia, the Satan's Sirens, might be interested in a Victoria Chapter. They were already operating up-Island in Nanaimo. Drew was sure that, in spite of Roger Kent's assurances, they would mount a challenge and he was not confident that he could fend them off. He wondered if Roger Kent could really help and decided it was his turn to arrange a meeting at the Five Mile House.

Drew was surprised to find himself on the defensive, as this was the first time that he was looking for something from Kent. He knew that Roger would want something in return, but he couldn't begin to determine in advance what that might be. Getting there first, he headed to their usual table in the back of the pub and sipped his beer nervously as he waited for Roger.

"Always a pleasure to meet you here," said Roger easily, as he suddenly appeared and dropped casually into the chair across from Drew. He called over their server and ordered his usual, a pint of pale ale. "How's it going?"

"It's been hectic, Roger, humming on all cylinders. I have to admit that our partnership has its advantages. I can see it has been good for both of us," he added, trying to establish in advance that if Roger was to assist him with his turf problem, he would only be helping himself.

"So I take it you want to explore some further initiatives, Drew?"

"Well, no," Drew replied hurriedly. "I'm looking at our long-term future and wondering about your assurance that we don't have to worry about outside interferences from others trying to muscle in on our operations here on the Island."

"I remember that conversation, Drew, and the promise that you wouldn't need to worry about any hassles from other mainland groups in running your lab in Vancouver. I didn't make any reference to what you do here in Victoria. We have already arranged for you to take control over most of the cocaine and recreational drug business here with the demise of the previous operation. Who else is there that could get in the way?"

"That's just the point, Roger. We are learning that the Satan's Sirens want to set up a Chapter here. Their B.C. headquarters is in Vancouver, so if you are able to control what they do there, you should be able to do the same here."

"Well, first of all, as a gang leader, you must know that no one controls the Satan's Sirens. In Vancouver we have an arrangement with them, but no one controls them. You have no need to know what our arrangement is, but it extends to keeping away from your crystal meth operation on the mainland, but nothing that you do here. There is no way I can provide that kind of assurance."

"So what would it take to get you to extend your arrangement to Victoria?"

"Well first of all, I would need to know more about their plans. Now, the best way is to find out directly from them by penetrating their organization here on the Island. I am pretty sure from my dealings with them that they will try to expand from their Chapter in Nanaimo. We would need to get an informant into Nanaimo."

"Anyone you have in mind?"

"Yes. Here in Victoria there is a woman who is very adept at providing a variety of valuable services to those involved in the drug trade. We've used her in the past. She's smart, very attractive and knows the drug business inside out. Do you know the background on the group who imported cocaine using motor homes on consignment?"

"Yes, of course. Their arrest is what led to our expanded cocaine business."

"Well, Thelma Frank is her name and she ran courier services for them, including transporting the money they collected from the drug users to an accountant they used for laundering. Thelma's name never came up when the operation was shut down and the key players were arrested. We don't think the cops even know she was involved."

"How come you know so much about her?"

"A little bird told me. The point is, if anyone can get inside the Siren's operation in Nanaimo, it's Thelma."

"How do we get to her?"

"I'll set it up and you can meet with her. From the reports I get, I think you'll find she's pretty easy to deal with."

"Alright, Roger, and what will you be expecting for this little favour?"

"As they say in the sports business, Drew, we'll be looking at future considerations."

DREW WASN'T SO SURE if Thelma was easy to deal with, but he found she was easy to look at. He had arranged to meet her in a suburban pub in Saanich where the customers were noisy, but not nosy. Typical of many Victoria pubs, the Animal House tried to cater to everyone. It consisted of one large room with a recessed centre packed with tables, each sitting two to six patrons and facing an extended bar with a long line of customers on stools competing for attention with an elevated bank of huge television sets, high above the bar. A raised floor with smaller tables for couples hugged a brass railing running around the outside of the sunken centre, and finally, secluded booths sat discreetly around the outer walls for the less extroverted patrons. It was in one of these that Thelma was waiting when Drew arrived. Given Roger's report, it wasn't hard for Drew to pick her out.

"Thanks for agreeing to meet with me," he began politely, after introducing himself under his cover name, Art Sampson, and drinks had been ordered. "An influential man I don't believe you have ever met thinks highly of you and I'm sure he has had one of his acquaintances explain the problem that he thought you may be able to help me with."

"Maybe you should explain it to me," she answered coolly.

"He said you can be fully trusted, so here goes. I head up a local gang here called the Desperados that has established a pretty active drug trade on the Island. Maybe we're too active. We're starting to get some unwelcome attention from the Satan's Sirens, who already have a chapter in Nanaimo and who are starting to interfere with our up-Island business. We need someone to penetrate their chapter and get an idea of their plans for Victoria. Once we do that, we will be in a better position to figure out how to deal with them."

"Why do you think I would want to do that? One could end up very dead if they crossed the Sirens."

"This man says you're very, uh, entrepreneurial, and are always looking for new opportunities."

"This man seems to think he knows a lot about me. Maybe I am looking for new prospects, but I'm also looking forward to breathing in the future."

"As I said, we're very active and can pay you well. We also are extremely discreet, and to date we have totally escaped the attentions of the law."

Thelma pondered the proposal. It wouldn't be hard for her to get inside the Siren's operation in Nanaimo. She had worked with them in the past when they needed a runner to carry money to Vancouver. Nevertheless, they were an obnoxious and unsophisticated crowd, typical of the old breed of bikers, taking most of their pleasure in cruising up and down the Island, harassing the locals and only raising enough money from drug sales to meet their obligations with headquarters. Besides, they had not paid her well and it was always distasteful to put up with their crude sexism and bullying.

Thelma also doubted that if the Sirens were interested in establishing in Victoria, they would do it through Nanaimo. They would probably use the Chapter to stalk the Desperados for awhile before moving in on them from Vancouver. But in the meantime, she could see how she could make some money from the situation with very little risk.

"Let me see what I can do," she finally answered. "If I think I can work with them and with you, I will let you know. In the meantime, you better come up with a pretty good offer. If I do this, it's my life on the line if anything goes wrong."

Chapter 19

BY DOUBLING HIS WORKLOAD, unauthorized drug gang research, in addition to his regular commercial vehicle inspection responsibilities, Tim had little free time to spend with Gloria. On her non-dialysis days, she enjoyed walking their dog on the Galloping Goose Trail, which was not far from their house in Metchosin. She was pleased when Tim offered to accompany them on a particularly warm fall Sunday morning in October.

"You mean you can pull your nose out of your files long enough to spend some time with your wife," she teased. "It's been awhile since you came with us."

They joined the trail near Matheson Lake and walked westward, parallel to the shore. Groucho, their eight-year-old black Lab, who was anything but grouchy, gambolled ahead of them, alternating between investigating various animal smells and searching for food. Tim had often thought that they should have named him Hoover.

The Galloping Goose is a beautiful trail, running from downtown Victoria, westward through the West Shore, before turning north, finishing at the Sooke Potholes, a parkland area about 45 kilometres from the trailhead. The section of the trail along the lake was once a rail line used in logging operations, but now catered to walkers, runners, bikers and horse riders, who all shared the wide flat path with little discord.

At this time of year, the trail was at its best. The deciduous trees asserted their characteristic attributes through their overhanging leaves, the maples showing off with brilliant huge yellow, brown and red specimens, while the oaks modestly clung to a smaller dull brown look. The aspens stubbornly retained a summer-like pale green, and finally, the arbutus, which refused to change at all, maintained their shiny, waxy, lime-green facade all year round. Completing the scene, the dominant coniferous firs and cedars acted as a backdrop, their long dark green needles blending together like an endless curtain, trying their best, but never quite succeeding, to hide the view of the water to the left and the rolling hills to the right. Here and there, the trunks of the maples also vied for attention, flashing their moss-covered bark furtively through the evergreen canopy. Finally, along the low banks of the trail, a few small wildflowers attempted to be noticed, their fading reds, purples and oranges making a last-ditch stand before the first frost could get to them.

Gloria was pleased that Tim had been able to join them. It gave her an opportunity to talk about her developing friendship with Sheila.

"I'm really surprised at how well we get along," she explained. "She seems to be so interested in the same things I am. Do you know that she wanted to be a nurse and got into paramedics as a first step before applying for the R.N. program? But then, after the paramedic training, she got to know quite a few police officers and decided to go into the RCMP instead. But she still is very interested in nursing work."

"No, I didn't know she had that background," Tim replied uneasily, wondering if Sheila's friendship with Gloria had become closer in spite of, or because of, Tim's earlier affair with her. Maybe some kind of guilt complex was behind it, he thought confusedly.

"Yes, and she wants to get involved in helping me with my patient visits at the clinic on my non-dialysis days. You know how the new kidney patients want to know what to expect when they start dialysis treatments? Well, I like to visit with patients who are considering dialysis and transplant options and help them to know more about the choices. As you know, the clinics don't explain the transplant option very well, but for those who can get one, it's a heck of a lot better than being on dialysis. Sometimes I think, because the doctors and nurses see so many patients on dialysis, they forget that many of them could benefit from a living-donor transplant, rather than wait for years and years for a deceased donor. Anyway, Sheila is very interested in all that and wants to come with me on my visits."

"How can she help when she's not even a nurse?"

"Because the newer patients in particular are so happy to see a healthy person from outside take an interest, the staff appreciates people like Sheila coming in. Besides, she knows from all the highway accidents where many deceased donors come from, so she can understand how important it all is."

Tim could see he wasn't going to dissuade her from increasing her friendship with Sheila, so he decided he better get used to it and learn to look at her in a new light. He decided he would let Sheila know that he appreciated her interest in Gloria. He could tell that it was making Gloria a lot happier and' let's face it, he hadn't been the best of company lately.

AFTER DECIDING SHE WOULD take on the assignment, Thelma called the number she had been given by the man she knew as Art. A little later he called back and arranged what she believed was a pretty attractive payment for her services considering the dangers involved. She then worked out a plan and set up a temporary residence at a motel in Nanaimo. She had elected to make her interest in working for the Nanaimo Chapter of the Sirens known by approaching one of their members, Reilly (Red) Black, whom she had dealt with previously. A tall, big-bellied brute, with a scraggly beard, Red was always dressed in a red checked shirt and greasy blue jeans that did nothing to hide his paunch. But Red was the best of a bad lot, as far as Thelma was concerned, and if she could get past his ingrained chauvinism, he could be counted on to let her know if there was work for her to do. She arranged to meet with him in the bar at the Worthington Hotel, a dark, dingy place and a preferred hangout for the Sirens, as it is located close to downtown and to their clubhouse.

"Well, hello, Thelma," Red yelled from his bar stool as she made her way through the gloom. "I just knew you couldn't stand being away from me any longer. Pull up a stool here, cutey, and tell me how much you missed me."

"Yeah, Red, I missed you like a dog misses being whipped by its owner. How about buying me a beer and bringing it over to one of these booths? I want to talk to you."

"Ooh, she wants to talk in private. This gets better all the time." Nevertheless, he did as he was told and slid into the booth beside her.

Thelma deftly slid over to the other side of the booth and said, "It's business I want to discuss, Red. The word has it that you guys are doing pretty good up-Island and you might need a reliable courier to haul all your money away."

"Well, even if that was true, pretty girl, why would you be interested? I thought Victoria was hopping these days."

"Not for me. You probably heard about the motor home bust a couple of months ago. Well, I was running for them and since they got busted, I have had to stay pretty low. It doesn't look like I've been connected to them, but I'm trying to stay away from the action in Victoria until things settle down again. In the meantime, I thought I might see if you guys have anything for me."

"Speaking about action, Thelma, I hear there's a new gang that's taken over the coke business since the bust, plus all kinds of other stuff. What do you know about them?"

"Not much. Like I told you, I'm keeping a low profile in Victoria for now. But I hear that they are doing all right. Anyway, my interest is here in Nanaimo for now."

"I suppose I can talk to Freddy. Now, just to show your appreciation, how about a little favour in return for good old Red, eh?"

"Forget it," Thelma laughed. "Now get out of here and go talk to Freddy."

Red made his call and came back with another beer, but nothing for Thelma. "You're in luck, gorgeous. Freddy says he can talk to you. He said to tell you he's in the clubhouse and will meet you right away."

"Thanks, Red, I will think of you in my dreams."

"Yeah, right," he answered, waving his already half empty beer bottle at her.

THE HEADQUARTERS of the Satan's Sirens Nanaimo Chapter was only two blocks away, located in a large, ramshackle house in an ex-residential neighbourhood that was slowly converting to commercial. The house was rundown and badly in need of a paint job. Four or five motorcycles were parked at scattered locations across the overgrown lawn and a huge Rottweiler barked and snarled at Thelma as she parked her car and approached the porch. A tall, thin, dark-complexioned man in his early forties appeared suddenly at the door, yelled at the dog and looked impassively down at Thelma.

"Hello, Freddy," Thelma called cheerfully, never knowing quite how to act with this volatile, quick-tempered leader of the Nanaimo Sirens, whose current mood was never expressed in his narrow, dour-looking face.

"Come in, Thelma," he answered, surprisingly cheerfully. "Don't worry about old Brutus here. He'll only take your leg off if I tell him to."

She cautiously made her way around the huge dog who stared at her balefully as she passed, seemingly lamenting the missed opportunity to make a meal of her. She followed Freddy into the kitchen where a half-dozen gang members were sitting around the table, appearing to be up to little more than playing cards and drinking beer. Probably waiting for the afternoon to pass, she thought, before commencing the usual evening's ritual of combined business and pleasure. They stared at her with obvious appreciation as Freddy led her down the long hallway, past a cavernous room where two more gang members were engaged in a game of pool, and into his sanctuary, a good-sized office where he directed her to a large leather chair facing a surprisingly bare and neat-looking desk.

"Red tells me you're looking for work, Thelma. That seems a bit odd when we haven't seen you up here for a couple of years. Why now?"

Thelma went through the same explanation she had given Red earlier, making sure to express as little knowledge of the Desperados as she could plausibly get away with. At any rate, Freddy seemed satisfied, or maybe it was just that her timing was good, as he admitted that he was indeed in need of a courier. He was also sure he could contract with her for a good price, as it was she who had come to him, in spite of the gang's having screwed her around in the past. Besides, he had always been impressed with Thelma's reliability and by the fact that, as far as he knew, she had never been picked up by the police.

"We do have a couple of shipments we need to make, Thelma. Our headquarters in Vancouver are after us, as usual, to get our quarterly payment in. We don't have a regular courier to do that, so there's no reason not to get you to do it. Also, we are starting to make some inroads in the Victoria area. We have a dealer in Mill Bay who has some coke customers on the other side and you can transport to him. A pretty girl like you, driving that old Chevy of yours, won't attract the wrong kind of attention. My guys are all known by the cops and it's getting harder for us to move stuff directly. Do this right and we can probably keep you pretty busy."

"Is it the same routine to Vancouver as ever, Freddy? I take a backpack to Stanley Park and switch with one of their guys?"

"Yep, it's the same as always, Thelma. We don't screw around with something that works. I will set it up for tomorrow and you can get to it. Same amount to you as always."

"You wouldn't have forgotten how much that is, have you Freddy?" she smiled sweetly.

"Of course not. Five hundred for Vancouver and three down-Island per trip."

"Okay, Freddy, it sounds good. I'll be ready."

"In the meantime, we're having a little soiree after tonight's action, here at the clubhouse. You're welcome to join us. There'll be lots of other broads coming, so you don't have to think you're the entertainment."

Thelma thought about it. Usually, she would avoid these slobs like the plague, but it was a good opportunity to find out their plans for Victoria, if there were any, and maybe give her something to pass on to the Desperados. "Why not, Freddy? What time?"

"Oh, around two. Gives everyone a chance to come over after the bars close."

"See you then."

THELMA WAITED until 2:30 a.m. before making her appearance. It was an ungodly hour to start partying as far as she was concerned, but by now the boys would be primed, and if they had plans for Victoria, she would likely find out about it. She had a nap earlier in the evening and she was feeling refreshed and alert. She made for Red who was holding forth with a couple of gang members, two or three hangers-on and a gaggle of groupies seemingly fascinated with his recollections of past exploits.

"So when the son of a bitch wouldn't let go of his wallet, I put the barrel of the twenty-two on the back of his wrist and shot his fuckin' hand off. Of course I was careful not to damage the wallet. Oh, hi, Thelma. Where you been?"

"Hello, Red. Spreading lies again, eh? I hope these naïve young bimbos don't believe a word of your bullshit."

Joining into the conversation, Thelma was eventually able to ask about expansion plans. "You guys seem to be doing all right these days, Red. You must be controlling most of the Island by now?"

"Yeah, except for those bastards in Victoria," piped in one of the other gang members, known to the group as Magic, based on his ability to get any locked car open and de-alarmed within twenty seconds. "But we have plans for those pricks, don't we

Red?" he bragged, obviously attempting to impress her, or maybe the vacant-looking brunette hanging onto his left arm.

"You can shut up about that," Red cautioned him quickly. "If we decide to move in on them, we don't need to tell the whole world about it."

She wasn't able to find out anything else during the rest of what turned out to be an exhausting night, as she was too often busy fighting off drunken advances from assorted sleaze artists and turning down invitations to participate in sordid party games. But it was clear, from a few subtle questions she asked from time to time, that the Desperados were looked upon with envy and great hostility, and the Sirens were convinced that they should be driven off the Island. Contrary to her earlier beliefs, it was now apparent to her that the Nanaimo Chapter was prepared to do this soon, by themselves, and that no direction was coming from Vancouver sanctioning a turf war.

EVEN AFTER A COUPLE of weeks of courier service, including carrying to dealers in a number of up-Island communities, Thelma was unable to find out more. She noted, however, that Freddy was calling a lot of meetings where only club members were invited and they all seemed a little cockier and more pumped-up than usual. She was pretty sure they were getting ready for a raid soon and she decided it was time to get the word back to the man she knew as Art. After another drop at Mill Bay, she arranged to meet with him at the Animal House.

After they had settled in with drinks and she had ordered a late meal for herself, she began by telling the Desperados' leader about her trip to Vancouver and to a number of dealers across the Island, including the one in Mill Bay. "You're antennae seem to be picking up pretty clear signals, Art," she added. "The Nanaimo Chapter is unhappy with the amount of drug action you have corralled here in Victoria and are planning to mount a raid on you."

Drew stared at her steadily. "And when can we expect their little visit?"

"I'm not sure. They're trying to keep their preparations to themselves, but the signs tell me it's not long. They hold a lot of secret meetings and the boys are all sticking close to the clubhouse these days."

"Is there any chance you will be able to give us a day or two's warning, so that we can be ready?"

"I don't know, but I'll stay as close to them as they will let me and will let you know if I learn more."

"Good work so far, Thelma," Drew replied, slipping a fat envelope under the table to her. "I've got to go. Enjoy your dinner," he added politely.

As he drove home, Drew thought about what he should do. It was pretty obvious that the Satan's Siren's executive were not behind the Nanaimo Chapter initiative, so he wasn't sure that Roger Kent would get involved. Nevertheless, Roger and the interests he represented would not want anything to interfere with the arrangement that was making all of them a fortune, so maybe he would find a way to discourage Nanaimo. But he couldn't count on it from what Roger had told him earlier, so maybe the Desperados better be prepared to defend themselves on their own.

Another thought came to him. A pre-emptive strike might be in order. If they could make it look like they were simply protecting their own turf, the Sirens might back off. The dealer in Mill Bay was very close to Victoria and many of his customers would be in the West Shore, and that was Desperados territory. Picking him off as he made a delivery would send a clear signal to Nanaimo that they were not to be messed with.

He also thought about Thelma. He obviously wouldn't need her anymore. In addition, she would figure out pretty quickly what was happening and that wasn't good, even if she didn't know his real name. He was pretty sure there was nothing she would do about it, but he didn't like her having the information. After the business with the Sirens was finished, he would need to deal with her. In the meantime, maybe the Sirens would solve that problem by getting to her first.

THELMA WAS HORRIFIED when she learned three days later, by reading about it in the morning newspaper, that the Mill Bay dealer had died in a traffic accident on the Malahat. The Desperados had obviously chosen the location carefully, as people were killed there on a regular basis, driving that narrow, mountainous section of the Island Highway. At the same time, the Nanaimo Sirens would know that it wasn't an accident and would take the message very seriously.

Why wouldn't Art talk it over with me first, or at least warn me, she wondered? Wouldn't he realize that he was putting her life in jeopardy, as Freddy would be sure to realize that the Desperados had learned about the dealer from her? She decided to call him immediately. When he didn't return her call, she knew he had determined either that she was expendable, or she could look after herself. She wasn't prepared to accept either alternative. She knew what she had to do, but first she had to get out of Nanaimo fast and then get out of sight. She couldn't go back to her apartment, so she booked a room in Sidney, well away from her usual stomping grounds.

Chapter 20

CORPORAL MURPHY COULDN'T escape the feeling that Parbeen Dhariwal wasn't working on his own. While there are many independent operators in the grow-op business, he learned from his research that the East Indian community tended to work in small gangs with close ties. Somewhere in the information he had gathered on the man and his various community connections there lurked a clue that would help him unravel the puzzle. He was at his desk, poring over this information when he got the call from Thelma that would take him in an entirely new direction.

"Corporal Murphy," he answered distractedly, reluctantly setting aside his files.

"Hi, stranger, how would you like to help a gal in distress?" she said flippantly, not sure how much to say and how to say it over the telephone.

"Who's this?" Tim replied abruptly, still annoyed about being disturbed.

"It's me, Thelma. Sorry if I caught you at a bad time, Murph, but I've got a big problem and I need to talk to you about it."

This time Tim detected the sense of urgency in her voice and started to pay closer attention. "Okay, do you want to come in?"

"Could you meet me away from your office? I'm not sure I want some people to know that I'm talking to the cops and they might be watching to see if I come there. How about that warehouse where you arrested that gunman awhile back?"

"Our phones aren't tapped, Thelma. We would know immediately if anyone was listening. Unless you're worried about your end, we can talk openly."

"Just the same, Tim, I'm scared stiff and I don't want to take any chances."

"Alright, there's a coffee shop one block south of the place you're talking about. I will come in civvies and meet you there in forty minutes."

Thelma was already there when he arrived at the Java Shoppe, a hangout for the warehouse and wholesale crowd that worked in that part of Royal Oak. Since he was required to wear his uniform again, after being sent back to Traffic Services, he had changed to a set of casual clothes he kept in his office for times he didn't want the public to know he was a Mountie. He bought a coffee at the counter and joined her at a booth in the back.

She looked as beautiful to him as ever. He thought fondly of their last meeting, but her anxious look was far removed from the cool, bemused expression that she typically portrayed. "So why all the secrecy, Thelma?" he began cautiously.

Having realized that her situation was extremely grave, she had decided that police protection was her best chance of remaining alive and she would leave nothing out. She quickly outlined her assignment with the Desperados, her experiences in Nanaimo and ended with the "accident" on the Malahat.

Tim was particularly interested in the information she disclosed about the Desperados. An obviously large and well-organized drug cartel was operating here in Victoria, right under the noses of the police, without them even being aware of their existence! Oh sure, they knew that a large amount of drugs was being traded in the city and, having discovered the two transporters, there must be some connection between the various growers that were obviously operating in the area. But to think that one organization was responsible for most of what was happening was startling. He could see why Thelma had decided her life was in danger.

"You've been very courageous by coming forward, Thelma. Many people would have chosen to get out of town and try to disappear. I think you probably know that rarely works. The first thing we need to do is get you into a police protection program where you can be really safe. As well, we'll need to go through the details and make sure we have every bit of information you can provide us with. In the meantime, the RCMP will book you into a nondescript motel. You will be safe there for a day or two until we can get you into the program."

Thelma wasn't sure that the police protection program provided that much security, either, but seeing little choice, agreed to go along with it.

AFTER ARRANGING TO GET Thelma settled in the motel, Tim immediately arranged an appointment with Inspector Fields. He repeated all that he had learned from Thelma and waited for his reaction.

"It's a pleasure to see that you haven't gone out to find these Desperados on your own, Tim," the Inspector began, only slightly sarcastically. "Based on the increase in drug dealings in the city, even since the bust of the motor home operation, we were pretty sure that another player had stepped in to fill the void. You are right, though, we have no information about them and weren't even aware that a biker gang was involved. We know about the Satan's Sirens Chapter in Nanaimo, of course, and have the information that they are not operating to any extent in the Victoria area. It may be that these Desperados are an example of the new breed of bikers who, in many cases, don't even have motorbikes. They have become very sophisticated white collar criminals that focus on business, not riding around the country, bullying the locals."

"So how do you think we can get to them, sir?" Tim asked innocently.

"I notice you said we, Tim. I have also been told that you are spending extra hours at work trying to track down connections between the drivers your commercial enforcement officers detected and the people they are hauling for. It might be time to bring you back in with us. I really don't like the way you operate, but you seem to be the only one around here that's getting any results. Consider yourself seconded back to the Combined Organized Crime Unit. I will handle the paperwork with Human Resources and free up a couple of officers to assist you in your research work."

"Thank you, sir. But I would still like a chance to further debrief Thelma Frank. I'm not sure she has had a chance to tell us all she knows."

"I think I will get someone else to do that. It's always advantageous to have different officers hear the same story. I think your good friend, Craig Ballard, from the City Police would be best, as he knows what to listen for. All in all, we will step up our efforts, now that we know we are dealing with one major player. Also, because we can expect a retaliatory strike from the Sirens out of Nanaimo, if not from Vancouver, these Desperados may become a little desperate themselves and we might glean a little information while they are vulnerable."

NEVERTHELESS, IN THE following days nothing happened. It hadn't been difficult for Roger Kent to learn that the accident victim on the Malahat was a member of the Nanaimo Sirens and he had met with Drew Pearson to learn the details.

"What's going on here, Drew? We agreed that you would find out what plans Nanaimo has to penetrate the Victoria market. You were never given an okay to mount a pre-emptive strike. Now you've opened a real can of worms. And where the hell is Thelma in all this? Was she part of your hare-brained scheme?"

"Well, no," Drew answered uneasily. "It was my understanding you were telling me you couldn't control the Satan's Sirens and it was my problem, so I was dealing with it, based on what I had learned from Thelma."

"Okay, so where is she now? Have you bumped her off too?"

"No, I haven't, at least not yet. I believe I can settle with her after the Nanaimo situation is cleared up. If not, I will do what is necessary. In the meantime, I think she has gone underground."

"Or gone to the cops?"

"She wouldn't do that, Roger. You told me yourself how reliable she is."

"You fucking idiot, Drew. I would have dealt with Nanaimo, once you gave me the information to work with. I had you talk directly to Thelma because I don't want her to know who I am. Now, for Christ sake, don't make any more stupid decisions on your own until I find out what is happening and can find a way to keep the Sirens from retaliating."

"You can do that?"

"Of course I can do that. I said we don't control the Sirens, but that doesn't mean I can't make an arrangement with them. And another thing, Drew, I want your gang to stay real low until I tell you otherwise. If the cops get wind of what you have done, you could jeopardize your whole operation here. I can't believe you wouldn't have realized that."

GAZING FROM HIS LARGE corner office high over the harbour, The Captain watched one of his container ships, the Golden Sea, as it glided quietly under the Lions Gate Bridge on its way into port. It was a half-hour before dark and the early-setting November sun lit a trail like a flashlight beam ahead of the ship, pointing the way to the city wharfs. The ship would dock after dark and its containers would be inspected by customs and border security agents, as The Captain had authorized. He had no reason not to. The cargo was a legitimate shipment of brand name Asian textiles, manufacturing tools, farm machinery and electronics equipment, destined for markets across the country.

The agents would not inspect the superstructure, however, and it was here, in a small accommodation block at the stern of the ship that The Captain had arranged to transport a separate shipment, a cluster of very frightened illegal Chinese immigrants. They were rural farm workers who had been promised a wonderful future in North America and had paid dearly for their cramped, unventilated space behind the ship's crew's quarters. Many were attractive young women who had been carefully selected and were destined for a vigilantly controlled life of prostitution. The few men in the group were young and in good health. They would find themselves as virtual slaves, forced into a life of hard labour as warehouse and dockyard workers, forever in debt in order to meet payments required for their squalid upkeep.

The Captain had arranged for one of the women, a pretty young girl about sixteen, to be brought later to his large, secluded home in West Vancouver. He was able to make such arrangements on a regular basis as a new shipment would arrive about every six weeks. He felt eminently qualified to indoctrinate these young ladies into their new profession and he looked forward with anticipation to the evening's lessons. Shortly before leaving his office, however, he received a call from Roger Kent, which served to alter his mood significantly. Later, having taken much of the brunt of The Captain's ire, the young Chinese girl would require comprehensive medical attention before she could leave Vancouver to begin her new life in America.

"What is it this time?" The Captain answered irritably, after Roger admitted that a new problem had arisen in Victoria.

Roger's description didn't improve his mood.

"Okay, Roger, I kind of understand why Drew thought he could deal with the Nanaimo threat on his own. They are an unsophisticated bunch and probably wouldn't have received much support from Vancouver in any case. I won't have any difficulty convincing Sirens' headquarters to get Nanaimo to back off. But leaving this Thelma Frank out in the cold doesn't make sense. We will have to keep an eye on the Desperados and be prepared to cut our losses in Victoria if need be."

"Do you think she might go to the cops?"

"That's easy enough to find out. Leave that with me. Oh, and Roger?"

"Yes?"

"That's two."

Roger Kent knew what that implied and once again he felt a chill of fear flow down his back.

Before leaving his office, The Captain made two quick phone calls, one to the Satan's Sirens B.C. leadership and one to his informant, Chit Batra, at RCMP District Headquarters in Victoria. The first call would require a future concession, the second, at this point, only his time. Both calls led to quick agreement to meet his requests.

TIM MURPHY WAS VERY pleased to have two other police officers to assist him in his research efforts. He assigned the first, RCMP Constable Debbie McGill, to tracking Parbeen Dhariwal and his wife in order to learn as much as possible about their connections to others in Victoria. The second, Saanich Constable Ray Denson, worked along with Tim in the office to follow the paper trail on Dhariwal and his associates. Like Tim, Debbie noted the regular visits between Parbeen's wife and Reena Chohan, obviously a close friend. Researching the documents on the Chohans soon caused Constable Denson to learn that, in addition to their home in View Royal, they owned a large rental property in Sooke.

"What do you make of this, Tim? Here's a guy who's a firefighter in View Royal, not making a big salary, but about two years ago can suddenly afford to buy a house in Sooke on a large chunk of land and has no problem renting it out for a pretty healthy monthly sum."

"It may not be that unusual. It doesn't take a big down payment to get into the real estate market these days, and with the low vacancy rates around Victoria it wouldn't be that hard to rent it out. Still, the fact the property is in Sooke is interesting. That's near where Parbeen Dhariwal's grow-op is located. There could be a connection. I think it's a good idea for us to find out more about the Chohans."

Tim set up surveillance on the Sooke property and from all appearances it was indeed the site of another grow-op. Now we're getting somewhere, he thought, and arranged for Debbie, Ray and himself to take shifts, monitoring all movement around the property.

At first they learned very little. The tenant didn't seem to be around much and when he was, he remained secured inside the house. Still, the signs confirmed a grow-op. While blinds covered all the windows, a faint glow filtered around the edges, indicating that lights were on day and night and yet the electrical bills recorded only minimal monthly consumption, meaning much of it was bypassing the meter.

It was two weeks before the next development occurred. One evening around eight o'clock in late November a pick-up truck drove onto the property and the driver and tenant quickly loaded a number of sizable bundles into the back and covered them with a tarp. Debbie was on surveillance and she quickly radioed in the information.

"Good work, Debbie," Tim answered. "Now follow the truck and see if it heads for a marina. Find out where he unloads and we will arrange surveillance on the cargo. I suspect it may be going either to the mainland or to an American destination. We won't make any arrests, but I think this will finally provide us an opportunity to learn how this gang operates. I'm pretty sure now that we're dealing with a bunch of grow-ops that are somehow all connected."

It didn't unfold the way Tim had predicted. The truck drove into Victoria and was unloaded in a warehouse rented by a previously fairly minor player in the local drug trade. From the warehouse, the marijuana was redistributed to local dealers and sold on the streets. It would be some time before they were able to connect the operation back to the Desperados.

Nevertheless, Tim's researchers were not back to square one. In addition to the surveillance on the rental in Sooke, Tim's team now focused on learning even more about the Chohans. They soon learned they were part of a large Sikh family, very active in the community and with influential ties to both the Federal and Provincial Progressive Parties. One of the family was Barinder Chohan, Jaswinder's cousin, who they quickly learned was the assistant to the Provincial Minister of Economic Diversification. Another was Harnam Gill, a cousin to both of them and an important executive member of the Federal Party in one of the Victoria area constituencies. Finally, they learned that Barinder was very good friends with Alan Diwan, not a grow-op owner, but a fellow assistant to a Cabinet Minister in the provincial government, Shelley Peregrine, Minister of Public Works. They had received their appointments at the same time and had previously been organizers for the federal Party.

Further research determined that the three cousins had more than politics in common: they were all landlords! Not only that, but they all owned rural properties and they all had tenants who made regular monthly rental payments that easily covered their respective mortgages. Surveillance on the Barinder- and Harnam-owned properties permitted the research team to discover these properties were also grow-ops. In the case of Barinder, Tim wondered if he wasn't perhaps taking his responsibilities in economic diversification a little too much to heart.

INSPECTOR FIELDS WAS AMAZED at the results that Tim and his team had accomplished. Instead of his usual aloof demeanour, he welcomed Tim into his office with a large smile.

"Good work, Corporal," he beamed. "Thanks to your research efforts, we have made a great start in breaking up a major grow-op here in Victoria."

"Uh, yes sir, but I think a few growers is all we have so far. We still don't know who's behind it, what else they're up to and where the stuff is going."

"That's right, Murph, and now we must figure out how to get to them. We are still hoping that by maintaining surveillance over the grow houses we will learn more. As far as we know, the renters are not aware of our surveillance and we don't think the Desperados know either. It's probably too early to think of arresting the cousins. While an owner is responsible for the criminal activities of a renter on his property, it's usually difficult to make the charge stick. Also, while we suspect the proceeds from the grow-ops might be partially going toward the Progressive Party and its operations, we don't yet know for what purpose. Maybe we can find out more by monitoring their activities?"

"It's unlikely, sir. From watching Parbeen Dhariwal and Jaswinder Chohan, all we have discovered is another owner. It seems that the owners have no connection to the renters, other than collecting their cheques each month. I don't think they ever visit the properties."

"What about Thelma Frank? Has Constable Ballard learned more from her?"

"Not yet, but I understand she's being very cooperative. It seems their interviews are going very well."

Tim was a little irritated to hear that, but he wasn't too sure why. Surely he wasn't jealous that Craig was getting to talk to her and he wasn't? "Do you think she would be willing to try and get the leader of the Desperados to surface?" he asked. "She probably doesn't know his right name, but she can identify him and if we could smoke him out, we could move in on the whole operation."

"Hmm, that's a thought, but very risky for her. Why would she go along with it?"

"I think she sees her life in danger as long as the turf war is on between the two gangs. As a witness for the police, she could give us enough information on the Nanaimo Chapter of the Sirens that we could make some arrests, but we still don't know why the Desperados put her at risk to begin with. Do you think she could try and arrange a deal with the Desperados to provide evidence against the Sirens in exchange for her protection?"

"So, let's see if I have this straight, Murphy. She tells the leader of the Desperados that, knowingly or unknowingly, they have put her life in danger. But if they promise to protect her and leave her alone in the future, she will come to the police and provide evidence against the Sirens, without involving the Desperados. It's a good deal for the Desperados because it ends the turf war and removes a threat to their operations here in Victoria. But while they are meeting, we maintain surveillance on her and find out who the Desperados' leader is and then start monitoring him?"

"That's right, Inspector," Tim answered, uneasily. "I know it sounds risky, but if we set it up right, I am sure we can protect Thelma. If this Art guy doesn't go along with it, we haven't lost anything. We just put her in the program as we have already planned."

"Do you want to talk to her, Tim?"

"I'll discuss it with Craig Ballard, sir. Maybe he and I should approach her together."

AFTER AGREEING IT WAS best to go together, Tim and Craig met Thelma that afternoon. Tim was amazed at how agreeable she was to the idea.

"You have no idea what it is like to think you may have to stay in hiding the rest of your life," she explained. "I still run the risk that the Sirens out of Vancouver will come after me, but if you can put the Nanaimo Chapter and the Desperados away without calling me as a witness in court, I don't think they will be aware that I have been working with you. But you're going to have to come up with an explanation how you found out that the Desperados were responsible for the death of the Mill Bay dealer that doesn't involve me. I don't want the Sirens in Vancouver blaming me for that."

"That shouldn't be too hard," Tim assured her. "We can release it to the media that the Desperados had known for some time that the Sirens from Nanaimo had been moving in on them, knew well in advance about the Mill Bay dealer and had chosen that time to remove him. There's no reason to think that Vancouver will connect it to you. We won't need to release anything publicly that you have ever talked to us. We'll make it seem like we have been after the Desperados for a long time and had been monitoring their actions and chose the Mill Bay dealer's death as the right time to move in on them."

"Okay," she said, satisfied. "Now, how do we set up this meeting with Art?"

"You said you met him twice before at the Animal House, so you arrange to meet him there again. First, you call and leave a message that you have a way to put the Nanaimo Sirens out of business once and for all. If he bites and calls you back, you tell him you are prepared to go to the police and tell them all you know about the Sirens without implicating the Desperados. But you also tell him you must meet him as you need him to assure you the Desperados will leave you alone and will help you go into hiding. If he asks why, you explain that you don't trust the police protection program."

"And what if he says he won't do it?"

"Well, then you suggest to him that you will tell the police all you know about him and the Desperados, including a good description of what he looks like. He thinks the police know nothing about them now, so he will be sure to treat your threat seriously. You again point out that all you want is security and the chance to be left alone."

"So what happens if he agrees to meet?"

"You work out the details of how he will get you into hiding and leave. We will take it from there."

"You think he will let me leave, just like that? If he believes the police don't know anything about the Desperados, why not just get rid of me?"

"Because he will be very glad to get the Nanaimo Sirens off his back and your statement to the police could do that. Maybe he will think he can deal with you after the Sirens are arrested, but we will have nailed him and the Desperados long before that can happen."

"You hope."

"I promise you, Thelma, we will never let you be in danger."

IT TOOK THE THREAT of exposure to convince Drew Pearson to meet with Thelma. By this point he felt the Desperados were better off dealing with the Sirens on their own and he didn't want any part of a plan that would let Thelma go to the police. He was now regretting that he hadn't hunted her down right away and gotten rid of her. She was becoming a loose end that needed to be cut away. He decided to dispose of her as soon as possible.

First, however, he needed to know if she was already working with the police. His call to Roger Kent led to an assurance that she had not met with the RCMP, at least as far as Chit Batra, The Captain's RCMP informant knew. What Batra didn't know, however, was that the police were meeting with Thelma at an out-of-town safe house and only Tim, Craig and the Inspector were aware that she had turned to the police for protection.

The meeting was arranged for their usual spot, the Animal House, for that evening. They met at their normal booth at 8:30 p.m. Drew had someone with him, an attractive woman about thirty, with short blond hair and big hazel eyes. She immediately made Thelma very uneasy.

"I thought we agreed to meet alone, Art."

"Hello, Thelma. This is Liz Blackburn. She's a member of our organization and she knows how to make people disappear. In your case, that might even be alive. Later, she will go over the details, so that once you have finished testifying to the police about the Sirens, you will be able to get out of town without a trace. First, however, let's go over the details about what you know about them and how you are going to put them away. If you provide even the slightest hint to the cops that you know about the Desperados and have been working with us, the deal is toast, understood?"

"Of course," Thelma answered quickly, signalling the waiter to come and get their drink orders.

Once they had finished their conversation, Drew left and Liz explained how their "layaway plan" worked. Basically, it had to do with getting her to Ontario by car so that her movements could not be traced and, once there, setting her up with friends of Drew's in Toronto. Liz would be responsible for ensuring she would travel with a contracted driver who would be unknown to the police and to the Sirens. The hardest part would be ensuring that once she had finished testifying she couldn't be tailed. A double would be used to throw anyone following her off the track and she would then be quickly smuggled off the Island by hiding in a vehicle during the ferry crossing. She would be switched to another vehicle after the crossing and again sometime during the trip east.

Once satisfied, Thelma finished her drink and the two of them walked together to the parking lot. She thanked Liz for her help and was digging out her keys when the sharp metal cutting edge struck her just below the shoulder blades and she collapsed to the ground after ricocheting off a nearby car. Two more sharp stabs followed. Satisfied with her work, her assailant jumped in her car and quickly drove away.

She was lying on the ground, not moving, when Tim got to her. "Damn it, Tim, you didn't tell me it would hurt so much. I feel like I was worked over with a hockey stick."

"Sorry, Thelma. I guess I should have also mentioned that you will have some nice bruises for a few days, plus maybe a couple of small holes in you that weren't there before. Now let's get you out of here while we cordon off the area and make it look like a crime scene."

The next morning when they had a better opportunity to talk, Tim admitted that the plan hadn't gone entirely as anticipated. "We didn't expect that Art would bring someone with him. Nevertheless, we were watching her very carefully, especially when she left the bar with you. If she had pulled out a gun, or even a blackjack, we would have stopped her immediately. Those vests are supposed to be bullet proof, but I wouldn't count on it. Besides, it wouldn't have helped much if she had decided to shoot you in the head. But, with a knife, it's almost always the case that an assailant will go for the body."

"Almost always, you say! Thanks for the vote of confidence."

"Don't worry, if she had decided to go for your head, we were right there to make sure she didn't get to finish. Craig had his revolver trained on her the whole time, didn't you, Craig?"

"Trust me, Thelma," Craig grinned, "we wouldn't let someone hurt a gorgeous woman like you."

As Thelma glared at him, Tim quickly interrupted. "The vest was our insurance policy, Thelma, but we admit we didn't expect to have to use it. But it works very much to our advantage. We can now use what happened to make out that you were killed. As far as what we tell the public, we don't have a clue why you were murdered, or who did it. This allows the Desperados to go about their affairs and it will be much easier to maintain surveillance on them. We have already tracked the man you know as Art to his home in Gordon Head. His name is actually Drew Pearson. He is thirty-eight, single and owns a medical chemical manufacturing business located in Royal Oak. We hope to learn a lot more about him soon."

"So does this mean I won't need to move to Ontario?" asked a quizzical Thelma.

"Not unless you still want to," Tim answered. "But I would at least like to see you out of Victoria for a time. If you want, we can arrange a new identity and get you established in Vancouver. With your talents you could make a very nice living as the manager of a courier company. How does the idea of making an honest living appeal to you?"

Thelma's index finger response gave him one answer, but her rueful smile let him know that she was very willing to give it a try. He knew she realized there was a small chance she could run into a Sirens gang member from Nanaimo or Vancouver who could recognize her. Yet it was clear to Tim that she preferred to take the chance.

Chapter 21

SUPERINTENDENT RITA CHAN was an extremely ambitious woman. A smart, third generation Chinese-Canadian, she had joined the RCMP as a way of breaking free from family demands. She found her parents insistence that she adhere to traditional Chinese customs and practises stultifying. They had pressured her into attending the University of British Columbia and majoring in Commerce, with the understanding she would become involved in the family's grocery wholesale business. They were highly displeased when she elected to continue her studies, completing a Master's degree in Criminology and immediately joining the Force upon graduation.

Rita took to the work immediately and rose rapidly through the officer ranks. It didn't hurt that she had a faculty for the work, came from a visual minority group, or that she was a woman. She was also adept at organizational politics and used her underlings ruthlessly in her quest for advancement. She had been promoted to Superintendent and posted to Victoria in charge of District Headquarters two years earlier at the ripe old age of forty-three. Her husband, Larry, a successful insurance sales agent, was content to follow her there, as he had with her other postings. He was also content with her practice of spending most of her time at work.

Rita Chan and Errol Fields rarely saw eye-to-eye. She was puzzled that he had managed to become an Inspector while seemingly totally indifferent to office politics and refusing to be intimidated by authority. Nevertheless, his ability to adeptly structure joint police organizations had always won approval from E Division headquarters and she knew better than to deny his requests for funding of his Combined Organized Crime Unit. Besides, the expanded police operations in Victoria, under the command of one of her officers, only served to increase her own authority.

WHILE INSPECTOR FIELDS was pleased with the progress being made by Corporal Murphy and his team, he knew they still didn't have the evidence to link the Desperados to the grow-ops. They tailed Pearson for a few days, determined the location of the lab and identified many of his contacts as members of his gang. But no shipments were received and none left the lab during that period. The Inspector decided it was time to use his organizational skills to put in place a thorough operation with an aim to connecting all the pieces. Once his plan was finalized, he received reluctant approval from the Superintendent to proceed with implementation and he assembled his troops.

They set up their operations centre in District Headquarters. Most of the officers were members of the Combined Organized Crime Unit and were either members of the RCMP or the City of Victoria Police, although a few were seconded from Saanich and Central Saanich. In all, the new anti-drug unit consisted of 23 officers. Fields met with his team in the building's largest meeting room to assign orders.

"We have two main assignments," he began. "One is to move in and shut down the marijuana grow-ops. We now know of five locations connected to the gang, and while there may be more, we will probably find out about them as we proceed with the operation. There is also an independent grow operation connected to one of the owners and we can shut it down, too, but it is not a high priority and we can get to it later. There is no reason for that grower to suspect that we are on to him."

"The second and more urgent task is to gather all the information we can on the Desperados before we move. We are now tracking their leader, Drew Pearson. We are very sure that a large medical warehouse he owns in Royal Oak is the shipping point for most of the marijuana crops and very likely the main distribution point for many other drugs sold in Victoria. We also suspect that a laboratory located in the warehouse is used for manufacturing illegal chemicals, and these are shipped, with the marijuana, to the U.S., although we haven't been able to verify this as yet. We do know that he legally ships other medical chemicals to Seattle and various locations in California."

"Why don't we just raid the lab and find out, sir?" a Saanich constable asked.

"We hope to maintain surveillance long enough to find out where the drugs are going, who his contacts for them are in the U.S. and what they are bringing back with them to Victoria. We also hope to find out who the dealers are here in Victoria and put an end to their entire operation, including their distribution network. Also, we need to get the goods on the other gang members."

"How long will all this take, Inspector?" the persistent Constable added. "Won't they eventually find out we are on to them?"

"Eventually, Constable, and if you let me finish my briefing we can get started before they all retire."

AFTER RECEIVING WORD from Roger Kent that Thelma Frank had been eliminated, The Captain decided it was safe for the Desperados to resume normal operations. It was also apparent to him that Frank had not gone to the police, based on their release indicating they had no suspects or leads in the case and because Chit Batra had no information to the contrary. Drew Pearson received approval from Kent to proceed with his work and the gang was soon in full swing. Within a week they had manufactured enough pseudoephedrine for a shipment and Drew ordered his gang members to bring in any marijuana ready for export. The next day he had a truck loaded and on its way to California.

Shortly after the truck had departed, The Captain received word that Chit Batra had an urgent message for him. He arranged for Batra to call him from a public telephone and took the call on his secure line in his office. Batra explained to The Captain that he had just learned about the new anti-drug operation and their surveillance of the Desperados' activities. He had also learned that just that day the new unit had observed a shipment leaving Victoria destined for the U.S.

"I don't understand this, Batra. A little more than a week ago, you tell me that Thelma Frank is dead and the Mounties have no information of any gang activity. Now all of a sudden there is full surveillance on the Desperados and the police seem to know all about them. Where the hell have you been?"

"I guess I picked a bad time to get the flu," he answered ruefully.

"So how the hell did they find out? Is Frank dead or not?"

"I don't know. There's no mention of her. I just found out about the operation before I called you. They know about the lab and the grow-ops and the shipments to the States, and they're planning a big raid, including the arrest of the American operatives."

"I'm not happy about this, Chit. I want you to find out all you can and get back to me with any developments. See if they have found out who owns the grow-ops and how much they know about the gang's operations in Victoria and elsewhere. In the meantime, I will do what I can to warn everyone. Damn!"

The Captain had two main concerns – that Barinder Chohan's party membership activities not be discovered and that the police remain ignorant of the existence of the medical chemical lab in Vancouver. He would make some phone calls to warn Drew Pearson and the Americans, but the downfall of the Desperados was not that significant, given the money flowing in from his other illegal businesses. He knew that the Desperados did not know about him and he knew that Chohan and Kent would never talk, so he was confident that there would be no linkage to him or to his conglomerate.

WHEN ROGER KENT called, Drew had been congratulating his gang members on their latest endeavour. They had just heard that the medical chemicals truck had cleared customs and was making its way southward through Washington State. Relaxing over a beer in the club lounge in the lab, they talked about their success in adding a large harvest from each of three grow-ops to the large supply of drug ingredients being shipped. All in all, it had gone like clockwork and would result in a large payoff. He hung up from the call, pale and shaking and slumped into his chair before passing on the message.

"We're trapped here, aren't we?" his second-in-command, Ryan Fuller, asked despondently after Drew had explained the situation. "There's no way to get off the Island without getting caught."

"Not yet, we're not," a defiant Drew answered. "The cops don't know we have been tipped off. We need to shut down the lab and hide as much as we can. If we do it right, they may not be able to prove just what we were manufacturing. Our official records indicate that we make legal medical chemicals, so let's make it look like we do. Also, we will need to radio the truck and get Jim Pallan to dump his load. Later we can say he was just on his way to pick up supplies. They won't be able to prove a thing."

"What about the grow-ops?" another gang member asked. "They will be able to connect us to them."

"That's right, and it's why we have to shut them down and get out of Victoria. We warn all the growers and tell everyone to split. If some of us get picked up, we deny everything. Even if they get some of us, growing and selling grass is a hell of a lot less serious than the other stuff we do."

"How much time do we have?"

"Not much. Our truck will be under surveillance, so we will be really lucky if he can get rid of the load without being caught. We will wait until Jim is in California before we tell him. If he can't figure out a way to dump the stuff, we will get him to keep driving until we are clear here."

"One way might be for him to shake off the surveillance long enough to drive the truck into the woods and abandon it. That may give him enough time to make a getaway."

"That's worth a thought," Drew agreed. "Let's work on that one. In the meantime, the rest of you get to work and clean up the lab. Ryan, call the growers and let them know what's going on."

What about the so-called owners?"

"Screw them. They will just deny they knew what was happening on the properties, anyway. Just make sure the growers don't panic, and they make their own arrangements to disappear. As soon as we finish with the lab, the rest of us will do the same. Meanwhile, I will figure out how to get the word out to anyone else we need to warn."

Drew knew what he had to do. He was sure that the laboratory was under surveillance and that there was a large enough police force to keep an eye on each gang member as they left. Once they realized the Desperados were attempting to flee, they would all be picked up. He had prepared long ago for just such a situation. Leaving the other gang members, he quietly left the lab and walked inconspicuously to his car and drove to his apartment where he packed nothing but a stash of large bills he kept hidden for just such an emergency. Next, he drove to a neighbourhood shopping mall in Royal Oak. Once inside, he quickly made two phone calls from the mall's public phones. The first was to Layne Bircham, a trusted associate who was not a member of his gang and would not be under surveillance. The second call was to Chris Cooper, an independent charter pilot, who flew a Piper Navajo out of the Victoria Airport.

He explained to Layne what he required him to do and asked him to pick him up just outside the north entrance to the mall within ten minutes. Layne agreed he could make it. Drew pretended to be shopping and even picked up a shopping cart inside the large Penny Wise food store and started loading on groceries. After ten minutes had elapsed, he pushed the cart casually toward the store's stockroom. Suddenly he dropped the cart and dashed into and through the stockroom, out the loading bay and into Layne's late model silver Acura, a powerful car that soon had them hurtling northward toward the Pat Bay Highway. They remained on the highway for a few minutes, turned left at Keating Crossroads and made their way westwards on back roads to the Island Highway, where they again turned north.

ALONG WITH A contingent of other unmarked cars in the area, Tim Murphy and Craig Ballard sat discreetly in their high-powered sedan a couple of blocks from the Desperados' laboratory. As Drew left the building, a Victoria police officer stationed closer to the scene radioed to them that he was leaving in his SUV. Craig easily picked up the signal from the tracking transmitter he had earlier installed on Drew's van and circumspectly followed as he made his way, first to his apartment, then the mall. At the mall, they remained well behind him and watched as he made his phone calls. Tim followed him into the Penny Wise Food Mart while Craig called the Telus operator and asked for a trace on the calls that Drew had made. As he hung up he was almost knocked over by a charging Mountie, ordering him to follow.

"Get in the car, Craig, the bastard has gone out the back!" Tim yelled as he jumped behind the wheel and peeled the car around the corner of the mall and headed in the direction he had last observed the departing Acura. Heading north, they decided Drew must be making for the airport or the ferries.

While Tim raced the powerful police car madly in the direction of the Pat Bay Highway, Craig calmly asked the Crime Unit Operations Centre for a licence and registration trace on the vehicle belonging to the owner Telus had identified as Layne Bircham. He radioed an all-points bulletin description of the Acura and turned his attention to finding out what he could about the pilot, Chris Cooper. After being notified that he chartered a Piper Navajo out of Victoria Airport, he radioed the airport's operation's centre to determine if Cooper had as yet filed a flight plan. He was informed that he hadn't but, according to the tower, he had departed under visual flight rules, only thirty minutes earlier, ostensibly for some local sight seeing.

"You know, Tim, we might be on a bit of a wild goose chase here. I bet the crafty bastard has arranged a pick-up at another airport or landing field. Let's see if we can find out what's available."

After finding out that almost all other airports to the north were located along the Island Highway, they elected to head in that direction while informing the Unit to keep a look out for the Acura on both the Island Highway and around the Victoria Airport and ferries. They were informed that no sightings had been made, but they had since arrested a sizable number of Desperados' gang members attempting to flee by a variety of transportation methods, including scheduled airlines, mainland and Gulf Island ferries and even chartered fishing boats.

"Well, that's good," Craig commented to Tim. "It looks like we have put these guys out of commission once and for all."

"Yeah, but we still need Pearson. He's smart enough to start up again somewhere else, plus he's the one who knows where the money is kept and we don't want him getting his hands on it. It's bound to be a sizeable chunk of change."

"At least we know there are not many places he can go. Someone will pick him up along the highway anytime now."

Fifteen minutes went by and there was still no sighting. Tim and Craig's cross-country trip ended when they joined the Island Highway at Langford. They had just started heading north when they received a call that the Acura had been spotted by a regular traffic patrol about ten minutes west of them on the Sooke Highway.

"Spotted on the Sooke Highway?" Craig puzzled. "There aren't any airports up there. Pearson must be sticking to the secondary roads to avoid detection. Maybe he plans to come out on the Cowichan Lake Road at Duncan."

"Well, let's get the hell over there. In the meantime, don't let that patrol car move in on them. Pearson is highly dangerous and they probably have weapons."

Craig hurdled across country again along Humpback Road, a narrow up and down trail used mainly as an access road to the water reservoir. He was barely able to keep the car on the road as it bumped and slammed its way over the rough and potholed surface. Within a few minutes, their hair-raising adventure ended as they intersected with Sooke Road and turned right.

"Jesus, Tim, I know had badly you want this guy, but could you get us to him in one piece? I feel like my teeth have all fallen out."

"Not to worry, Craig, it's all clear sailing now."

"Yeah, but for how long? It gets pretty rough again north of Sooke."

The patrol car followed at a safe distance behind the Acura and the driver reported to Craig that he didn't believe he had been noticed. Even so, he was travelling at a pretty fair clip and it took another half hour before Tim and Craig closed in on him, by now well north of Sooke. After spotting the patrol car and radioing him to stay close, they passed and picked up a visual on the Acura. By now they were into Jordon River, a small community along the shores of the Juan de Fuca Straights, at one time a forest company town and now just another stop along the way for the tourists.

"Where the hell is he going?" Craig exclaimed as the Acura suddenly turned right at the top of a steep hill past the village, just as they were about to close in.

"Darned if I know, but this should make it easy to trap them. This has to be a dead-end road. I'll be damned! There's an old temporary airstrip up there. The logging companies must have used this. Maybe they still do, for all I know."

In front of them the terrain had flattened out and the first-growth timber had been stripped bare for miles in all directions. The airstrip was short and bumpy and didn't exactly look like it would replace the Vancouver International anytime soon. On either side, second growth timber had reclaimed much of the land and was squeezing in on the strip, like a flesh wound that slowly gets crowded out by encroaching healthy tissue. Nevertheless, as rough as it was, it was clear that Cooper had brought the Navajo in for a safe landing.

"Yeah, now where the hell did that fucking car go? There, Tim, down at the end of the airstrip. There's the Navajo and they are already piling into it. We need to get down there fast."

"I can't go any quicker, Craig, or I'll take the bottom out of this thing."

"Christ, now they're in and heading back toward us."

"Hang on," Tim yelled as he pulled the police car into the middle of the narrow airstrip. "This should get them to stop."

"You crazy bastard, Tim, they're picking up speed. They'll never make it!"

"Get out, get out!" Tim ordered as he shoved his door open and ran for the trees.

Craig followed him quickly. They were just able to get off the airstrip as the pilot, in a desperate attempt to get airborne, pulled back on the stick at full throttle. The plane lurched into the sky, but the undercarriage caught on the windshield of the police sedan and slammed forward into the dirt, the engines bursting into flame and wreckage careening in all directions. The three occupants were killed instantly.

Part Four

Political Crimes

We live in a political world
Love don't have any place
We're living in times where men commit crimes
And crime don't have a face

Bob Dylan – Political World

Chapter 22

TIM WAS BECOMING very attached to the picture of the Queen hanging behind Inspector Field's desk. Errol Fields, on the other hand, was less than enamoured with Tim's increasingly frequent visits. Unlike their previous meeting, the Inspector was far from jovial and, after beckoning him to a chair, he ripped into the Corporal like a school of hungry piranhas fastening onto an innocent calf that had wandered indiscreetly into the wrong stream.

"You might not think your life is worth a plugged nickel, Corporal Murphy, and you'd probably be right," he began. "But unfortunately, the City of Victoria has invested a lot of time and money to train and prepare Constable Ballard for his duties, just as the RCMP has, unfortunately, done for you. As a result, I don't take kindly to your irrational obsession for positioning our expensive automobiles in the way of onrushing vehicles. It was bad enough when you did it on your own, but when you're willing to risk the lives of other police officers, you go too far. Not to mention, of course, that you manage to take the lives of others every time you do it."

"I was concerned that Pearson would get away scot-free, sir," Tim mumbled pathetically.

"Christ, Murphy, the armed forces have interceptors based just up the road in Comox. They could easily have had someone tracking the Navajo within ten minutes. And we would have picked them up when they landed. Once again, you have jeopardized your own life and, in this case, the life of another valuable officer for no good reason."

"Yes, sir."

"Consider yourself off the case and this time it's for good. I don't even want you back on traffic services, Tim. You're too dangerous on the highways and too foolhardy to even work with others in an operational situation. As you seem to have an affinity for research, I will arrange for you to review cold case files until I can get you removed from the District. I would suspend you immediately, but we are so short of officers with this joint investigation I don't even have the time to work with Human Resources to arrange your transfer. Now, get the hell out of here and report to Staff-Sergeant Rudnick in Investigative Research."

After Murphy had left his office and after he had had a chance to calm down, Inspector Fields contemplated what they had learned so far. They had broken up a sophisticated criminal operation that had played a very major role in supplying drugs for the Victoria market, as well as for export. They had also picked up the southbound medical chemicals truck before the driver could abandon his valuable cargo. As a result, they had the evidence that the lab's activities were much less than legal. Finally, they had the information that the owners of the grow-ops included some influential members of the Progressive Party and that one of them was also an assistant to a Cabinet Minister in the Provincial Government.

As the renters of the grow-ops had all been arrested, the owners of the properties would be expecting the same would be happening to them shortly. The Inspector knew he would have to move fast. After receiving the approvals from a reluctant Superintendent Rita Chan and from E Division headquarters, he arranged for a raid on the homes of the owners and on the offices of Barinder Chohan and his fellow Cabinet Minister assistant, Alan Diwan, in addition to the homes or offices of other Progressive Party officials, including Harnam Gill, who Fields knew worked closely with the two aides.

The raids would also include Jaswinder Chohan, who could very likely shed some light on his cousin Barinder, as well as on his friend Parbeen Dhariwal, whose grow-op was clearly separate from the gang's operations. He was also sure that he could get at least one of the owners to talk and decided to have a good heart-to-heart with each of them in the near future. Also, he would hold off on arresting Dhariwal until after this talk in order to gather more evidence about this curious independent arrangement.

By this time, Inspector Fields had learned enough to know that the political activities of Barinder Chohan and his associates were highly suspect. He had no proof, but he was confident the monies raised from marijuana sales were being funnelled to the party organization. It was easy enough to make a connection from the cash obtained from the grow-ops to Chohan's success in recruiting new party members, especially on the Island and on the Lower Mainland.

The Inspector was able to receive warrants for the searches, ostensibly as part of the on-going investigation of the marijuana grow operation, but he also hoped to learn a lot more about the membership-buying scheme. He even convinced a sympathetic judge that searches of the homes and offices of party officials connected to Chohan's recruitment drives was warranted. The Court Services budget had recently been severely slashed by the Provincial Government and perhaps the judiciary were in a mood to get even. At any rate, the judge issued the warrants, including those that approved of a search of offices and tape storage facilities right in the legislature.

Over the next few days, Inspector Fields carefully planned out the arrests. He assembled his team and briefed them on their responsibilities. By the third week of December he had completed his organizational arrangements, received the required approvals from headquarters and settled on the date to carry out the raids.

UNFORTUNATELY, AN ENTERPRISING Chip Batra learned about the raid before it happened. He was brought in to arrange for a large fleet of vehicles for the morning in question, and while he was not told why they were needed, his curiosity was naturally aroused. After a few casual enquiries, a loose-lipped Sergeant with an exaggerated sense of his own importance bragged to Chit about his inclusion on a "secret" mission. Using a bit of flattery, Chit was able to get enough out of him to learn it had something to do with a vote-buying scheme and some Cabinet Minister's office. He reported this to The Captain who naturally was able to determine from this what was about to occur.

The Captain pondered his next moves. He was enraged that the legislature would be subject to a search, as he now realized that the party's membership purchasing activities would be in jeopardy. Still, they could not be traced back to him, and with Drew Pearson dead, there was little likelihood that even Roger Kent's role would be discovered. Also, no matter what happened to him, Barinder Chohan would never talk. Nevertheless, he would need to warn him. Unfortunately, his call to Kent went unanswered and The Captain was forced to rely on Chit Batra to get the word to Barinder. And with all the work involved in arranging the vehicle fleet for the raid, Chit somehow managed to forget to call him.

Next, The Captain considered the information that other party officials were also targeted for searches. He knew that Paul Husband and Leif Johannsen were smart enough to cover their tracks and he doubted they could be connected to buying memberships. But did the Mounties have any information to suspect that these influential backroom activists in Vancouver were part of a scheme to manipulate the upcoming federal election results, or were they simply attempting to connect them to Chohan? After warning Paul Husband, he arranged a meeting with Johannsen. Leif was the party's west coast communications genius and had agreed to mastermind The Captain's idea of altering election results in B.C. He worked closely with Husband, but while Husband worked with the party organization to manipulate constituency matters, Johannsen worked with the voters and their voting intentions.

Leif Johannsen was a colourful and talkative little man whose main ambition in life was to advise others on how to become rich and influential. He owned a research company called Bridge Consulting that assisted business owners who wished to better understand the market for the products they sold and how to reach these target markets. He would use his researching skills to determine for The Captain which voters in which ridings could be targeted and convinced to vote for the federal Progressive Party and at what price.

The Captain, while impressed with Johannsen's abilities as a researcher, did not much care for his bold and cavalier method of operating. He suspected that if the police were to get a lead on his plans, it would be through Johannsen and his big mouth.

"Are you aware the Horsemen have arranged to conduct a search on your home and office, Leif?" he began bluntly, after leading him to a chair across from his desk. "Is there any reason to think they may have connected you to Chohan's membership purchasing program or to our current project?"

"Of course not," a startled and indignant Johannsen shot back. "I don't keep that kind of information where anyone can find it and use it against me. I've been in this game long enough to have figured that out. And what are you talking about, anyway? Why would the Mounties want to search my offices?"

"It seems they have connected Barinder Chohan to our marijuana project over in Victoria and are about to make a raid on all his connections, including those that are part of our party membership drive."

"That won't prove anything. Barinder won't talk and I don't have any records to implicate me."

"Sure, sure, but what about Paul?"

"You have warned him, haven't you? You have to give us a little credit."

"I gave Barinder some credit too, and look at his screw up."

"When is this raid supposed to take place anyway and who else is involved?"

"I don't know yet, but very soon I think. Chit Batra passes on what he knows as he learns it. However, my guess is that along with Barinder, you, Paul and Alan Diwan can expect a visit. Anyway, enough of that. I've mainly asked you in to review how our plans are coming along for voter profiling in key Lower Mainland ridings, Leif?"

"Everything is in good order," Johannsen answered with his usual bravado. "I have identified twelve ridings where the margin of vote was less than five percent in the last federal election. That means that if about 3000 voters had voted differently, the results would have gone to another party."

"Wouldn't some of these ridings be held by the Progressive Party anyway? We wouldn't need to change the results in ridings we already hold."

"Yes, but in those ridings we will need to ensure the results remain the same. In addition, the remaining close ridings will need to shift to our candidate. In those ridings, our candidate was second. Keep in mind, these are all volatile ridings and the results are always close, but unpredictable."

"Are these ridings all in the Lower Mainland? Can we focus on one ethnic group to affect the results?" The Captain was hoping to use his influence in the Indo-Canadian community to get what he wanted.

"No and no," Leif squirmed uncomfortably. "But the good news is that with the exception of a northern riding with a large native population, they all have significant ethnic minorities that are first or second generation and still subject to community leadership pressures. In addition, many are poor, have no political affiliations of their own and can be easily bought for a nominal fee. In fact, according to my records provided by Paul Husband, many potential voters, particularly in the Lower Mainland, have already been given party memberships and voted, under direction, in the nominating meetings."

"So, Leif, do you think we can actually buy ourselves an election?" The Captain feigned amusement, but he was deadly serious and he wanted Johannsen to be too. The next federal election was expected to be very close and B.C. was looked upon as the key to success. If the Progressive Party received the largest number of seats of the three major parties contending in the province, they would potentially win the federal election. If this happened, The Captain would be a major influence within the party and could count on support from the Federal Cabinet for his plans for the province.

"Absolutely, but two things must happen. First, even though they are apathetic, the voters we buy must actually believe they are doing a good thing by voting for the Progressive Party. They are then more likely to do what they agreed to do and that is to actually vote for the party when they get in the voting booth. Studies from other countries show that buying voters results in only 70 per cent of them actually casting their vote for the party when they get in the booth. And secondly, you have to ensure they get to the poll in the first place and that means a big enough payment to provide an incentive, plus drivers to get them there. I suggest a $50 payment, $25 up front to the ones we identify in each riding and the other $25 after they vote and after they pass a simple test."

"What kind of test?"

"What the candidate's name is that they voted for and where on the ballot his name is located – third, forth, whatever. In that way, you can be better assured they actually paid attention and did what they were supposed to do."

"What would be the total cost?

"Well, it's simple enough. Twelve ridings times 3,000 voters times $50 and that equals $1.8 million."

"That works, but all 3,000 voters would need to switch their vote to our party in the ridings that did not go Progressive the last time, assuming of course that other events don't cause a complete change in the way people vote. Just to be sure, what about 5,000 voters?"

"It's your money."

"Yes, it is, and I mean to get the results I am looking for. If there is the slightest indication that the authorities learn about this before it happens, I will want to know why. Is that clear?"

"Of course," Johannsen answered quickly, the colour draining out of his face even while he attempted to retain his bravado appearance. "You are paying me well for this research and I want the same for the party as you do. You can count on me to maintain full discretion, as always."

"What are the next steps?"

"You are going to need a whole lot of workers. I suggest you get Paul Husband in on this and start organizing. Also, you need to start working on Canadian Universal Media. I know they already are behind the party and they are close to maintaining a media monopoly in the province, but they are going to have to ensure that the voters see our party as vastly preferable to the others. Finally, you have to get the ethnic community leaders onside. Many of them already are, I understand, but they will need to know that good things will happen for them if the party gets elected."

"When the party gets elected," he corrected. "I have that in hand, Leif. Now let's see how well you can profile the individual voters we need."

What a prick! Johannsen thought, as he left The Captain's office. If the man wasn't so damn powerful he would never have agreed to work for him. Nevertheless, he was in too deep now to refuse his orders and he knew that he would surely regret it if he decided to go against The Captain's wishes. He had decided to keep his little arrangement with Barinder to receive bribes from a company interested in bidding on a portion of the BC Hydro privatization initiative to himself. The Captain would not be pleased to learn he was illegally meddling in provincial politics without his consent, or even his knowledge. Surely Barinder wouldn't have been dumb enough to keep a record of their lucrative little scheme, would he?

Chapter 23

BARINDER CHOHAN HAD NEVER considered that his office in the legislature would be raided. It wasn't until the media reported it in the afternoon that he even knew it had happened. When the police search party had come to his house he knew the jig was up on his grow-op ownership, but he had not maintained any records at home that related to his other activities, particularly his party membership records. The irony was, because he was sure they would be safe in his office, that is where he had kept them. Who would have thought a judge would ever grant a warrant to permit a search of the legislature?

If Barinder had ever felt stressed in the past, it was nothing compared to this. He was confident he could beat any charges that came out of ownership of property where a grow-op was maintained, but he didn't know what to expect from his other activities. The membership purchases were bad enough, but his little initiative with Alan Diwan and Leif Johannsen was sure to get him in real trouble, not only with the law, but much more seriously with Roger Kent and his more powerful party associates who had never sanctioned their little ploy.

The point was, being an assistant to a Cabinet Minister had made him feel influential and this perceived importance had gone to his head. While the money wasn't great, he felt entitled to use his position for his own benefit. In fact, that was what he thought he was supposed to do and why he had been rewarded with the job in the first place. Everyone had told him what great work he had done signing up new party members and his assignment to Cabinet was his well-deserved reward. So when he received inside information that BC Hydro was to be privatized and he and Alan Diwan were to be responsible for assessing the interested candidates, why shouldn't he use this information for his own benefit? That's what others did with inside information. He was just playing the game.

It didn't hurt that he was responsible for vetting the Expressions of Interest process and the subsequent Request for Proposals that would go to private sector firms that may be interested in purchasing a chunk of the huge Crown Corporation once it was put up for offers. He could use this information to tip off any companies that may be interested in putting in a submission. Also, Alan knew how to use this knowledge to best political advantage, and he, in turn, had brought Johannsen in, mainly because Johannsen could arrange effective lobbying for whoever was willing to submit a proposal. Once a potential candidate was identified, Barinder could then ensure the RFP was "tailored" to give that candidate the best chance of winning the competition for that particular chunk of the action. He wouldn't have much input on the final decision, but he knew many companies would pay well just for the chance to receive a very lucrative monopoly service contract.

Like Barinder, Alan Diwan had worked for the federal Progressive Party ever since he was recruited as a student at UBC. He had helped to recruit new party members and dabbled in organizational work under the tutelage of Paul Husband. He had come to Victoria as a reward for his work as an assistant to party organizers. He was much more politically astute than Barinder and had many important connections at the federal party level. He did not have Barinder's street gang background, however, and when asked if he would like to be the owner of a grow-op property he had quickly declined. Nevertheless, he maintained close ties with Barinder, especially after they had both been made assistants to B.C. Cabinet Ministers. This connection had led to the issuance of a search warrant for his home and office, as it might likely lead to further evidence of his and Chohan's involvement in membership irregularities, given their close association.

Barinder decided that he and Alan had a lot to talk about and he arranged to visit him. As they both lived in an upscale neighbourhood in Gordon Head it didn't take long for Barinder to drive over on a cold, dreary, weekday afternoon soon after the raid. Alan's wife, Darshi, would be out with her young children at a local daycare cooperative where she worked as a volunteer. The houses here were large and, unlike much of Victoria, included a good-sized yard where some space could be maintained between neighbours. Barinder hurried from his car at the end of the long, wide driveway as the rain, an oppressive presence after the good weather that had occurred such a few short days before, leaked from a grey saturated sponge that surrendered its burden of water reluctantly and seemingly endlessly. The wet weather, like an unwanted houseguest, had settled in for a long, long stay.

As Alan led him into the house, he took time to look around. Like Barinder, Alan maintained the trappings that corresponded to their previously perceived importance. The rooms were large and filled with high quality furniture, paintings and plants. Toys were scattered in almost every room, discarded randomly by Alan's two high-energy pre-schoolers as their interests flitted spontaneously from one temporary object of amusement to another. They made their way through the jumble of dolls, puzzles, stuffed animals and racing cars and found refuge in Alan's den, where he quickly poured each of them a stiff glass of Scotch. They then settled into the blue leather furniture and got down to business.

Already since the raid, Barinder had been fired and Alan suspended from his duties. The first item on Barinder's agenda was to review their unhappy situation. "I think I have the most to lose here, Alan," he led off. "The biggest problem will be the BC Hydro privatization contract. I doubt whether the charges on the grow-op can stand up and the party membership purchases will be hard to prove."

"Oh, no, Barinder! Don't tell me you had records in your office of our arrangements. Do you mean to tell me you had stuff in your files that will implicate all of us?"

"Where else was I to keep the information? My files are private and no one could know that they would be subject to search. I had no knowledge that this would happen."

"Okay, so what was in these files? Everything we arranged and all the deals we made? What about Leif's lobbying kickbacks? Is that in there too? And what about the list of companies I gave you to approach? Did you keep a record of that, too?"

"Yes, yes, Alan, but what else could I do? If Western Utilipower Corp. had reneged on our agreement and not paid us for tailoring the RFP in their favour, we would have had nothing to leverage them with. And remember, Leif had promised us very good jobs in Ottawa after the federal election. How could we hold him to that if I didn't keep something to show the kickback arrangement? I didn't have anything that implicates him directly, but I had copies of receipts showing lucrative payments to Leif from the lobbyists who supposedly hired Leif for consulting work. I knew I could use that information if we needed Leif to keep his promise."

"And just how did you get those copies?"

"I know his secretary very well and I told her I needed them so that I could see that we were getting our 10 per cent of whatever Leif received."

"That's ridiculous, Barinder, and you know it. You don't keep that information where anyone can find it and use it against you. You have to trust others to honour their agreements. I suppose you also kept records of the money paid out for party memberships?"

Alan groaned as Barinder nodded affirmatively. Alan realized that he would be implicated once all the information in the files was analyzed, along with Leif, although in both cases it may take the police awhile to connect all the dots. He would have to think carefully about his defence. At the very least, once the charges came out, he could probably stall off going to court for quite some time. At this point, he was just suspended and he knew that he could not be implicated in the drug deal. Also, he hadn't been directly involved in the membership payments, so that would be Barinder's problem to face alone.

So that only left the privatization of B.C. Hydro. There was nothing to directly connect him to the kickback scheme, other than the list of companies interested in the privatization of the huge Crown Corporation. Also, the list could be easily explained as simply part of his activities connected to managing the purchase contracts. It wouldn't hurt that Western Utilipower Corp. hadn't been awarded one of the first contracts that had since come out of the privatization process. For its own reasons, the Cabinet had chosen a larger firm, Cascadian Power Corporation, an American-owned company that had been a BC Crown Corporation in the past and which would allow the Howe Street in-crowd to more directly share in the spoils.

"How do you plan to fight this, Barinder?" he asked, making it clear that he planned to distance himself as much as he could. "We should probably arrange our defence teams separately, so that we can better make it appear that there was no conspiracy. Also, I will need to tell Leif what you have told me, so that he can be prepared in case he gets dragged into it. After all, they have already searched his offices, so let's hope he didn't have anything in his files to connect him to the kickback scheme, or to us. Perhaps in his case, they were only looking for information about the membership purchase and didn't even learn anything about that."

"Okay, well, I guess I better find myself a good lawyer," Barinder replied ruefully. He got up slowly and left Alan's office in a daze, tripping over a large purple hippopotamus as he walked through the living room, banging his head on the side of the door frame. What else can go wrong, he wondered, as he dodged his way through the relentless drizzle and slid slowly into his car seat.

IT WAS A QUIET Sunday morning and Tim Murphy looked out his kitchen window and stared absentmindedly at the dull grey sky. Earlier he had reported to Staff-Sergeant Eric Rudnick in Investigative Research as ordered, but he was very depressed and his interest in his work was lacklustre, at best. He had worked at his duties the past few weeks like a robot, routinely and without thought or imagination. Rudnick, a wise, long-in-the-tooth officer, was a patient man, and knowing Murphy's situation, he was sympathetic and gave Tim the time to adjust to his new reality. Now, finally, as he stared out at the trees, he was indeed coming to grips with his situation.

At the moment, his thoughts were on his up-and-down career. He had many differences of opinion with his senior officers over the years, but never had anyone been as upset with him as Inspector Fields. The odd thing was, in spite of his by-the-book approach, he liked the Inspector and thought he had the best of intentions for the force and for his subordinates. But why was it that the Inspector couldn't understand it was sometimes necessary to take the bull by the horns to get something done? He would never concede, for instance, that allowing Drew Pearson to get airborne would have resulted in his inevitable capture anyway. Hell, they could have ditched the Navajo anywhere, long before an air force interceptor could locate them. Once out of sight, Pearson would have had the money and connections to make his way across to the mainland and into the States, by boat, for instance, and simply disappear.

More importantly, what was Tim to do now? Should he fight his transfer, or find another line of work? He was still young enough to take up another career and knew he was determined enough to do anything he decided to take on. It would be tough, though, especially as Gloria, with her debilitating disease, very much needed him. Also, the time and money to get established in something else would be extremely taxing. Besides, he liked being a Mountie and all he needed was a good job where he could be himself. Undercover work would be perfect for him as he could work by himself, or with another independent partner, like Craig Ballard, for instance, and he wouldn't have to worry about a lot of stupid bureaucratic rules. Why couldn't that pigheaded Inspector understand that? Tim decided he would fight to remain at the District Office.

First, though, he would talk it over with Gloria, so he proposed an afternoon's walk on the main Thetis Lake trail. This would give them an opportunity to give Groucho some much needed exercise, in addition to providing a good venue for airing his thoughts. He had learned that a pleasurable stroll through one of Victoria's most scenic nature parks put them both in the mood for sharing ideas and making decisions. Also, the main trail was flat and open, and Gloria could manage it without tiring too quickly.

For a change, it wasn't raining, and notwithstanding the gloomy sky, the walk was charming and captivating. In spite of its name, Thetis is two lakes, Upper and Lower. The main trail winds pleasantly around the outside of the lakes, providing a good view of the water and its surrounding hills. At this time of year, the coniferous trees dominate the skyline, while many of the leaves from the maples and alders cover the ground, providing a yellow, red and brown montage that softens the ground and makes it seem as if ambling along a plush, never-ending carpet. From time to time, as if reluctant to leave the trees, a transparent canopy of huge maple leaves filtered the light and cast a pale yellow glow on the trail ahead.

Groucho ran ahead of them and scurried through the tree trunks on either side of the trail. Periodically he stopped and carefully analyzed the posted canine odours, as if classifying them through some complex reference system known only in dog world. Frequently he came back to check on them, determined to show Tim and Gloria that in spite of his concentration on this task, he was also paying attention to his over-arching responsibility for their safety.

While he absently eyed Groucho's movements, Tim reviewed his dilemma with Gloria and defended his decision. She agreed with him that he should take whatever steps were necessary to remain in the District.

"Maybe the fact that Inspector Fields has not started the paperwork to have you transferred is an indicator that he is not sure what to do," mused Gloria. "I think if he was serious in having you gone, you would have been suspended by now, and the transfer process would have been immediately initiated. To blame it on a shortage of officers is hogwash. What's so critical about research work that he needs you there now, especially on cold case files? I think maybe you should just keep working quietly and conscientiously and at the same time review what options you have to prepare a defence if he does decide to go ahead."

"Okay, but if I do fight to be retained here, even if I win, it would likely be the end of my career. I could probably look forward to a life of traffic patrols."

"Oh, I don't know. One senior officer rotation later and there is no one around to remember what happened." Besides, it's too early to worry about that. Just do your assignments to the best of your ability, as you always have, and you will be all right. Everybody knows how good you are and they will want to keep you on."

"You know, Gloria, I'm lucky to have you. I will try my best to keep my nose clean. Besides, how much trouble can I get into doing research work?"

"Knowing you, plenty," she smiled. "Wasn't it from research that you eventually found out about the Desperados?"

"Touché," he grinned. "Now let's enjoy our walk," he added, picking up a stick to throw for Groucho, who was urgently trying to get it across that he had an insatiable desire to immerse himself in the freezing cold water.

"Remember how you had to rescue him from drowning here when he was still a pup? It was about this time of year, too."

"Yeah, a Labrador Retriever who couldn't swim and all because of a little ear infection. I thought I would die of exposure before we got back to the car in my sopping wet clothes. Well, look at him now! I guess he doesn't remember."

"Or he's as stubborn as you are."

"Be careful, or you're next in," Tim replied, steering her toward the edge of the water.

"Watch it," Gloria laughed, "or you'll have to rescue me and I don't even have an ear infection. Now get serious, because I, too, have a predicament to lay on you."

"What, you need a ride to your dialysis run tomorrow? Why not? Being on research duties means I am flexible again."

"No, it's not that, but thanks anyway. I want to talk about something Sheila York said to me."

Tim felt himself go pale. "What's that?" he asked cautiously.

"Well, you know how involved she has become in working with me and visiting other dialysis patients. She should really have become a nurse because she has so much concern for all of us and wants to help so much. She told me she wants to be tested to see if she can give me one of her kidneys."

"Wow! That's wonderful, Gloria. But why does she want to do that?" Once again Tim wondered whether Sheila was still on some kind of guilt trip related to their earlier affair.

"She has been looking into the dismal state of organ transplantation in this province. I don't think you know, but for one thing, she has been working to encourage the members of the police and firefighting forces in the city to register their organs."

"Yeah. It can't but help to get as many people as possible to register. But as you know so well, the consent only takes effect after you are dead, and even then it depends on how you died."

"She knows that. I explained to her how, except for kidneys and some liver situations where you can use organs from live donors, many of the organs come from the small proportion of people who have died from brain death causes. I also told her that at one time even most kidney transplants were from people who had died, but that has changed and most now come from live donors."

"So what did she learn from her research on the topic?"

"She was dismayed at the eight or even ten years wait for a transplant and the number of people who don't make it."

"And did she learn why people have to wait so long?"

"Sure. As we know, B.C. has the worst record for transplants of almost all the provinces and one of the worst in the western world."

"People say they want to help, but very few actually get around to registering," Tim retorted. "Then the relatives often won't provide consent when they don't know the wishes of the would-be donor. It's a hell of a screwed up situation."

"So, it's up to all of us to get as many people registered as possible in order to help improve the chances of increasing the number of transplants," Gloria answered patiently.

"What does all that have to do with Sheila's decision to provide you with a kidney?"

"She's looked into that as well. Most live donor kidney transplants still come from other family members, but increasingly other kinds of people have started to donate too. These include spouses, workmates, friends and even anonymous donors who will never know the person receiving the kidney."

"And she wants to be a donor? Pretty risky, isn't it?"

"She recognizes there is a risk, about the same as for any operation where an anaesthetic is required. But she also knows that a person can live just as well with one kidney as with two."

"Doesn't she have to go through the same detailed process that I went through to see if she can even be a donor?"

"She does, but the B.C. Transplant Society makes it as straightforward as possible. You probably remember that the key points are that the person must be very serious about being a donor and be absolutely healthy. The assessment phase starts when someone who wants to be a donor is referred by a patient's kidney specialist to the transplant team. As part of the initial assessment, she will have several tests including blood work, laboratory and x-rays, and cardiac and vascular studies. Then she must go through a series of consultations with all the team members, including a transplant nephrologist, transplant surgeon, clinical coordinator, social worker and even a psychologist. And after all that she will be given an angiogram to make sure her blood vessels are in good shape."

"I recall all that. But then there's her recovery time. She would have to be off work after."

"Oh yes, she would need time to recover. But she has already found out the RCMP would cover her salary while she is off, which would only be about two months at the most."

"Well, I think it's great that she would want to do this. I know you would have a much better life than you do now on dialysis. So, what's the predicament?"

"It was bad enough when you offered to help me and we found out you were the wrong blood type. How can I agree to have Sheila do this when she has only been a friend for a few months and it would mean being off work and everything?"

"It sounds to me like she is going to do it anyway. If I were you, I would support her decision. It's for her, too, you know. It's the greatest gift one person can give another and she will get as much out of helping as you will from receiving her kidney."

"Okay, I won't try to stop her, but I still worry that something will go wrong."

"It's only natural you should feel that way, but she can see how much it will mean for you, even though there is some risk on her part."

"You know, Tim, this must be the best walk we have ever taken."

Tim could only agree as he resolved to find out how good a researcher he could be.

Chapter 24

JAKE GREENE HAD REASON to be pleased. His media empire continued to expand across the country and his control over news in British Columbia was now nearly total. Over the years, he had competed ruthlessly, buying out smaller media broadcasters and merging with once-huge newspaper chains. Today, with the exception of two much smaller TV networks and a few independent weekly papers, his corporation was the opinion-formulating catalyst for all important issues affecting the province. Most radio stations had long since given up trying to provide an alternative news perspective and the other TV broadcasters simply echoed his stories, and at any rate shared his pro-business philosophy.

He had also lobbied hard to reduce the influence of the public broadcasting network and had succeeded. Twenty years of political pressure by himself and his predecessors had convinced the federal government to cut the budget of the state-owned network to the point where it was now a pathetic voice in the wilderness. Its alternative perspective had become weakened by an inability to hire and properly pay good reporters, and now its listeners and viewers were a small minority and the network lacked the capacity to influence political and social opinion.

It had not always been like this for Jake. Born and raised in rural Manitoba, he had watched his father struggle to eke out a living for his mother, two brothers and himself on a large wheat farm that had once provided a good income for Jake's ancestors. However, the effects of globalization, foreign agricultural subsidies, Wheat Board policies and protectionist measures by the Americans ignoring the "free trade" agreement had steadily eroded the price of grain. Two years after his despondent father committed suicide and his mother and brothers had scattered across the country to live with sympathetic relatives, Jake had made his way to the coast where he knew he could at least stay warm.

Jake vowed he wouldn't stay poor. He had found work with a Vancouver newspaper publishing company, at first merely delivering the paper. He worked extremely hard, tirelessly expanded his route and was soon responsible for the delivery schedules of many other carriers across the east side of the city, a poor area, which other route managers had not desired. He controlled his carriers ruthlessly, insisting the paper be delivered daily, regardless of weather conditions or health problems. As a result, he caught the eye of management and was soon made a circulation manager, at which he excelled.

Jake's aptitude for, and interest in, the business side of the company eventually gained the attention of senior managers. When he was approached to take a small bursary to pursue a formal education under the company's sponsorship, he jumped at the chance. He selected the University of British Columbia and majored in Commerce. The bursary was small, but, used to hard work, he was content to exist on scholarships, macaroni and part-time waiter jobs.

It was there that Jake had met The Captain. They were both seen as outsiders, Jake because he was poor and The Captain because of his crippled leg. While not close, they had shared an interest in sailing. Jake had been willing to race with The Captain in spite of his harsh treatment of his crew, which Jake tended to admire anyway and tried to emulate in his own dealings with subordinates later in life. The two of them would sometimes get together for a beer and eventually learned to confide in each other in business matters. Nevertheless, they drifted apart after graduation, The Captain pursuing his Master's degree in Business Administration and Jake returning to his newspaper career.

Eventually, Jake's talent for business resulted in a vice-president position, but his desire for independence and wealth drove him to leave the company and start his own weekly paper. Through careful investment of his profits, he accumulated the money to open other weeklies in smaller communities across the province, and soon he was the owner of a publishing chain. The chain continued to grow until he gained the attention of Peter Schwartz, the owner of a burgeoning conglomerate of media outlets and daily papers called Canadian Universal Media, who strongly desired to add Canada's weekly papers to his empire. The bargaining was fierce, but eventually Jake sold his chain to Peter and joined him as a junior partner.

In spite of being his partner, Jake soon learned to detest Peter. Unlike his father, Mort, who ran the conglomerate before him, Peter had no interest in preserving a strongly pro-Canadian editorial slant in his publications and broadcasts. He allowed his editors to express an independent viewpoint, as long as they continued to represent the pro-business interests of the country's elites. Peter had little concern that globalization and foreign takeovers might eventually lead to a lack of dominance in the country by Canada's upper classes. Nor was he worried they may become little more than agents for outside owners. Peter was confident that Canadian elites could hold their own and favoured the no-holds barred philosophy of global free trade.

Jake, on the other hand, had seen the effects of so-called free trade on his own family and he knew what it meant to junior players, like Canada. He was certain that Canada's business elites would gradually be shoved aside attempting to compete against the world's dominant economic powerhouses, particularly, as he saw them, the ruthless and unscrupulous Americans. Nevertheless, Jake, quite ironically, was confident he could get the upper hand in his dealings with Peter and would soon be able to steer the conglomerate in the editorial direction he preferred. Over time, he was able to improve his economic position within their partnership, but he continued to be frustrated by his inability to obtain editorial control and he began to look for a way to gain the dominant position in the boardroom he so obsessively desired.

He recalled his conversations with The Captain from their university days and remembered how The Captain had detested the willingness of the "Howe Street Boys" to act as sell-out agents, or "compradors" as he sneeringly referred to them, to

American interests in order to increase their own wealth and position in B.C. society. He knew that many of their well-off fellow students were now members of this Howe Street business group and enjoyed political power through the Provincial Government, a government willing to sell out the long-term interests of British Columbians for short-term prosperity and promises of important jobs. Jake was certain that The Captain would be sympathetic, and having become wealthy in his own right and influential in Federal political circles, may have a suggestion on how to solve his dilemma.

The Captain had indeed been sympathetic and had a solution, although to Jake it had taken some time to consider it seriously. The Captain had made it clear that he knew someone that would remove Peter "permanently" from the situation, thus allowing Jake to "transition" to the CEO position within Canadian Universal. Reluctantly, Jake had eventually gone along with it. The Captain had been true to his word and Peter had soon after suffered a sudden and brutal death at the hands of Roy Carpenter, The Captain's hit man.

They had not even been subtle about it. Carpenter had shot him symmetrically between the eyes while Peter was sitting in his car in his underground parking lot in company headquarters in downtown Toronto. Jake had, of course, been a suspect but without proof he was allowed to go free and carry on in his quest to gain full company control, which he accomplished within a few short years.

Jake had maintained sporadic contact with The Captain since, although they had never discussed the incident until now. The Captain had called two weeks previously and had invited Jake to come visit him on a business trip, which he had assured him on the phone would be to their mutual benefit. Jake had quickly agreed to come, knowing that The Captain's invitation must be very important and, at any rate, would be one he could hardly refuse.

As The Captain abruptly led him into his expansive office and sat him in the chair directly across his desk, Jake began to get the uneasy feeling that this was not a cozy meeting of two long-separated university buddies. The feeling was reinforced as The Captain, ignoring any pleasantries and nostalgic recollections, soon explained why he had "called" for him.

"We share the same philosophical position, I believe," he began, staring intently at Jake across the desk, adding to his unease. "I am pleased with the success you have made of your companies, Jake, and generally with the editorial direction you have taken them. Here in B.C., your approval of our provincial government's legislative changes has helped to create much support from the public. The forceful coverage of your pro-business opinions has allowed government to get away with its anti-labour laws and has made it more difficult for those who represent the interests of working people to remain well-organized. In addition, you have been sympathetic with their initiatives to reduce the benefits of government employees and the pension perks of seniors. Also, I note with approval how you side with the interests of the business elites, while agreeing with government that social programs should be weakened and two-tier health programs introduced. Finally, I very much see eye-to-eye with you that initiatives to privatize government Crown corporations need to be supported and encouraged."

"I'm pleased that you and I agree so much," Jake nodded cautiously.

"However, Jake, I want you to take it a lot further," The Captain added, ignoring Jake's interjection. "We need to emphasize how the privatization of government businesses is good for British Columbians, especially when it is Canadian companies that take over these businesses. Up until now, most, if not all of these companies have fallen into American hands. Even CN is now American-owned. While I know, like me, you disagree with that happening, I don't believe you have been critical enough. These businesses, in addition to those in the private sector that come up for sale, must go to Canadians, not outsiders."

"It sounds to me like we are on the same page here," Jake again nodded. "But I don't know what you mean about not being critical enough. We made a big deal of it when BC Rail was taken over by CN and we were quick to ridicule their excuses when they experienced all those subsequent train derailments. What more do you want?"

"No, no, that was fine. It's just that others haven't received enough critical opinion. I would like you, for instance, to convince the B.C. public that the privatization of BC Hydro must only occur with Canadian companies taking over their operations. I would also prefer to see the same thing with the Insurance Company of B.C. and other Crown corporations when they go private."

"You are saying I should become much more disparaging of the Provincial Government's privatization initiatives?"

"No, Jake," The Captain irritably replied. "Just in respect to the eventual owners of the new companies. The government shouldn't even be considering outsiders as owners. The way to do this is to emphasize that the Federal Government has a role here and should be preventing foreign takeovers."

"We do that now. You know I agree with you on that."

"Okay, but here's what I want you to do. There's going to be a federal election soon and I want the Progressives to be re-elected with a majority. You have been pussyfooting around with the other business-oriented parties and I don't believe they care enough about foreign takeovers. I have here a list of nominated candidates for the Progressive Party who believe in the same things we do. I want you to help me see that they get elected."

"What exactly are you asking?" Jake asked uneasily.

"I want a smear campaign on those candidates they are running against that may have a chance of winning. I want a full exposition of the virtues of our party's candidates in these ridings and I want a continuing barrage of approval for the positive policies of our party, especially in its support for minority interests and immigration policies. I want you to convince the voters that without an influx of overseas workers, business interests are threatened, the economy of the province will suffer and the pensions of retired workers are at risk. In short, I want nothing less than full media support for a policy of easing immigration requirements, especially for those individuals coming from Asian countries. This will assist in ensuring that we receive the electoral support of the Asian-Canadians who already live in these ridings and keep them from considering voting for candidates from other parties."

"I believe we are already doing all of these things, with perhaps the exception of supporting the easing of immigration policies. Do you really want that to happen?"

"Of course not, you fool. We are talking here about election promises, not the long-term interests of the province and the party. If we were to actually let in more offshore immigrants, it could lead to a lot of social problems that would not be good for business and the interests of those of us who run the province."

"Okay, I don't know how far I can go in supporting a smear campaign, but the rest seems fine. I have to be conscious of the risk of libel suits."

"I don't care if you are sued. If you are, just don't mention it in your media outlets. I want the candidates whose names I give you to be seen as vile and unethical and unworthy of support from the voters. I will provide you with information, much of which will be true at any rate, and it will be up to you and your reporters to exaggerate and embellish it. You also simply don't publish any comments they make in their own defence that may elicit sympathy from the voters."

"I don't think I can go as far as you want me to. I have my reputation and the reputation of my corporation to consider."

"What a bunch of crap, Jake. You will do it anyway or you will have more than your reputation to worry about."

"Just what is that supposed to mean?"

"You haven't obtained your position without a little assistance from me, you may recall. It would be a shame if certain information were to be disclosed."

"Don't be ridiculous. You couldn't do a thing without implicating yourself. Just what information do you think you have that would prove anything?"

"Well, as you know, Jake, the police keep the evidence from all unsolved crimes, including, I would suggest, a certain bullet that Peter Schwartz so conveniently stored in his brain when you had him murdered. It would be a shame if the police were to receive an anonymous tip where to find the gun that fired that bullet, especially if it was to be found in your possession."

"You can rest assured if that ever happened I would take you down with me."

"I don't think so. While there would be evidence to convict you, Jake, there is absolutely no proof of my involvement. There also would be no reason for anyone to believe you. Now, I suggest you leave quietly and get on with it. An election will be called any day now and you have a lot of work to do."

"This isn't the end of this by any means," Peter said, glaring furiously at The Captain as he rose to leave. "You think you have me now, but there will be a day of reckoning. I will see that you suffer for blackmailing me."

"Have a nice day," The Captain chuckled, as he closed the door on the retreating media czar.

Chapter 25

THE CAPTAIN WAS the most influential of a powerful group of federal Progressive Party activists whose primary objective was to ensure a better economic deal within confederation for British Columbia, particularly for its pro-nationalist business elites. They maintained an uneasy alliance with the provincial Party, which tended to favour a more continentalist economic strategy and were more philosophically aligned with Canada's other right wing federal party, the Unity Party.

In the previous election, the federal activists had worked ruthlessly to ensure party candidates were nominated and elected who supported a leadership candidate that promised to support their objectives. However, the party had not received enough seats in British Columbia to allow it to form a majority government and the new Prime Minister had not felt it necessary to maintain his promise. The Captain had vowed that wouldn't happen again and was committed to ensuring the results in B.C. for the next federal election would provide him the power and prosperity he was convinced he very much deserved. He had also convinced the other members of his group and they were very supportive of his aggressive moves to improve the party's fortunes in the next election.

Perhaps the most brutal of The Captain's henchmen was Paul Husband. He lived for political power and all his actions were centred on improving his own influence in senior political circles. At one time, he had worked exclusively with the provincial Party and had even married a member of the legislature, mainly to get closer to government decision makers.

Over time, he had become jaded with their small-time thinking and, after his wife Maureen had become a Cabinet Minister, he had learned through her that they were in favour of selling out the province to American interests, simply to increase their own political wealth. Paul had no qualms about increasing his wealth, but he was sure that the provincial strategy was short-sighted and the Americans would eventually renege on any personal promises made to government ministers once they had achieved economic dominance in the province. As a result, he had switched his allegiance to the federal Party, a decision that had earned him the hostility of the provincial Party and a fair amount of grief at home.

Nevertheless, Paul worked tirelessly on behalf of the federal Party and was totally in agreement with The Captain's objectives, in spite of detesting the man personally. He had been ruthless in removing constituency presidents in ridings that had agreed with the provincial party's philosophy or who had remained loyal to the previous Prime Minister during the federal leadership competition. He had stacked constituent meetings with new members who agreed to support the new leadership candidate and ensured they represented their ridings at the convention. Now, using the information from Leif Johannsen, he prepared his campaign for influencing the results in the next federal election, in particular the twelve swing ridings that could determine whether the Progressives formed a majority government and give B.C. the political influence in Ottawa that he was convinced it deserved.

Paul was prepared to ensure that nothing was left to chance. Today he was meeting with Parambir Gill, a powerful leader of one of the Indo-Canadian gangs that were so prevalent in East Surrey, a riding that had been won by the Progressives in the last election, but by less than 800 votes. He was concerned that the gangs would take advantage of the vote-buying scheme and demand the payments from the selected voters as they came out of the polling stations. It was his intention to head that off by getting the gang leaders onside. He had chosen Parambir as he had been made aware that his gang was powerful enough to take the lead and could discourage other gangs from interfering in the process.

Paul had arranged for them to meet at the Elk Tavern which, in spite of its name, was a sports bar where athletes in action were seen running, kicking, swimming and manipulating various-sized balls with assorted implements on at least a dozen different television sets mounted strategically around the walls. Paul had chosen this location as it was the one spot he could be sure a white businessman and an Indo-Canadian gang leader could be seen together without attracting the slightest attention. Parambir, or Par as he soon made it clear he preferred to be called, was there ahead of him and was easy to recognize with his youthful good looks and overconfident bearing. Parambir means great warrior in Punjabi and Par looked like he fit the description. He beckoned Paul over to his table, located in a raised section of the bar where he had a good overview of the patrons as they made their way in and out of the tavern's entrance.

Paul reached across the table and introduced himself with a handshake which Par acknowledged cursorily without rising and signalled for Paul to sit. Paul decided to get quickly to the reason he had come and, after ordering a mug of ale, he began to provide an explanation.

"I know why you are here, Paul," Par quickly interjected. "Since your call I have asked around and I have become aware of your involvement with the federal Progressive Party. I also know that an election will be held soon and the results here are always close. Finally, I know that the minority groups in the riding, especially the Indo-Canadian voters, are key to winning the riding and you are hoping to win us over. Maybe you think I have some influence with them and can convince them to vote for your candidate?"

"Well, not quite, Par, but you are indeed important to me," Paul answered quickly, impressed with the preparations that Parambir had made for their meeting. "I also know a little about you and that you are an important leader with, uh, a young group of fellow Indo-Canadians here in Surrey. I think with your help we can ensure the Progressives take enough seats in B.C. to effect the results of the election and that will be good for both of us. The ability to conduct certain businesses in the province will be easier with our party in power. Moreover, during the campaign I have been authorized to make payments to leaders like yourself in exchange for supporting our objectives and allowing your fellow Indo-Canadians to follow their voting wishes without any restrictions."

"Why would I want to restrict them?"

"Well, let's just say that we will be providing certain inducements to selected voters to follow their hearts in the voting booth, and we would want them to fully enjoy those inducements."

"I see. So you will also provide an inducement to me to ensure that my young fellow Indo-Canadians and I allow all the inducements to occur without restriction. What kind of inducement might I expect?"

"Well, Par, I have been authorized to provide a generous donation of $15,000 in order to assist your organization in pursuing its civic duties. In exchange, you would encourage unrestricted access to the voting booths and an unimpeded exit after each vote. You might look at it as a reward for being so community-minded."

"I am always willing to meet my community responsibilities, Paul. With an additional $10,000 donation I might even be able to help convince my numerous acquaintances and their families to see the advantage in voting for your party."

"I think I can arrange that, Par. You will hear from me when the election is called. In the meantime, I wish you good success in all your business endeavours."

As Paul left the Elk Tavern he couldn't help but be amused by the ironies of the exchange. The Indo-Canadian gangs on the Lower Mainland were absolutely ruthless in their dealings with each other and their conflicts were responsible for a large percentage of the killings that occurred each year in the province. Nevertheless, the municipal police forces responsible for investigating these killings rarely made much of an effort to solve the murders as long as the gangs were content to eliminate each other. Also, buying protection for the voters would do nothing to increase civic-mindedness in the riding, but would only provide Paul an increased opportunity to buy himself more influence in the party. In addition, increasing the number of apathetic voters making it to the polls had nothing to do with improving the democratic process. All in all, not much civic-mindedness had gone on in his bargain with Parambir Gill. By and large, he could see that the bargain had much potential and he would attempt the same tactic in at least four other close ridings where Asian-Canadian gang leaders were influential and disinterested voters could be bought.

Paul's next initiative was to meet with the band leaders of the First Nations settlements in the huge northern riding of Cassiar-Ominica. Again, the results in this riding had been very close in the previous election, but in this case, the left-leaning opposition party, the New Labour Party, had won the seat. The problem was one of neglect. Because the riding was so large and so remote, it was very difficult to influence the outcome from Ottawa or Victoria. The opposition had taken the time to send their party leader to two of the riding's larger communities and enough of the voters had expressed their appreciation on the ballot form to get their candidate elected. Paul wasn't sure he could convince the Prime Minister to visit the riding, but knowing the power of the band leaders amongst the native people, he felt he could at least get them onside and that might be enough to swing the results back to his Party in the upcoming election.

Vote buying was again the tool that Paul would use to change the results. In this riding, though, he would visit the communities where the percentage of eligible voters who actually voted was especially low and provide the motivation for the band leaders to get out the vote. Because the riding had gone to the opposition previously, the First Nations communities did not receive the largesse that went to communities in other ridings that had elected Progressive candidates. Thus, Paul had two tools he could use: a payment to the band leaders for each voter from their communities that had not voted in the last election and who voted this time, and the promise of increased goodies for the band councils to be shared with their friends and families after the election, providing the party formed government. Very few controls were in place to ensure the councils allocated monies from Ottawa fairly, and the process was open to abuse, something he was sure a majority of band council decision-makers would appreciate.

Paul flew to Prince Rupert and chartered a small aircraft to fly him to a dozen remote, but reasonably-sized communities across the riding. He had allocated six days to the initiative, two communities a day. His first stop was Mary's Cove, a small fishing village on the Salem Inlet, north of Prince Rupert. Here he had arranged to meet in the council offices with Chief Emily George, an astute politician who had been band leader for the last eight years.

As the floatplane came in for a landing in the small, narrow harbour at the end of the cove for which the village was named, Paul was struck by the beauty and privacy of the location. Huge mountains, like sentinels, stood guard over the harbour and rose immediately and majestically out of the water on either side of the bay, changing from green to blue and finally to a brilliant white as they at first gave up their tree cover and then hid the bare rock that made up their bulk behind a deep blanket of snow on their higher elevations. As they taxied to the docks, the sun peered over the peaks on the far shore, highlighting the colours on the mountains behind them and spotlighting their arrival for the villagers and their lofty guardians.

Only a small flat area on either side of a narrow creek where it emptied itself into the ocean provided a location to construct the village. It was as if the mountains had somehow momentarily let down their guard and had permitted this one opportunity for outsiders to gain a foothold at the base of their otherwise foreboding, impenetrable cliffs. As he climbed out of the Cessna and made his way along the walk, Paul had the feeling he was seen as a hostile presence that was only grudgingly being allowed by these guardians to enter their territory. He hoped the villagers would be more welcoming.

In fact, they weren't. Chief George met him, as his arrival was announced to her, with suspicion and unfriendliness. It was as if too many years in the village had let the mountains affect her attitude with strangers. What it really was, however, was her previous encounters with outside politicians and their various assistants and hangers-on. Too many broken promises and bitter disappointments had made her jaded and cynical.

Emily George had been born in the village and loved it with a passion. In spite of the many challenges facing the residents, her hardworking parents had seen to it that she had been protected, loved and well-cared for. She learned to appreciate the tranquility of the setting, the close interactions with nature, even the rituals of the band that altered with the seasons. Emily could see that in spite of the poverty and turmoil that made up the lives of most band members, there was also a pride in maintaining native customs and their Nishka language.

She had found it extremely hard to leave when her parents insisted she move to Prince Rupert to complete her education, as the village school only went to grade eight. In the residential school, however, she met other First Nations students from across northern B.C. and learned that they experienced similar problems of poverty and unemployment. Emily determined she would go on to the University of Northern British Columbia in Prince George and complete a degree in social work, which she believed would prepare her to at least make life a little easier for her own people.

She had returned to Mary's Cove resolved to improve life for the members of her community. Her hard work and dedication gained her the respect of many village elders and she was often included in their deliberations, especially in attempting to resolve ongoing social problems. Within a few years, she had been elected to the band council as the spokesperson for those who wanted to bring about social change. Politically adroit, she was made Chief after successfully spearheading a movement to remove the previous Chief, whose main talent had been collecting various grants and handouts from the Federal Government and using these to line his pockets and those of his selected friends within the community. He had made the mistake of not recognizing Emily as a threat, as in his mind she was nothing but another harmless overeducated squaw.

After her eight years as Chief, Emily had become adept at dealing with outsiders who promised much, but rarely had any intention of arranging substantial improvements to the lives of northern First Nations peoples. She calmly escorted Paul Husband to a seat in her office and prepared for his pitch.

His exuberant manner and flattering statements soon made Emily annoyed as Paul outlined the reason for his visit. He explained how a majority government would make it easier to fund the projects that would bring safe drinking water, hospitals and better schooling to her people. He promised that a majority Progressive Party government would see to it that poverty and unemployment were eliminated from the north and drug and alcohol programs would lead to the demise of substance abuse and dependency. By the time he finished, he would be promising to pave the streets with gold, she thought.

"We have had many years of majority governments in the past, including those from your Party, Paul, and none of these have led to substantial change. Why would it be different now?"

"Because B.C. is poised to become the pivotal province in creating a majority government in the country," he explained. "Ottawa will have no choice but to meet the demands of the elected members and their supporters in our province. With your help, I can ensure that the Cassiar-Ominica constituency returns to our party and, in return, communities in the riding will receive the rewards they deserve."

"And as one of those supporters, will you be helping to see that we receive these rewards you so grandly promise us, Paul?"

"Yes, I will, Emily, and like we have done in the past, I will see to it that the programs come with the dollars that allow you and your council members much discretion in determining how the money will be spent," he hinted.

"You mean we will have the ability to allocate spending as we see fit, without a lot of red tape and bureaucratic interference from Ottawa?"

Paul beamed from ear to ear, not noting the irony in her reply. "Yes, of course," he replied enthusiastically. "And just to show our goodwill and how prepared we are to help you get your people to vote for our candidate," he hurried on, "I am authorized to provide you personally with a small subsidy of $3,000 for, uh, publicity purposes. I am also authorized to add another $3,000 should more than half of the eligible voters in the village cast their ballots for us."

Emily was flabbergasted. She had dealt with enough shady politicians to know that they often allowed monies to flow to the village council in ways that left much discretion in the way the money was spent. This was usually the main cause for the rampant corruption that permitted band leaders to spend lavishly on themselves, their extended family members and their cronies, while ignoring the needs of the majority of the villagers who remained out of the loop. But never before had she heard of a Chief receiving a direct bribe, simply for persuading other band members to vote for a particular federal Party. She also knew that she had influence with the villagers and many, if not most, would be willing to support the candidate she recommended.

Still, she could go along with this conniving arrogant man for the time being until she had the proof to expose his corrupt little scheme. The $6,000, while not a lot of money, would still be useful to help "her people" and to meet some of the village's most pressing emergency needs. Also, if she collected the evidence in the meantime, should the Progressives win the election, she could use that information to ensure the party actually met the significant social and economic needs of the north.

"I will think about what you have said, Mr. Husband, and let you know," she finally replied cautiously. "If I agree to help you and your Party, when will I see this money and how will it be delivered to me?"

"As soon as the election is imminent, I will arrange for the candidate to come and visit Mary's Cove to campaign and to deliver the up-front money. After the election, if we are successful, I will return personally and we can discuss the needs of the village and what programs we can provide funding for. At that time, I will bring the rest of the subsidy."

"In cash?"

"Of course," he smiled as he rose and shook her hand.

As Paul made his exit and headed for his plane, Emily headed for the bathroom and washed her hands.

Chapter 26

AFTER THE WEEKEND and his talk with Gloria, Tim
Murphy went back to work with a new resolve. Staff-Sergeant
Rudnick was impressed and relieved to see his interest in his
work. Researching cold case files was often seen as a duty
performed by officers unable to work effectively in the field or in
responsible staff positions. Nevertheless, the work was arduous
and required much patience and highly developed analytical skills.
Unfortunately, his seniors rarely appreciated the value of the
work and most of the researchers assigned to him did not possess
the required talents or personality for the job. In spite of his
impulsive nature, Corporal Murphy's sense of curiosity made him
a good candidate as long as he was assigned cases that interested
him.

Rudnick had assigned Tim a homicide case that had taken
place in the West Shore a number of years previously. It involved
a typical drug deal arrangement gone wrong. A pusher in Victoria
named Martha Swanson had decided her abusive user husband
Phil was ripe for making a deal with the police and she had
decided he needed to be done away with before she could be
implicated. As she was also having an affair with her supplier,
Larry Eamer, Martha could greatly benefit from Phil's demise and
had convinced Larry to help her get rid of him.

They had enlisted the help of a couple of Larry's clients, who
had arranged to drive Phil to a remote gravel pit late at night and
light his car on fire with Phil still in it. Witnesses had seen the
vehicle earlier in the evening with the three men inside. Later,
Martha and Larry had become the chief suspects, but as the two

clients who had actually done the job had never been identified, the Colwood RCMP detachment had no proof that she had initiated the crime and she had never been arrested. The file had ended up in Staff Sergeant Rudnick's hands a year later after homicide investigators had finally given up locating the two accomplices.

For the past few weeks, Tim had spent his time patiently reviewing the case file and talking with previous investigators tied to the case. While he had collected bits of information from them that were not in the files, he had learned little that was new. Now he decided to review the files one more time and attempt to discover any gaps of information in the case, including people mentioned in statements that did not have a corresponding interview report in the case file. Included in the evidence was a vague reference to a native woman who might be an acquaintance of Martha's, but the reference had not been seen as important and had never been investigated. Tim had not seen the reference earlier, as it had been included in a long-winded report by one of the original investigators that, while containing a lot of convoluted information, had never seemed to directly relate to the case. As a result, Tim had been too quick to analyze it carefully and he had skipped over it. Now he thought it might be worth pursuing.

Knowing that Thelma Frank had been familiar with the goings-on of the native communities in and around Victoria, he wondered if she might be able to shed any light on the matter. Tim knew that Thelma Frank had taken the position in Vancouver that was arranged for her and she was doing very well as manager of a courier company. The company specialized in the discreet handling of valuable packages that had to be transported quickly where armoured car services were seen as too slow and awkward to meet client needs. Jewellery companies and those that handled precious metals were their main clients, but even banks, which required a quick transfer of foreign currency, would often employ her company's services. Of course, Thelma had been required to go through a security check, but as she had no record, and the police were vouching for her, the courier company was pleased to give her the job. As manager, Thelma was able to provide a service she was well suited for and where she could still maintain a low profile. She was very satisfied with the arrangement and enjoyed the job immensely.

When Tim called and asked to meet her, she agreed reluctantly. "If you do anything to blow my cover, I will never forgive you. It may have been your idea for me to take this job, but it doesn't give you any right to risk it."

"Don't worry, Thelma, I'm not working on active drug deals or organized crime cases. There's no reason for anyone to have any interest in what I am doing, so no one will be tracking my movements. But if you wish, we don't need to meet in your office. Perhaps we could meet at a bar or restaurant near where you work?"

"Alright, meet me tomorrow at 10:30 a.m. at the Moonglow coffee shop on Howe Street. And it better be important."

Tim knew it wasn't really that important to see her in person. He probably could have interviewed Thelma on the phone and at least determined if she had even known Martha. But he wanted to see her. Tim still felt guilty about risking her life in the sting operation and forcing her move to Vancouver. Also, although he wouldn't admit it to himself, he was still very attracted to her and just wanted to see her again.

After catching an early ferry, Tim arrived at the coffee shop as scheduled the next morning. The Moonglow was one of those urban hangouts that appealed to those with lots of time on their hands and who liked to spend their idle time in a comfortable setting where they could be seen and not have to part with too much money. He wasn't sure why Thelma had recommended it until on his arrival she beckoned to him from a partially hidden alcove in the back of the shop, where the few customers who liked their privacy could find it.

He acknowledged her wave and stopped long enough to purchase a small cup of plain black coffee, which caused the very young man behind the till, used to filling tall, fancy orders of lattes and flavoured cappuccinos, to stare at him in wonderment.

"Out of your element I see, Tim," Thelma said by way of greeting. "You're probably used to gulping down a strong java at one of those plain-folks places where the blue collar crowd hangs out. Welcome to the big city."

"Uh, thanks for the welcome, I guess. Good to see you, too. What's that you're drinking? Looks like a chocolate milkshake."

"Never mind, you wouldn't like it anyway. Now, tell me what brings you all the way over here that you couldn't have asked about on the phone?"

Tim filled her in on his secondment to cold case research, his current assignment and the reference in the files to the native woman.

"It must be an old file, Tim. To be politically correct, it should refer to her as a First Nation's woman," Thelma smiled ironically. "At any rate, I knew about Martha, but I never had any dealings with her during my time in Victoria. She was part of the RV drug organization I worked for, but it was years ago when she arranged the hit on her husband. She was forced to go clean after and was never connected to Ross Stubbs or the motor home operation. I have an idea who the other woman might be, though. There was a dealer I know, who at the time was operating in Victoria. She didn't do much, other than sell some coke and grass to the band in Saanich. I don't even know if she is around anymore, especially since the cops put them out of business, but she may have still been buying later from the Desperados or from an independent."

"Do you remember her name?"

"Sure, we even went to school together for awhile. Her name was Millie Harvey, now Millie Salmon. I don't remember her husband's first name, but they used to be pretty wild. She might even still live on the reserve in Brentwood Bay, if she's still alive. She was using drugs herself, so anything could have happened to her by now."

"Anything else you can tell me about her, Thelma, or about other people who might know Martha?"

"No, anything I would know about Martha would already be in the files. Like I said, I didn't have anything to do with her."

"Well, I better go then. I'm keeping you from work, but I'm glad I came over to see you in person. It's been good to see you again, Thelma."

"You too, Tim, but what's your rush? Maybe you don't have to go back until tomorrow?"

"I wish I could stay," Tim replied, his face reddening. "But I have a ferry reservation for early this afternoon and my new boss keeps me on a short leash."

"Well, I wouldn't mind putting you on a short leash. Good bye, Tim, and good luck. Next time you come over, stay for awhile."

"You bet," he responded, his legs weighing about a ton each as he slowly made his escape.

THE BRENTWOOD BAY reserve had seen better days. For years, both levels of government had made an issue of allowing First Nations peoples on the Island to run their own affairs by providing band councils anything they required, short of real assistance. As a result, monies were never made available to improve the economy of the reserves, which would have allowed the band members to escape their poverty-stricken conditions. Unemployment was rampant, and the reserve, even though in a beautiful setting, was remote and away from the normal tourist routes. Most of the residents existed on social assistance or were employed in part-time service jobs that did little to make their lives more comfortable.

Tim didn't let Millie know he was coming. He had found a listing for William Salmon in the phone book, and as it was the only one for a Salmon on the reserve, he decided to take a chance that it was the right one. He didn't want to scare her off by setting up an appointment. Hearing from the police after all this time might lead to a complete refusal to become involved, leading to the issuance of warrants and other painful legal processes that Tim would rather avoid. Just dropping by, driving his own vehicle and out of uniform, on the other hand, may keep her at ease and lead to a willingness to talk to him.

As Tim drove along West Saanich Road, he was struck by the solitude and the beauty. At ten-thirty in the morning, anyone who had a place to go had already gone. The few cars that he met along the wide curving road crept along slowly as if their drivers, like lovers on a deserted beach at sunset, were attempting to make the pleasant adventure last as long as possible. From time to time, Tim caught a glimpse of the bay, the sun glistening off the small whitecaps the ever-present breeze stirred up as it spilled across the water from its origins in the Malahat mountains on the far shore. Once again, Tim was awed by the range of pleasant scenic views to be found across the small confines of southern Vancouver Island.

He turned left off West Saanich Road at a nondescript street leading into the reserve. Wide non-landscaped properties along the water side of the street each held a single dwelling, all badly in need of repair. On the right, a small untended cemetery sat forlornly, squeezed between a dilapidated church and a small general store. Using a map he had brought from the office, which listed property numbers, Tim quickly located the house he was looking for. Old rusting automobiles, disgorging their useless innards, covered the front lawn, surrounded by various scraps of wood, plastic and assorted metal objects. It looked like a malicious giant child, tired of its large toy collection, had torn each apart, scattered the pieces and left them neglected and forgotten across the weed-infested ground.

Tim parked his car and was greeted by a thin collie-cross canine that incongruously wagged his whippet-like tail while its simultaneous barks and snarls communicated a conflicting message. He cautiously disembarked while the dog alternatively approached and drew back. It continued its noisy cacophony until a shout from the house finally silenced him. A tall, tired-looking woman in her late thirties or early forties stood at the top of the front steps and peered suspiciously down at Tim as he slowly approached, while the collie-cross reluctantly retreated. Tim put on his best disarmingly wide smile and stopped at the bottom of the steps.

"Good morning, ma'am," he began cheerfully. "I'm looking for Millie Salmon."

"And who are you and why are you looking for her?" she answered quietly and firmly.

Tim quickly judged that this was Millie and he should be completely up front with her. "I'm Tim Murphy and I am with the RCMP. I'm here to ask about a police homicide case from years ago that you might be able to help us with."

"I don't see how I could possibly help you with a homicide case. Have you got any ID?"

Tim showed her his identification card and she scrutinised it carefully. "You better come inside," she finally said. "I have a kid in here and I imagine you will be wasting my time with a long story and a bunch of silly questions."

"Thank you," he answered politely. "I will try and keep it short."

She led him through the front door which immediately entered into a small kitchen, dominated by a table in the middle of the floor where a boy of about four or five sat with a colouring book and a busted set of crayons, most of which had long ago mysteriously lost their wrappings. The boy ignored Tim and continued to studiously fill in the chartreuse horse that stood out from its multi-coloured grassland surroundings.

"Sit down," she ordered. "Do you want some coffee?"

Tim politely replied that he would and outlined his reason for calling on her while she brought him his coffee and refilled her own.

"Yeah, I know Martha," she said when he was finished. "But that was a long time ago and I'm not involved in any of that stuff anymore. I cleaned up my act and now I live here quietly with Bill. He still drinks too much, but he doesn't do any drugs and he supports us as best he can by working as a mechanic. He doesn't get too much work, eh, but with our government cheque we get by. We have two more kids in school and life is a lot different than it was in those days."

"Well, that's good, Millie. What I would really like to know is do you have any idea who the two men are that helped Martha Swanson kill her husband?"

"You mean Phil? He was no loss, I'll tell you that. Sure Martha was pushing, but he was a lazy good-for-nothing that lived off her and at the same time figured he could make some money from the cops by telling them who her clients were. I knew she and Larry Eamer were a number and it's no surprise the two of them would want to get rid of the bastard."

"Okay, but it's still not right for her to murder him. There had to be a better way."

"Maybe, but at the time she probably didn't think so. Anyway, she and Larry split long ago and Martha is pretty pathetic these days. She's not really any good for anyone anymore, including herself."

"Well, Larry's still not talking, though, and we would still like to see justice served. We think you could really help to put an end to this if we can find out who the men are that helped him. We likely won't have to involve you if you can tell us who they are."

"I sure wouldn't have had anything to do with it at the time, but it probably doesn't matter now. I'm pretty sure one of them is my cousin and he lives right here on the reserve. His name is Andy, Andy Harvey, and he's a useless bastard that makes my life miserable. He keeps bugging me for money and when I won't give him any he gets the chief, who he is close to, to harass me. As a result, I never get anything but trouble from that goddamn band council. If it doesn't come out that I told you, it will help make my life easier, but even if it does, it just means I will only be harassed by the chief instead of both of them, so what do I have to lose, right?"

Tim nodded reassuringly.

"The other one is an old white guy named Al Whitelaw who lives over in Colwood. A real cokehead, but he and Andy used to like to hang out together and get drugs wherever they could. They are also the kind of guys who will do anything for a buck, so it's not surprising they would do this for Martha, for a price, of course. They're both kind of useless though, so if they are the right guys, I'm surprised you haven't found out before now."

Tim's head was going a mile a minute. Christ, he thought, Al Whitelaw! It didn't appear possible he could have had the courage to pull this off. It wasn't a surprise he was never a suspect, as it seemed unlikely he had the initiative to be involved in something like this. Still, he had to get money from somewhere to feed his habit and he had to agree with Millie, maybe somebody should have wondered.

Tim was quite sure now that if Millie was right, he wouldn't have to involve her further. Finishing his coffee, he thanked her profusely and without promising not to trouble her further, he suggested it was unlikely that anyone else would need to know about his visit or that she would be called as a witness. He suggested to her she could tell her neighbours, if they should be so nosy as to ask, that he was conducting interviews for a consumer survey and her name had come up.

She saw him to the door and closed it behind him with relief, glad to have had the opportunity to get what she suspected off her chest, and maybe, eventually, her money-demanding cousin off her back.

Back in his office, Tim thought about what he had learned. It was clear the murder had not been a professional job. While Phil's body was partially burned, it was still obvious that he had been badly beaten before the car was set on fire. The instigators had not even bothered to dose him in gasoline. As a result, while the car had exploded, and probably satisfied them that the evidence had been destroyed, the interior of the car was left fairly intact. Eventually, the coroner had been able to determine that Phil had actually died from toxic poisoning.

Not only that, the police had managed to collect blood samples, some of which were not Phil's and were likely a result of the beating. The men had probably used their hands and had gashed a knuckle or two. While the investigators had attempted to match the samples using DNA with all known suspects, they had been unsuccessful. Nevertheless, they had never released the information that they had collected the samples and they still maintained this evidence in police storage.

After he shared his findings with Staff-Sergeant Rudnick, warrants were issued for the two men and they were quickly arrested. DNA testing determined that Andy Harvey had carried out the beatings, and while he denied it, Al Whitelaw had been quick to make a deal in order to receive a lighter sentence. The prosecutor now had all the evidence needed to go to trial. Eventually, the four were all found guilty and sentenced to lengthy jail terms. It was not necessary to call Millie Salmon as a witness and her role remained confidential. Life on the reserve improved for her shortly thereafter.

Chapter 27

DURING THE RUN UP to the approaching federal election, The Captain was kept very busy. It took all his energy and formidable organizational skills to ensure all his powerful henchmen kept events moving in the proper direction. He was pleased that Jake Green had ensured his reporters and editors reflected the actions of the Federal Government in the very best light, while ridiculing and belittling those of the opposition parties. He was also pleased that Canadian Universal's newspaper editorials relentlessly criticized the Provincial Government for its pro-American privatization policies. He tracked Leif Johannsen's political polling results carefully and noted how public opinion gradually echoed the views of the formidable media empire. Media concentration certainly has an effect on influencing the democratic process, he thought approvingly, and it's clear that B.C was not immune to it.

The Captain was also satisfied to see that his behind-the-scenes efforts had ensured the results from the police raid on the legislature had received a minimum of media coverage. He was also happy to see that, for its own reasons, the Provincial Government continued to stall on bringing the accused to trial. He was amazed that because the media had followed his orders to keep the raid's aftermath out of the spotlight, the public had actually lost interest in the matter. Here was one of the most significant historical events that had ever hit the province, a raid on the most sacrosanct of institutions, the people's parliament, and no one was even talking about it! For that matter, by the time the accused went to trial, the public would barely remember what it was all about.

It had been his wish that the trial would not convene until after the Federal election. As time went by, he began to believe he could ensure the accused wouldn't go to trial at all. It had taken months just to decide on charges and even then it was only the two provincial cabinet ministers' assistants who were being focused on. He was enraged when he had learned about the side deal that Barinder and Alan Diwan had struck with Leif Johannsen to profit from the BC Hydro privatization deal and he had been quick to rebuke them. Nevertheless, when the only charges against the two centered on their role in this little scheme, it appeared that their connections to him and the other Federal Party organizers in B.C. would receive little attention and this could only work to his advantage. Somehow, all the police efforts to obtain search warrants and gather evidence connecting grow-op property ownership to the purchase of party memberships wasn't going to result in a single related charge.

It was here that The Captain had proven how powerful and influential he was. He had pulled out all the stops to ensure that none of his organizers would be implicated, even though a number of them had initially been subject to searches after warrants had been issued. All evidence connecting Barinder Chohan's membership purchases to the Federal party organization in B.C. had been destroyed. Nothing was found that would show who was organizing the membership purchasing scheme, even though lists of party members were found in Chohan's legislative office. Follow-up would later show that in many cases these new party members hadn't even realized they had been recruited. Of course, many of them were dead when they had been recruited, so it would have been difficult for those ones to deny anything.

The federal Party was adamant that it was not a target of the raids. Even the Prime Minister denied that the federal Party was connected. Pressure was placed on the Provincial Government to keep them out of it and they complied. At any rate, they were convinced that focussing the charges on the BC Hydro fraud would allow the two accused to become scapegoats and the Provincial Government would also escape sanctions. Stalling on the charges was also in their interests as they had their own election to contend with, and when it was finally called, the raid did not even become an issue during the campaign. Of course, it had helped immensely that they had issued a court order to keep the reasons for the legislative search warrants secret until after the provincial election. It also helped that a second order was issued, which helped even more, as it did not even permit reporting on the raids themselves until the trial was over. That is, if it was to ever be over or even convened.

So now, The Captain was free to concentrate on winning as many seats as possible for the federal Party in the upcoming election. He had done what he could to ensure the media were onside. Now he would ensure the other party organizers redoubled their efforts, using every tool and dirty scheme in the book to gather a maximum of votes in the applicable ridings they could win. He decided to call in Paul Husband to see where they were and what more needed to be done.

"I felt it was time we did a complete review of where we are in ensuring we maximize our seat winnings here in B.C, Paul. How are things looking?"

"Well, other than the Prime Minister doing everything he can to damage the party's re-election chances nationally, I would say here in B.C. things are stacking up very nicely."

"Nevertheless, he is still the best person to protect the long-term interests of business people across the country, including here in B.C. Have we done everything we can to ensure we have the best people representing each riding?"

"You bet. We had a few candidates seeking the party nomination who were not onside, but they were unsuccessful."

"How did you manage that?"

"Oh, you know - the usual stuff. Convincing popular candidates they are so likely to win that we ask them to run in another riding, thus picking up two seats. Then we stack the meeting to ensure they don't get the nomination and leave them out in the cold. Another useful technique has been to book a large hall, change the location at the last allowable minute, then load the new, smaller meeting room with supporters of the preferred candidate. The supporters are asked to come an hour before the meeting start time. Oh yes, and my favourite is to parachute a high-profile candidate into a riding where someone thinks they are a shoo-in, simply because they have been loyal to the party. Usually these are uncharismatic types that wouldn't appeal to the voters, but have the support of the local riding executive. Again, you stack the meeting with newly-purchased members and vote them out. We even had one guy crying after he lost the nomination. It was a good day for the party!"

"Good to see you enjoying your work, Paul. Now, what about maximizing election wins?"

"Well, to begin with, the media are doing a tremendous job in digging out dirt on the other party's candidates where we have a chance to gain an upset win. Some of the stuff is close to libellous, but Jake Green seems to know exactly where to draw the line. He's also been able to soften up the voters to believe the government is doing an effective job. In spite of all the dirt coming out of Ottawa, it mainly gets overlooked here in B.C. It's almost as if we're going to be fighting a different election. The electorate even believes, thanks to Jake, that the opposition is set to bring the government down, just in spite. The press is also playing up the wasted expense associated with another election and the fact it could be seen as undemocratic, as it will likely be called in the summer when most voters are travelling and won't be able to vote."

"And what about buying a win in close ridings?"

"That's going well. Leif has been experimenting with interviews. It seems where potential voters, in response to a survey, indicate they are unlikely to vote because it is a waste of time as they see all politicians as corrupt, will also sometimes agree that voters should receive a payment for taking the time to go to the polls. You would be surprised how many people, especially younger and less well off ones, think this way. At any rate, follow-up interviews identify a significant minority will agree to vote for a particular candidate for a small fee. Furthermore, many of these don't see anything unethical about it and would readily agree not to disclose the arrangement."

"It seems like Leif has narrowed the criteria down quite a bit. Does that still leave us with enough earmarked voters?"

"No. There are about 85,000 potential voters in each riding. We only need 6 per cent of them to change their vote and Leif's stats show we have 4 per cent in this group alone. The good news is they don't need to be poor to go for the arrangement. The group he has identified see it as an entitlement and they deserve the money for taking the time to go to the polls."

"So, what about the difference? Where do we get the rest?"

"The other 2 per cent are made up of those who are poor and who have indicated they are unlikely to vote because they don't think it matters who they vote for as none of the parties represent their interests. In other words, they are apathetic and feel disenfranchised. The interviews show that after a spiel on how our candidate will help them, many of them are convinced the $50 payment is an indicator of the candidate's intentions. This group is larger than the first, but could be more likely to talk about it later, thus there is more risk of exposure for us. Leif believes, again through interviews, we can determine which are less likely to do this and can eliminate the risk, at least until the election is over."

"What about workers? Who is going to do all these interviews?"

"It's not as many as you think. We need about 50 volunteers in each riding doing about 100 interviews each. We can easily recruit that many party loyalists at election time, especially with a generous payment to cover their expenses. In addition, they can make the first $25 payment at the end of each successful interview. After they vote, the selected voters return to an agreed upon location, and after answering the test question, they collect the other $25."

"So what's the total bill for all these volunteer party workers?"

"Well, figure it out. You are looking at fifty workers in 12 ridings. Perhaps you need $500 to cover the expenses of each worker. So you will need about $300,000. Still, it's only a fraction of the cost of buying the votes at $50 each."

"It's well worth it if we get the results we are looking for. Have you thought about ways to stuff the ballot boxes or manipulate the vote count?"

"I have and I am afraid that is next to impossible. In this day of modern technological voter information and vote counting, there's no easy way to accomplish that. Even if we could get to the election officials, there is not much that can be done to affect the results. The whole process has just become too sophisticated and too accurate."

"Still, if the polling surveys don't look promising we may need to consider it."

"I would look at it as a last resort."

"You do that, Paul. In the meantime, I am sure the media-sponsored polls will indicate how well our candidates are doing."

"That's what we pay them to do. Their poll results always paint the best picture for the Progressive Party candidate. In the meantime, we also run a party-sponsored poll for our own purposes which paint the most accurate picture of voter intentions. It's only that poll that we count on to make our internal party decisions."

"Okay, Paul. It looks like you are on top of it. Keep me posted once the election is called."

INSPECTOR ERROL FIELDS was deeply troubled about the lack of further evidence he needed to consolidate the charges against the subjects of the raids he had initiated. He had stuck his neck out to get the search warrants for some very senior Progressive Party officials, as well as to convince a very reluctant judge to permit the search of legislative offices and records facilities. Further interviews with Barinder Chohan, his cousins and his associates in the grow-op ownerships had produced nothing. The ever-politically astute Superintendent Rita Chan was also on his case, making life miserable for him. His police career was on the line if he couldn't produce some results very soon.

While frustrated it was taking so long for the prosecutor to take the case to trial, he was nevertheless relieved. It was giving him the time he so desperately needed to find the evidence to make the charges stick and to find further evidence to convict the other players. He knew the case was potentially huge and getting the proper convictions would have historical significance for the province in cleaning up political corruption at the highest levels of the governing federal party's organization in B.C.

There was one glimmer of hope. The raid had produced a list of party members in Barinder Chohan's files that had obviously had their memberships paid for by the party. Unfortunately, though, the list did not indicate from where the money had emanated and who had actually paid for the memberships. Interviews with these new members had produced very little. Many had not even known they were party members until they had been asked to attend nomination meetings and vote for particular candidates.

It was unlikely that Barinder had personally paid for all these new party memberships himself and the connection to other party officials needed to be established. The money trail was proving to be very elusive. Somewhere there was an individual collecting the monies from the grow-ops and funnelling this into the organization to make the purchases. That someone would need to be close to Barinder and likely resided here in Victoria. Transferring the illicit funds was a risky operation and if Barinder had done so personally, there would have been a money trail. It had to be someone else and all Barinder's connections would need to be further researched and analysed to see if it could be determined who it was.

Adding to his woes since the raid, Rita Chan had decimated Inspector Field's Combined Organized Crime Unit. After the biker crime gang, The Desperados, had been exposed and eliminated, there was perceived to be little need for the expensive and sophisticated Unit's services. The RCMP was experiencing severe resource shortages anyway and the other police forces were no longer willing to contribute police officers to a combined force that had perhaps outlived its purpose. So now Inspector Fields was forced to fight organized crime with a mere skeleton force, mostly members of his anti-drug unit, compared to his earlier operation. His personnel-reduced unit was kept busy full time dealing with the remaining criminal elements on the Island and, while less effective and organized than the Desperados, they, and in particular the Nanaimo Chapter of the Satan's Sirens, still kept the RCMP busy in order to keep them in check.

As a result, Inspector Fields did not have the officers available to conduct the research required to make the connection between the grow-ops and the party membership payments. He would need the assistance of Staff-Sergeant Rudnick's effective Investigative Research Unit and in particular the services of one Corporal Tim Murphy, who not only was totally up to speed on the whole case, but had shown he had a talent for research that his own officers did not possess. While he would never live long enough to understand, never mind condone, Murphy's methods, he couldn't dispute his results, as so clearly shown with the recent closure of the Martha Swanson cold case file. Eating a little crow was in order, he decided ruefully.

After explaining the situation to Staff Sergeant Rudnick, he obtained his agreement to interview Murphy personally and involve him in his investigation. So when Murphy heard that the Inspector wished to talk to him, he was apprehensive that Inspector Fields had decided to proceed with his transfer from the District. Nevertheless, Tim hoped to use the meeting to convince the Inspector he could still be useful in the right capacity, such as in undercover work.

Tim was surprised by the Inspector's greeting when he arrived for his appointment. He was prepared for the cold, almost hostile reception that had accompanied their last meeting, but instead the Inspector received him quietly and politely, and almost seemed embarrassed in his opening remarks.

"I would like to congratulate you, Tim, for your excellent work in solving the Swanson case. It seems your ability to get results with research work has paid off and I am pleased that we reassigned you to this kind of work."

"Thank you, sir. A little bit of luck, I think, and once more some good information from Thelma Frank is what really made it possible." Tim was puzzled by the reassignment remark. Hadn't he been sent there to give him something to do until he could initiate his transfer? Hardly a reassignment. Maybe Gloria was right. There never was any intention on the Inspector's part to have him transferred, in spite of his so clearly expressed comments.

"Just the same, Tim, you have shown that in the right circumstances you can make an important contribution and that needs to be recognized. Perhaps you would be willing to take on an extremely important assignment that makes full use of your abilities?"

"I, uh, would like to help where I can have a useful part to play, sir," he answered cautiously, wondering where the Inspector was heading with all this. Not another cold case, he hoped.

"I understand your hesitation, Tim, but I think this will be right up your alley. It relates to our longstanding case with organized crime and the connection to the federal Progressive Party. You played a major part in bringing the Desperados to justice. Now we need your help to cement the connection from them to the political organizers who used the proceeds from their drug operations to fund their party membership purchasing scheme. Before the case comes to trial, we need to get the evidence that makes the connection between them. I truly believe that a key member of the party must have been working with the locals involved in the membership recruitment program and was coordinating the money transfer from the illegal grow operations to the membership-purchasing operation. I want you to find that person and we can probably blow this case wide open before the trial starts."

"No disrespect, sir, but I thought with the arrests so far that you would have had that evidence before the raid was sanctioned."

"Well, so did I, Corporal Murphy, but it has turned out that those who handled the membership recruitment side, in particular Barinder Chohan and Alan Diwan, have been very unwilling to implicate the power-brokers in the party, and as it is in the interests of both levels of government to see the case fall apart, we are receiving no help from that end. In hindsight, I am amazed I was ever able to get search warrants to raid their offices and homes."

"Just what do you think I can do that you and your team haven't been able to accomplish?"

"You seem to have the capability to get others to do or say things that most other officers can't. And frankly, Tim, I no longer have the research resources available to go through the materials and interviews to find the evidence we need."

"Would I be able to carry out further interviews with those who may be willing to provide additional information, sir?"

"I understand what you are saying, Murphy, and I want you to stay within the law. I'm by no means sanctioning your usual unorthodox methods of operating."

"Yes, sir. Just one other thing. Will I be staying on with the District Office for awhile?"

"Get me the evidence I am looking for, Tim, and you will be so solidly entrenched that no one would ever dare question you again."

"Perhaps I would be able to think of a transfer to the drug squad, Inspector?"

"Don't push it, Corporal," the Inspector answered with a begrudging smile.

Chapter 28

DUNCAN HENDERSON very much enjoyed being a fairly big fish in a reasonably large pond. During the short period the Progressive Party had governed with a minority government, he had become an important Cabinet Minister and powerful member of the party elite in British Columbia. Still, he worried about the future of the party and the ability of the current Prime Minister to maintain them in office. The man had the uncanny ability to turn political advantage over to the opposition in B.C. through his amazing ignorance of the West and his talent for discounting the suggestions of his western ministers. Duncan was the only one from B.C. that he favoured, and even then he saw

Duncan as his chosen disciple to spread party messages to the western subjects, rather than incorporate his advice into party policies. This was sometimes frustrating to Henderson, whose main aim was to improve the business climate in B.C and to ensure that provincially-based corporations received at least their fair share of government-arranged contracts.

Still, Duncan believed they could keep the party in power as long as the voters in the province supported the Progressive Party. He also understood the pivotal role B.C. could play if the province could provide enough seats to allow the party to form a majority government. As a result, he was very willing to endorse the manoeuvrings of The Captain to improve the chances of the party, and as one of only a handful of influential party members in the province who even knew of the plan, backed his vote-buying scheme. Nevertheless, he was careful to ensure that he had nothing to do with those who were assigned the task of putting the plan into action. In fact, other than providing counsel at inner circle meetings, Duncan was not often involved with day-to-day party happenings in the province. Still, as a Cabinet Minister with national responsibilities, this was understandable, and he was able to keep his distance from these manoeuvrings without causing resentment or suspicion. Consequently, he maintained the trust of The Captain and the other inner circle members.

Duncan's favourite expression was "keep your options open." But it was more than an expression; it was something he continually practiced. And while he fully supported the idea of improving the business climate in the province that The Captain advocated, he was not so sure it could only be achieved by promoting nationalist policies. Thus, he could just as easily support the ideas of the Provincial Government and the other pro-business federal opposition party, The Unionists. As a result, he also maintained contact with representatives of these groups and confidentially expressed his willingness to maintain their common interests. This also served the purposes of The Captain when he wanted these parties to maintain a united front, such as in promoting the province's privatization policies, or in de-emphasizing the importance of the raid on the legislature. All in all, Duncan maintained an important and pivotal role heading into the federal election and he was not surprised when he received an invitation to attend a discreet meeting with a senior representative of the opposition Union Party.

Bill Morris had been with the party forever, and while he did not plan to run in the next election, he was given the role of ensuring the party was able to field a slate of pro-business candidates in the West, particularly in British Columbia. He had the full support of the Union Party leader when he extended an invitation to Duncan to meet with him. He chose the Vancouver Club.

Every Canadian city has as an influential centre of activity in the heart of the business district where its members can meet other influential people without arousing suspicion or the curiosity of the media. In Calgary or Edmonton, it is the Petroleum Club; in Ottawa, the Rideau; in Toronto, the National; and in Victoria, the Union Club. The Vancouver Club fills this role for its city's elites very nicely. Located close to the city's convention centre and the heliport at the bottom of Hornby Street, the Vancouver Club has been meeting its member's needs for well over a century.

Bill chose to meet Duncan in Bar 3 at 5:30 p.m., a usually busy time when members can down a bracing drink before heading out into the city's congested streets for the unnerving drive home. Bill had chosen the time because he liked the food at the club, and as it was a Wednesday, he could stay around after the meeting and order the calf's liver with bacon and onions, a favourite meal that his wife, Anna, refused to cook. Duncan was also a member, of course, and he was there ahead of Bill, contently sipping his single malt scotch.

The bar was crowded with other members and their cronies, still mainly men, in spite of the long-since accepted decision to permit equal gender access. As an indication of his standing within the club, the membership coordinator, Kerrie Thomson, personally escorted Bill over to Duncan's secluded corner where he slid into the overstuffed lounge chair across from Duncan as easily as if the two of them met like this every afternoon.

"Good to meet you here, Duncan. I see you often enough in Ottawa, but we rarely get a chance to talk here in our home city. Thanks for coming down."

"Not at all, Bill. This place used to be a second home to me when I was still in business. I still like to drop in as often as I get the chance."

"Me, too, and I may have plenty of chances from here on in. You probably know I am not running in the next election. Maybe I will become one of those old curmudgeons who hang out here all day, boring everyone with how good it used to be in the old days."

"I can't imagine you doing that, Bill. I suspect you will have your fingers in plenty more pies before you're really through. Why aren't you running, anyway?"

"Things are changing fast, Duncan, and I am not sure I can move with the currents. Our new guy has his own ideas and some of us old farts can't keep up with him. I'm no Red Tory, but I still feel there's a requirement to look after the basic needs of those who slip through the cracks. We need some younger and more versatile people around who can keep him in check. People like you, for instance."

"What are you trying to say, Bill? You know I have committed myself to running for the Progressives. If the election goes like it should, your guy won't matter anyway. In fact, he'll probably abandon your Party pretty quickly after."

"Yeah, but I see the results differently. You guys are doing okay out here, but they're pretty pissed off with you in the rest of

Canada. Maybe we won't get a majority, but I'm pretty sure we will be forming government."

"Dream on, Bill. They're not that pissed off."

"Just the same, you should be thinking of coming over to our side. Look, both parties want the same thing. Thanks to your party's cosy relationship with Canadian Universal here in B.C, the voters think we are the bad guys, but we want the same things. I doubt you see that much difference. What would you do in opposition anyway? A guy like you would be bored to tears, totally frustrated, or both at the same time."

"Just suppose we did lose. I would still be a member of the Progressive team and if I did lose my seat, which is totally unlikely, I wouldn't be of any use to you anyway. And it would be ridiculous of me to change allegiances now. I would be shot down in flames."

"On the other hand, if you crossed the floor after the election, you would have plenty of value, and frankly, we can use your talents."

"My constituents would be in an uproar if I did that. They would have my head."

"I think you give the voters too much credit, Duncan. Within a week they would forget you had done it. It happens all the time, as you know, and those who change parties still get re-elected in the following election. The memory of the electorate is pretty damn short. With proper media manipulation, you can get away with anything now. And it's just going to get better and better. Elections serve a great purpose by keeping the public in check because they think they are making choices, but the choices are pretty well all made for them now, long before they get in the voter's box. Sure, they think the parties are different, but it's mainly around the means. We all want to organize the economy to benefit the business owners."

"Quite a speech, but because they think we are different, I wouldn't be able to switch parties right away if I did lose. They would remember that until the following election."

"Again, I believe you are wrong and I would be very surprised if you hung around long enough for another election anyway, if you did win your seat, assuming, like I do, that our Party forms the government. But supposing that happened and you waited a decent period of time as an opposition backbencher and then switched to our Party. We could wait awhile and then make you a cabinet minister again. Your voters would certainly understand that."

"Well, as you know, Bill I like to keep my options open. I am willing to consider that because I know I would be forced to resign my seat if I went with your first idea, but the whole scenario is pretty unlikely anyway, since our Party is going to win the election."

"We'll see, Duncan, we'll see. But I am pleased to see you will consider joining us. You are too talented to waste away on the opposition backbenches. In the meantime, I will only share our conversation with the party leader. How about another scotch?"

"All right, Bill, and how about something to eat? You know, I really like the liver and onions they do here."

Chapter 29

TIM MURPHY LOOKED FORWARD to his new assignment from Inspector Fields with a combination of excitement and apprehension. He was excited because a successful result would lead, not only to his remaining in the District, but to a much more satisfying career path than he had been recently experiencing. Nevertheless, he had to be apprehensive. How could he expect to get results when the Inspector's Combined Organized Crime Unit had gotten nowhere in unearthing the evidence that would allow the linkages between the grow-ops and the Progressive Party to be exposed? At any rate, it sure beat cold case files and he was determined to tackle his assigned task with a vengeance.

After carefully reviewing the files, Tim determined that a linkage through the local Indo-Canadian cousins was the way to go. He knew that the Inspector had taken this route earlier and had even personally interviewed them. The interviews had included Harman Gill, who, although he was not personally a grow-op owner, had assisted Barinder Chohan in recruiting party members on the Island and was currently an executive member of a Victoria-area Progressive Party constituency. Also interviewed was Jaswinder Chohan who was an owner, but who had also worked independently with Parbeen Dhariwal to set up another grow-house outside the local Desperados-controlled operation. Finally, and most especially, Barinder Chohan, who was definitely a grow-op owner, but also had primary responsibility for the membership recruitment program. Barinder had unfortunately kept a list of new party members in his legislative office and had been interviewed by the RCMP on many previous occasions.

Missing from the Inspector's list was Parbeen Dhariwal. According to the report from the interviews included in the files, the Inspector had concluded that the independent grow-op had no bearing on the larger case and Parbeen was to be tried separately for trafficking.

Tim was puzzled that Parbeen was being overlooked. The key was to get something on the cousins that would eventually put pressure on Barinder to break his silence. He decided he would start by having a good chat with Parbeen and see where that led him. Parbeen Dhariwal had been released on bail after his charge of trafficking in marijuana. Determining once again that there was no time like the present, Tim made an appointment to interview him early the next morning at his home in East Sooke.

Tim left his own house in Metchosin about twenty minutes before the interview. By taking Rocky Point and East Sooke Roads along the coast, the distance between the two communities was short and the drive was pleasant. The route allowed him to meander through the Beecher Bay First Nations reserve, a beautiful area where the winding road provided an ever-changing view of rolling hills, sparkling waters and majestic fir trees, interspersed with the unusual arbutus, with its peeling orange bark, partially exposed dull walnut-green trunks and shiny lime-green leaves. As he drove past the arbutus, bending out over the roadside ocean waters, they made him think of shut-ins in an extended care facility, leaning out open windows to absorb the bright sunlight. For the hundredth time, Tim wondered to himself how the area in such a picture-perfect setting could ever have received the name Metchosin, which in the local native language meant the land of the stinking fish. On this day, the sky was a deep solid blue and the atmosphere completely devoid of pollution, thanks to a cleansing westerly breeze blowing in from the Pacific that started thousands of miles between this land point and the closest sources of air contamination. It was the kind of day the local residents lived for and made it so easy for them to tolerate the long, dull, rainy season that preceded it.

Tim arrived at the Dhariwal home off Coppermine Road in plenty of time for their meeting. The house was stationed well back from the road and greatly secluded behind a cover of towering fir trees. The large yard was filled with a number of outbuildings associated with Dhariwal's fishing business, including a storage shed for nets and fish boxes, a garage for his three-ton panel truck and a large open lean-to where he stored his boat during the off-season. Everything looked well used, as it was the middle of the early spring fishing season and it appeared that an impending charge in drug trafficking was not about to stop the ever-efficient owner from pursuing his normal occupation.

In fact, Parbeen was not at all pleased to meet with Tim, as it meant a late start to his day and he had only agreed to talk because Tim had indicated he had new information that related to Parbeen's charge. Tim entered the large kitchen, noting that Parbeen's wife, Taninder, seemed not to be at home. Perhaps she preferred to let him deal with his self-inflicted problems on his own, he thought idly. Looking around, Tim could see no clues to indicate that the house had recently been the site of a large marijuana cultivation business, but as the house was huge, it was probably grown and harvested well away from the living quarters. At any rate, Tim was sure that there would be little left to suggest that the place had ever served as a major grow-op.

Parbeen poured Tim a cup of coffee and waited expectantly for Tim to get on with the reason for his visit. When it seemed that Tim was content to sip on his drink and idly contemplate his surroundings, he irritably asked him why he was harassing him and keeping him from his work.

"Harassing you? Not at all, Parbeen. In fact, I believe I might be here to do you a favour. We know full well that you didn't initiate your marijuana cultivation business here in your own home all on your own, but we note how your partner, Jaswinder Chohan, is content to allow you to take full responsibility for it and the charges related to growing and selling the stuff. Meanwhile, he gets off scot-free, not only complicit in your partnership operation, but also as an owner of his own grow-op. He has denied being your partner, as well as having any knowledge of the illegal activities of his renter, and to this point has escaped prosecution and may never be charged for anything. Now, do you think that is fair?"

"I haven't got a clue what you are talking about. The fact that I owned a grow-op and was found out has nothing to do with Jaswinder owning one and which I knew nothing about."

"Not so, Parbeen. You might not remember, but you weren't arrested until after the raids that shut down the houses growing crops for the Desperados. Who do you think gave us the information about you? Your grow-op is not connected to that operation and we would likely have never found out about it."

"That's ridiculous. You must have discovered my crop way back when that traffic cop first stopped me and inspected my truck. I bet you were following me all that time before my arrest, hoping you could connect me to the other grow-ops."

"Not at all, Par. Why do you think Jaswinder hasn't been arrested? Can't you see that he gave us the information about you as part of a deal, in order to save his own neck? I'm afraid you have been made a scapegoat in all this. That's why you're potentially facing a stiff sentence. We got you for trafficking. Why, even the gang's members who were growing the marijuana in their rented houses were only charged with cultivating. You've been set up, Parbeen."

"Jaswinder would never do that. We have been friends for a very long time. He is like a brother to me."

"So, now you don't deny he was your partner?" Tim took a long slow sip of his steaming coffee, letting the flavour sink in as he waited for his question to do the same.

"Now you are putting words in my mouth," Parbeen finally answered.

"Parbeen, your buddy has obviously let you down to save his own neck. All we want you to do is agree that he put up the money to finance your grow-op. If you do that, I should be able to get the charges against you reduced. We might even be able to show that you were simply growing and hauling, but not actually selling. That would reduce the seriousness of the felony quite significantly."

"Yeah, and what would happen to Jaswinder? Even our wives are good friends. She would never let me forget it and I don't think I could live with myself."

"Look Parbeen, it's not Jaswinder we really want. I know that the two of you got talked into this by others who you thought were your friends. If you can agree to do this, it's these other people we want to go after. The courts will likely be very sympathetic toward you, as you were just helping a buddy. It's also quite likely, if he helps us, that Jaswinder won't be charged for trafficking."

"But what if he won't help? What if he denies everything? Then I am still left hanging out to dry and I have lost my best friend and even my wife will be angry with me."

"Here's what we can do. You sign a statement that Jaswinder was your financial partner in the grow-op here in your house. That won't necessarily mean he was a party to trafficking, but it could likely allow me to make a deal to get the charges against you reduced before you go to court. We will use the information to get Jaswinder to tell us who he was working with in the larger grow operation and see what we can do to reduce the charges against him if he cooperates too. If he agrees, there is a good chance that we will never need to tell the public how we found out about him, and if it all works out your wives may never need to know about our deal."

"Well, I will still lose my friend if I agree to sign your statement."

"Some friend he is! Think again about how we found out about you. Sign a statement and probably only Jaswinder will see it. Maybe later you can iron this out and be friends again."

"Alright, I will do it, but I hope only Jas will know."

"I really hope so too, Parbeen."

Later, as he drove away with the signed statement, Tim reflected on how he really did hope he didn't have to show it to anyone, other than Jaswinder. If it ever came out how he obtained it, it might very likely never be accepted as evidence. Mind you, Tim had never said that Jaswinder had told the police about his and Parbeen's grow-op, he had simply asked him rhetorical questions, such as 'who do you think' and 'can't you see'. Mind you, he doubted whether the courts, not to mention Inspector Fields, would appreciate the distinction and the Inspector, in any case, would be less than amused with his methods.

Tim's next challenge was to get Jaswinder Chohan to point the finger at his cousin Barinder. He knew he would have to move fast before Parbeen thought too much about why his good friend, Jas, would have implicated him in the first place. After all, it could potentially trigger an investigation, leading to the police finding out that he was a partner in Parbeen's grow-op, a charge much more serious than being an owner of a place where he could show he didn't know what his tenant was up to. He suspected that Jaswinder would be a lot more sophisticated than his fisherman friend about such matters and he would need to use different techniques.

Probably simply showing him the statement and going for a deal would work best. After all, it was clear evidence and Jaswinder couldn't know what methods Tim had used to obtain it. Still, he would need to arrive at an agreement quickly, before Jaswinder could get a chance to discuss the evidence in detail with Parbeen. At least Tim could honestly say to himself that, should Jaswinder be willing to implicate his cousin Barinder, he would be more than happy to never use the statement again. He was content to let Jaswinder get off if need be. However, if that happened, he could only hope that Parbeen didn't decide to start publicly questioning what had happened to his deal with Corporal Murphy. Oh well, Tim sighed to himself, I'll jump off that bridge when I come to it.

TIM DECIDED TO FIND a location away from work, which would also be agreeable to Jaswinder. Tim was aware that the Victoria firefighters who worked at Fire Hall Number Three were accustomed to hanging out at The Superb Coffee House, the specialty coffee shop on Bay Street. The Superb was a comfortable place where the firefighters could go when they needed to get away for a short break, or found it necessary to conduct business away from work. Nor was if far from the RCMP District Office and Tim figured it would be a good spot to have a chat where it could be conducted informally, yet in a location where the staff and customers were used to seeing customers in uniforms.

Jaswinder had, over the preceding months, gotten used to Inspector Fields and his officers from the Combined Organized Crime Unit grilling him about his real estate holdings. These meetings were always held in RCMP offices and, as it was a relief to him that Murphy was suggesting a neutral location, he agreed to the meeting readily enough. Tim arranged to meet Jaswinder at ten o'clock, a time Jas could arrange to be away from work, in between community safety briefings, which was his area of responsibility when he wasn't required for regular firefighting shifts.

The Superb Coffee House was different than the large chains in that it didn't try to impress its clientele with either fancy or rustic furniture. It settled for conventional and functional tables and chairs in the centre of the room, together with padded booths along the walls for people like Corporal Murphy who wanted to keep their conversations private. Tim arrived first and ordered a large plain cup of black coffee and settled into a booth along the back wall where he could keep an eye on the door. While he waited, he scanned the Coffee News, a free ad-filled newsletter that a local entrepreneur made available for various Victoria fast food places so that their customers would have something to do while passing the time. Jaswinder Chohan arrived about ten minutes later, making no apology for being late. He signalled the waiter for an herbal tea and waited expectantly for Tim to begin the conversation. Tim's immediate reaction was to dislike the man and decided this would make his task easier.

"You're obviously a very busy man, Jaswinder, with all those responsibilities at work and looking after your real estate holdings. It's probably very difficult for you to fit everything in with the little time you have available in the day."

"Having to meet with the police constantly doesn't make it any easier," he shrugged. "I was fortunate to find a few minutes between meetings. But I must warn you, I need to deliver a fire safety briefing for the school kids at S.J. Willis at eleven o'clock, so I can't stay long."

"Like I say, you're a busy man. Well, it's obviously not your firefighter duties I'm here about. I'm much more interested in your sideline interests that you seem to find plenty of time for. All these property holdings must keep you very busy indeed."

"What do you mean - all? Except for my own home, I only have the one place in Sooke, which I could only afford because property prices are cheaper there than here in Victoria. Even then, my wife had to help me with the down payment."

"Looking at the rent payments you receive from it, it couldn't have been that cheap to buy. Otherwise, it's hard to see how you could justify charging the rents you do."

"Look, Murphy, I have been over this again and again with your colleagues. I had no inkling my renters were using my property as a grow-op. You guys keep telling me I am responsible for my tenants and then the Residential Tenancy Office tells me I can't inspect my own house when I want to because that is an infringement on my tenant's privacy. Do you think if I make an appointment to inspect them they are going to leave the evidence around that they are cultivating marijuana in the place?"

"Have you ever arranged an inspection?"

"There would have been no point. Besides, these charges are foolish and you know I will not be convicted. It's a stupid law to make the owner responsible for what their tenants do and it will soon be ruled invalid and struck from the books."

"You seem to know the law very well, Mr. Chohan. What does the legislation say about co-owning a business where the owners are intentionally and personally cultivating an illegal substance? Will that soon be ruled invalid too?"

"Why should I care about that? I don't co-own any businesses, except property ownership with my wife, and I have told you and your fellow henchmen a hundred times now that neither she nor I had any idea it was being used as a grow-op."

"Come now, Jas, you know I'm referring to the property in East Sooke where you, in partnership with your good friend, Parbeen Dhariwal, were maintaining an independent grow-op. We know that you were Parbeen's partner and you have left him to carry the can for trafficking. It looks like you were content to let him go to jail while you got off completely in two illegal businesses you were involved in."

"Even if what you say was true, which it's not, you would have no way to prove it. It would be Parbeen's word against mine."

"You would be very surprised what a little research can uncover, Jaswinder. It's very difficult to be involved in a business financially and not make expenditures that can be tracked. Together with this signed statement from your good friend Parbeen Dhariwal, I believe we have the goods on you, so to speak."

"Let me see that. Jaswinder signed this? Why?"

"I guess he wanted some company over in William Head. Those federal penitentiaries can be real lonely when you don't know anyone."

"You will never make this stick. It's still my word against his."

"Having already determined that you are the owner of one grow-op property, it will be very easy to convince the courts to find you guilty. You see, Jas, no one is very happy you haven't already gone to prison for that one. You can rest assured this will be more than enough to put you away this time. Look Jaswinder, we know the situation. You are an influential member of the Indo-Canadian community here in Victoria. You are also active and have, or at least did have, an executive position with your Progressive Party constituency association. Finally, we know that your wife and Parbeen's are very good friends and they don't really understand what is going on. You have a lot to lose here."

"You're trying to tell me something, Corporal Murphy?"

"To be honest, Jaswinder, I would be very happy to see you go to jail for a very long time. You are an arrogant son of a bitch and you think you're above the law. You were even willing to let your best friend go to jail without saying a word while you got off completely. Nevertheless, in spite of how important you might think you are, you are only one very small fish in a very big pond. There are some very big fish behind the dirty business you are involved in and those are the ones we really want."

"You're saying you want to make a deal with me? What kind of a deal?"

"You're always thinking deals, Jas. Alright, here's one for you. Give me a statement like the one Parbeen signed, explaining that it was your cousin Barinder who convinced you to own a grow-op. I will make the same deal with you that I made with him. I will attempt to convince the prosecution, in exchange for your cooperation, to reduce the charges from trafficking in an illegal substance to simple cultivation with intent to sell. With the change in charges you may never even face jail time."

"Barinder is my cousin, like you said, and I would never go against family. Besides, he is hardly a big fish. He is nothing but an assistant to a government minister."

"Yes, and as you fully know, he was involved in a dirty political party membership-buying scheme and was using the proceeds from your grow-op businesses to fund it, as well as being embroiled in a kickback scheme in a Crown corporation sell-off. He might be a small fish, but he has been doing business with some really big smelly ones."

"And you think I would help you implicate him in all that?"

"Not at all. In fact, you could say I am trying to help save his neck. I am not sure if he really appreciates who he is dealing with. He probably thinks he is okay as the Desperados have all been arrested and their leader is dead, but they were only a tool in a bigger scheme. The people behind this are very ruthless and Barinder has to help us get to them before they decide to get to him."

"Why don't you go to Barinder and just tell him that?"

"That has already been tried by my seniors, and because Barinder thinks we have nothing on him that will stick, other than the BC Hydro fraud, he is unwilling to listen. You can help us make him listen."

"But if he goes to jail they will be sure to get him if they are that ruthless."

"He's going to go to jail anyway, if he lives long enough. We already have enough with the fraud charges, so it's just a matter of time before he goes to court. In the meantime, those who are behind this are going to be fretting that Barinder will eventually talk anyway. So again, he needs to help us identify them before they get to him. And you can help Barinder by helping us."

"Does Barinder need to know that I ratted on him?"

"I'm afraid so, Jas. You are the best one to make him pay attention."

"Well, okay. I don't like it, but I will do it. Not because of any arrangement we might make about my deal with Parbeen, but to help my family. Barinder is family."

"You're doing the right thing, Jaswinder."

"What do I need to do?"

"Just a simple signed statement like Parbeen's will do it. Then I can go to Barinder. Here is my notebook. Just write it out on one page and sign it and you can go back to work. It's that easy."

"It's not that easy."

After Jas left, Tim sat for awhile and thought about what he had accomplished so far. It was clear that, in spite of his arrogant and generally self-centered attitude, family connections were important to Jas. Perhaps they would be to Barinder too. Tim decided he better talk to him soon, before the Inspector asked for a progress report.

Chapter 30

BARINDER CHOHAN WAS DEPRESSED, frustrated and broke. Since losing his position as a Cabinet Minister's assistant months before, he had spent his time alternatively looking after his children and trying to find a job. His wife, Asha, had already been forced to find work, as a cleaning lady no less, as the payments on their upscale Gordon Head home refused to go away. Barinder's own assets had been frozen since the raid, including his bank account and his grow-op home. Even should he be found innocent on the charges against him, it was unlikely he would be able to keep any of his ill-gotten gains. Not being financially astute, he had neglected to open a hidden bank account where, by now, he could have squirreled away a tidy sum for a rainy day.

Now he was having many rainy days. He hadn't been able to afford a brilliant criminal lawyer, but some members of the Sikh community in Victoria had come to his assistance. Having respect for his efforts to increase Indo-Canadian political involvement, they believed he may have received a raw deal, as he was the only grow-op owner facing trial, albeit for other charges. The lawyer they recruited on his behalf had been influential in persuading the prosecution not to charge Barinder for purchasing Progressive Party memberships. He had successfully argued that they would have had little chance of proving that Barinder had done anything more than compile lists of potential members and add them to the roster after they had qualified for full membership. Still, all that was months ago, and although the only remaining charges against him related to his scheme to obtain monies from the privatization of B.C. Hydro, he realized there was still a good chance he could serve time in prison.

To make matters worse, he was being shunned by his former friends and relatives, including Alan Diwan, who had steered clear of him since Barinder had admitted maintaining incriminating evidence in his legislative office. Even his cousin Jaswinder was avoiding him, even though, or maybe because, he hadn't been charged with owning a grow-op. Barinder was sure that Jaswinder was upset for persuading him to ever become an owner, but as he refused to talk to him, he couldn't be sure if there was more to it. At the same time, Barinder remained puzzled that Jaswinder's friend Parbeen had been charged with also owning a grow-op, and more seriously, for trafficking. He was confused and frustrated in not knowing how and why that had ever come about.

Barinder made the rounds of former friends and associates in his search for employment, but to no avail. While they may have been sympathetic, they considered their own reputations and determined that having Barinder onboard could only be bad for their own businesses. At home, not used to domestic duties, he found his two pre-schoolers hard to deal with. Asha had always dealt adeptly with their squabbles and minor accidents, so to Barinder it was all a mystery how they could so quickly alternate between quiet, cooperative playing and full-blown screaming, fighting and crying.

There was also Asha, who had always been close and loving. Now she seemed distant and at times acted as if she resented Barinder for their predicament, although never voicing her opinion and remaining loyal in her contacts with others. Probably, he thought, she was mainly confused how their situation could change so suddenly, so that almost overnight they had transformed from respected community figures to social pariahs. It didn't help that she was exhausted after her long, physically-demanding days cleaning up other people's houses, only to come home and face Barinder's indifferent attempts to maintain order in their own increasingly messy home.

It was late in the afternoon and Barinder was going through his perfunctory attempts to get their place in order before Asha's expected return when he received the call from Corporal Murphy, asking for a meeting. By now, Barinder was very used to formal police methods of doing things and their relentless and constant interviews, and he found the idea of a "meeting" rather strange. He protested that he was fed up with talking to the police and would rather not, but finally agreed to slip out for a coffee after the Corporal's less than subtle suggestion that he might find their meeting to be in his best interest.

It was about eight o'clock that evening when they sat down in a franchise coffee shop on Mackenzie, about five minutes from Barinder's house and a long way from Tim's home in Metchosin. Neither of them was actually very keen about drinking coffee at that time of day and they finally settled for herbal tea. Barinder attempted to keep his annoyance at dealing so frequently with the police to himself and waited relatively patiently for this latest representative of the law, albeit dressed in very casual civilian clothing, to begin his interrogation.

"You know, Barinder," Tim finally began, "you are actually a very lucky man. By now you should be in prison, facing a whole lot of years for a whole lot of criminal activities. Instead, you're only facing a couple of fraud charges and even then you have been out on your own recognisance for months and months now, with still no trial date to look forward to. It seems to me, between the work of your lawyer and the reluctance of government to get you into a courthouse, at least until a couple more elections have been held, that you may be running around loose for a long time yet."

"I would hardly call it luck, Corporal. I am facing charges for matters where I am completely innocent and in the meantime I have lost my job and no one talks to me."

"The way I understand it, Barinder, all kinds of official people have been talking to you. The trouble is, as I see it, you haven't been too willing to tell them very much."

"Look, Corporal, I have been very cooperative with the police, and if you have only come here to tell me that I haven't, then I suggest you stop harassing me and we can both go home."

"No, Barinder, I am here to tell you that your luck is finally running out. I have a sworn affidavit from a grow-op owner stating that you persuaded him to get involved in your nefarious business. Also, in the statement he claims you told him you would ensure he received a lucrative return for his involvement and would be able to keep the house he was provided after the grow-op was no longer required. Now Barinder, this is very serious as it means you can now be charged with both cultivation and trafficking. I am afraid these statements could quickly lead to that lengthy prison time you have tried so hard to avoid."

"This is ridiculous. None of the owners where marijuana was being cultivated were ever charged, so why would one of them now claim to know that it was? He would only be setting himself up to be charged."

"The thing is, Barinder, this owner has come forward in a bid to have the charges reduced against him. In other words, we have the evidence to convict him for cultivating and probably trafficking as well, and he has made a deal by implicating you."

"Are you going to tell me who it is?"

"Not if I don't need to at this time, but let me add that with this evidence we can probably implicate all the owners that were involved, and that would include your cousin Jaswinder."

"Are you here to arrest me then?"

"Not yet. A very serious and ruthless organization has been operating here in B.C. for some time. You have been involved, Barinder, and have played a significant part. Nevertheless, others more senior to you in this organization are masterminding a bigger scheme and have used you and the Desperados to help achieve their aims. One of those organizers has obviously involved you in buying party memberships as part of a plot to ensure the Progressive Party remains in power after the next federal election, not to mention the Provincial Government after its next election, as well. To allow this to happen is a direct threat to the democratic process in this country and it has to stop. You need to tell me the name of this person and the people he reports to."

"I don't know what you are talking about. I don't know any such person. I have already explained that I was merely recruiting members to the party and that is why I had membership lists. You know I haven't been charged for buying members."

"Well, that's just the point then, isn't it? If you didn't buy the memberships, which dozens of members have admitted were purchased for them, then who did? Give me that name, Barinder, so we can put an end to this."

"I don't know who it was."

"Come on, you were obviously reporting to him. Who was it?"

"I can't say."

"Well, then I guess you and I are off to jail. And after you, my next stop will be your cousin Jaswinder's place."

"Are you telling me that if I was to give you a name you wouldn't arrest me?"

"No, I am telling you I wouldn't be arresting you right now and that later I would try to persuade the prosecution to have the charges reduced, just as I will try to do for the owner who came forward."

"You're talking about Jaswinder, aren't you?"

"I am not permitted to tell you that."

"If I give you a name, will that person be told it came from me?"

"No, there's no need to do that. Once we have the name we will use that information to work our way up the ladder, unless you want to tell me who's directing this whole scheme?"

"I can honestly tell you I don't know. I know it must be a very senior party official, probably here in B.C., but I don't even know that. All I know is the person I report to," Barinder lied.

"All right, I believe you. Now give me the name and we can both go home."

"His name is Roger Kent and he lives right here in Victoria."

"What's the address?"

"He lives at 1133 Random Avenue. Also, he works for the True Value Insurance Company."

"Very good, Barinder. You will thank me for this in the long run."

Barinder often felt anxious and later that night he began to feel much stressed indeed as he wrestled with the dilemma of whether or not he had done the right thing. On the one hand, he thought he had. He was pretty sure that the owner who had given Murphy the information was Jaswinder and that he had done so because he was likely involved in the independent grow-op that his friend Parbeen Dhariwal was arrested for. Yes, Jaswinder had griped because he had convinced him to become an owner, but he wouldn't have turned on him, unless it was extremely necessary to save himself and Par. And while he was still angry at

Jas for informing on him, he could understand him doing it. In addition, he was family and Barinder felt that by providing Roger Kent's name he would be helping Jas, as well as himself.

On the other hand, he couldn't help but be concerned that Roger would guess that he had given Corporal Murphy his name. He didn't know all that much about Roger, but he knew that behind those cold blue eyes was a man who wouldn't take kindly to being crossed. Not to mention that Roger had powerful friends who could be very ruthless in order to get their way. Maybe he should warn Roger and he could get away before Murphy picked him up. It wasn't too late, as the Corporal would likely wait until morning to arrest him, and in the meantime Roger could make his escape. Barinder would then have kept his end of the bargain with the Corporal, and by escaping, Roger couldn't be tracked to others in the party. Barinder felt like a man who couldn't swim caught on a burning boat miles from shore. But where, oh where, was the life jacket?

Maybe Paul Husband would know what to do. He had lied to Murphy when he said he didn't know any other senior Party officials involved in the membership purchasing scheme. He knew the Corporal would be content with the one name, so why jeopardize things more than he had? He decided to call Paul and ask for his advice. To do so was to be exposed, but he was beginning to convince himself that was going to happen anyway, so he might as well try and cut his losses. Besides, he trusted Paul and Paul would try and do what was best, wouldn't he?

It was close to eleven when he called, but Paul took his call and listened carefully to Barinder's dilemma. "Don't worry too much about it, Barinder," he answered soothingly. "I appreciate the warning and I will take it from here."

Paul immediately called The Captain and explained the situation, and while hardly in a soothing manner, The Captain in turn said he would take it from there.

Barinder went to bed somewhat less stressed than earlier and feeling he had probably done the best he could.

AFTER LEAVING the coffee shop, Tim had decided he could wait until morning before picking up Roger Kent. He had had a couple of very productive days and was extremely pleased that he had accomplished so much in so little time, especially considering Inspector Field's officers had gotten nowhere after months of investigation. Now, as he wound his way along the darkened roads on the long drive back to Metchosin, he had to decide whether he should bring the Inspector up to speed on his progress or pick Kent up first. It should be easy enough to nab him, he decided, provided I am there early in the morning. Also, it would likely be easier to convince the Inspector that his somewhat unorthodox techniques had been required in order to finally get some valuable information out of Barinder Chohan.

It was close to midnight when Tim arrived home, yet he was up by five in order to get to Roger Kent's apartment before he left for work. Over the years, the daily drive to work downtown had become almost unbearable, but at this time of the morning he was ahead of the commuter traffic. It was a delight to flow along the Island Highway, sharing the road with a fraction of the cars and trucks that would be clogging the intersections only an hour later in the morning.

He streamed effortlessly through downtown and into the centre of James Bay with relative ease, arriving on Random Avenue well before seven a.m. Kent's apartment was in one of the old original buildings from the 1880's that had been preserved to remind Victorians they had a history. Just the same, it was a funky mishmash of a neighbourhood, with tall condominiums and modern apartment buildings, interspersed with crowded-in and rundown boarding houses and much smaller, but relatively newer, houses converted to neighbourhood grocery stores and hair dresser salons. It was as if the city fathers had relaxed the residential zoning regulations as an experiment to see what the area's building owners would do with their properties. Nevertheless, it all actually worked quite well and the area was one of the few in the city that could boast of having a community spirit.

Tim doubted his target shared that spirit. He was also sure that nabbing Kent could lead to a break in a criminal case that had now become one of the largest in the history of Victoria. Certainly the effort expended on it, before Superintendent Chan cut the heart out of the Combined Organized Crime Unit, was the most extensive in all the years the RCMP had been in the city. As he approached the apartment building, Tim felt a rising sense of excitement that he could play a major role in finally determining who was behind it all.

For a change, Tim had worn his uniform, and as he approached the door to the apartment, a woman leaving for work smiled and held the door for him. That's convenient, he thought. At least he wouldn't have to announce his arrival, making it less likely Kent would have an opportunity to look for an escape, should he be so inclined. He located Kent's name on the mailbox and climbed the stairs to the third floor and knocked on the door. No answer. He knocked again. There was still no answer. Reaching for his wallet, he pulled out his handy plastic key and inserted it deftly between the door and its jamb and lowered it, pushing the lock back while he turned the knob and opened the unresisting door. There was no inner door chain to impede his progress and the door opened quietly.

Cautiously drawing his revolver, Tim entered the room. He was in the main living area and the room was unlit. He walked quietly across the floor and peered warily into the unoccupied kitchen-dining area. Stealthily now, he moved quickly along the darkened hallway to the bedroom. The door to the bedroom was open and the bed appeared not to have been slept in. Tim holstered his revolver and dialled the number for the True Value Insurance Company. He was rewarded with a very pleasant female voice notifying him office hours were eight to four every week day and eight to noon on Saturdays.

Tim concluded that Roger Kent was a fastidious earlier riser and had already made his bed and left for work. At the moment he was likely at Smitty's, or some such place, having breakfast and would soon be on his way to the office. Tim decided he would wait a few minutes before making his way downtown to the insurance company. In the meantime, he decided he might as well have a quick look in the other rooms of the apartment. He opened the bathroom door and there was Roger, slumped on the toilet seat, his throat slashed from ear to ear and his fully clothed body covered with copious quantities of his own blood. More of it was coagulating on the non-absorbing linoleum beneath his feet.

Part Five

Homicide

Tyrannical Leaders
of which you're the best
Can only be happy
As the only one left

Pennywise - Premeditated Murder

Chapter 31

INSPECTOR FIELDS FOCUSED his impressive thought processes on Corporal Murphy's puzzling message. An early riser, he had already been at work for well over an hour when he had answered Tim's cell phone call, outlining his find. He had thoroughly probed for details and had learned enough to know that he and the Corporal would be requiring another long, heart-to-heart conversation. Once again, Murphy's unorthodox methods had resulted in havoc and yet had the potential for providing a significant advance in their investigation. He suspected that the discovery of a major player, Roger Kent, could possibly lead to an important break, but the statements that Murphy had acquired, and especially the manner in which he had obtained them, might easily scuttle their whole case. It didn't help that Murphy had illegally broken in to Kent's apartment without a warrant in order to make his would-be arrest.

At any rate, he had immediately ordered Murphy to inform Sergeant Mark Scandiffio from the Homicide Unit of his discovery and to remain at the scene long enough to answer his questions, but not to disclose why Barinder Chohan had offered up the name of the victim. Once his interview with Homicide was complete, he was to report immediately to the Inspector's office.

It was almost two hours later that Tim had gotten away and was able to report. He had never seen Inspector Fields so coldly hostile. He beckoned Tim to a chair across from his desk and over the next hour he methodically grilled him on each and every sordid detail of his recent activities, with heavy emphasis on the techniques he had used in obtaining the signed statements from the grow-op partners.

Once satisfied there was nothing more to learn, he simply asked, "Was it your intention to use the signed statements in court?"

Immediately, Tim could see where the Inspector was going with this and why he had requested he not inform Homicide of the reason for Chohan's tip. "Yes, sir, it was," he quickly answered. "Never in my interviews with any of the three of them did I ever state outright that one of the others had provided me information that they in fact hadn't. I always couched it in questions, such as 'Who do you think gave us the info?' 'Why is so and so getting off while you go to jail?' and 'Another owner has confessed,' etc. Nor did I ever promise outright that I could get them a shorter sentence. It was always that I would do what I could, I will try my best – that kind of language."

"Corporal Murphy, your methods are devious, underhanded and unscrupulous. You know that I could never condone the way you operate."

"Yes, sir. What do you think we should do with the statements, Inspector?"

"I'm satisfied that they are acceptable evidence and can be used in court. In addition, it means we can probably lay more charges in the case and can move forward with the investigation. Nevertheless, in gathering these statements, you have been extremely close to crossing the line and I am not very happy about that. And when it came to Kent's would-be arrest, you did cross the line. Why the hell couldn't you at least wait until you had been issued a search warrant?"

"I was afraid he would find out we were on to him and skip out."

"Even though you went home to sleep on it, before going back to the city to pick him up," the Inspector added sarcastically.

"Yes, Inspector. How do you think we should proceed with the investigation?"

"Murphy, you are so presumptuous. What do you mean, we? I am of a mind to send you to Iqaluit and let you rot there. This case is much more than an investigation into organized crime and political misdeeds now. It has become another homicide investigation and as such, I have a new kettle of fish to deal with."

"I believe I can still be useful, sir. Barinder Chohan will need to be brought in for his own protection and I can spend more time questioning him. He might be willing to provide us with additional names if he thinks it is the only way to save his own skin in the long run. As well, I wouldn't mind doing the research on Roger Kent. We should be able to find out who his contacts are and see where that leads us."

"Just the same, I can't have you running around like a loose cannon. I believe the solution is to put you under Sergeant Scandiffio's control. I am quite confident he can keep you in line and you might be useful to him, being as you are more up to speed in the case than anyone else. Nevertheless, I will ask him to let you proceed with your two suggestions. But he calls the shots and I expect you to listen to him and do what he says. Is that clear?"

"Yes, sir, that's perfectly clear, Inspector Fields."

A FLUSTERED AND IRATE Paul Husband sat across from The Captain, other emotions overriding his usual unease in the man's presence. The item on the noon news had provided a good description of Roger Kent's legitimate insurance business and work background, but seemed to be oblivious to his extracurricular affairs. The police had been quoted as being unaware of the reason for his murder, but were investigating. He knew that was hogwash as Barinder had made it clear he had informed on Roger and had even admitted that Roger was his contact between the party and the Desperados. It was bad enough that The Captain had not informed him of the murder, but much worse was the fact he had arranged it in the first place.

"When you told me that you would take care of it, I didn't for a moment consider that this was what you had in mind. Don't you think the whole west coast party organization is now in jeopardy? The police will never leave us alone until they have discovered who is behind this. Buying a few party memberships is one thing, but murder? They will never let it rest."

"Calm down, Paul. Let's not get emotional here. I did what you very well knew needed to be done. If there was another way of dealing with Roger, you would have done it yourself. You know full well you could have tried to get him out of Victoria before the police had descended on his apartment, if you thought you could have pulled it off. Just why didn't you?"

"Because I knew that even if I got to Roger in time he would never have agreed to go into exile, even if I was able to get him out of Victoria. Also, if anyone was likely to make a deal to save his own skin it would be Roger. I called you because I thought you might have some solution I hadn't considered and I thought maybe you did when you said right away that you would look after it."

"No point in trying to shift the blame, Paul. You know as well as I that we are in this together and you have already admitted that we couldn't trust Roger.

"How did you manage to have him killed on such short notice?"

"You know that I have a bias for action. As soon as I hung up from talking to you I called Roy. He was able to make the late ferry to Nanaimo and drove down to Victoria, did the job and caught the first ferry back from Schwartz Bay this morning. And now we know he can't lead the police back to us."

"No, but Barinder might."

"I'm very surprised that Barinder gave the RCMP Roger's name. Maybe they got close to someone that Barinder is now trying to protect. Did Barinder have any family members involved in the grow-op?"

"Yes, his cousin was an owner."

"Okay, that's probably it. Barinder has probably said all he is going to say and only what was going to help his cousin anyway. I think we can sit tight until we figure out how much the police know. He did tell you that Roger's name was the only one he gave them, right?"

"Yes, and as you know, I am the only other senior person in the party organization that he has dealt with and I am very sure that he hasn't given them my name."

"And we are very sure that if he has, you would take the full blame for the whole membership scheme, wouldn't you, Paul?"

"Of course, you know that. Plus, they will never be able to figure out who murdered Roger, never mind who arranged it."

"That's right, Paul. Now let's just keep working on the campaign and let this matter rest. We only have two weeks to go and if the Horsemen start asking questions, we will stall them until after the party wins the election. After that, we should have enough influence to get the PM to tell the Mounties to back off."

"All right. Leif says the polls are looking good for us in B.C. I just hope there is enough support in the rest of the country."

"We'll soon know, Paul. We'll soon know."

SERGEANT MARK SCANDIFFIO was a squat, barrel-shaped man in his early fifties. He had joined the RCMP right out of school and except for basic training and the few specialized courses the force insisted he attend, he had attained his present rank strictly as a result of practical field achievement. He had little patience or respect for those who had achieved higher rank because of their academic credentials or skill at bureaucratic political manoeuvring. Nor was he impressed with those who employed questionable methods to solve cases. He was no-nonsense, by-the-book and doggedly persistent. He was also highly respected and the man that his seniors turned to when they wanted a job done properly. He was the perfect police officer to head up a homicide investigation.

The Sergeant was not particularly pleased to have Corporal Murphy on his team. He knew of Murphy's reputation, he intently disliked his spontaneous actions and he was not impressed that the man had no experience in investigating murders. He received Tim into his office with no enthusiasm and a bare modicum of civility.

"Come in, Corporal," he ordered, cursorily beckoning at a chair while remaining firmly fixed behind his cluttered desk. "You are no doubt aware that I have been asked to make you a temporary member of the Homicide Unit while we investigate the death of one Roger Kent. Frankly, I am much more interested in you as a witness and in what you can tell me about his death and who you think might be involved. Nevertheless, I have my orders, so let's make the most of it. We can begin by having you sit down with one of my team and get you to go over all the details of your discovery and what led up to it. After that, I can figure out how to best employ you. Is that clear?"

"It sounds fair enough, Sergeant." Tim was still relieved that Inspector Fields had kept him actively involved in the case and he was actually looking forward to working with Homicide, one of the police specialties where he felt he belonged. He knew that usually officers worked murder cases either alone, or in pairs, and he was confident his personality would be reasonably well suited for this line of work. "When can we get started?"

His quick agreement caught the Sergeant by surprise. He had seen Murphy around the District Office over the years, but having had no experience working with him, he had based his judgements of the man on his reputation as individualistic and being something of a loose cannon. As a result, he had expected Murphy to be hot tempered and arrogant. Instead, here was a polite, courteous officer, quite prepared to be cooperative.

"I will arrange for Constable Ballard to interview you," he carefully answered. "He's with the Victoria Police and since the murder took place in their jurisdiction, they would normally be fully responsible for looking into it. It's only because of the continuing investigation into organized crime that Inspector Fields is heading up, as I know you are fully aware, that we are involved at all. Now, the Inspector's team has been cut back dramatically, but because Ballard is still part of it, he has been assigned to work with me. The City seems to be okay with that, even though their resources are severely stretched. They have also assigned one actual homicide officer to the case and it has been agreed he will also report to me."

"Were you aware, Sergeant, that Craig Ballard and I worked closely together earlier in the case?"

"No, I wasn't, but maybe that will make it easier to get the information out of you. Just don't get too palsy. I expect you to provide him with every detail that you know and for him to bring that information directly to me."

"No problem, Sergeant. We all want the same thing here and that is to find out who is responsible for this. It will help that Constable Ballard is up to speed on the case."

"All right. Get to it then."

CRAIG BALLARD was his normal chipper self and had apparently forgiven Tim for risking their necks at Jordon River. Nevertheless, he listened carefully to Tim's story, questioning him frequently in order to fully come to grips with the logic of his step-by-step approach to learning Roger Kent's identity from Barinder Chohan. Finally satisfied, he asked, "Tim, do you think we can get any more out of Chohan? He must know others in the party hierarchy that were involved."

"I'm sure he does, Craig, but short of letting him wander free and see who comes after him, I am not sure how we will find out who they are. I think Barinder still believes they will leave him alone as long as he takes the rap at the trial flowing out of the disclosures from the raid on the legislature, if it ever does."

"Hmm, allowing him to walk around freely and following him may not be such a bad idea. If we get desperate enough, we might want to consider that. In the meantime though, in spite of his optimism, I agree with you that he is a marked man and we will need to keep him under wraps for his own protection. Maybe he will finally realize that and give us more as a way of best protecting his own skin in the long run."

"So, do you agree with me that the best we can do in the meantime is to research Kent's background and see if we can discover something from that?"

"Okay, Tim. For now, why don't we break this up? I will go to the insurance office and find out what I can about his contacts and associates and you follow the paper trail. The man must have some information somewhere that can lead us to the people calling the shots on this. Also, we might want to tackle it from the other end. We can start looking into the backgrounds of the senior Progressive Party people and see if any of them are hiding something. Given what's been going on here, if we turn over enough rocks we are sure to find some very strange creatures."

"Somehow you've managed to arrange to get the fun part, Craig. It's only that I know you would be useless doing research that I will reluctantly agree. But if you find out anything interesting from the interviews, I will want to know immediately and we can investigate together, okay?"

"Hey, we're partners, aren't we?"

"And that reminds me. Keep Scandiffio in the loop. He's not the kind of guy you want to screw around with."

TIM WAS TIRED from his busy morning and decided to go home early after a quick scan of Roger Kent's financial profile. On the surface, the information provided little of value. He maintained a chequing account with a few monthly transactions, all of which looked totally mundane and related to the business of daily living. There was no record of hobby or recreational purchases, zero indication of domestic or foreign travel, or even much that was related to his entertainment. He managed to locate a very small insurance policy with his aging mother in Vancouver as beneficiary, and to Tim it seemed as if he needed to have the policy just to justify his occupation as a life insurance agent.

His tax returns seemed to be straightforward, prepared by a local accountant and showing a modest income from salary and commissions, augmented with some insignificant capital gains from a few blue chip stock purchases. About the only item of interest was included in his expenditure listings, related to his insurance income. He seemed to make many regular trips to Vancouver, although his customer records indicated only two clients there, one of which was his mother. Was this just a minor expense padding transaction, or was there more to these visits than insurance business? Here was one avenue for Tim to explore, but a very narrow looking one indeed. He decided he could wait to research it after he had rested up.

Tim had also decided to leave early as Gloria had been very unhealthy for the last few weeks and he had attempted to be with her as often as he could get away. It had been a distressing period for her, with her dialysis treatments resulting in complications. The clinical nurses had been experiencing great difficulty in getting the huge dialysis needles into her, and rather than use her arms, they had often been forced to access veins in her hands and neck and even the soles of her feet. They were preparing a permanent catheter near her left collarbone that would allow better access, but which would restrict her exercise activities.

Another complication had resulted from an inability to stabilize her during treatments, and she had often become very dehydrated, resulting in painful cramping that left her exhausted and unable to sleep properly. All of this was causing much distress to her body, and if it continued, would make it difficult for her system to cope and could lead to even more complications, such as heart failure or slipping into unconsciousness during her dialysis runs. These were problems that were all too common amongst kidney patients that had been required to undergo dialysis treatments for an extended period. For many of them, the complications and strain on their bodies after years of dialysis eventually led to their deaths.

Thus, Tim was very surprised to find a tired but smiling Gloria welcome him home that afternoon. "Well, you look very pleased about something. Did you win the lottery today?"

"In a matter of speaking I sure did. Sheila went through with the testing to see if she could be a donor for me and it turns out, not only that she can, but that she would be a terrific match. It means, if we go ahead with the transplant, which she says she is totally prepared to do, I will get a good kidney that is less unlikely to reject and I can be back to normal. Isn't that exciting?"

"Oh, that's wonderful news! When can you expect that they will schedule the operations?"

"It may only take about four or five weeks. Sometimes it takes longer to fit it into the operating schedule at one of the Vancouver hospitals where they perform organ transplants, but because of the difficulty I have been going through, they will try and speed things up. So it will probably be sometime next month or in early October."

"That's terrific. I will book some time off so I can be with you while you recover."

"Oh, my goodness, how could I forget? It was only this morning when you got up so awfully early to go and arrest that man you talked about last night. Has something bad happened?

"I should have called you. Apparently it's been on the news already. Haven't you been listening?"

"No, I have been too excited to do anything. Why, what's happened?"

"Well, I still have my job," Tim answered, and described everything that had happened that morning and how he was now working on a homicide investigation.

"But how will you get time off? You can't just drop a homicide investigation, can you?"

"You bet I can. Nothing is as important as being with you while you recover. And besides, my role is not that critical. It's mainly doing some research on this Roger Kent guy. And who knows, maybe we can have it rapped up by then."

"Yeah, right. It seems like forever since this whole investigation started. Now you're going to wrap it up in the next month?"

"Well, at the very least, I deserve some time off. One way or another, you can rest assured I will be there when you get your transplant."

"Okay, and thanks for coming home early."

Chapter 32

OVER THE NEXT TWO WEEKS, the homicide team continued the investigation with little to show for it. Sergeant Scandiffio had become an irate and perplexed man who was beginning to feel his homicide team was really not up to the job, although all of them appeared to be doing their best. He had to admit they were a bit of an odd group to be involved in a homicide case. Only one was an actual homicide detective and he worked for the City Police. The other two were an undercover drug cop, also on loan from the City, and a jack-of-all-trades RCMP Corporal, who was a bit of a loose cannon to boot.

There were absolutely no clues from the crime scene to help them. The Sergeant was sure the killing was done by a professional who knew his business, and it was obvious that Kent hadn't received the slightest warning he was about to die before it happened. Craig Ballard was getting nowhere with his interviews, other than to determine the victim was a man who kept to himself and barely had acquaintances, never mind friends. Others in the office where he had been employed for three years kept their distance from the man, his aloof manner and cold blue eyes never inviting their friendship. And the best Tim Murphy had been able to come up with was the observation that anyone with such a boring background had to be hiding something.

"No kidding," Scandiffio had retorted, with obvious exasperation.

Tim knew the homicide team must leave no stone unturned if they were going to find anything of value from Roger's death that would help lead to the killers. Comparatively, it was only a pebble in the great gravel pile of possibilities, but he decided he could make himself useful by arranging to go to Vancouver and visit Roger's mother. He hoped to learn more about Roger and thought a history of his upbringing might provide some clues. Also, he might learn more about Roger's travel expenses and perhaps his other Vancouver client could shed some light on his regular visits to the city.

He decided to go by ferry as he would need his car when he arrived on the mainland. He left home in time to catch the 7:00 a.m. sailing in order to make it back in time to pick up Gloria after her afternoon dialysis treatment. The city's patient services bus, the HandiDART, was able to get her there in time for her afternoon run, but couldn't be counted on to be ready to take her home after she had finished.

Contrary to the old poem, the red sky in the Straight of Georgia on that morning appeared to be a promise that another magnificent sunny day was in store. The huge ferry slipped from its berth and was soon up to speed. It quickly streamed past Piers Island and into the maze of Channels - Shute, Swanson and Navy - before it slowed slightly to squeeze through Active Pass, then picked up speed again as it left Lighthouse Point and the Gulf Islands to enter the open waters of the Straights. It was flat calm on the open water and the sky was soon sparkling clear as the sun rose quickly, melting the pink particles in the air, leaving a deep crystal blue. Ahead of them and off to the right, the shimmering white peak of Mt. Baker stood out high on the horizon and served as a beacon to guide even the poorest navigator across the water to Roberts Bank and the ferry dock at Tsawwassen. As he contemplated the scene from high on the outer deck, Tim felt like an explorer as they skimmed along the water, miraculously, if only temporarily, devoid of other water traffic. But all too soon they were across and the P. A. system blared out its approach messages, ordering all automobile drivers to the car deck to prepare to disembark.

Any impressions Tim may have felt of being an early explorer were quickly and abruptly put to rest as he left the ferry and faced the reality of seemingly endless traffic crawling into downtown Vancouver. He crept up Highway 99 and through the George Massey Tunnel, feeling like a can of tuna bumping slowly along an infinitely long conveyor belt. By ten o'clock, he finally made it across the Oak Street Bridge and into the city.

The address he had for Roger Kent's mother led him to a large, stately, but run-down house on Angus Drive in the South Granville area. Like many of the mansions along the street, Bernice Kent's place had seen better days. The expansive front lawn was long, scruffy and faded to a dead bleached brown. The house fit in well, the once deep blue exterior paint peeling away to expose a washed-out beige undercoat. Windows and doors sagged and gapped, and many of the eves looked ready to break away from the broken-shingled roof.

Tim had called ahead, but there was no sign of life as he rang the doorbell. After rapping firmly on the doorjamb for the third time, the door finally opened to reveal an elderly, tired-looking woman dressed in a faded and tattered house gown. She looked at Tim quizzically. "Can I help you?" she finally offered, feebly.

"Yes, ma'am, I'm Corporal Murphy. I called earlier to talk to you about your son."

"Oh, no, you must be mistaken, my son Roger is dead," she corrected him.

"Uh, yes, Mrs. Kent. That's why I called. I was hoping you could tell me about him so I can try and find out why he died."

"He was killed, you know. But why would anyone kill Roger? He sold insurance. In Victoria I think."

"Yes, that right, Mrs. Kent. But I'm wondering about his time here in Vancouver. You know, where he worked, who his friends were, where he went to school, that sort of thing."

"Oh, he had a nice school. Roger went to school at St. Albert's, you know. That was before Jim lost all our money and Roger couldn't go to university. Roger sold insurance, you know."

"Yes, Mrs. Kent. He sold insurance in Victoria. Did he sell insurance here in Vancouver as well?"

"I think so. He was so busy, you know, what with politics and all."

"Can you tell me about the people in politics that he worked with?"

"Oh, I don't remember their names. It was such a long time ago."

Tim could see he wasn't going to get much out of her, but he kept at it. Eventually, he learned that Roger had worked with the Progressives where, as far as she knew, his duties were quite basic, including canvassing and envelope stuffing. But then she couldn't remember if that was years ago after graduation, or more recently, before he moved to Victoria. Nor did she have a clue why he had moved to the capital. In fact, she wasn't sure when he had last been home, although she didn't think it was long ago. She seemed to remember that he visited her fairly regularly.

He asked her if Roger had a room here at home and she agreed he did. After getting her permission to look at it, she took him to a large second-floor bedroom with all the appropriate furniture, but absolutely nothing to indicate that Roger had ever made the room his own. It was apparent that he had removed all his personal effects when he left for Victoria. Searches of other bedrooms, readily agreed to by Mrs. Kent, also bore no indication that her son had made any part of the house his home. However, she again recollected that he often came to Vancouver to visit her and would sometimes stay overnight, and seemed to think he had done so fairly recently, but wasn't really sure when.

Finally, having determined that he wouldn't learn anything else of value, he bid her goodbye and drove to a smaller home a few blocks away, near the old tracks by West Boulevard, where, except for his mother, Roger's lone Vancouver insurance client lived. The client explained that he had known Roger's mother and had agreed to let Roger take him on after meeting Roger at a dinner they had both attended at her home. But he hadn't talked to him since setting up the policy and hadn't even seen his mother in the three years since. At this point, Tim was feeling that his trip had been a very big waste of time.

He returned on the 3:00 p.m. ferry sailing feeling more like a downtrodden traveller than an adventurous explorer. Even the sky had clouded over and he had to wonder if the old ditty about red skies was right after all. For this leg of the journey, he sat in the crowded fifth deck passenger lounge and reviewed the meagre information that Roger's senile mother had been able to recall about her son.

Gone was his earlier optimism, to be replaced by a sense of futile disappointment. About the only thing he had learned was that Roger had gone to an exclusive private school and perhaps had made contacts there that had led to his involvement with the Progressive Party, although if his mother was right, he was not exactly in the centre of Party decision making. But then, if he wasn't making regular trips to Vancouver for insurance purposes or to visit his dementia-stricken mother, why was he doing it? Maybe he just had a girlfriend? Or maybe his position with the Progressive Party was more involved than his mother thought? He obviously still had a lot to learn about Roger Kent. Back in Victoria, he picked Gloria up from the hospital and drove home, slightly depressed and more than a little disappointed.

Nevertheless, in the following days, Tim kept researching. He eventually discovered that Roger's accountant was none other than Bill Taylor, the accountant who had been assassinated in the Victoria Court House, and that might mean something. At the very least, it probably explained why his tax returns were so mundane. The assassinated accountant had been an expert at money laundering and Tim surmised he was possibly doing the same for Roger in his nefarious second life, whatever that was, other than acting as a middleman in a dope-funded party membership purchasing scheme.

THE RESULTS OF THE federal election were announced quickly after the polls closed on the first Monday after the Labour Day weekend. Far from any of the Vancouver constituency election centres, The Captain sat with Leif Johannsen and Paul Husband, reviewing the results. In spite of the best efforts of the media, and in particular the Canadian Universal's blatantly biased pro-Progressive Party news stories, the attention of the electorate was elsewhere. A summer campaign had been necessary after a vote of non-confidence had passed immediately before Parliament was to have recessed, but it was an ungodly time to get the citizenry interested in politics. On the West Coast, in particular, a beautiful summer had focussed everyone's attention on trips to the cottage, golf, sailing and lazing in the sun. As a result, the turn-out on Election Day had set an all time low, and generally speaking, those who did bother to vote were in the mood for a change and had turned against the Progressives and voted for the even more right-wing Union Party that was now poised to form a minority government.

An exception was the twelve ridings in British Columbia where the Progressives had focussed their vote-buying scheme. It had worked, virtually without a hitch. The usually disinterested voters paid to vote for the party had turned out to collect their easily made $50 and were able to tip the scales in ten of the twelve constituencies. It hadn't made much of a difference overall though, as the three main parties had split the B.C. seats three ways, and other than making it extremely difficult for the Union Party to form an effective coalition with any other party, had little national effect.

Gone was The Captain's opportunity to be a major influence in Canadian politics. Even the Prime Minister, whom he had worked so hard to re-elect, announced on election night that he would be stepping down, meaning a new leader would likely emerge with whom The Captain had no ties. Should a new election be necessary within the next year or two and the Progressives were to once again emerge successful, it would still be unlikely that he would have time to regain the influence he was beginning to enjoy with the old leader.

All was not lost, though, as Leif pointed out. "We have learned that the model works and it can be used again in other elections. We now know that not only is the electorate jaded and apathetic, they are willing to be bought, seeing it as just an extension to what Canadian politics has become."

"I'm not sure how that can help us make the changes we want to see," The Captain answered, despondent that his chance for power seemed to have slipped from his grasp.

"What about employing the same strategy in the next Provincial election?" Leif continued. "We have discovered we can successfully replace the executive members in individual ridings and put in place candidates that share your philosophy. We can easily turn to the same party members we have already recruited to take out provincial party memberships and override the current candidates of their existing party establishment. Then, when the election is called, we again focus on a couple dozen key ridings to get the results we obtained here. So far, no one has come forward to announce they were paid to vote a certain way, and with any luck it will never become public knowledge. Then we can probably get those cocky Howe Street bastards out of Victoria pretty easily and turn the province around."

"In the meantime, the whole country could be sold off to outsiders by this new bunch in Ottawa who can't wait to suck up to the Americans."

"They won't last long. They're a minority now and none of the other parties will be able to work with them. In the meantime, we get the media to keep hammering away at any and all signs of corruption and arrogance, and there will be plenty. The voters will soon be willing to return to our Party. I wouldn't give them more than two years and they shouldn't be able to do too much damage. They have to worry about not showing their true colours too soon and forcing an even earlier election."

"Okay, but we will still need plenty of money to cover the financing for a provincial campaign. Also, I will need to back off on illegal shipments for awhile until I determine whether the new Federal Government wants to start snooping around my business affairs. For now, I will call a halt to all cross-border smuggling, including both trucking and shipping operations. Still, we have a pretty solid surplus in our offshore accounts, so I guess when the time comes we will be okay."

"There's no great sense of urgency, but we must do a fair amount of groundwork," Leif added. "The provincial election won't happen until next May, so there's about nine months to get ready. However, we will still need to get our candidates in line to replace the existing ones when the nominating meetings are called in each of the ridings we want to control."

"Yeah, and there's the little matter that we don't control the provincial party the way we do the federal one here in B.C.," Paul added. "The good news is the lack of restrictions under the provincial constitution. We can sign up as many new members as we can buy, so that in addition to those who are already federal party members, who can easily be persuaded to take out provincial Party membership, we are free to recruit new ones."

"It seems to me, Paul, that the two of you need to get started right away. Don't worry about the financing. I will see that the money is there when you need it."

By this point in the meeting The Captain had regained his normal sense of confident assurance and looked forward to the fight. He had to admit to himself his real aim was to get those arrogant assholes in Victoria out of power and once that was done he could at least ensure that British Columbia's assets were used for the betterment of people like himself, who knew that in order to maintain real power, you could never allow yourself to be simply an agent for outsiders. He was in the game for the long haul and wanted to ensure that by the time he was finished, he would be so dominant that all his actions would be unquestioned.

Chapter 33

TWO WEEKS LATER, all hell broke loose. First there was the announcement that Duncan Henderson had gone over to the Union Party in exchange for the promise of a future cabinet position. Then Paul came to The Captain to inform him that his wife had "got wind' of their vote-buying scheme in the federal election and was threatening to take action against them. And just to add to his woes, The Captain had discovered that the new government was taking a keen interest in not only his, but all businesses that engaged in cross-border trucking operations. And, in spite of his clampdown, it seemed one of his Indo-Canadian drivers had independently decided to complete "just one more run."

The latter case was easy enough to deal with. All his drivers were independent haulers and knew they were on their own, should anything happen. Nevertheless, the border guards knew they were hauling for The Captain's company and had increased inspections at all crossings into the United States. He had quickly ordered a complete freeze on the movement of illegal substances and other contraband and arranged for these goods to be removed from his warehouses and relocated to other storage facilities controlled by the Satan's Sirens, who were quite willing to stash them for a healthy fee.

The betrayal by Duncan Henderson was another matter altogether. He was enraged that he had taken this step. While it was quite acceptable, from The Captain's standpoint, for someone to look for opportunities to better their own status in life, it was not acceptable to do so in a way that would cause him to be disadvantaged. And The Captain would be very disadvantaged indeed, should Henderson, who was privy to the B.C. Progressive Party decision makers' most secretive deliberations, decide to inform the Union Party leaders of their nefarious activities. The man would have to be dealt with and very quickly. Additionally, he would need to deal with the Paul and Maureen Husband situation in the very near future, as well, but at least she was only threatening at this stage.

He arranged a meeting with Roy Carpenter. This was very easy to do as the man lived on The Captain's secluded estate in West Vancouver, employed as his handy man, which in fact he was, in more ways than one. He had his own good-sized cottage, well removed from the main house, but positioned to allow Roy to observe the comings and goings of The Captain's infrequent guests. The arrangement had resulted from a conversation the two men had years before, when Roy had been recommended by a previous leader, since deceased, of the Vancouver Chapter of the Satan's Sirens. The arrangement suited both of them perfectly – The Captain because Roy was so convenient when he needed him and for Roy it provided the cover he required for his main profession. He was at liberty to contract out to others who knew of his line of work and he was often called on to do this, usually by biker gangs and other criminal organizations who were aware of the voice mail arrangement he used to mask his identity.

Roy was a true professional and took great pains to develop and perfect efficient methods of disposing of his targets. He was an expert with many types of firearms, knives, ice picks and even a crossbow. He knew how to construct a very lethal car bomb from everyday parts, making it next to impossible to trace its origins.

One of his favourite techniques and one that had become almost a signature trademark, was a nasal spray bottle that could quickly and quietly administer a lethal measure of cyanide solution into a victim's face. He was so adept with this little tool that he had been known to mete out a quick dosage on a busy urban sidewalk and make his unnoticed exit before the hapless recipient hit the pavement. Once The Captain had outlined his latest requirement and, after studying his target's habits, he concluded that Henderson was an urbane kind of guy and concluded the spray bottle would be an appropriate weapon for the situation.

Roy knew he had to move quickly, but at first Henderson proved to be a little more unpredictable and less subject to routines than he at first expected. His move to the Union Party had disrupted his usual social and business acquaintance patterns and he was moving through a transition as he adapted to new ones. He was even avoiding the Vancouver Club, being reluctant to cross paths with his previous political allies. He was also avoiding locations where his constituents might accost him, as many of them were less than pleased with him for crossing the floor, particularly those that had worked on his campaign.

Soon, however, through careful and persistent tracking of his movements, Roy obtained the information he needed. Through some library research, he learned in the social pages of his neighbourhood weekly that Henderson was a family man. When he was in town and when he had the time, he very much enjoyed the company of his relatively young children. The article mentioned that he often accompanied his fourteen-year-old daughter, Amanda, to the Kerrisdale Arena for her Wednesday night figure skating lesson. Since his party switch, Henderson was indeed in town, attempting to avoid his new political enemies and the Ottawa media.

Roy decided the Kerrisdale Arena would make a nice location to complete their transaction. He followed them into the arena that very Wednesday, his chosen weapon in his pocket, and discreetly found a seat in the stands a good distance from his target. Sure enough, about forty minutes after arriving, Duncan became bored and restless and headed off in the general direction of the snack bar and washrooms. Roy gave him about twenty seconds before following him into the men's room and found him alone at the urinal. Deftly he applied the spray before Duncan even realized he was there, and then, quietly and completely overlooked, left the building by the main entrance.

HENDERSON'S DEATH naturally caused a sensation. The Vancouver Police had no reason to suspect murder, but it was obviously an unusual place for a person to suddenly die and the coroner was quick to hold an autopsy. On discovery of the cyanide in his lungs, the cause of death was quickly changed from suspected heart attack to homicide. It took a few days, but eventually the police decided not to rule out political differences as a motive. Nevertheless, it was difficult to believe that anyone would want to kill the man simply because he had changed party affiliations!

Within the Vancouver Island District of the RCMP, however, political differences were seen as a plausible motivation. Roger Kent's death had likely occurred to ensure that powerful people were not exposed and Corporal Murphy and Sergeant Scandiffio agreed that Henderson's death may have come about for the same reasons. They agreed to take a new tack on their own investigation, focussing much more on learning what they could about all the senior officials within the B.C. wing of the Federal Progressive Political Party. They also agreed to meet with Inspector Fields, as they suspected they would be requiring political support from their own senior officials if they wished to push their investigation in this direction.

Inspector Errol Fields listened to their arguments with great interest. He had arranged the raid on the legislature to begin with as there was reason to think that provincial politicians were possibly involved in the activities of Barinder Chohan and Alan Diwan. And while that hadn't gone anywhere, a connection to the

Federal Party had been established through the membership-purchasing scheme and the party member recruitment activities, particularly of Chohan. Finally, it had been established that Roger Kent had also worked for the federal Party, although from Murphy's investigations, it was thought at a very low level. He couldn't see why the cases were necessarily connected, although he agreed that it was possible someone very senior in the party could be calling the shots, so to speak, on both murders.

"But why," he asked them, "do you believe that?"

"I know it seems pretty nebulous, sir," Tim answered hesitantly, "but Roger Kent's regular trips to Vancouver were for a reason and we already have Barinder Chohan's confession that he was getting his directions from Kent. It's not hard to conclude that Kent was killed because someone didn't want to be identified, someone obviously very powerful who can arrange, on very short notice, to have a man murdered. Also, we're talking about someone who desperately wishes to remain anonymous, to the point he would kill, rather than be exposed as the ringleader for the relatively minor crime of arranging the purchase of party memberships."

"Okay, we know that, but what does that have to do with the latest killing?"

"It seems to me to be very likely that Henderson knew about this person's activities and perhaps much more that he doesn't want exposed. It could be that this person desperately wants to continue to influence the party in the future, even though they are no longer in power federally."

"All right, if you think your theory holds water, just who in the federal wing of the party would you suspect of these desperate crimes. You have to admit, Murphy, it's a little unlikely the average politician, in office or behind the scenes, would want power that desperately."

"Well, I'm at the point," Tim continued uncertainly, "where I have the names of the most senior officials and powerbrokers of the BC organization, together with their backgrounds. They are, without exception, wealthy and influential business owners, but as yet I don't know enough about their backgrounds to pinpoint any one individual, or even to suggest that one person is acting alone. I strongly believe that more than one is involved in the membership purchases, but for the murders, perhaps not. However, for orders to be carried out, less senior party people would need to be involved. It seems very apparent that Barinder Chohan tipped someone off about ratting on Kent, but it seems highly unlikely he would be working directly with the senior decision maker, or makers, and may not even have a clue who was directing the membership purchases, never mind the killings."

"Okay, Murphy, but where do you want to go with this? What are you suggesting we do next?"

"Let me keep digging into the backgrounds of these senior people in the party and see if I can discover anything. If I do, we may need to go to Vancouver to follow up. If we get to that point, sir, we will need to work with E Division and the Vancouver City Police."

"Alright, Tim, I will let Rita know what we are doing. Get to it."

AS USUAL, SUPERINTENDENT Chan was reluctant to see Inspector Fields broaden his investigation. Budget restrictions had been imposed even further than usual across the RCMP and she was having great difficulty maintaining even normal operations, never mind agreeing to one that crossed into another jurisdiction. There was another reason, however, that she was reluctant to disclose.

"Look, Errol," she began, "messing into the affairs of a major federal party is not very smart. I know the Progressives are out of office now, but they are still extremely powerful and they won't be too pleased if we start investigating their senior officials. Besides, we're dealing with a minority government situation and they could conceivably be back in power before you know it. And you think we have budget restrictions now?"

"I can't believe I'm hearing this. You're telling me we should back off from a murder investigation because it might affect our budget?"

"Don't be so naïve, Errol. It has to be handled discreetly and you should simply hand over all information to E Division as quickly as you discover it. It's their jurisdiction and they are quite capable of conducting their own investigation in their own city, for God's sake."

"Yeah, right. Like their investigation of the pig farm murders. That one took years and the police forces there still haven't learned to cooperate fully, in spite of all the work I did setting up joint investigation and enforcement units. Sometimes it seems like politics and budgets are more important than solving cases."

"Unless you can come up with a very good reason to get involved, I won't give you approval for sending anyone to Vancouver, or even ask if we can be part of the investigation away from the Island. Is that clear?"

"No, we wouldn't want to interfere in your own career advancement, would we?"

"Now you're bordering on insubordination. Get the hell out of my office and restrict yourself to Kent's murder. You don't seem to be accomplishing all that much there, never mind trying to involve the District in an out-of-town case."

As he left her office, in spite of his anger at her, he had to agree. There had to be something about Roger Kent they were overlooking.

TIM MURPHY was more than a little disappointed when informed by Inspector Fields he was to back off on his investigation of senior Progressive Party officials and restrict himself to the murder of Roger Kent. It seemed to him, especially after his talk with Roger's mother, that further investigation here was futile. Also, Tim knew that it was only a couple of weeks until Gloria was due to enter Vancouver General Hospital for her kidney transplant and he had hoped to kill two birds with one stone by arranging a secondment to the Vancouver investigation of Henderson's murder. It looked more and more as if he would have to arrange leave to be with her during her operation and recovery period.

Still, he was determined to do what he could in the meantime, and assuming he wasn't getting anywhere, he was sure he could always arrange his leave at the last moment. He decided to review what they had on Roger Kent and try and determine whether they may have overlooked anything. An obvious place to start was with the connection to the accountant, Bill Taylor. Perhaps his interest in Henderson's death and the various leads to the Progressive Party had coloured his thoughts. He probably should have pursued this one first, given that both Taylor and Kent had been murdered in Victoria. Who knows, there was good reason to think that all three murders were connected and perhaps he could still find the link that would lead him back to Vancouver.

Over the next few days, like a man swimming through molasses, he waded through all the information in the files related to Taylor's death. Like Kent, the man had been very discreet, and while Tim learned a lot more about money laundering techniques and operations, he found very little in the files that related to his personal life and connections that they didn't already know. It seemed that his accounting practice had acted as a good front, and unlike Kent, he maintained a large legitimate client base. Of course, he also had an even larger group of customers for whom he provided a more questionable service, including the Desperados, the party membership purchasers, and of course, Roger Kent. Now, if he could only find out what it was he was doing for Kent, in addition to looking after the books for his very modest insurance business.

Stubbornly, Murphy kept digging. Taylor's personal records showed he too was born and raised in Vancouver, and while Inspector Field's team had explored these connections in the earlier investigation of his murder, there was little in the files to go on. His records indicated he had grown up in a moderately well-to-do section of North Vancouver, but had attended a private school in the west end. Later, he had gone to UBC, majoring in Commerce and had followed this up by completing a Chartered Accountancy program. His documents also showed that he had moved to Victoria shortly after this and had been practicing in Victoria for quite some time. All in all, it was a pretty bland paper trail and very similar to the nondescript information he and Craig Ballard had gleaned on Roger Kent's personal life. They both appeared to be single hermits with almost no social life and with little regular contact with friends and families.

And then he wondered. The school Taylor had attended in Vancouver was none other than St. Albert's, the same school that Roger Kent had gone to. Comparing the files, Tim also learned they were the same age. Perhaps all this meant nothing, other than that they had known each other and this was all just another old boy's net that had naturally led to Bill becoming Roger's accountant. Except, of course, each had been engaged in illegal activities, each had been murdered and each had at least an indirect connection to the Progressive Party.

Tim was able to get a copy of the St. Albert school year-book from the microfiche files at the Victoria library, and sure enough, both were listed, although their pictures and descriptions provided nothing of interest. Oh, what a frustrating case, he thought to himself.

Methodically, he turned next to Taylor's contacts at the University and the Chartered Accountant School of Business. It was pedantic work, and while he was able to persuade the Inspector to assign Craig Ballard to assist him, their progress was very slow. For days, their time was spent conducting interviews of classmates by phone and attempting to learn about their social networks and course requirements.

One big item of interest was Taylor's part-time work assignments. It had been necessary for him to complete a number of these in order to meet the requirements of the business school. They were all listed, including ones with large Vancouver companies engaged in the retail sector, manufacturing, forestry and a huge conglomerate that, amongst others, included a shipping company, where he had completed a six-week stint. Again, in order to follow these up properly, Tim would need to go to Vancouver to interview the businesses that had engaged Bill Taylor so many years before.

Doggedly, he and Craig kept at it, interviewing contacts by phone. Finally, though, Gloria's appointment date approached and Tim was forced to apply for time off and leave the research work to Craig. It was more than a little frustrating to think that they were getting nowhere in finding Kent's killer. Meantime, the police in Vancouver were having no more success in tracking down the culprit who had done in Duncan Henderson. In a last bid to pull the cases together, Tim turned his attention back to the senior Progressive party officials in Vancouver.

Chapter 34

THE CAPTAIN AWOKE screaming from a very bad dream. In the dream, he was resting in his luxurious cabin on his motor yacht while on an extended ocean cruise. Looking up, someone was entering his bedroom unannounced. Three men silently made their way to his huge bed and gazed down at him accusingly. The men were Bill Taylor, Roger Kent and Duncan Henderson. Then The Captain noticed their faces. Taylor and Kent, instead of mouths, had large gaping holes in their throats. As he stared at them in trembling fear, the hole in each man began to widen and a vaguely familiar tune began to play, like an old juke-box which had been prompted by inserting a quarter. He recognized a few words from an old Who song: *looks like we're fooled again.*

Then he shifted his attention to Duncan Henderson. He was wearing a gas mask, which he slowly removed to expose a face with no nose. He said nothing to The Captain, but stared at him intently and kept moving his hand to his side and up to where his nose had been, over and over, like a clock pendulum, up and down, up and down.

Suddenly, all three men stopped their actions, turned quickly and left his cabin. The boat had become deathly still, but then a low rumbling noise came to him, followed by creaking, splintering and the snapping of wood. The cabin walls were squeezing inward, relentlessly moving toward his bed and diminishing the space around him. He lunged for the overhead hatch and pulled himself up onto the deck. Outside it was completely quiet and he could tell that he was alone on the boat. While millions of stars twinkled intently overhead, nothing else was visible: no lights, no crew, no shore, no boats, including his own lifeboats, nothing. And, of course, the yacht was slowly sinking.

As he awoke, his body drenched in sweat, The Captain realized what was happening. His vision for the province was being thwarted by incompetent underlings who couldn't seem to fulfill their responsibilities without bungling and acts of deception. Damn it, he had recruited the best, he had provided jobs and nurtured the loyalty of people he had known for many years. They would share in his ambitions. They could be powerful men, assisting him in controlling the destiny of the province and eventually the whole country. How could they all screw up when it meant so much? Why couldn't they all quite understand what would result from absolute control? Together, under his stewardship, they would ensure future prosperity for the nation, led by leaders who could count on unquestioning obedience from the public.

Yet, in spite of the setbacks, he knew he was still on the right track. He had control of the media in the province and soon he would control the provincial party in power. The public was apathetic and felt powerless after experiencing the effects of "lowest common denominator" globalization, the loss of control over the nation's wealth under "free" trade, reduced wages, the stripping of work benefits and the relentless propaganda by business-controlled government at all levels of society.

He was so close. To hell with his stupid dream, he decided. He could still make it all happen. He would increase his resolve yet again and keep his remaining key lieutenants on track. So he had lost a few bad apples. The rest were still loyal and he would move forward to gain his prime objective, total power. Step one would be to meet with Paul and get this business with his trouble-making wife, Maureen, resolved immediately. It would also be a good test of Paul's loyalty, the one person he trusted more than any other, with the possible exceptions of Michael Chan and Roy Carpenter. He would arrange to meet with him that very day.

IT WAS THE SAME DAY Gloria and Sheila were required to travel to Vancouver to prepare for their transplant operations. Tim had scheduled his leave to be with her, and Gordon had arranged to meet them later. Gloria and Sheila had decided to travel together and Tim had agreed to drive them. After picking up Sheila, they headed for the ferry terminal in time to catch the 2:00 p.m. sailing. The arrangement was for them to check in that evening, where they would be "prepped" for their respective operations, which would occur the following day. As they boarded and settled into their seats on the ferry, both Gloria and Sheila were feeling a mixture of excitement, apprehension and curiosity, which combined made them more than a little giddy.

"You know it's not too late to chicken out, Sheila," Gloria teased, knowing full well that Sheila's resolve was steadfast, and who was, at this stage, even more committed than Gloria was.

"No chance, my dear, it's merely routine. Why, in a matter of days I could be back at work, crashing cars with your accident-prone husband. Now, that's a much more scary thought than having a kidney removed."

"Hey, not so fast," Tim retorted. "The chances of anything going wrong through the operation and recovery period may be next to nothing, but it's still major surgery and you won't be running the 100-yard dash for a while after."

"That's quite all right with me. I haven't run that far since we went after those street racers who backed into us and took off by foot. I have no desire to do it again. What about you, Gloria? I bet I can make it down to your room after the operation before you can get to mine."

"No chance of that. There's a lot more to getting one of your kidneys out than there is to getting it hooked up inside of me.

They just plunk it into my abdomen, but with you they have to get at the kidney through the back, moving ribs and other organs out of the way."

"Yeah, but with the procedures they use now, they only make an incision big enough to pop the kidney out. Apparently my bikini scar will only be about four inches long. That's not even a good conversation starter as hardly anyone will notice it."

"It still takes time to recover. Some doctors downplay the process by referring to them as drive-by kidney transplants, but rest assured you won't be going home for a couple of weeks at best. In my case, however, I could be home within a week, if everything goes as planned."

"Is that so? Well, in that case, I have changed my mind," Sheila laughed.

"Oh well, back to the waiting list. What's another eight years of dialysis treatments?"

As they continued to talk, they teased each other about going shopping and dining while the other recovered and eventually sidetracked into a discussion of Vancouver amenities they hoped to take advantage of before returning to Victoria. Tim could sense how well they related to each other and contentedly settled into his own thoughts. Naturally, those thoughts soon turned to the homicide investigations and the research he hoped to accomplish while Gloria and Sheila convalesced.

Over the last few days at work, Tim and Craig had continued to conduct phone interviews with the academic institutions and businesses that Roger Kent and Bill Taylor had attended. The linkages between the men were established, but no headway was made in connecting them to others who may have been involved in their murders. Craig continued to plug away at it, but in spite of Inspector Field's orders, Tim began using more and more of his time to investigate the backgrounds of Progressive Party officials in Vancouver in order to discover a tie to either of the murdered men.

He had narrowed in on three senior officials. In addition to all being rich and powerful business owners, they were about the same age as Kent and Taylor, so perhaps they may have crossed paths earlier in life that would have led to one or both of them being recruited into active Progressive Party work. The three were Norton McCullough, Brenda Fox and Allan Carrigan, all graduates of UBC and all members of the party since they were students. At this point, he knew their formal academic and business backgrounds, and their positions, all very senior, within the party establishment. He did not know much about their private lives, however, other than learning that Fox was married with three children, while Carrigan and McCullough were both single. But what was perhaps more important, Bill Taylor had completed his Chartered Accountancy student work assignments with companies owned by each of the three. Here, he had concluded, was the connection he needed to focus on. But it would have to wait until after Gloria and Sheila had their operations.

They left the ferry just in time to face the oncoming bottleneck traffic streaming out of Vancouver heading for the Fraser Valley and the suburban communities from Surrey to Chilliwack. At least it was mainly heading the other way, but they were forced into narrowed access lanes as they approached the George Massey tunnel, narrowed so that one of their lanes could be opened to the homeward bound commuters. They crawled along slowly, finally reaching the Vancouver General Hospital after five o'clock. Conversation between the two women had petered out and they now sat silently, individually contemplating the next day's weighty events.

Tim had arranged for a hotel room at the Holiday Inn on West Broadway, a location that would be convenient to both the hospital and the university, where he hoped to conduct most of his research. After getting Gloria and Sheila registered and settled into their rooms at the hospital, he checked into his new home away from home. It was going to be expensive staying here, he realized, but he was prepared to pay the cost, rather than bunk in at the Mountie barracks at the training school, where he could be seen to be interfering with E Division's ongoing investigation of the Duncan Henderson murder. He would much rather be free to conduct his own investigation anonymously and with little chance that anyone would know what he was up to.

At any rate, the next day the operations went perfectly. Sheila's surgery team assembled and she was given an anaesthetic. Once she was completely unconscious, her left kidney, along with a piece of her kidney's artery and vein, was removed and placed on ice. Then it became Gloria's turn. After again applying an anaesthetic, an incision was made in her lower abdomen on her right side and a vein and artery accessed for blood flow. Once it was clear she was able to receive it, the kidney from Sheila was inserted and the bloodlines were connected. Soon blood was coursing smoothly through the organ like electricity flowing through a plugged-in kettle.

The following day, when both had recovered from the anaesthetic, Tim and Gordon, who had arrived earlier, were allowed to visit them. While she was still groggy, Tim could tell that Gloria was feeling very euphoric.

"I know this sounds silly, Tim, but I feel better already. I could even pee like you wouldn't believe this morning!"

"Well, you look pretty darn good, but I doubt you're ready for a stroll down to Sheila's room yet."

"No, but I bet I can make it by tomorrow, or the day after. I guess I will be pretty sore, but they are planning to get me to stand up later this afternoon."

"This is great, Gloria. I can't wait to take you home."

"Me too," she answered with a weak grin. "We've got to make up for some lost time."

"Get some rest, lady. You're going to need it."

TIM'S RESEARCH took him first to the headquarters of Fox's Realty, Brenda Fox's real estate company. It was early in the morning when he went to see her, too early to visit Gloria, who wouldn't be up to a visit until her nurse, lab technician, therapist and doctor all had a go at her, in that order. Tim wasn't sure how much time he would be able to spend with Mrs. Fox, but he wanted to finish his interview before noon, and she had agreed to see him at 8:30 a.m.

The Fox Realty headquarters was located in a huge office building on Georgia Street that was owned by another Brenda Fox company, Vixen Holdings. Fox's Realty had been a major player in the Vancouver area for over fifty years and had prospered under the astute marketing skills of Brenda's father, George. Brenda had taken over the company twenty years before. She was more of an organizer than her entrepreneurial father, and was able to steer the company forward as a result of her ability to hire the right people at the right time, allowing her to effectively manage the various functions of her burgeoning businesses.

Although it wasn't very far from his hotel, Tim had left early enough to allow himself plenty of time to fight his way through Vancouver's morning commuter traffic. The section of Georgia Street where the office building was located was an awesome place for a country boy like Tim. The street was a canyon of office towers sliced by a stream of traffic fighting its way into the downtown from its habitat in West and North Vancouver. Still, it was almost 8:30 a.m. by the time he found a parking lot meter willing to empty most of the bills from his wallet in order to park his car for a few hours. As he walked briskly to the towering office building, he couldn't help but crane his neck to stare at the uppermost floors of the imposing edifice. Nevertheless, he hurriedly made his way to the elevator and up to Brenda's huge corner office on the twenty-eighth story.

Brenda Fox was a quiet and gracious lady who, after he showed her his identification, welcomed Tim into her office. She led him to a corner alcove where, settled into comfortable lounge chairs in an L-shape arrangement, they gazed through the floor-to-ceiling windows at the view over Stanley Park and English Bay. Sipping contentedly on a steaming cup of coffee, Tim had difficulty in maintaining the firm inquisitive cop manner he hoped to use to gather the information he required.

"Thank you for agreeing to meet with me," he smiled. "As I explained in my call, I am investigating the recent murder of a man named Roger Kent and a possible connection to an earlier homicide investigation involving an accountant named Bill Taylor, who I understand may have once done a Chartered Accountant Program work assignment with your company. I think, to start us off, I would ask if you can recall him completing an assignment with you?"

"Oh, all these horrible killings. Just a few days ago the Vancouver police were here trying to get information connected to Duncan Henderson's murder. Now this. But, yes, I do recall Bill Taylor. I make it a practice to encourage my human resources people to take on students completing work assignments like that. I don't normally get involved myself, but because he also became an active member of the Progressive Party I can make the connection. I was so upset at the time when I heard he had been murdered."

"Would you happen to know how he became involved with the party? Had you recruited him?"

"Corporal, are you suggesting that Bill's murder had something to do with the party?"

"Frankly, ma'am, I can't be sure. At this stage, I am just trying to find out what I can about his background."

"I prefer Brenda. To answer your question, I am not sure how Bill got involved, or even what he did for us. I have to admit I am not that active, even though I have been on the BC executive of the federal Party for a long time. I go to a few meetings each year, particularly when an election is called, but I don't really get into the day-to-day stuff."

"Perhaps you might have some idea of what he might have done with others in the party or whom he may have reported to?"

"I know he did some campaign work in an earlier election, and it wasn't that long after he did the work assignment with my company. It seems to me he might have had some old boy's connection to one of the other executive members, probably through sailing. A couple of the senior members of the executive are good at bringing in fresh new blood that way."

"That could be helpful, ma'am, er Brenda. Can you give me their names?"

"Oh, I guess that would be all right. The most likely is Al Carrigan. He's an outgoing guy and has a knack for convincing his old classmates to become active in the party. I think he calls it press-ganging, as he probably had most of them as crew on his sailboat at one time or another."

"Okay. What about the other one?"

"It's much more unlikely, but that would be Norton McCullough, another sailor. He's a pretty cold fish, though, although he's probably the most powerful person in the party on the west coast. He seems to have a pretty good grip on party affairs, and at the very least might be able to give you more information than I can. Sorry, I should be able to tell you more. I do know that Bill was an earnest student and he probably became a very good accountant."

"What was the nature of his assignment with your company?"

"It had to do with setting up a system to manage our offshore accounts. We do a lot of listings with immigrants from places like Taiwan and Hong Kong. If I remember right, he was specializing in accounting for fund transfers between banks in different countries, with different exchanges and whatnot. It was all a mystery to me. Why, is it important?"

"Oh, probably not. I was just curious," Tim answered glibly. "Now, I would also like to know about Roger Kent. I understand he was also active in Party work here in Vancouver for awhile. Did you know him?"

"No, I don't believe so. Party workers come and go. There may be a record at party headquarters on Main Street. You could check there. Does he know Bill Taylor?"

"Did, ma'am. They went to school together. Now he's dead, too."

"Oh dear. How did he die?"

"He was murdered too, Mrs. Fox. Didn't the Vancouver Police mention that?"

"No. Oh, I am really out of the picture. I can't believe all this is happening."

Deciding he wasn't going to find out any more, Tim thanked her for her time and made his exit. He went back to his hotel and thought it over. He determined his best bet was to talk to McCullough first, glean what he could about the party's west coast operations and how Bill Taylor and Roger Kent fit into that. Then he would talk to Allan Carrigan, who he suspected was his man. He was pretty certain the "old boy" thing had to be the key and Carrigan seemed like the kind of man who could charm his associates into getting involved in political matters.

He then made arrangements for interviewing each man the next day. Allan Carrigan readily agreed to see him at 2:30 in the afternoon. It wasn't nearly as easy getting McCullough to agree to an appointment, but he finally granted him half an hour in his office early in the morning.

Chapter 35

WHEN THEY FOUND her body in the morning, the base of
the light bulb was clutched tightly in her hand. She lay spread in a
contorted position, her legs split a full 180 degrees apart, as if she
were in full stride when the asphalt interrupted her midair sprint.
Soon after the Victoria Police arrived, they determined that her
descent had begun from her fourteenth floor apartment behind
the legislature on Michigan Street. It was there they also found
the ladder and the empty light socket, and at first they jumped to
the wrong conclusion. It wasn't until they began their forensic
investigation that they decided to call in homicide, and because of
who she was, they also notified the RCMP. This time it was easy
for Inspector Fields to convince Superintendent Chan to call in
the joint homicide investigation team.

Immediately upon their arrival at the crime scene, Sergeant
Scandiffio and Constable Ballard were met by the Victoria Police
Department Forensic Officer, Corporal Roberta Whyte and her
superior, Sergeant Frank Schmidt. In his typical brusque manner,
Scandiffio began the conversation by asking Schmidt what they
knew so far.

"And a good morning to you, too, Mark. Would you like to
brief the good Sergeant and his sidekick, our very own Craig
Ballard, on what you have found so far, Roberta?"

"Good morning, Sergeant, hi Craig," she smiled weakly.
"Well, obviously you know who we have here, or you wouldn't
have been asked to become involved so quickly. But for the
record, the victim is Maureen Husband, Provincial Government
Cabinet   Minister   responsible   for   Children   and   Family

Development. Evidence gathered from the scene has so far determined that she died last night, I would guess around ten or eleven, from a cause that at first seemed to be accidental. On the surface, it appeared as if she simply fell while attempting to change a light bulb on her balcony. One could conjecture that she may have been changing the bulb so she could stay outside and take advantage of the unusually warm evenings we have been experiencing this summer."

"Seems reasonable," Mark agreed. "What caused you to think otherwise?"

"Well, for one thing, while it may seem logical to grip tightly onto any object in such a circumstance, no one would actually clutch a light bulb as they fell to their death from an apartment balcony. Forensic studies have shown that the natural human reaction is to reach out grasping for something to break your fall. As a result, ones hands would be empty and open in a futile search to find something to hang on to.

"Secondly, the pattern of the scattered light bulb fragments doesn't appear to jibe with what you would expect after smashing into the ground after such a rapid descent. The bulb should have shattered in a long, narrow, reasonably straight line in the direction the body was pointing when it hit the pavement in the parking lot, but instead they were simply scattered around the body as if they had been sprinkled there after the fall.

"Finally, many of the pieces should be quite small. In fact, in close to the body where the impact occurred, you would expect the glass to be ground almost to powder. But the pieces are larger, as if someone had broken the bulb by striking it on a hard object and then placing them around the body later."

"Anything else?"

"Yes. There is a severe contusion behind her right ear, as if the victim had been struck by a heavy object, which could have killed her, or at the very least, knocked her unconscious."

"Couldn't that have happened from the fall?"

"I don't think so, Sergeant, although that is what we were expected to believe. We know that the body landed upright in a spread-eagled position and there was no opportunity for her head to hit the ground in a manner to cause it to be bashed like that."

"Could she have struck it on the balcony as she fell?"

"That's possible, but there are no marks or tissue residue anywhere on the balcony to indicate that is what happened."

"So you definitely believe it was murder?"

"Let's just say that the death was suspicious enough to get you involved, Mark," Sergeant Schmidt interjected.

"Have you notified the media, Frank?"

"So far we have been able to keep it quiet. As you can see, the apartment is on the side facing Irving Park and away from the legislature. Also, a couple of cars blocked the view of her body from most of the apartment units, so that may explain why it took until almost eight-thirty this morning before anyone found her. An elderly lady noticed her when she went out to walk her dog in the park and she called us right away. So, except for the other apartment dwellers, who we have asked not to discuss the find, we have had all this time to investigate without having to make a statement of any kind."

"Okay. Let's recommend that we try and keep it quiet. When they do find out, simply say we are still investigating."

"Fair enough. As I understand it, your team is now in charge, so I will refer any media enquiries to the RCMP."

"Well, that should get them curious, but I guess we don't have much choice. Will you arrange for Corporal Whyte to join our team and continue her investigation? It looks like you have done some very good work here, Roberta."

"Thank you, Sergeant. I will be pleased to be part of your team."

AT ROUGHLY THE same time that morning, a dazed and bleary-eyed Paul Husband met with The Captain in his office.

"How did it go, Paul?" The Captain asked cautiously.

"Horribly. I can't believe you got me to do this."

"It was a joint decision, you know that, and it was necessary."

"I should have kept working on her. There must have been some way I could have convinced her it wasn't necessary to inform the Provincial Government about our membership strategies."

"Well, it wasn't so much the membership strategy, Paul. It was the fact you let it out to her that we were also buying votes and most especially that she suspected we might be planning to use the same techniques in the upcoming provincial election."

"I didn't tell her all that. She seemed to have figured it out from just observing my movements the last few months."

"Nevertheless, she knew, and that would have caused irreparable damage to our operation. You did the right thing."

"I know, I know. I just wish we hadn't had to kill her."

"I thought you said she was pretty miserable to live with. I think you are taking this harder than you need to. She's not the first we had to do away with and you got through the others okay."

"I didn't live with the others and I didn't have to be directly involved."

"What did you mean when you said it was horrible? Did Roy handle the job okay?"

"Yes, but it was horrible to watch him and to be part of it. He's so cold-blooded and matter-of-fact about it all. You would think he was taking out the garbage."

"Well, in a sense…uh, but did everything go as planned?"

"Yes. I took him to her apartment about nine-thirty, as we agreed, and I made sure that no one saw us. Maureen was preparing for a Cabinet meeting that was to have taken place today, so she didn't expect us, but she let us in without complaining too much. I explained that Roy was a good friend from university that I hadn't seen in many years and we ran into each other at a party meeting I had come over to attend. She accepted that, even though she was surprised I hadn't told her I was coming to Victoria."

"Did Roy take long to complete the job?"

"No. He said he didn't wish to leave any clues that we had been there, so I simply asked her if she would make us a cup of tea. While she was filling the kettle, he struck her with the revolver he was carrying under his jacket. Then he carried her out to the balcony, looked around for about half a minute and simply threw her over into the parking lot."

"What about the light bulb change?"

"Well, I knew the utility ladder was there in the hall closet and we left it lying next to the balcony, along with the burned out bulb I brought with us. Then we went down to the parking lot after ensuring we had left no signs of our visit. There we scattered the bulb after breaking it on the pavement near her body and then we squeezed her fingers around the base before we left."

"Did anyone recognize you at any time, either in Victoria or during the crossings?"

"No. Also Roy and I travelled separately. I caught the first ferry at seven and he waited for the eight o'clock sailing. After we docked I came straight here."

"It all sounds good so far. Do you have an alibi for last night?"

"Yes, Leif agreed that I was with him until about twelve o'clock downtown at the pub in the Prince Edward Hotel. He even went there with a guy from the Federal Party who looks like me, in case we need it later. Leif didn't much want to do it but I convinced him I know more about his part in the BC Ferries bribery case than he would like the police to be aware of."

"Okay, so go get some rest and prepare yourself for the inevitable police interview."

All in all, The Captain decided, another important detail had been taken care of. While they would all have to lay low for a month or two, he expected they could still proceed with their plans for the provincial Party without further interference. That is, if he could figure out what this RCMP Corporal from Victoria was after and how he might deal with him. He could only hope that he was merely poking at the very cold ashes of the Bill Taylor case and his calling him at this time was merely an awful coincidence. If so, he wasn't about to give the Horseman anything he could use to fan the flames.

AFTER HIS INTERVIEW with Brenda Fox, Tim had been able to be with Gloria the rest of the day. He was amazed at how quickly she was improving, and although she was still very sore, she had been able to get out of bed. She was still hoping to take that stroll down to Sheila's room sometime that very afternoon.

"Maybe you will even be here and can walk down with me?"

"I'm all yours until they kick me out," Tim assured her.

Tim sat with her while she periodically dozed, only to wake every twenty minutes or so to talk excitedly about anything that came to mind, including the strange dreams the after effects of her anaesthetic were still giving her. Finally, about three o'clock, the therapist arrived to get her out of bed again.

Gloria dreaded the thought of the pain and soreness, but she was determined to recover quickly, and she was assured by the therapist that getting out of bed and moving around was the quickest way to do that. Once on her feet, her intravenous pole providing support, she very slowly moved across the room.

"Are you okay?" Tim asked apprehensively. "Do you feel dizzy or anything?"

"No, Tim, I'm fine," she answered with a grimace. "Let's go."

"Can she do this?" Tim asked the therapist. "She wants to walk down the hallway."

"Sure. Just stay close to her and come right back if she gets light-headed or wants to sit or lie down."

Slowly, oh so slowly, they inched their way forward down the long corridor. Gloria knew that Sheila's room was about fifty feet away, four rooms down on the opposite side of the hallway. Then, looking up, Tim saw a strange apparition coming toward them. Dressed in a blue hospital gown and dragging along with her own pole was an equally determined Sheila York.

"It's a tie!" Sheila grinned weakly as they finally came together. "But I bet I can get a discharge before you."

"Well, you've both done damn well," said Tim, "but I think you better get back to your beds before *I* faint. I swear this is harder on me than it is on you two."

The hours seemed to fly by as he sat with Gloria the rest of the afternoon, but by 7:30 p.m. she was sound asleep and Tim was convinced to let her rest for the night. After a late supper, he was so tired he went straight to bed. Before falling asleep he managed to listen to the ten o'clock news report, including an item reporting the death of Provincial Cabinet Minister Maureen Husband, who had apparently fallen from her James Bay apartment in Victoria. There was no indication the death had been in any way suspicious.

AT 8:00 A.M. THE following morning, Tim was escorted into Norton McCullough's huge office. The grim businessman and senior party official brusquely directed him to the chair facing his expansive desk.

"My time is limited, Corporal. I understand you are following up on a very old investigation into the death of an accountant in Victoria. Now, how could I possibly be of help to you in such a matter?"

"Well, sir, there's a couple of reasons why you might be able to help," the instantly irritated Mountie began. "To begin with, the accountant's name, as I mentioned on the phone, was Bill Taylor. You should know him as he used to work for the party here in Vancouver before he moved to Victoria. Also, as a Chartered Accountant student, he was hired by your company to complete a work assignment."

"Do you know how large this company is, Corporal? I couldn't possibly keep track of all the people who have done part-time work here over the years."

"What about the party work? Someone had to have recruited him."

"Well, as you probably know, the party has a lot of volunteers, even more than my company has employees," he shrugged.

"I don't recall mentioning he was a volunteer, Mr. McCullough. How would you know that?"

"Because if he was a staff member, I would very likely know him. The party doesn't have that many paid employees."

"Fair enough. Now, how about Roger Kent, another volunteer, I believe?" Tim detected just the slightest twitch before McCullough slowly answered.

"Now, that one I seem to recall," he answered cautiously. "I can remember someone by that name doing some party membership work. But that was quite awhile ago and I don't remember seeing him for quite some time. Why do you bring his name up? Is he a suspect in your investigation of Taylor's murder?"

"No, sir. He was also murdered in Victoria. Quite recently, as a matter of fact. I am surprised you hadn't heard about it."

"Not everything that happens in Victoria makes the news here in Vancouver, Corporal Murphy."

"Still, it's interesting that each of these men once worked as volunteers for the Progressive Party here in Vancouver, wouldn't you think?"

"Life is full of coincidences, Corporal."

"So, you wouldn't have had anything to do with recruiting either of these men to the party?"

"Nothing whatsoever, and if you are finished, I must get on with my day."

"Oh, just one other thing," Tim added, as he rose to leave. "Do you do any sailing?"

"Sure, all the time. Why?"

"Oh, I was just wondering. I will find my own way out."

SERGEANT SCANDIFFIO met with his homicide team the morning after Maureen Husband's body was found. Roberta Whyte's continuing research and investigation had made her more certain than ever that Husband had been murdered. The Sergeant decided it was time to get moving and he quickly assigned them to their tasks. It would be up to Craig Ballard to travel to Vancouver to inform Paul Husband of the circumstances of his wife's death. Maureen's sister, Helen, who lived in Victoria, had already agreed to identify her body. While interviewing him, Craig was also to carefully check out Husband's alibi. Too many deaths were connected to the Progressive Party to rule anyone out of their investigation.

Craig arranged for the interview and caught an early afternoon ferry. He arrived at Tsawwassen on another unseasonably warm afternoon and drove his car to Paul's office in the federal Progressive Party's humble headquarters on Main Street. There was only a small nondescript sign on the door to denote the occupants. As he stepped inside, the plain furnishings and drab surroundings also seemed to reflect an intention to disguise the prestige of the power-brokers who met here.

The receptionist smiled politely and asked Craig to wait while she personally walked to an open door only a few yards from her desk, knocked on the doorframe and announced his arrival. The small wiry-looking man who came forward to welcome Craig didn't appear to bear the countenance of one burdened by the very recent death of a loved one. He led Craig to his small windowless office and beckoned him to a chair beside his desk. Craig took the initiative before Husband could speak and quickly expressed his regrets for his wife's recent death.

"Yes, I am afraid I am still numb from the awful news, Constable. I tried to stay home and absorb it all, but there are just too many reminders of her. I came here, hoping to bury myself in work, but I must admit that's not working either."

"Still, it must be hard just to make an appearance. I must say I truly admire your fortitude."

"Well, thank you, Constable. We all have different ways of trying to cope, I suppose. Now, how can I help you? I must say I am a bit surprised that the City of Victoria would send someone over to personally notify me of Maureen's death. You do know that your Chief called me yesterday morning, right after she was officially identified by her sister, Helen?"

"Yes, he made me aware of that. Well, I'm afraid to say, Mr. Husband, that my being here is more than an official notification. It's not easy to say this, but we have reason to believe that your wife was murdered."

Paul Husband went very white and remained expressionless for what seemed to Craig a very long time before replying. "Murdered?" he finally gasped. "But why? Who could want to murder her?"

"That's what I've been asked to assist in finding out. I have been attached to a homicide investigation team to explore the circumstances of her death and to answer that very question."

"Alright," Paul slowly replied. "But how could she have been murdered? Your Chief said she had fallen off her apartment balcony."

"The evidence seems to indicate that she didn't fall."

Paul slumped forward and buried his head in his hands. "Oh, my God, how could this be?" he sobbed.

"Can you think of anyone who would want to see her dead?" Craig asked gently, watching Paul's reaction carefully.

"No, no, of course not. Oh sure, there are threats sometimes from people who think that the Provincial Government should be doing more for them. Children and Family Development is not the most popular ministry in the province, but I couldn't begin to imagine anyone going to that extreme. But what happened to Maureen? Was she pushed?"

"I'm sorry, but I can't really go into the details, Mr. Husband. The investigation is still ongoing and it's too early to make definite conclusions, except, as I have said, that foul play is evident. What about in the party? Did she have any enemies there that you know of?"

"No. Well, we don't, I mean didn't, talk about it much, but the political parties at the two levels aren't much connected and she might have some enemies that I wouldn't know about."

"So, was this a source of friction? Is there an animosity between the two party levels and two levels of government?"

"I didn't mean that. I simply meant that we agreed not to bring work home all the time. Sure, there's some competition between the parties, canvassing for funds, recruiting good candidates, that sort of thing. But nothing like you're suggesting."

"I'm not suggesting anything, Mr. Husband, just trying to determine whether there is someone who would like to see her dead. It's my job to explore all the leads."

"Yes, I know. I'm sorry, but I can't think of anyone who would want to kill her."

"Now, just for the record. Can you tell me where you were two nights ago, when she was murdered?"

"You don't think I did it, Constable? Why would I? I would have had nothing to gain."

"I'm merely eliminating possibilities, Mr. Husband. As you know, your wife is not the first politician in the province to be murdered recently. Do you have an alibi for the night in question?"

"What are you getting at, Constable? Are you implying now that there is a connection between Maureen's death and that of Duncan Henderson's?"

"As I said, Mr. Husband, I am merely eliminating possibilities."

"For Christ's sake, call me Paul. Yes, I have a goddamn alibi, as you insist on calling it. I was at a local pub that night with The Capt, no, I mean …. Damn, now you're getting me all upset. I was at the Prince Eddy drinking with a couple of friends. Call Leif Johannsen if you don't believe me. He was with me."

"I haven't said I didn't believe you, Paul," Craig said soothingly. "Could you tell me how long you were there, please?"

"Quite awhile, I'm afraid," Paul smiled thinly, regaining his composure. "We went there about eight-thirty and stayed until close to midnight. The peelers were putting on a pretty good show."

"Okay. Now who's this man you were referring to, The Cap, I think you said?"

"No, no. I have been working closely on a project here in the office lately with another party official who goes by the moniker The Captain. The name doesn't mean anything. It just came out because we've been working together."

"Alright. Well, I guess that's all for now. Thank you for your cooperation, and once again, my condolences. If you think of anyone who might have wanted your wife dead, please don't hesitate to call me."

"I will be sure to, Constable. I hope you get whoever did it."

"I'm sure we will, Mr. Husband. I'm sure we will."

Craig left Paul's office, smiled his goodbye to the receptionist and went out to the street. He waited about a minute on the sidewalk before going back inside. Paul Husband's office door was now closed.

"I wonder if you can help me?" he asked the receptionist politely. "I need to go to Waterfront Road and I have to admit I don't know the city that well. Could you give me directions?"

"That's an easy one," she laughed. "Just follow Main Street downtown and when you get to the end you will be there."

"Oh, of course, thank you," he laughed. "Also, Paul gave me the name of someone I should talk to. He told me his name, but I have already forgotten it and I didn't write it down. Sometimes I don't think I'm a very good police officer. But he did refer to him as The Captain?"

"That would be Norton McCullough. I don't think he likes his name very much, so he chooses to be referred to as The Captain."

"Does he come to the office here a lot?"

"Hardly ever. But he sure seems to know the party well. Everyone here is always saying, 'well, I better ask The Captain,' or 'I'll check that one with The Captain' or 'The Captain will know.' For a man who's so invisible, he sure seems to run the place."

"Well, I've sure heard the name Norton McCullough before. He's a pretty well known businessman, isn't he?"

"He sure is. And probably one of the richest men, if not the richest, in the province. You would think he would have too much to do to spend so much time on party stuff."

"Well, thank you, miss. You have been very helpful."

"Oh, you're welcome. Have a nice day."

"I'm sure I will," Craig answered with a huge smile. "I'm sure I will."

Chapter 36

NOW IT WAS TIME for Tim to get ready for his interview with Allan Carrigan. He still felt very sure that Carrigan was behind the murders. In spite of McCullough's seemingly scanty knowledge of Taylor and Kent, his unhelpful manner and his flippant remarks, it appeared to Tim that the man wasn't the type who could persuade anyone to volunteer for anything. Nevertheless, in spite of McCullough's remark about coincidences, it had to be more than a fluke that people connected to the federal Progressive Party were dying like flies and McCullough must know more than he was letting on. He hadn't even commented on Henderson's death, which was a bit of a puzzle, as surely the Vancouver police would have talked to him about it by now.

Tim also knew he wasn't supposed to stick his nose into the Vancouver investigation, but somehow he had to find out what they had learned so far. If he pressed his own suspects too much, one of them was sure to complain about police harassment and he knew he couldn't risk Inspector Fields wrath, which would lead to a direct order to stop what he was doing immediately. He would keep his fingers crossed and hope to hit pay dirt with Carrigan.

Tim's research had allowed him to learn that Carrigan, like McCullough, was involved in a number of different enterprises, many of them having to do with transportation. Amongst others, he had an import-export company, a shipping operation and a healthy chunk of the rail interests in the province. Tim couldn't help but think that he and McCullough must be business rivals in spite of working together as senior officials in the B.C. wing of the federal Progressive Party.

Allan Carrigan's office building was also close to the water. I guess it was logical, Tim thought, that wealthy business types would enjoy the prestige that went with a large upper story office looking over the harbour and the mountains, especially when they were also into sailing. But didn't any of them like to look over the city streets where the workers were bustling about, making them even richer? He decided he was just jealous and would give up an eyetooth to have the same view of the world.

Carrigan's greeting had to be the friendliest of the three. While Brenda Fox had been pleasant and polite, Carrigan acted as if Tim were a long lost buddy, which was rather odd, as he was here to determine if Allan was a multiple murderer. Of course, Carrigan couldn't know that. Tim had used the same routine on the phone as he had with the others – that he was here to follow up on some new leads in a very old investigation.

"Sit down, sit down," he said, leading Tim to a couch and chair in a corner of his office. Carrigan beckoned a secretary to bring them coffee before Tim could politely decline. "Now, how can I help you, Corporal?"

Tim went through the same routine as he had with Brenda Fox and Norton McCullough. Finally he got to the point where he asked if he had anything to do with the recruitment of either Taylor or Kent. That's when the surprises started.

"Oh, no," he answered assuredly. "It would have been Norton who got them involved. He has a way of press-ganging his old school and college cronies into joining the party. Especially in Bill Taylor's case. He would have had their time in University to work on him. Taylor was often crew for Norton in those days on his sailboat. Norton and I used to race competitively and he usually beat me, simply because he was so determined and because he had a way of getting his crew to take it all so damn seriously. Bill Taylor was one of them and he was as serious as Norton about it all."

"What about Roger Kent? He was never in university, I believe?"

"No, Roger was with us well before Bill arrived. I think Norton relied on their schoolboy connections to persuade Roger to join us."

"So, Roger was an active volunteer for the party here in Vancouver, even before McCullough completed his university years?"

"That's right, but you have to remember that Norton and I have been involved with the Progressive Party for a very long time. In my case, it goes back to a high school debating class that got me started. Norton, on the other hand, was simply following in his father's footsteps and carrying on the family tradition."

"But Kent didn't stay with the party?" Tim asked, trying to steer the conversation back to the homicide investigation.

"Well, I am not sure about that. He moved to Victoria, but I think he kept his connections to The Captain after he left. Another party member, Paul Husband, who is closer to Norton than I am, mentions his name once in a while."

"Wait a minute, who's this Captain you referred to?"

"Why, Norton of course. He hates the name Norton, so he has tried to insist that everyone refer to him as The Captain. The way he says it, even the 't' in 'the' sounds like it should be capitalized. Of course, I try not to use it in his presence because I know he hates to be called Norton, so I make a point of calling him that."

"Interesting. Now, you also mentioned Paul Husband. Is he not the husband of Maureen Husband, the Provincial Cabinet Minister that died in a fall in Victoria only two days ago?"

"The very same. He looks after recruiting new party members across the province, an area that Norton and he take a special interest in."

"What about you, Mr. Carrigan? What party affairs do you take a special interest in?"

"Oh, for me it's the party organization. Party constitution, riding matters, conventions, that sort of thing."

"You and Norton McCullough seem to be the driving forces in the party's west coast operations? You must work very closely at times."

"At times, although it's always been a bit of a chore. We don't always see eye-to-eye. We worked hard during the last campaign to get the right people into the constituency executive positions, especially riding presidents. Norton's methods are sometimes a little brutal and he makes things difficult, although we were both very much in agreement to do what we could to ensure we ran candidates who supported our ex-Prime Minister."

"So, the two of you are brutal enough to remove anyone who may interfere with your plans, including at last count, two party workers and one party MP who defected to the new governing party?"

"Is that what you think, Corporal? Christ, Taylor's death goes back now a couple of years and you can't possibly believe you can link Kent's and Henderson's deaths? They had nothing to do with each other. I'm not even sure Kent was still with the party. I can't accept that you think that this is all connected!"

"Why not? Are you telling me it's just a coincidence so many individuals connected to the party have been murdered? What about McCullough? Is he brutal enough?"

"Why would he be? The man has more money than he can ever possibly need. Sure, he likes power and he lords it over everyone. But I really don't see him killing people, just to get his own way. There must be another explanation."

"Maybe there is, Mr. Carrigan. Oh, just one more thing. How did it come about that Bill Taylor completed a work assignment for you during his days as a chartered accountant student? I understand he also completed assignments with Brenda Fox and

Norton McCullough. You have to admit, that's more than a coincidence."

"It wouldn't have been that strange for him to use his party connections to get those jobs, Corporal. Nor would it have hurt him to have gone to university with Norton and Norton's own Financial Officer, Michael Chan. That's what the old boy's club is all about."

"Well, thank you for your time, Mr. Carrigan. I am sure we will talk again."

"Good luck with your investigation, Corporal Murphy. I am confident you will find that Bill Taylor's death had nothing to do with the party."

"I wish I shared your confidence, Mr. Carrigan. We shall see."

As he left Carrigan's office, Tim reviewed what he had learned. Tim was surer than ever that there was a very close connection between the three deaths. And while he was still uncertain whether Carrigan was being straight with him, he had to assume that Norton McCullough had been lying through his teeth. If Carrigan's story held up, McCullough knew both Taylor and Kent very well indeed. He would need to check out this link to a common high school. He hadn't noticed if McCullough was a student at St. Albert's earlier, but then he had no reason to look for it. And what about these close university ties to Kent, including sailing together in races?

He should talk to Paul Husband next. It appeared the man was close to Norton McCullough and he could probably shed some light on the case, as he had been involved in the membership side of the party. And wasn't it buying party memberships that partially got Tim started on this investigation so long ago? Finally, was it simply just another coincidence that Husband's wife had just died a violent death, even though at this point there was nothing Tim knew that would lead him to believe it was anything more than an accident? He would have to be very circumspect. Inspector Fields would be terribly unhappy if he knew how much Tim was getting involved in the Vancouver side of the investigation.

AS HE LEFT the west coast headquarters of the Progressive Party, Craig Barlow was thinking, "The Captain, The Captain, where have I seen that before?" Then it came to him. Wasn't that the nickname of one of Kent and Taylor's classmates at St. Albert's school? He was sure he could remember seeing it in the school year-book when he had reviewed it as part of his and Tim Murphy's research on the two murdered party workers.

He drove as quickly as he could to St. Albert's school. As normal, traffic was heavy. It was close to 4:00 p.m. and he had to hurry before all the staff left for the day. The school was located on West 7th, not far from the Kitsilano area. It was in a secluded location, surrounded by Lombard poplars and set well back from the street. There were two main buildings, a long, low single-story shed-like affair and a two-story structure, neither of which were particularly pleasing to the eye.

Craig wound down the long paved driveway and into an oversized parking lot, almost empty of automobiles. He hurried to the main door of the two-story building, fronting a sign indicating that the school's administration office was located here. Immediately inside the doors, a large receptionist counter signified that he was in the right place. Craig identified himself and explained his request to a slightly annoyed fiftyish-looking woman obviously making preparations to leave. She quickly directed him to a computer station after assuring him it would be unlikely he would easily find a hard copy of the year-book he was searching for. She sat impassively, offering little assistance as he fumbled his way through the school's internal website to locate the school's history and finally the year-books, going back to the early 1920s.

He found the year he was looking for easily enough and turned to the grade 12 class. Sure enough, Roger Kent and Bill Taylor were there, although their pictures didn't look the same as he remembered. But no Norton McCullough and no one nicknamed The Captain. "What now?" he thought. Perhaps he would find them all in the grade 11 class. There they were again, and this time a stern, gangling and lonely-looking Norton McCullough was there as well. The caption on him quickly made the point. A brilliant hard-working student, the write-up explained, who would likely be among the few students who would write their senior matriculation exams this year. It went on to describe how he still managed to find plenty of time to pursue his passion for sailing, to the point that he preferred to be known as The Captain. His lack of popularity was perhaps hinted at because the legend went on to indicate that most students nevertheless called him Nort.

Craig profusely thanked the very fidgety receptionist for her patience and left the school triumphantly. The connection was now impossible to ignore. He left the school, drove into Kitsilano and found a phone book in a large Consumer's drug store. He found the number for McCullough's shipping company and was soon connected to his office secretary. He explained who he was and that it was urgent for him to meet with her boss.

"My goodness," she exclaimed, "Mr. McCullough is certainly popular with Victoria police officers today. This morning it was an RCMP Corporal and now a City of Victoria Constable. But I'm very sorry, Constable Ballard. Mr. McCullough has left for the day. In fact, you were fortunate I was still here as it's getting close to six. Perhaps you will find him at his home in West Vancouver. I remember he commented as he left that he'd had a very trying day and he thought he would skip sailing tonight and just relax at home."

Craig wondered if she would chat all night. Perhaps she was just lonely, or is one of those people who are overly helpful, he thought. He cut in and asked for directions to Norton's home, having decided an element of surprise, rather than a formal appointment, might be in order. She readily supplied the directions.

Finally Craig asked, "By the way, who was the Corporal from the RCMP?"

"I have it right here," she replied promptly. "It was a Corporal Tim Murphy, and I believe he said he was looking for some information related to an old case in Victoria that Mr. McCullough might be able to help him with."

"Well, I very much appreciate your help, miss. By the way, is Mr. McCullough ever referred to as The Captain?"

"Oh, all the time. For business, I am required to call him by his formal surname. But people close to him call him that. In fact, I know he encourages it. Would you like to be called Norton?"

"I see your point, miss. Thank you again for your help."

"You're welcome, Constable, and please, just call me Prudence."

IT WAS VERY LATE in the afternoon when Tim located the phone number for the Progressive Party offices and called Paul Husband to arrange an interview. In spite of the time, Husband was still in his office and agreed to see Tim right away. As he drove to the headquarters, Tim decided it was kind of odd that a man grieving over a very recently deceased wife would be at work, but then everyone seemed to have their own way of coping with personal loss. When he arrived, Paul escorted him into his small busy office and nodded to the plain, hard-backed chair next to his desk.

"Look, I understand the need for the police to conduct a homicide investigation, but was it really necessary for the Victoria City Police and the RCMP to both question me on the same day?"

What's he talking about, thought Tim? I haven't said anything about homicide. Was Maureen Husband's death now considered a murder as well? That wasn't indicated on the report he had heard on the news earlier. He would have to do some fast thinking.

"Uh, my condolences, Mr. Husband, and my apologies, but we just need some follow-up information."

"Well, I don't know what I can tell you that I didn't already share with Constable Ballard earlier."

Craig Ballard was here, thought Tim. Obviously Mrs. Husband's death is connected to the larger investigation and Inspector Fields sent him over to find out what he can about the circumstances of her death. I should be treating Paul Husband as a suspect, he realized. Perhaps he could start with the connection between Paul and The Captain. After all, their joint involvement with party memberships was certainly connected to Roger Kent and maybe Craig hadn't gone too far down that road. At the very least, it would bring his reason for being here back to his part of the whole investigation. Paul Husband was now eyeing him curiously.

"I've just come from a chat with The Captain," he began slowly, knowing that certainly Paul would use that name for him. "He tells me you two work very closely together."

Immediately, Husband turned very pale and cut in excitedly. "Look, I already told Ballard that The Captain wasn't there. It was Leif Johannsen who was with me at the Prince Eddy the night she was killed. You guys should be talking to him, not The Captain."

Tim had no idea what Paul was talking about, but the look on his face and this strange reaction to what Tim thought was an innocuous lead-in question meant he had struck some kind of chord. Was he trying to confirm some kind of alibi and why had Craig tied Maureen's death to her husband and The Captain?

"Well, I guess if The Captain wasn't with you and can't provide an alibi for you, then you can't provide one for him, can you?"

"Why would The Captain have anything to do with Maureen's death? He doesn't have anything to do with her."

"No, but you do," Tim continued, thinking hard and fast. "Maybe you have been blabbing little pillow talk secrets and The Captain found out about it. Maybe you even admitted to him that you'd told her more than you should. And just maybe that got The Captain worried. Enough people who know your dirty little secrets have been killed already, that one more wouldn't make any difference."

"That's ridiculous," Paul answered too quickly, his face now having turned an ashen white. "I don't tell her anything about what we are doing."

"So, you admit to having dirty little secrets? Just tell me one thing, Paul. What are the two of you up to that is worth killing so many people over, even your own wife, for god sakes?"

"Nothing, we're not up to anything," Paul yelled fearfully. "Leave me alone! I didn't do it, I didn't do it," he sobbed.

"I think you did, Paul, and you will be much better off to tell me about it. I am sure you know now that we will find out anyway. This alibi of yours sounds a little too pat."

"I have nothing to tell you. And anything else I have to say will be said with my lawyer present," Paul answered, regaining his composure. "Now I would ask you to leave my office."

"Only one more thing, Paul. Until our next conversation, it will be in your best interests to keep all this to yourself, unless of course, other police officers also wish to interview you. Now, before I go, I need McCullough's home address."

"There's little point. He won't talk to you outside of his office."

"Let me worry about that."

"It's your funeral," he shrugged. "He's in West Vancouver at 4280 Desman Drive."

"Thank you, Paul. Our next conversation will be very soon and it will be at the police station." Tim quickly rose and left a shaken Paul Husband standing dazed by his open door.

Tim had to get to Craig and he had to get to him fast. But where was he? Damn, why did he leave his cell phone back in Victoria? As quickly as he could, he found a payphone and called dispatch at RCMP District Headquarters in Victoria. He was told that Craig had been sent to Vancouver to inform Paul Husband of his wife's murder and to question him in order to determine whether Paul should be considered a suspect in her death. District Headquarters then assured Tim that they had no idea where Craig was now as he had not reported in. However, this wasn't considered unusual, as he probably had nothing of interest to say and he was very likely making his way back to Victoria on the ferry as they spoke. Tim asked about the circumstances of Maureen Husband's death. The dispatcher, Chit Batra, then asked about Gloria's operation and after an abbreviated chitchat, they hung up.

Chit then found a temporary replacement, left the office and called The Captain's home on a payphone. He told him about Craig's call and that he wondered whether both Craig and Tim might be investigating Maureen's death. The Captain thanked him, told him he was pleased to receive the information and that he had also talked to Corporal Murphy earlier and his questions seemed to be of a routine nature. Nevertheless, The Captain then wondered why Murphy had ostensibly questioned him about a very old case when such a fresh one, connected indirectly to him, would go ignored. In fact, Murphy had said nothing about Maureen's death, which, come to think of it, had to be very curious. He would have to find out what Corporal Murphy was really up to.

Chapter 37

IT WAS WELL AFTER SIX when Craig set out for West Vancouver and the large estate of Norton McCullough. The traffic had thinned out considerably as he crossed the Burrard Street Bridge. Looking ahead, the West Vancouver office towers gleamed like sharks teeth in the brilliant glare of the setting sun. As he drove off the bridge and motored through the heart of the city, a few tardy office workers scurried to bus stops and parking lots, hoping to get home in time to salvage at least some of the pleasant early fall evening. Craig's thoughts, however, were a few miles away and focussed solidly on the case and his important rendezvous with the man who called himself The Captain.

He pondered how to deal with the man. He had enough information now to suggest that McCullough was the mastermind of a scheme to manipulate the fortunes of the Progressive Party on the west coast. What was it the receptionist had said? "For a man who's so invisible he sure seems to run the place." But while he had information to tell him that The Captain was behind the moves, everything was circumstantial. If he was behind the party membership purchases and was ordering killings, no one was saying so. Nor could he see any good reason for such drastic actions. In fact, what did he really have on the man, other than a hint that he may have helped Paul Husband arrange an alibi while Paul set about killing his wife? And he was a long way from being able to prove that as well. Oh well, he thought, a good bluff might at least get him through the door.

Craig followed Lions Gate Bridge Road as it sliced through Stanley Park and across the magnificent First Narrows overpass.

The sun had almost slipped below the horizon and the light was beginning to fade as he turned left on Marine Drive and into West Vancouver. Along the water, the large mansions of Vancouver's millionaires came and went from view as the road followed the wavy coastline along West Bay and Sandy Cove. Eventually, he spotted the circular Desmond Drive that brought him to the gates of The Captain's place. Far down an arrow-straight driveway bordered by large weeping willow trees covered in shimmering golden leaves, he could see the house sprawling along the shore with a magnificent view of Point Grey across the water to the south.

Craig sucked in his breath and buzzed the intercom. He provided his identification to the voice that promptly answered and explained that he wished to see The Captain on a police matter of some urgency.

"You will have to be more specific, Constable," the voice replied curtly. "The Captain is not in the habit of granting impromptu audiences to anyone calling without proper notice."

"Tell him I am checking an alibi for Paul Husband in an investigation of his wife's death. Tell him I apologize for seeing him at home, but that I have come from interviewing Husband and I would like to confirm the alibi before I return to Victoria on the last ferry this evening."

"Just a minute," came the answer, and Craig was left to ponder the silence. Finally, after what seemed to be a very long time, but was in fact only about four minutes, the gate clicked and slowly slid quietly open. Paul nosed cautiously forward and just as quietly the gate closed behind him. Ahead, a man stood beside the driveway and beckoned Craig to stop. Paul could see a small replica of the house on the beach behind the man, partially hidden in huge fir trees that seemed to cover much of the massive waterside estate. Quietly the man slid in beside Craig and pointed to the estate without a word. Craig drove up the circular roundabout in front of the main entrance where his silent passenger bid him to stop.

As they walked up to the large double doors, a much older version of the stern boy in the year-book stood in the wide doorway. After carefully studying Craig's identification, he ordered him to follow him into the house. He led Craig to a large sunken den-like room filled with ornate furniture, large pictures of sailing boats and display cases full of trophies. Everything reflected a nautical theme. Even the fireplace, constructed of large stones and a mantel made out of driftwood, was covered in chunks of fishing net attached with round white-painted floats, all interspersed with dull grey sausage-shaped sinkers. Definitely a bachelor's room, thought Craig, as The Captain beckoned him to a cushion-covered wicker chair behind a low beachwood coffee table.

Sitting himself directly across from Craig, he asked bluntly, "Now, tell us what you know, Constable. What's this about an alibi for Paul Husband?"

Craig immediately found the man irritating. Acting recklessly on some instinctive intuition, he abandoned his carefully rehearsed plan to gradually tie The Captain to Husband's alibi and went for the jackpot. "That was to get me in the door, Mr. McCullough. I'm sure you will not be pleased to know that your trusted friend Paul Husband is accusing you of being behind his wife's murder. He tells me he has a good alibi for the night of her death, but that I should ask you about yours."

"That's all very amusing, Ballard, but hardly enough for you to be making your own accusations," The Captain replied without hesitation. "You will be quite disappointed to find out I was with a lady friend that night and we were together at a social event here in Vancouver. Many people were present who can substantiate that I was there."

"I'm sure you are right, but Husband says you would have arranged someone else to actually carry out the murder." Craig was groping, but knowing that other victims in the case were likely murdered by a hired killer, he could easily make the accusation with a fair chance of being right.

"This gets more far-fetched all the time. Just why would I want Maureen Husband dead?"

"Because you were worried that she knew too much about your membership purchase scheme and your plans for the party. I'm afraid Paul has been getting cold feet and has decided to finger you."

For the first time, the Captain seemed to lose his natural self-assurance, some of the colour draining out of his well-tanned face. He asked quietly, "Who besides you has Paul Husband been telling these wild tales?"

"Right now, just me, but knowing he is ready to confess, it will be just a matter of time, and not much of that, before he makes a full confession of all the details."

"So you came here alone with this wild story to do what, Constable, arrest me?" The Captain glared threateningly.

"Not now. But your reaction tells me there is something to his assertions. In the meantime, I would caution you not to plan any trips. As they say in the movies, I'll be back."

"Actually, Constable, I don't think you should leave just yet. In fact, I would insist on it. Take him to the games room, Roy. I think we need to learn a lot more about just how much our good police officer knows and who else he has told."

Roy stood behind Craig, holding a 9mm Browning pistol to his back. "This way, Ballard," he said gently. He marched him out of the den and along a long corridor toward the water. He steered Craig toward a large room near the back of the house, facing away from the closest neighbours. Next to a closed door, he ordered Craig to face the wall with his hands high against it and to lean forward until he was almost off balance. Only then did Roy Carpenter deftly unlock the door, grab Craig by the neck and expertly push him into the room, switching on the light as Craig stumbled forward.

The room was like nothing that Craig had ever seen before. The floor and walls were muffled in pale blue vinyl-covered carpets and the ceiling was finished in thick acoustic tiles and covered in large mirrors. Fastened to the walls were more mirrors, along with iron shackles and leather straps at different heights, some high overhead and others at knee height. Low cushioned tables and waist-high hobbyhorses were scattered about, all fitted with stirrups and handcuffs in curious placements. In one corner was a long, low bed, again outfitted with handcuffs along its edges and on its headboard. A sink, some large easy chairs and a couple of cupboards, upon which were distributed an assortment of whips, handcuffs and ropes of various thicknesses, added to the room's furnishings. There were no windows, but an assortment of lamps and overhead fixtures provided the proper lighting for every mood.

"What in hell is this?" he blurted out, but The Captain, who had followed them into the room, ignored him and ordered Roy to strap him into a chair.

"Now, let's talk some more, Constable. I am very curious how you really found out about my political activities and who else you have shared this information with. I know that Paul would never have betrayed me, as he is in too deep. I will warn you to cooperate, as Roy here can make your life very uncomfortable."

"It's like I told you, McCullough. Paul Husband determined the jig was up and shifted the blame to you. He said he only went along with your schemes because you had too much on him, but his position had become impossible after you had his wife killed."

"Well, that's not how it happened, Ballard. I think maybe the Constable could use a drink of water, Roy."

Roy left the room for a minute and came back with a large bucket of water and a narrow rubber tube. The bucket was placed high on a table beside Craig's chair and the tube was inserted into the water. Craig's head was then tilted backward and strapped against the wall behind him. Roy sucked on the thin hose to get the water flowing, shoved the tube with its trickle of water into Craig's mouth and taped it firmly in place so he couldn't spit it out. He also taped his nostrils shut so that he could barely breathe.

At first, the sensation was only uncomfortable as Craig struggled to catch his breath. Then the panic set in as the water ran down the back of his throat and he could no longer breathe. As his lungs filled with the water, he felt as if they were bursting. As he started to black out, he was sure that he was about to die.

Just as he slipped into unconsciousness, Roy took the tube out of his mouth and removed the tape from his nose. The end of the tube was covered in blood. Slowly, his lungs burning, Craig felt himself regaining awareness as he gasped for breath.

"Perhaps you would care to tell us the real story now, Constable?" The Captain asked quietly, as Carpenter unstrapped his forehead and sat him back upright.

"Alright, alright." Craig had no intention of going through that again, and in spite of what else was to happen to him, he could see little further point in deceitfulness. "When I interviewed Husband, he let it slip unintentionally that you may have had something to do with his alibi the night of the murder. When I followed up, I learned more about you and your position in the party. In fact, the receptionist at the west coast party headquarters admitted that you pretty well run the operation. I deduced that you and Husband were likely behind the membership purchasing scheme …"

TIM MURPHY had to quickly decide what to do. He first checked with B.C. Ferries, but Craig had neither made a reservation nor used a credit card to pay for a return sailing to

Victoria. It didn't mean he hadn't left yet, but it was more likely he was still in Vancouver. Now, that stupid fool wouldn't try and interview McCullough at his home, would he? If McCullough figures out that we are closing in on him, there is no telling what he might do. Craig may have no idea just how dangerous the man is.

There's only one way to find out, he decided. And besides, he had to confront McCullough with all that he had learned. Catching him off guard at home might be the way to do it, even if Craig hadn't got there first. But he would be sure to keep the upper hand.

Tim then called the hospital and asked the nurse on Gloria's ward to inform her that he would not be able to make visiting hours. "Tell her not to worry," he added, "but something came up I must attend to." He also fleetingly thought of Inspector Fields and whether or not he should let him know what had transpired to this point. Maybe when I learn a little more, he rationalized. He set out quickly from downtown, feeling only a little guilty.

By the time Tim drove to West Vancouver, it was almost dark. He found the address easily enough, but the gate was closed and locked. He noticed the intercom but decided to maintain an element of surprise. He walked along the fence until he found a spot where, with the assistance of an overhanging tree, he was able to scramble over. He made his way back to the driveway and cautiously approached the house. He noticed the darkened smaller house to his left as he passed, but with no signs of life emanating from it, he crept past silently. Closer to the big house, he noticed the car.

That's Craig's car, he thought excitedly. He had made the right decision. Now to make sure he is okay. He crouched low, moved around the car and sidled along the heavily landscaped front wall of the house and up to the door. He pressed the latch slowly. It was unlocked. He listened carefully, heard nothing, and quietly and slowly opened the door and eased into the empty front hall. Lights were on in the hall, so he crossed quickly to the far wall and stopped beside the long hallway leading to the main rooms of the house. Still hearing nothing, he passed the den where The Captain had briefly received Craig earlier and continued along toward the back of the house.

Now he could hear muffled voices emanating from a room in front of him to his right. The door was closed, and as he inched up to it, he drew his revolver and listened carefully. Craig was talking and he was explaining how he had determined that McCullough might be involved in the party membership scheme and its cover-up.

"...as Paul was in charge of membership matters and the two of you were known to spend a lot of time together," Craig concluded.

"Who else did you share these brilliant deductions with?" Tim heard The Captain ask sarcastically.

"No one, I swear." Craig answered hurriedly and Tim could detect the fear in his voice.

"You say that, but I am informed that Corporal Murphy called his office in Victoria checking on your whereabouts. The nosy bastard was in my office earlier today, supposedly checking a new lead on a very old case to do with an accountant named Bill Taylor that I was required to permanently silence. You're telling me that you two are not working together."

"No, no. I haven't seen Murphy in days. As far as I know, he currently has nothing to do with the case and probably doesn't even know about Maureen Husband's murder. He is supposed to be over here to accompany his wife who is in hospital, and he wouldn't be conducting any investigative work."

"Well, what do you think, Roy? Should we believe the lying bastard or give him another drink?"

"Please, I heard earlier from your secretary that Murphy had talked to you, but I didn't know why and I haven't talked to him,

I swear. It would make sense for him to follow up on the information about Taylor. We had been working together on the case and had found out about him and Roger Kent going to school together. But I still don't know why that would lead to you. At any rate, only the two of us knew the connection between Kent and Taylor."

"Well, I guess it's obvious to you that we can't let you get out of this alive, Ballard. The only question is, do we take your word for it and assume Murphy and maybe others haven't made the connection to me, in which case we arrange an accident for you and lay low until this blows over? Or do we decide others know what you know and finish you off quickly and arrange our permanent offshore vacations."

"There's no way anyone else would know," Craig interjected quickly, hoping to stay alive at least a little longer.

"Maybe we can wait," Roy added. "If the police know anything, Batra can tip us off in time to make a getaway. I'll make the arrangements and we can be flying south within an hour of Batra's call. We can be in South America before an alert is issued and quickly disappear under our contingency plan."

"You've gone to a lot of trouble to set up this whole scheme," Craig blurted out, hoping to switch the conversation away from him. "But why? You are one of the richest men in the province. Why are you doing all this? Even killing people who get in your way. You have already mentioned having Taylor killed. Did you kill the others, too, and for what? Just so you can help your party leader become Prime Minister? It doesn't make much sense."

"There's very little you understand, my naïve friend. It's picking the right Prime Minister that counts. One who can be persuaded to do the right thing, so that the country remains in the hands of those that can ensure our destiny. The country, including this province, is full of short-sighted fools who are all too willing to sell out to outsiders for short-term rewards. In the right hands, we can continue to control the wealth that is generated here for the benefit of those of us who understand what that means."

"And what does that mean?"

"It means total decision-making powers for the betterment of the country, so that it will continue to prosper and grow. It means total and absolute power, once my plan is fulfilled, so that all my decisions will be unquestioned by anyone. There is so much waste and inefficiency that needs to be eradicated. We can do so much better once we are rid of all this ineffective bickering and squabbling."

"The people would never let you have that kind of power. You could never take away their democratic rights. The world, especially the Americans, would never stand for it."

"I don't need to change the system, just manipulate it. People are dolts and democracy is but a façade already. Once I control the media across the country, as I do already here in B.C., I can ensure decisions are made without opposition. The people are already apathetic, cynical and willing to be led. Look how easy it was for me to buy enough votes to elect so many Progressive Party candidates in the last federal election. There is so much corruption in the present system that I bought all those votes and no one admitted it had happened. They were already of a mind-set to believe it was simply their due."

"You're mad. Look at all the people you've had to kill already. You don't control anything."

"Can't you see how close I am? I have already put in place the plan to get control of the province in the next provincial election. My method works and I will buy myself to power. Then I will be in a position to extend my control of the media across the country and go on to win power federally. Fools like you will only slow the process down."

"But you have already made contingency plans in case your hare-brained scheme is uncovered."

"You know, you are so naïve that I am beginning to believe you really are operating alone, Ballard. Take him to your place, Roy, and chain him up until we can figure out an appropriate accident for him that will get the police off our case."

"I believe it's too late for that, McCullough," Tim interjected quietly, standing unnoticed inside the doorway. "The police are already on your case. Don't bother to go for that gun, Roy. I assume you must be Roy? Now keep your hands where I can see them and please don't give me any opportunity to shoot you. I am having a hard enough time avoiding doing that as it is."

The Captain's reaction was of immediate shock, followed quickly by a sense of great loss and finally of profound anger. "Why, you interfering son of a bitch," he yelled, and in a fit of uncontrolled rage came straight across the room, lunging for Tim's throat. Tim fired quickly, hitting him high in the right thigh. McCullough went down quickly, yelling and rolling in pain, his blood draining and running freely over the vinyl covered flooring.

Roy Carpenter took advantage of the distraction to draw his own pistol. He brought the pistol up quickly to take aim at Tim's head, but not quickly enough. Tim shot him squarely between the eyes before he could squeeze the trigger and he dropped to the floor like a sack of potatoes falling off the back of a truck. The blood spurted from his forehead, commingling with the rapidly expanding mess from McCullough's leg.

Tim confirmed that Carpenter was dead, ignored the howling man on the floor, and turned his attention to Craig. "Well, Craig, are you just going to sit around here all night, or would you like to get out of this place?"

"It's delightful you decided to make this timely appearance, Corporal Murphy. Now if you would be kind enough to undo these straps, it would be my pleasure to accompany you away from this hell-hole."

Tim quickly removed the straps. Reluctantly, he returned to McCullough, chose a pair of handcuffs from the cupboard top and locked his hands securely behind his back. Next, he selected one of the thicker ropes and used it as a tourniquet on McCullough's leg. He ignored his howls and tightened it until the blood finally ceased to flow. Finally, he directed Tim to keep an eye on him while he left the room, found a phone and called the Vancouver police and an ambulance.

When he returned, McCullough had finally calmed down. In fact, he was beginning to look a little groggy and Tim almost hoped he would pass out before the ambulance arrived. As they waited, he looked around and finally asked, "Craig, what do you make of this place?"

"It's something, isn't it? McCullough referred to it as 'the games room.' It seems he was in the habit of entertaining his guests here. It also seems he wouldn't take no for an answer when they appeared to be a tad reluctant to join in."

"You know, Craig, I suggest we are dealing with one twisted, sick bastard here."

"You want to believe it, Tim. You want to believe it."

Chapter 38

INSPECTOR FIELDS FLEW to Vancouver early the next morning for a debriefing. He insisted on interviewing the two exhausted police officers in E Division headquarters as soon as he arrived from his 8:00 a.m. harbour flight. After hearing their stories, he saved his greatest wrath for Tim.

"Once again your actions are reprehensible, Corporal Murphy," he began. "You can't be trusted, even when you are on leave, to refrain from poking your nose into the affairs of other officers and other jurisdictions. Just because you blundered into a solution for this case doesn't make your actions acceptable. You are truly irresponsible and the only thing saving your skin right now is that your illegal trespass probably saved the life of Constable Ballard. Nevertheless, when we get back to the District I am going to take action to put in place a permanent solution to your unending insubordination. I just can't deal with you anymore."

"Yes sir."

"And you, Corporal Ballard, have become just as bad. I believe that working with Murphy has allowed his undisciplined behaviour to rub off on you. You had no right to go to McCullough's house checking on alibis, never mind accusing the man of being a master criminal. You are very fortunate you are not dead right now. What's the matter with you two, anyway? You have the combined resources of at least three police forces in two major population centres at your disposal and you insist on acting as if you were the only two cops around for a thousand miles. I'll never get it," he concluded, the note of despair in his voice settling heavily in the quiet room.

"You're right, sir, but if we hadn't acted, it is quite likely that Craig would be dead like you said, but also McCullough would have been free to carry out his awful plan, at least until someone else discovered what he was up to."

"All right, so what else do you know so far?"

"That McCullough felt he could control the political process in B.C. and eventually all of Canada by manipulating the vote in close ridings to influence the final outcome of an election. He also believed he could ensure party candidates were selected who would be loyal to him and his ambitious plans. And finally, that once in power he could dominate both politically and financially, and could decide the very economic future of the country, including the ownership of major industries and resources."

"It still seems a bit far-fetched that he believed he could do all that."

"Well, when you consider that he was able to significantly affect the results of the last federal election here in B.C., it's not all that far-fetched," Murphy added. "If he was given the time to obtain total control over the media in the rest of the country like he did here, he might have changed the overall results."

"Who do we know so far that knew of his plan and was working with him on this?"

"Only the names I passed on to you last night, sir. Roy Carpenter, Paul Husband and Leif Johannsen here in Vancouver are the only ones we know of for sure that were in on the whole plan. We suspect that Jake Green, owner and CEO of Canadian Universal Media was in on it, given the total unconditional support of his media empire to the B.C. wing of the Progressive Party, but we haven't been able to get McCullough to admit to anything. Husband and Johannsen were arrested by the Vancouver Police last night."

"Okay, Murphy. Based on your information, we also picked up Chit Batra. I believe he was only a conduit for passing on information and probably knew very little about McCullough's full scheme. Who else fits that category?"

"Amazingly enough, other party officials knew parts of it, but only as it applied to increasing the votes for the party here in B.C. Allan Carrigan probably knows more than he is willing to admit, but I suspect he and Brenda Fox were trying very hard not to know, if you see what I mean. Then there are all those who took part knowingly in illegal operations that The Captain has been involved in for years. His Chief Financial Officer, Michael Chan who, it turns out, was in the same university program as McCullough and Bill Taylor, ran the money laundering end of the business. He has been picked up. Duncan Henderson probably knew more than he should have, unfortunately for him. Then there are gang members, managers in his corporate empire who handled various smuggling operations and perhaps countless others who took part in the vote purchasing end of things, whose names we don't know."

"Okay, Tim. Have you two had any sleep?" he added, his voice softening slightly.

"Not much, sir. Craig and I crashed in my motel room about four. At about six we got the word to meet you here, so here we are."

"Alright Tim, I will discuss your future in more detail after we get back to Victoria. In the meantime, I want the two of you to be available for a conference of all the police officers involved in this operation this afternoon. In the meantime, try and rest up. I want you both to be in full uniform and all spit and polish. Is that understood?"

"Yes sir," they answered resignedly and in unison.

THERE WAS A good-sized crowd of police officers present by the time they were all assembled in the auditorium of E Division headquarters at 1:00 p.m. The media had somehow already learned of the sensational arrest of Norton McCullough and eagerly flocked around the headquarters entrance, attempting to learn what they could. The grim-faced Inspector ignored their attempts to get his attention and walked up the steps and through the wide entrance of the stately building on West 37th Avenue. A hush fell over the assembly as he made his way to the podium and prepared to talk.

Tim wasn't looking forward to it. He was expecting a lot of references to "unorthodox methods" and "unauthorized acts." Instead the Inspector surprised him by referring to the brilliant deductive work and daring initiatives of two very courageous police officers who had independently unravelled the biggest and most complex police investigation in British Columbia in years.

"Because of their untiring research and willingness to pursue this case over and beyond the call of duty, an officer of the RCMP and another from the City of Victoria police force, have put an end to a reign of terror that has threatened the very foundations of our democratic traditions. The arrest last night of Norton McCullough, one of the richest and most powerful men in B.C., has put an end to an investigation that has consumed years of work and the attentions of many, many police officers. Our task today is to review what we know to this point and to move quickly to roundup all those who had a part in this nefarious scheme to control the political process in this province and perhaps the whole country."

This is certainly different than the reception I received earlier, thought Tim. As the Inspector went on, reviewing the complex maze of illegal operations the fanatical McCullough had masterminded, his mind drifted away to thoughts of Gloria and their future. Even if it wasn't to be with the Mounties, at least they could start again, both in good health. But how could Fields compliment him in public and then arrange his release later? Tired and confused, his thoughts wandered over all that happened to him the past two years and his own impetuous actions. Maybe when this was over he could get a rest and think matters out properly. He tried to bring his thoughts back to the present as the Inspector coordinated the assignments of the police officers in bringing the case to a close.

When he finally finished, Tim wasn't even sure whether or not he had been assigned any further tasks. He left the conference in a bit of a daze, accepting congratulations from various officers he didn't know. He eventually got away, drove back to the motel and slept until six o'clock, when he rose somewhat refreshed and drove to the hospital to finally visit with Gloria.

TIM STAYED IN Vancouver on leave until Gloria had recovered enough to go home. She was told she would be required to return frequently for follow-up care for the first few weeks after leaving hospital, but these visits would gradually diminish and she would then receive attention from nephrologists in Victoria. Tim used the time to relax to think about his future. A surprise call from Inspector Fields gave him even more to think about. He decided not to share what the Inspector had to say until he had fully digested it himself.

He also arranged a meeting with Thelma Frank to let her know what had happened. They met in Moonglow's, the same upscale coffee shop they had gone to on his previous visit. He brought her up to date, including the meeting with Millie Harvey and how that had resulted in the arrest of Martha Swanson and put to bed a case that had been cold for years.

"So what's my reward?" she asked coyly.

"Just that you no longer need to maintain cover and are free to resume your own identity, if you wish." He went on to enlighten her about McCullough's capture, his connection to Roger Kent, the Desperados and even his hit man, Roy Carpenter, all potential threats to her.

"You're forgetting about the Sirens in Nanaimo. I'm sure they still wonder if I had anything to do with the accident of one of their dealers on the Malahat near Mill Bay."

"That's history now, as well, and word has it that Freddy has been replaced, so is no longer their leader. Apparently, the higher-ups in Vancouver decided he was just too old-fashioned. I'm pretty sure the current leadership has no idea of your role in the death of the dealer."

"Gee, Tim, you mean I can return to Victoria and push drugs for a living again? Thanks for meeting me and putting my mind at ease, but I have a cushy job here and a new life that I quite enjoy. This is what I have always wanted and why I have been willing to work with you guys all along. I'm just fine where I am, thank you very much."

"Well, I owe you a lot. You have not only assisted the police when we needed it, you have helped put a lot of criminals away."

"So give me a medal, Tim."

"Well, if there's anything you need, I will do anything I can to help," he answered feebly.

"Anything? Well I have a very nice new apartment that still needs a good house-warming," she teased.

"Uh, almost anything. Very tempting, though."

"What a coward you are, Murphy. I don't know why I waste my time on you. Still, you were fun once. Now get out of here," she added with a rueful smile.

"Okay, Thelma. I won't forget what you've done."

She wiggled her fingers goodbye as he rose and headed slowly for the street.

FINALLY THE DAY CAME when Gloria could go home. Tim made the arrangements for the ferry and picked her up at the hospital in plenty of time to make their sailing. In the meantime, Sheila had recovered and she and Gloria had arranged for her and Gordon to accompany them on the same trip home. They were all in good spirits and looked forward to getting home to Victoria.

As they set sail, Tim found them a quiet corner in the top-deck lounge and brought them all hot drinks. Once settled, he again expressed his gratitude to Sheila for her donation.

"Oh, in the end it wasn't such a big deal, Tim. I am sure that if things were reversed Gloria would have done the same for me."

"Nevertheless, you are a true hero. You have given Gloria the gift of a real life and I am truly grateful. I've had time to think about all that has happened the last few months and I realize how much I have to be thankful for. A few days ago, I had a telephone call from Inspector Fields and what he had to say surprised me and got me to thinking about my and Gloria's future."

"You never mentioned his call, Tim," Gloria interjected.

"Well, I wasn't sure how to react, but now I know. He had earlier indicated he was going to take steps, as he put it, to deal with me once and for all. When he called, he admitted that he finds me impossible to work with and has taken the initiative to remove me from his command."

"Tim, you haven't been released have you?"

"No, Gloria. In fact, he said he had to acknowledge that, in spite of my reckless actions, I had to be rewarded for all that I had accomplished to help solve the most significant criminal case ever to occur in British Columbia. He asked if I would be willing to receive a promotion to Sergeant, providing I was to accept a position as head of research in the District office."

"But why you, Tim?" Sheila asked. "You've almost always been involved in front-line stuff where, as you are so fond of saying, the action is."

"It seems that Staff-Sergeant Rudnick is retiring and he felt I have a real talent for research work and would like to recommend me for the position. Inspector Fields said the real bonus was that I would no longer be under his direct command, as research is not part of operations."

"What did you say to him?" Gloria asked quietly.

"I said I would think about it and now I have. I don't know. All this action lately and with your operation and our chance to finally have a family, I think I would like to take it. Let's face it, I can't change my personality and I believe I owe it to the two of us to stay out of trouble long enough to enjoy some good years together. What do you think, Gloria? The funny thing is, while I was working in research, I actually did enjoy it. It was so damned satisfying to solve that Martha Swanson case and later to find out so much about Norton McCullough, alias The Captain, by following his audit trail. It was all very rewarding."

"Well, all I can say, Tim, is go for it. Nothing could please me more than to see you get away from all the trouble you get yourself into."

"Oh, I don't know if I will stay entirely away from trouble, but at least I should reduce the odds," Tim laughed.

"Well, congratulations Sergeant," Gordon piped in. "Now let's hear some more about your investigation. Do you think The Captain could really have gotten away with it?"

"It sounds unlikely, but he might have eventually, if we hadn't found out about him when we did. The day after Craig and I arrested McCullough, Inspector Fields arranged a meeting of all the police forces involved in the case. At the meeting, while I wasn't always with it because I was so damn tired, I still managed to pay attention to a political analyst the Inspector had asked to attend to answer that very question. He explained how the political climate in B.C. is at a stage where it is feasible for someone like McCullough to succeed."

"What do you mean by the political climate?"

"He said the stage has been set because of many years of corrupt business-oriented governments being in power in the province and across the country. Especially in B.C., their policies have made the electorate truly cynical, apathetic and downright defeatist. When you combine that with a monopolistic media that supports their agenda, the voters feel that they can do nothing to change the situation and are truly open to manipulation."

"Hold on. You don't feel that way, do you? I know I don't. Just what do you mean?"

"He said you have to look at the effects of privatization and globalization to begin with. Wages and benefits have been driven down in real terms across the western world as businesses increasingly look to manufacture their products offshore. Then they put in place laws that removed the right to strike for most public sector workers, destroyed the public health care system and cut back on pensions and workers' compensation benefits.

This has created an atmosphere of fear amongst the working class.

"Naturally, you would expect them to turn to pro-labour parties to form an alternative government, but the media has hammered away at the dastardly consequences should they ever again obtain power. Enough people are afraid to change that they continue to re-elect right-wing governments, which continues to worsen their conditions. Eventually, they began to feel helpless and unable to affect the system.

"Next, you add corruption. Voters become cynical as they witness greedy governments and businesses working together to reward each other's friends. They observe elected members voting themselves huge salary increases and switching parties to further their own economic and private interests. Then the media reports how the 'punishment' for blatant infractions only goes to minor players and even whistle-blowers. This, in turn, causes the public to determine it is fine to take advantage of the system the way it is, as long as you don't get caught. In fact, this analyst thinks the political climate is now such that a majority of the electorate believes it is permissible to accept money for casting their vote and it's especially okay to be paid for voting for a particular party."

"But again, Tim, not everybody feels that apathetic."

"No, Gordon, but enough do that the same governments continue to be re-elected no matter how greedy and corrupt they are. At least McCullough was attempting to ensure business profits would be re-invested here in Canada. According to this analyst, the province, and now the new federal government don't even care about that, as long as they can receive their own immediate rewards by selling out public resources to offshore owners."

"So, is McCullough the first to take advantage of this business-dominated political climate to attempt to obtain total control of the government anywhere in Canada?"

"Yes, and if we don't learn quickly from this lesson, he won't be the last."

"You say it is the first, but wasn't there a similar episode a few years ago that started out the same, with a raid on the legislature?"

"Yes, that was one of the very few times a Parliamentary office in Canada had been raided, and yes, some of the circumstances were the same, including the police pinpointing a couple of cabinet ministers' aides who were accused of taking advantage of their positions to better themselves economically. But it turned out they were just a couple of two-bit players who may have been trying to benefit from the provincial sell-off of a Crown corporation by feeding insider information to one of the bidders. I don't even remember what, if anything, they were eventually charged with, but it pales in significance to this operation."

"So, you wouldn't put McCullough's scheme in the same category?"

"No. Over the last ten years matters have become a good deal worse than they were then. People are willing to play for keeps and be very brutal to get want they want when the rewards for success are so much more meaningful. After all, this is 2013!"

ISBN 141209309-0

9 781412 093095